SPRING MUSIC

SPRING MUSIC

ELVI RHODES

BANTAM PRESS

LONDON · NEW YORK · TORONTO · SYDNEY · AUCKLAND

TRANSWORLD PUBLISHERS LTD
61–63 Uxbridge Road, London W5 5SA

TRANSWORLD PUBLISHERS (AUSTRALIA) PTY LTD
15–23 Helles Avenue, Moorebank, NSW 2170

TRANSWORLD PUBLISHERS (NZ) LTD
3 William Pickering Drive, Albany, Auckland

Published 1998 by Bantam Press
a division of Transworld Publishers Ltd
Copyright © Elvi Rhodes 1998

A catalogue record for this book is available from the British Library.

0593 043871

Typeset in 11/13pt Plantin by Kestrel Data, Exeter, Devon.

Printed in Great Britain by
Mackays of Chatham plc, Chatham, Kent.

This is for my granddaughter, Emma Rhodes,
with much love

Acknowledgements

I am greatly indebted to Olwen Holmes, friend and musician, for telling me about teaching the piano to children. Also for our discussions about what music Naomi would choose to play. Thank you, Olwen.

I also thank my son, Stephen, for his help in changing my too-English dialogue into 'New York speak'. Also for the inspiration which his beautiful Manhattan roof garden gave me.

ONE

'That's it then, madam! We'll be off!'

The foreman of the removal firm stood in the doorway, his two assistants behind him. Aside from the fact that they were all three dressed in white overalls with the company's name, MoveAll, embroidered in red across the breast pocket, they were an ill-assorted trio: the foreman tall, thin, hungry-looking; the middle one stocky, with huge hands and a red face; and the third, the one who had carried in, single-handed, the oak chest which Naomi hoped would fit in the hall, was small and puny-looking, as if a strong puff of wind would blow him over.

'You'll soon have everything in order!' the foreman said encouragingly.

She nodded, not because she agreed with him, she doubted everything would be in order again, but she was too tired to dissent. Also, she had discovered, he was one of the world's talkers and she didn't wish to encourage him any further.

'We'll be off then,' he repeated.

She said nothing lest a single word should set off a further conversation. She had given them a reasonable tip with which they'd seemed pleased. There was nothing more, was there?

'Thanks for the tea!' he said. 'Cheers!'

To her great relief he turned and led his small posse out of the flat.

Without rising from her seat she watched them through the window which, she noted, needed cleaning, as they fastened up the back of the van, climbed into the front and drove away into the late afternoon traffic.

They'd been all right, she supposed. Agreeable, good-tempered, though not very clever. But then she had almost no experience of removal men, she'd lived in the same house all her married life. Perhaps none of them were good at putting the right furniture in the right rooms? Perhaps she hadn't instructed them properly? Maybe it was her fault that she was sitting on what was manifestly a kitchen chair, and shabby with it, in the middle of her sitting room? Not yet *her* sitting room, though. She and the room, indeed the whole flat, were strangers to each other. She hadn't, either on first viewing it or subsequently, by any means fallen in love with it. She'd had to find something quickly: it was a place to live.

Why am I here? What am I doing here? she asked herself. 'I don't believe it!'

She said the last words out loud. So am I now going to start talking to myself? she wondered. Or will I talk to the walls, like Shirley Valentine?

The telephone rang, the sound in the unfamiliar room startling her so that her whole body jumped and she leapt up from the chair. She had arranged for the phone to be connected yesterday and checked first thing today that it had been done, but since then it had remained silent, and now, in the untidy mess which had accumulated, she couldn't even remember where it was. She searched frantically for the source of the ringing, calling out, 'I'm coming! I'm coming!' until she found it on the floor behind the sofa. She bent down to it and, as she clasped her hand around the receiver, the ringing ceased.

'Damn!' she said. 'Damn, damn!'

It could have been Isobel. Though if it was, she thought, it would not have been to ask about me. How are you, Mummy? How are you getting on? Is there anything I can do? No, it would have been something about the baby. Sure to be. Harry was four months old and filled Isobel's horizon almost entirely. His feeding, his sleeping, the colour and consistency of the contents

10

of his diapers, every movement of his hands, feet, eyes were of consuming interest to his mother. The small windy quirks of his mouth were *not* caused by wind, they were full-blown smiles at the world around him. Any day now, Naomi expected to hear he had taken his first steps, said his first words, and cut half a dozen pearly teeth. If they had had a video camera, it would all have been recorded. Not, of course, that Naomi didn't adore him! Of course she did.

Sometimes she felt sorry for Patrick, Isobel's partner – if anything as definite as the word 'partner' could be applied to him. He got short shrift these days, not because Isobel held anything against him, not even the fact that he'd made her pregnant before she'd hardly got to know him, but simply that the baby was all. Patrick's crowning glory was just that he had fathered this wonderful child. Isobel would think further about Patrick, about whether they would or would not get married, as he sometimes suggested, when she had time; which was not now.

If it had been Isobel, she would ring again.

Naomi picked up the phone and placed it on a shelf which, when she had unpacked them, would hold books. She had no idea where the books were, except that they were in tea chests. They could be in the bathroom, or the larder; they could be anywhere.

She looked beseechingly at the phone as she put it down, begging it to ring again so that someone, anyone, could briefly inhabit the room with her. Even a wrong number would do. One could prolong a wrong number into a short conversation. It looked back at her, mute, silent.

She would make a cup of tea. Not that she wanted one, she was awash with tea, had been all day. When the removal men had arrived at Four Winds at eight o'clock this morning it had been plain that they couldn't start the day without strong tea to get them going, and thereafter they had hinted about it, or asked outright, every hour on the hour. A week or two ago she had read an article about moving house. 'Pack a basket with everything essential for tea-making,' it advised. 'See that it's last to go on the van before you leave and first to be unloaded at the new place.' There'd been other advice too, stuff about putting coloured stickers on the furniture and corresponding ones on the doors of the rooms for which it was intended, but she couldn't be bothered with all that. And now I'll pay the price, she thought.

Nevertheless she would have yet another cup of tea and then she'd make up the bed so that she could fall into it when she wanted to. *Our* bed. It was how she still thought of it though for many months now she had occupied it alone, still keeping to her own side as though Edward might at any moment join her after sitting on the edge, his back to her, for several minutes, which he did every night. She had never liked to ask him what he was contemplating. He was not praying, she knew that, since Edward did not believe in God. God was not logical. Sometimes she wondered if he was contemplating his rather nice feet.

Did he do it now? she wondered. Now that he had a new and younger bedmate. Did he keep her waiting while he locked every door and window, turned off every light? Or did he drag her upstairs by the hair of her head, throw her onto the bed and jump on her?

She had been thunderstruck – 'gobsmacked' as Cecily would have put it – when Edward, coming home late one evening and finding her sitting up in bed, had told her, in his mellifluous, beautifully modulated voice, that he no longer loved her, well, not as he *had* loved her. He had, he explained, fallen in love with someone else. Her name was Helen. She was twenty-six.

'*Deeply* in love!' he'd emphasized. 'So you see . . . But don't think,' he had added kindly, 'that I don't respect you, don't like you. Of course I do! You are an eminently likeable woman!'

'Thank you,' she'd said automatically, because she was on auto-pilot, so astonished, so disbelieving, that the agony had not hit her until he'd left the following morning after spending the night in the guest room. She had had to wait until the evening to ask the questions which had hammered at her all day.

They sat on either side of the dinner table while he explained his position, which he did in a kindly, matter-of-fact manner as if she might be a client whom he was advising on the niceties of making a will. It was not unlike discussing a will.

'I shall not shirk my obligations,' he'd said. 'I shall, of course, provide for you. I will give you a modest allowance and when we

12

sell Four Winds your share of the proceeds will buy a flat, or a small cottage.'

'Sell Four Winds? You mean I can't live here?' They had moved into Four Winds straight after their honeymoon. It was a solid, Edwardian house, the kind of house where the children had brought their friends and would, eventually, as she saw it, bring their own offspring. She had expected to live there for the rest of her life.

'Of course not!' Edward had said patiently. 'I shall have to make economies. In any case it would be far too big for you!'

It was she who would have to make the economies, Naomi quickly discovered. Since Helen's father was the owner of a large department store in Bristol and she was his only child, there would be no need for scrimping and saving there.

'And then there's . . .' Edward had hesitated slightly '. . . and then there's the baby.'

'The baby? What has Harry to do with this?'

'Not Harry! Helen is expecting a baby. My baby! Which is why I want a divorce quickly.'

She'd stared at him. Edward Fletcher, upright, straightforward, kind, conventional, a little bit dull but she hadn't really minded that. Even his profession fitted him. A square peg in a square hole. Yet suddenly, it seemed, he was none of those things! Had she never quite known him? For how long had this other self been bubbling away beneath the unremarkable surface before it had erupted? Falling for a younger woman was one thing, though in Edward's case quite out of character; fathering a child was mind-boggling. Though regular and consistent, and giving and taking moderate satisfaction in his sex life, he was so careful, so controlled that he would seem capable of deciding which day of the week any child of his might be born. He was not given to mad passion, or moments of abandonment. Or at least not with me, Naomi thought. So what did this other woman have, to have wrought this change in him?

'You do see that, don't you?' he'd persisted. 'You do see why I need to settle this quickly?'

'Oh, I see! Well you would, wouldn't you!' She'd tried to keep

13

calm though now her whole body was trembling. She'd gripped the sides of her chair, trying to keep control of herself. 'And who better than you, a family solicitor, to know the best way to go about such a thing?'

Don't do this to me! she'd wanted to shout. Don't do it! Come back to me!

She'd looked down at her plate. They were eating, or, rather, not eating, Dover sole with a shrimp sauce, one of his favourite dishes. Fierce anger swept through her. She wanted to pick up the plate and land the contents full-square on his face. She looked up at him and saw, in her imagination, the fish caught in his hair, the sauce dripping down his face, tiny shrimps caught in his neat beard.

And that was another thing, she'd thought frantically, wildly. Why had he, who had always been somewhat suspicious of men who sported beards, considered them raffish, suddenly over the last months grown one? Why hadn't it alerted her?

It was, stupidly, the sight of his beard which had brought the tears to her eyes. She'd opened her eyes wide, held them rigid so that the tears shouldn't fall.

The moment passed. She pushed her plate away, steadied herself.

'And what about your own children? I mean the ones you already have?'

'I shall do my duty,' he said. 'Of course I shall. Hugh seems to be scraping along in the theatre, though it's a precarious career, as I warned him at the time, but if ever he wants to set up in a proper business then I'll listen to him.'

'And Isobel and Cecily?' she prompted.

'Isobel has made her own bed and she must lie on it!' he said. It was an unfortunate metaphor in the circumstances, Naomi had thought. And not only for Isobel.

'As for Cecily,' he'd continued, 'of course I shall look after her as long as she's in university. After that we'll see. But she'll be all right, I promise you!'

'I'm sure!' Naomi said. Cecily was Daddy's girl, always had been. She probably thought that what he was doing was perfectly in order, the thing to do. When the music stops everybody

14

change partners. The University of Sussex, though it might approve of them, couldn't be blamed for giving Cecily her ideas. She had always had them.

There had been practically nothing else to say to Edward. He was besotted. Totally besotted.

And the first economy, Naomi realized, as she began to look in estate agents' windows, take home sheaves of details, was that no way could she afford even the cheapest house. Not if she wished to live in or near to the centre of Bath, which she had decided was the only thing to do. She must at least make an effort to be where the action was. Indeed, it was at this point that she'd realized that to stay at Four Winds, situated in the stretch of country between Bath and Bristol, was not the best possible idea.

She had friends of course, and they would be kind. They would invite her to things, especially at first, though she would be the extra woman at the dinner table. She would upset the seating, even causing two women to have to sit side by side. *Quelle horreur!*

They would start asking her to female tea parties instead of to dinner. She would be an appendage on the edge of their lives – at which thought she wiped away a tear and then pulled herself together, squared her shoulders. No-one must be sorry for her; nothing could make her feel more of a failure than that. No! She would pull up her anchor and sail into new waters, even if it was only in a small houseboat on the Kennet and Avon canal!

To be practical, and with an effort she had talked herself into a practical mood, she had faced the fact that she must look for a flat, and not too expensive at that. She tore up and threw away all the agents' details which didn't fall into that category, including the description of a house in the Royal Crescent, wildly beyond her means, which she had kept to read as a sort of fairy tale.

This flat, which at the moment resembled a council tip, had been chosen because the living room was roomy enough to have her piano and, being on the ground floor, included the garden at the back. It was also no more than a ten minute brisk walk

15

from the town centre, in the hinterland behind Pulteney Street and close to Sydney Gardens, so that when she got a job she would be able to walk to work. No bus fares.

She went into the kitchen and put on the kettle. It was such a small kitchen. 'Compact' the estate agent had called it, in the special language they used.

She poured the boiling water into a mug, swished the tea-bag around in it until the liquid was exactly the right strength, then scooped it out again. Then she cut a slice of wholemeal bread and a piece of Cheddar cheese and took the whole lot back to the sitting room. This kitchen was not a place in which to eat, even if she could have found a chair which was not piled with objects.

Four Winds had had a roomy kitchen with a large square table in the centre, at which, when the children had come in from school, they'd always had tea. She had strong memories of beans on toast. But what did she want with a large kitchen? Here, she argued, she could conveniently reach almost everything without moving more than two or three steps.

Stop it, she ordered herself, you are beginning to *think* like an estate agent!

Of course, there was no reason why she should be perched on a corner of the sofa, eating this frugal meal. There were plenty of cafés nearby. That was one of the good things about Bath, everything was more or less within walking distance. But she wasn't in the mood for eating out nor, she realized, having caught sight of herself in the mirror which the previous owner had left behind in the hall, was she fit to be seen. She was pale and dishevelled and her sweatshirt and jeans, though good enough for moving house, had seen better days. No, when she had eaten she would make up the bed, take a shower and call it a day. Not the best day of her life so far, but tomorrow would be different. She would make it so.

She was in bed and reading the new Inspector Morse she had saved especially for now, something absorbing, when the telephone by her bedside rang. She grabbed it.

'I rang earlier. I didn't think you'd be out!'

'Edward! What? Why?' He was the last person she'd ex-

16

pected to hear. 'I wasn't out,' she said. 'I just couldn't find the phone!'

'*Couldn't find the phone?*'

She felt ten years old, and incompetent. On the other hand, what had it now to do with him?

'Did you ring for anything special?'

'I just wanted to make sure you were all right,' Edward said. 'Naturally.'

Naturally? Was this the way things were conducted, then? He sounded so damnably civilized, which was not at all how she felt. She felt full of primitive passions; furious!

'Are you settled in?'

'Settled in?' She looked around the bedroom. Except for the large square of her bed it was chaotic. And how dare he telephone her in this calm manner? Why wasn't he lying right here beside her? He was hers!

'Not quite,' she said. 'Not yet.'

'We'll pop across and see you as soon as Helen's able.' He made it sound like a treat in store. 'She's not too well at the moment. She finds the cold trying.'

I find the whole of life trying, Naomi thought. What in the world did he mean by all this? Were they all to be cosy friends together? Was that what he expected? Was she to be asked to *sympathize* with Helen in her pregnancy? Would she, later on, be requested to babysit?

'If there's anything at all I can do for you . . .' he was saying.

'You mean like the bathroom tap needs a washer and the kitchen sink's blocked? And yes, and I shall need new shelves putting up all over the place? Is that the kind of thing?'

'Not . . . precisely,' he floundered. 'But if there *is* anything . . . And in the meantime take care of yourself!'

'Take care of myself!' she shouted. 'You should be taking care of me!' But she didn't say it until after she had slammed the phone down.

She went back to her book, but it was no good, she couldn't concentrate, the words ran together. Even Inspector Morse failed her. She had been thoroughly upset by Edward's call. When she found herself reading the same sentence for the

17

third time she gave it up, closed the book and switched off the light.

I will think about tomorrow, she decided. And the day after and the day after that. I will make plans. She would give herself two weeks to put the flat to rights, to walk around Bath at leisure, to visit her mother. She would have her hair done and then she would look for a job.

TWO

When she wakened next morning for a moment or two Naomi did not know where she was, and assumed that she was still asleep and dreaming. After all, every morning for twenty-five years, give or take a few holidays away from home, she had opened her eyes to a pastel-coloured wall, the shade changing occasionally when the room was redecorated, and meeting her eye had been the watercolour of the harbour at St Ives which Edward had bought for her when they were on honeymoon there in 1969.

Her first, incoherent thought was that the picture had been stolen by thieves in the night, but quickly following that came the realization that it was not the picture which had been stolen from her – that was around somewhere – but her husband. And as her eyes travelled around the bedroom there *was* the picture, leaning against the wall, waiting to be hung. Well, she wouldn't hang it that was for sure. She would give it to the Help the Aged shop. Did they take pictures? Never mind, someone would, if only the dustman.

She got out of bed – the rugs had not been laid and the floor was cold to her feet – crossed to the window and drew back the curtains which had kindly been left by the previous owner. 'You might as well have them,' she'd said. 'No curtains ever fit any other window. It's a rule of life!'

Looking at the garden was the first thing she had always done every morning, but it was strange now, seeing this one almost on a level instead of from a first-floor window. It was strange, but rather pleasant since there was a feeling of being in it. Not that there was much to see on this chilly, damp February morning. Close to the house, purple *Iris reticulata* were in flower and there were yellow crocuses in a wooden tub. On the wall to the left, winter jasmine was breathing its last. The grass, waiting for its new spring growth, was dull and tired-looking, but would not be so much longer. Spring came early here. Already the daffodil spears were several inches high, with the buds starting to swell. But in spite of the signs, it was not yet spring. It was not even one of those days which, with deeper colour in the shafts of sunlight, offered a tantalizing foretaste of what was to come. Beyond the bottom wall the mist took over, blotting out the view which she knew, from a previous visit, included the abbey. If she went into the town today perhaps she would pop into the abbey.

Shivering a little, she turned away from the window, put on her dressing-gown and went into the kitchen. She looked forward to doing something with the garden when she had the time. It was small, but that was not the chief thing against it. The trouble was that it was dull and conventional, with a rectangular lawn, straight, too-narrow borders planted in rows, like soldiers on parade. It needed imagination, it needed redesigning and she would see that it got both.

As she made coffee and put a slice of brown bread in the toaster, she couldn't help but think of the garden she had left behind at Four Winds. That had been the achievement of a twenty-five-year labour of love; with its lawn, an arbour smothered in the springtime in *Clematis Montana*, the pale pink one; a small statue, half-hidden, of a boy; trees now grown to maturity. There was a pond where six koi – she had given them all names of poets – swam with goldfish too numerous to name, and into which, and it was the delight of her life, a small waterfall tumbled. On summer evenings, waiting for Edward to come home from Bristol, she would sit close by, glass of wine in her hand, enjoying the sound.

20

She pushed the thought away from her. There was no mileage in looking back and she would not do it.

Needing only to make a right-angled turn, she placed her coffee and toast on the ledge which was an extension of the window-sill. 'Integral breakfast bar,' the agent had described it as. She fetched a sheet of paper which she firmly headed 'THINGS TO DO!' and then stared at the blank sheet while she ate and drank. In the end she wrote down:

> Phone Mr Betts
> ditto Isobel
> unpack music

And then gave up. The rest she would do as it came to her. The surrounding chaos would supply all the inspiration she needed.

First things first! Mr Betts was the piano tuner. Her poor piano, in spite of the fact that she had hired, not the Three Stooges, but a specialist firm that had known how to deal with it carefully, to bring it over the day before the general move, as befitted its station as a Bechstein, must be suffering from disturbance. Much as I am, she thought. But where is the Mr Betts who will retune me?

Mr Betts, who lived close to Bristol, promised to call in two days' time.

'First thing in the morning!' she reminded him.

On the day her piano was newly tuned she always followed the same routine. She lovingly washed its keys with milk then indulged herself by sitting down to play for the rest of the morning, answering neither the telephone nor the door.

'Very well, first thing,' Mr Betts agreed. 'But let her settle down until then. She'll be all the better for it!'

Perhaps *I* would be all the better for settling down first, Naomi thought, clutching at a straw, looking around at the appearance of the room. Maybe I shouldn't even attempt to get everything into place quickly, perhaps I should take it a little at a time? After all, there is no-one to stand over me with a stopwatch, no-one other than me to give a damn what it looks like.

21

She would phone Isobel next. She would not wait for Isobel to phone her, partly because her daughter, unprompted, might not do it, partly because, Naomi told herself, though with little conviction, my daughter might be needing me. After all, she had a young baby, she was inexperienced. Mostly, she admitted, she would phone her because she simply wanted to talk to someone, and someone with a little more conversation than Mr Betts. True, both he and Isobel had one-track minds, pianos or babies, take your pick, but Isobel was the more articulate.

'He's just gone off to sleep!' Isobel said quietly. 'Bless him!' She added this invocation to most things she said about Harry.

'Bless him!' Naomi replied dutifully, forbearing to add that babies sometimes did go to sleep. 'I thought I might pop in and see you. This morning?'

'Aren't you too busy, Mummy?' Isobel sounded doubtful.

'Not really!' Naomi lied. 'Everything's under control.'

'Well I'm sure Harry would like to see you,' Isobel said. 'I'm sure he'd say so if he was awake – in his only little way, bless him! And I know you'd like to see him.'

'Of course! I'll be down later, then!'

And before I go, Naomi thought virtuously, I will unpack my music. Well, not all of it, there was too much of it to do all at once, but at least she would see to her music cabinet which always stood, and still would, not far from her piano. The top drawer housed what she was currently working on, in this case Grieg's 'Remembrances' and Liszt's 'Consolation Number 3'. Unlikely bedfellows, Grieg and Liszt, she thought. Yet perhaps not in another way since, if she remembered rightly, Liszt had been very helpful to Grieg.

There was no way she should allow herself to sit down at the piano right now. There were far too many things screaming for attention, and in any case she ought not to use the piano until Mr Betts had ministered to it. All the same she was going to. She was going to sit at the piano and she was going to play, 'Remembrances' first and 'Consolation' afterwards. She had chosen both pieces shortly after Edward had left her, so that by now she knew them well. But she would not be able to let them go, not just yet; they had come to mean something more than the music.

22

In the untidy, rather chilly flat she played the piano with confidence, and knew she was playing well. They were well-named pieces. She wondered under what circumstances Grieg and Liszt had composed them. Oddly enough, she thought, when you were down, to play sad music *was* consoling. When the last notes had died away she sat for a minute. Then she closed the lid. 'That's the last time I touch you until you've been tuned!' she promised. And that was also her last ration of sadness for the day. Next stop, Isobel and Harry!

I shall walk to Isobel's, Naomi decided. It was to be yet another feature of her new lifestyle that she would drive around less, take more exercise. In any case, parking in Bath was hellish. Yesterday only by the skin of her teeth, seizing the opportunity the second someone else moved out, had she sneaked her Peugeot into a space reasonably close to her flat. And if she moved it would she ever get the space back again? She pushed aside the question of what use a car was if it only existed to fill a space.

Edward had considered it somewhat common to park one's car permanently in the street. The place for a car, when not in use, was in the garage, and that was where he drove his dark blue BMW every evening when he arrived home, not leaving it, which she suspected he did with a little goodnight pat, until it was safely tucked away.

Isobel lived in a flat part-way up Bathwick Hill, over premises occupied during the day by a firm of dentists, Brane and Manners. It was not ideal, or so Naomi thought, but Isobel seemed happy enough with it. The sound of traffic, and it was muted a little because she was a storey above it, didn't worry her, and the position was handy for Patrick, who was an assistant in the university library. The number 18 bus – he earned a pittance and could not afford a car – stopped right outside the dentists' door.

It was in the last year of Isobel's degree in English that Patrick had joined the library staff and it became the year in which she spent a great deal of time working in the library. She was not alone – females, arts or science, it made no difference – were strongly attracted to this new young man who, they agreed, was

23

a cross between Byron and Heathcliff, but more outgoing than either. Isobel it was who won him. The fact that she was having his baby, even though she wouldn't agree to marry him, gave her the edge over those who would have married him like a shot, and waited for a baby.

'We shan't always live here, Mummy,' Isobel had said in answer to Naomi's look when she had first set eyes on the flat. 'It's a starting place. When Patrick has passed his exams we shall move on.'

And who am I to criticize? Naomi asked herself now, as she turned the corner past the church and began to climb the hill. My flat is a finishing place, it's what I've come to in the end.

She let herself into the building, peeked into Harry's pram which was parked in the hall, though of course he couldn't possibly be in it, not out of his mother's sight, and climbed the stairs to the first floor. A smell of disinfectant mixed with anaesthetic hung about the stairs, which made her dicey back molar, which should have been attended to a month ago, jump with guilt. She really must go into Bristol to see Mr Fanshaw before he sent one of his polite reminders. But he wouldn't know when to send it, would he? And perhaps with all this new life business she would strike out with a fresh dentist? She would ask Isobel about this one, Mr Brane or Mr Manners as the case might be.

Harry's cries came loud and strong even before she rang the bell. Isobel came to the door with him in her arms. He was puce in the face.

'What do you know about four-month colic?' Isobel asked by way of greeting. 'He just goes on and on! Bless him!'

'All I ever want to know,' Naomi said. 'But including the fact that it does pass. Eventually. Let me get rid of my coat, then I'll take him.'

She held him over her shoulder rubbing his back. For a moment his cries ceased. He belched loudly, then started to cry with renewed vigour.

'Does he need feeding?' Naomi enquired.

'I fed him half an hour before you arrived.'

'Then that's it, he has indigestion!' Naomi said.

'Indigestion?' Isobel bridled. 'How can his mother's milk give

24

him indigestion? It's perfected by nature for its purpose!'

'It's easy enough to thwart nature, dear. You've only got to eat pickled onions, for example.'

'Oh Mummy! As if I would! I'm extremely careful what I eat. I know my responsibilities.'

'I didn't say you would, darling. I only said you *could*.'

Harry gave a final whimper, then stopped crying. A self-satisfied expression crossed his face.

'Anyway,' Naomi said quickly, 'perhaps you'd better have him back. His nappy needs changing. Babies are so primitive, aren't they?'

'Who's a clever boy, then?' Isobel cooed.

While she dealt with Harry's little offering her mother stood by the window, looking out onto the road. Does she really like babies? Isobel wondered. *Really* like? Did she like us? Impossible to say. One couldn't remember anything at all about being a small baby, and if asked her mother would say, 'Of course I did!'

She'd been a perfectly satisfactory mother; caring, fun-loving, encouraging them to do all manner of things which the mothers of their friends wouldn't allow. She'd helped them with their homework, chauffeured them to Brownies, parties, dancing classes. Perhaps she liked us better when we were older, Isobel thought.

She massaged cream into Harry's bottom before putting on his fresh nappy, carefully, so that not even the slightest crease could irk him. It was quite sad, really, that unless she told him later he would never know just how much she loved him at this moment. And it wasn't something you could tell a grown boy, was it?

'There!' she said brightly. 'All done! A nice clean boy, bless him!'

Naomi turned back into the room. 'It still looks misty down in the town.'

'It's a misty place,' Isobel said. 'Especially down by the river. Have you settled in then, Mummy?'

'More or less,' Naomi said vaguely. 'I might go and see your grandmother this afternoon.'

'Well, give her my love. And Harry's. I know she'd just love to see him but I'm not sure it's the place to take a young baby.'

25

'Oh, I don't *know*!' Naomi said. 'It might do the old folks a world of good. And it wouldn't hurt Harry. They're not infectious. Just old, and some of them a bit dotty.'

Isobel smiled at her mother.

'But that's what I mean, darling. I wasn't thinking Harry would catch something nasty . . .' She broke off, suddenly uncertain. 'But I mean . . . well . . . I mean, babies are so impressionable, aren't they? I do think they should be with people who are *whole* and *sound* and, well, *beautiful*! Don't you?'

'I think babies are as tough as old boots,' Naomi said.

Isobel looked uncertain, then laughed.

'Oh Mummy, you are so funny. Sometimes you say the oddest things!'

'Do I, dear?'

Or is it, Naomi wondered, that you and I don't speak the same language? The thought saddened her. She needed, at the moment, to be closer to her family, not more distant.

She stayed for another hour, during which time Harry slept the sleep of one whose bodily functions were at last in total harmony.

'How is Patrick?' she asked. Her visits, though not by design, seldom coincided with Patrick's presence.

'Very well. Working hard, studying hard.'

'And are you and he . . . ?'

'He does want us to marry,' Isobel said. 'But really I have to concentrate on Harry. Marriage is such a big production, but having a baby is even more so.'

And you have got them the wrong way round, Naomi thought. Or perhaps it was she who was wrong? It would be quite nice, though, to have one child conventionally married, one grandchild with legally bound parents. Hugh showed no sign whatever of settling down and no-one in the world could foretell what Cecily would do.

'I would quite like to see you married.' She spoke as casually as she could; no pressure, no hectoring.

'Oh, I expect we'll get around to it one day,' Isobel said.

And why would I wish to rush anyone into matrimony? Naomi asked herself. Where has it landed me? But quick as a flash the answer came: it has landed you with three children who, though they might not be entirely as you would have designed them, are yours to love and to be loved by, and with that dear little infant, sleeping like an angel in his crib.

She stood there, Isobel beside her, both of them looking down at Harry.

'He has a distinct look of you, Mummy,' Isobel said. 'Dark hair, and those well-defined eyebrows.'

'I hope my hair's a little less sparse,' Naomi said. 'Though of course he has the advantage of no stray grey bits.' As far as her eyebrows, well it was better to have handed those down than her rather short tilted nose, which would have been all right on a baby but was not serious enough for a grown man.

'Fortunately,' she said, 'he has inherited your father's aquiline nose. Anyway I must go!'

'What are you going to do?'

There was no doubt what she should do, she should go back to the flat and tackle the mess.

'I think I shall walk into the town,' she said. 'There are one or two things I need.'

The day was fractionally brighter than it had been as she set off down the hill. At least the mist had dispersed. Though she eventually found herself outside the abbey, its west front almost totally obscured by scaffolding, she didn't go in. The mood to do so had left her, she would wait for another day. As she crossed the abbey churchyard lunch was being served in the Pump Room, but today she would seek somewhere simpler. She turned right and walked towards Milsom Street.

Eating her cheese-and-tomato sandwich, which was tastefully garnished with a few strands of cress and half a lettuce leaf, Naomi wondered whether she would or would not visit her mother this afternoon. When living at Four Winds she had driven over once a fortnight or so. Many of the relatives of the guests at River View, she knew, visited on the same day at the same time each week, a regularity appreciated by their elderly dependants, who liked to think they could set the clock by them. It had not been so with her mother for some time now. Though physically fit and seemingly happy she seldom knew which day of the week it was or even which year she was living in. Time had lost its meaning. She would greet Naomi with surprise, saying, 'But you were only here yesterday, dear!' or with reproach because she believed she had not been near her for months.

So this afternoon or tomorrow, Naomi thought sadly, what difference will it make?

Her mother had moved into River View less than three years ago after almost eighteen years of not unpleasant widowhood. Indeed, it had turned out to be the most pleasant period of her life, since her husband, Ronald Campbell, had proved soon after their marraige to be bad-tempered, bullying, oppressive and mean. He had, however, by working all hours in his native West Yorkshire, made a deal of money as a builder who could and did turn his hand to anything, especially in the immediate post-war years. There was so much to be done and if materials were short Ronald Campbell always knew where to lay his hands on what was needed. Whether he found it on the black market or not, no-one wanted to know. Builders were as Princes of the Blood.

Naomi could not remember a time when she hadn't disliked her father, mostly because he was so nasty to her mother. In turn, he disliked Naomi. Apart from the fact that she was not a son, who could have followed him into the building trade, she was too spirited. He couldn't squash her. Women should be capable of being squashed.

It had been a godsend to Naomi – quite apart from the fact that she was head over heels in love with him – when Edward met her when he was in Leeds, married her, and whisked her off to his native Bristol. The pity was that when Ronald and his wife Doris visited the newly-weds a year later, Ronald fell hook, line and sinker for the West Country. He went back to Yorkshire, sold his business at a substantial profit and returned, aged sixty, to buy a house in Cheltenham. There he darkened their lives, and the lives of all who met him, for no more than two years before he died of a heart attack.

What a pity, Naomi thought, not for the first time, that Mother hadn't married again. She'd been eligible enough – a lively sixty, slim and pretty, owner of a mortgage-free detached house and in receipt of a substantial, well-invested income.

But what I know now that I didn't know then, she thought,

moving to the cash desk to pay her bill, is that older men would rather have two women of thirty than one of sixty!

She decided as she left the café that she would put off the visit to her mother until tomorrow. She had, after all, made one family visit today. Passing Jolly's store, she nipped in, not because she needed anything but because it looked so bright and inviting. Could I get a job here? she wondered. She knew nothing of salesmanship, but then what *did* she know anything about? Whatever she decided to do – or more likely whatever she could find to do – she would have to learn about it from the ground up.

She bought a lipstick – Red Passion – it seemed mean to buy nothing, then left the store and walked back through the chilly afternoon to her flat. Turning the key in the lock, walking in, for the first time coming back to it, she suddenly thought, This is my home!

THREE

When Naomi went into her sitting room next morning, and this time she did not have to pick her way around obstacles because she had spent last evening making this room at least reasonable to live in, she looked with longing at her piano. She wanted so much to play it, but she had promised herself not to and she would keep that promise. Its lid would stay closed until Mr Betts had done what he had to do.

She would not have played either the 'Remembrances' or the 'Consolation' this morning. She was in a different mood today, more hopeful, almost looking forward. It had started at that moment yesterday afternoon when she had put her key in the lock, and had thought, This is my home. She had cooked a tasty meal for herself, worked hard in the flat, gone to bed late, slept well, and had realized as soon as she had wakened at daybreak that the better mood had not left her.

I would still play Grieg, she thought, but something less reflective, more positive. There was plenty in his music to choose from. In fact, she felt close to Grieg this morning, perhaps because last night she had been thinking, unusually for her, of her time in Yorkshire. Those years had, after all, been the formative ones. They couldn't be denied. By now she had lived longer in the south-west than she had in the north, but every drop of blood in her body, from both sides, was northern as far

30

back as anyone had bothered to trace it. And it was a matter of history that Viking blood flowed in many a northern vein, so it was small wonder that Grieg, who painted pictures of his native Norway in his music as clearly as did any artist with oils and canvas, whose notes were redolent of lakes and mountains, frost and ice and fast-running water, spoke to something deep within her.

But definitely no piano today. She turned her back on it and looked out of the window. Not only did she feel brighter, but the day itself was sunny, one of those days which came occasionally in February to remind one that spring was on the way. There was no mist this morning, not even by the river. The abbey stood out high and clear above its surrounding buildings. Her car, she was pleased to see, was still in its place.

While she watched, a man came out of the house and walked down the front path. He was presumably the man who occupied the first-floor flat. She knew of him, although until now there'd been neither sight nor sound of him. Surely he must have been away on the day she'd moved in or he'd have appeared? They shared the front door and the first part of the hall, but four steps from the bottom of the staircase a door sealed off his domain, and a yard or so along the passage another door guarded her privacy.

Presumably they shared the pocket-handkerchief-sized front garden? Or was that his because she had the back? If so, he clearly didn't care two hoots about it. Even allowing for the time of the year it looked as though nothing grew there.

As he made a half-turn into the street she stepped back from the window, not wanting to be discovered watching him. He was tallish, perhaps five feet eleven, wore beige trousers and a green anorak, and his fair hair was cropped short, which gave him the appearance of not having much of it. His face remained turned away from her as he watched for a break in the traffic in order to cross the road. She wondered where he was going. Probably, at this time of day, to work.

She would get to know him, of course, but all in good time. She was in no hurry and, living in such close proximity, something entirely new to her, it would be as well to take things

31

slowly. It was also possible, she reminded herself, that he might not be bursting to make her acquaintance!

She planned, this morning, to work really hard in the flat and then after lunch to visit her mother. No tripping off into the town today. She had discarded her previous idea of putting things to rights a little at a time and was now determined to sort everything out as quickly as possible, no procrastination. Only when she had done that could she start living a life, joining things, going places, not to mention looking for a job.

She set to work unpacking the tea chests and large cardboard boxes which had been loaned by MoveAll. That was a priority because they were anxious to collect them.

Why in the world had she packed all this stuff, she asked herself, bent double over the fourth box, with several more still to go? Why did I think even half the contents of Four Winds would fit into a small flat? All this detritus of another life, what do I want with it? Edward had taken almost nothing. Most likely, Naomi thought, Helen had refused to have things. For one glorious moment she toyed with the idea of packing everything she didn't want, or had no room for, back into the boxes and sending them off to Bristol.

She compiled a list in her mind of the items she would return to him: the crinoline lady lamp, which he hated and so did she, but it had been a present from his aunt, and a set of *boules* they had brought back from a holiday in France, and had never used again. And she could include the painting of St Ives, now propped against the bedroom wall. He could give that to Helen, though he had probably given her one of St Lucia, where they had recently spent *their* honeymoon.

She straightened up, stretched herself and rubbed her aching back. Why don't I just put every damned thing I don't want, which was about half the stuff around her, back into the boxes and get removal men to deliver it to a charity shop, or the Salvation Army or something? Or throw it on the tip? She hated almost everything. She would like to have just the basic essentials – table, a few chairs, bed, cooking pots – in a bare flat, paint the walls white, and start again from the beginning. No memories. No excess baggage.

Hey, she admonished herself, you were supposed to be in a bright mood! This was going to be a good day! Snap out of it! She broke off, made herself a cup of coffee, ate a piece of shortbread, then went out into the garden and walked around. There was nothing much to see. What had met her eye on the first occasion was all there was, but already her mind was setting to work, reshaping, choosing colours, planting.

It was a walled garden, which pleased her immensely though the wall, of golden Bath stone, was not as high as she would have liked it. She could still see into her neighbour's garden, and be seen. Perhaps she might be allowed to add eighteen inches or so of trellising to the top and grow climbers over it. Roses, honeysuckle, clematis: something for each season. She was thinking about this when a woman emerged from the house next door, carrying a basket of washing. As she began to peg tea towels on the line, she looked up and saw Naomi.

'Good morning!' she called out. 'You must be my new neighbour. I'm Emily Simpson. Have you settled in?'

'Good morning! I'm Naomi Fletcher. No, I haven't quite. Still a few things to do.'

Her neighbour was heavily pregnant, due any day now, Naomi decided. She pushed away the thought that Helen – the second Mrs Fletcher – would now look like this, at least in shape, though not otherwise. She herself had not met Helen, but Cecily had, and had reported that she was blonde and blue-eyed.

'Quite pretty, really!' she'd said. And then, kindly, 'But not as striking as you.' Whatever that means, Naomi had thought.

Mrs Simpson had red hair, drawn back in a pony tail, and pale, heavily freckled skin.

'If there's anything I can do, anything you're short of,' the new neighbour said, 'do pop around. Not that I'm much good at *doing* at the moment, and not that I'll be around much longer!' She patted her swollen abdomen.

'When is your baby due?' Naomi asked.

'Next week – if I last that long! My first, so I'm a bit apprehensive. I'll be glad when it's over, and so will my husband. I think he's more nervous than I am!'

'You'll be all right!' Naomi said. 'My daughter has a young

33

baby. Just four months.' As if that had anything to do with it! 'My elder daughter,' she added. 'My younger one's still at university.'

'So you've had two children. You'll know all about it!' Mrs Simpson said.

'Three! I have a son.' Did that make her an expert? She had never felt like one. Looking back, she thought she'd probably muddled her way through. But it had turned out all right, or at least the children had, more or less.

'I haven't met my neighbour on the first floor,' she said.

'Mr Sheridan? He's been away. He's a teacher. I think it was an exchange visit. He's very nice.'

'Good!' Naomi said. 'I don't think you should stand outside in the cold.'

'You're right!' Mrs Simpson said. 'A chill is all I need. Nice to have met you!'

'Sheridan,' Naomi said, going back into the house. It was a rather nice name. She wondered if he was Irish.

As she closed the door behind her, the telephone rang.

If it was Edward she wouldn't talk to him. She had had enough. Any day now, she thought, he'll be phoning to tell me that the second Mrs Fletcher has had her baby. A dear little boy, seven pounds eight ounces, mother and child doing well. Well he could break that bit of news to someone else.

It was not Edward. It was Cecily.

'I thought I'd come down this weekend, Mummy! Is that all right?'

'Of course! That would be lovely, darling!'

'Will you meet me at the station? Friday night?'

'I'd rather you got a taxi. I'll pay!'

How to explain that if she used her car she'd never get the space back, certainly not on Friday night? How very stupid this car business was! She would have to solve it.

River View was on the Warminster Road, too far out of the town to walk on a bad day but this afternoon was pleasant. Three years ago, when her mother had become frail, Naomi had wanted her to come to live at Four Winds, where she would look after her.

34

There was ample room, she needn't have impinged on their own living, but Edward would not hear of it.

'Your mother would be far better off in a proper rest home,' he'd said firmly. 'She's bound to get worse, and when she does she'll have professional care. It isn't as if money was a problem. She's well able to pay for something decent!'

So many places had been inspected and River View had been chosen. At that point Naomi would not have chosen anything quite so far from Four Winds but, as it was, it had worked out for the best. In any case, it was the one her mother had taken to, partly because the room she was offered, at the rear of the house, overlooked the valley, with all of Bath laid out before her, but even more because she discovered that a strong bridge school operated in the home. There was the prospect of several games a week without having to leave the premises.

Now of course there were days when to play bridge was not possible. She couldn't remember the cards, her bids were wild, her partners got furious with her. On other days she played like a champion.

It was one of those days when Doris Campbell was living in the past. Naomi recognized that as soon as she entered her room. It was the reason why she was still in her room instead of in the day-room, where she would normally be when she wasn't expecting a visitor. Naomi had phoned River View in the morning to say she would visit later in the day but the nurse had said, 'I won't tell her, it'll be a nice surprise. Sometimes if you tell them early they start looking out of the window straightaway, and then it makes it such a long wait.'

'How are you, Mother?' Naomi enquired.

Mrs Campbell smiled, submitted to being kissed, but Naomi could see the puzzlement in her eyes. She is working out who I am, she thought. It might or might not come to her.

It seemed to Naomi that her mother was often happier when she was living in the past, especially the distant past before she'd married. In any case, Naomi reasoned, when you were in your eighties wasn't the past richer than the present or the future?

Nevertheless she would try, as always, to bring her mother into the present.

35

'I went to see Isobel yesterday,' she said. 'Harry's doing well. He's a lovely little baby!'

'Yes, Uncle Harry was a fine young man,' Doris said. 'He looked lovely in his uniform when he came home on leave. He was a sergeant in the artillery. But I don't remember him as a baby. I wasn't born then. Was he a lovely baby?'

'Not that Harry,' Naomi said. 'I'm talking about your great-grandson! Don't you remember, darling, you're a great-grandmother now? Harry is Isobel's baby.'

'If you say Harry was a lovely baby then I'm sure he was. But look what's happened to him. He's been killed on the Somme. I shall miss him. He's always been my favourite uncle!'

It was one of those days, Naomi recognized, when her mother was living her very early childhood, in the First World War, or even living what *her* mother had told Doris about it when she'd been a little girl.

When she went so far back it was more difficult to recall her, not that she was any trouble at these times. She sat quietly living it through, particularly grateful when, as now, she had an audience to listen, or even to be a participant in the scene, Naomi thought, depending on who she thinks her audience is.

'The Zeppelins were over again last night,' Doris said. 'And poor Ben's been drowned in the *Lusitania*! I don't know why ever he went to sea. He always hated water. Mother had the greatest trouble trying to get him to take a bath!'

She rambled on in her gentle voice. A tray of tea was brought, daintily served, they did things well here; a flowered tea-service, buttered scones.

'I've brought you some chocolate biscuits,' Naomi said.

Her mother ate steadily through everything and drank two cups of tea.

'We have to think of the brave sailors bringing this tea for us through seas ridden with torpedoes!' she said.

It was not always easy to know which war her mother was in, but did it matter? And the nice thing was that though it was always the tragedies she recalled, she never seemed unduly distressed by them.

Naomi stayed for more than an hour and although even in the

end her mother didn't know who she was, except that she was some relative or other, she was glad she had come. She had, for a little while, taken the place of whoever her mother wanted her to be.

And then, in a flutter of lucidity which was not uncommon, she called out after Naomi as she was walking towards the door.

'Did you say Edward had left you?'

'Yes,' Naomi replied.

'Then be thankful! I wish your father had left me twenty years before he did!'

Naomi stood there, smiling at her mother.

'And do you know,' Doris continued, 'I worked out I've played four thousand one hundred and sixty games of bridge since I moved south. We played whist in the north, you know!'

The thing was, Naomi thought, that her mother had probably got the number right.

Ought I to have her to live with me now? she asked herself as she walked home. Now that I have a place of my own?

But if she did, she wouldn't be able to take a job – and she must do something away from the house to preserve her own sanity and to earn some money. And would my mother be happy with me? she wondered. What would we talk about? After all this time, even when she was lucid, what would we have in common?

No, better not, she concluded. She seemed happy enough at River View. Perhaps she would have her for a holiday.

Friday evening, Cecily had said. There was no telling what time that meant and it was never any use asking her. Clocks were anathema to Cecily. It would be a miracle if she caught the train she'd planned to. However, Naomi thought, one thing was certain, whether she arrived early or late she would be hungry, so to cater for that a substantial lamb stew, with herb dumplings, which could be popped in the moment Cecily showed up, was gently simmering on a low heat. The only thing which could scupper that would be if Cecily, on a sudden whim, had turned vegetarian overnight, which was by no means impossible. In the meantime the stew's appetizing aroma filled every corner of the flat making Naomi sharply hungry. But she would wait.

There was nothing more to do. The table was laid, she had opened a bottle of red wine – was Cecily on or off alcohol? – made up the bed in the small bedroom. She had even dashed out around teatime and bought fresh flowers – deep purple irises, pale pink carnations – from a shop around the corner. The gas fire was lit, its flames leaping high through the artificial coals with the utmost realism, the coals themselves now beginning to glow red. She would have shuddered at the thought of such a contrivance at Four Winds but here it seemed quite right, it fitted in. And there would be no mess to clean out in the morning!

Mr Betts had been. He'd arrived early, as promised, and when he'd left and she'd cleaned the keys she'd seated herself at the piano, pushing aside all thoughts of the jobs which were crying out to be done, and played for more than two hours. She'd played whatever came to hand, whatever entered her head: Schubert, Debussy, Scriabin, songs from the shows. When she'd finally torn herself away she'd been a person renewed.

She could, of course, play now while she was waiting. Nothing made the time fly by more quickly for her than playing the piano, but she was too restless. Why am I so nervous when any one of my children is coming to see me? she asked herself. It was not as if she didn't get on with them, of course she did. But once one's children had flown the nest, when one was no longer in control, one felt somehow left behind. We inhabit different countries, she thought. One felt judgement in the air whether it was there or not.

It was a quarter to ten, the stew had been turned off and on and off again when the doorbell rang and continued to ring. That was certainly Cecily. Her way with doorbells was to continue to lean on them until the door was actually opened.

As Naomi rushed out of the room she stopped to pick up her purse. She could guess what would be required of her. At the same time she heard quick footsteps on the stairs, and the man from the first-floor flat appeared, reaching the front door and opening it fractionally ahead of her.

Cecily, standing on the step, looked past him.

'Mummy!' she cried. 'I've no money for the taxi!'

Naomi thrust a five-pound note into her daughter's out-stretched hand.

'I'm sorry!' the man said as Cecily ran back down the path. 'I didn't quite know who the bell was for. I used to have an agreement with your predecessor, one push on the bell for me, two for her. I didn't quite know what this was.'

Yes, he was Irish! A soft, pleasant accent, probably from the south-west.

'You wouldn't!' Naomi said. 'My daughter combines six of anyone else's rings into one. I'm sorry she disturbed you.'

'It doesn't matter in the least,' the man said. 'I can't think why we don't have separate bells. Perhaps we will now.'

Cecily returned. On her upper half she wore a shapeless, padded garment which looked as though it could have been made from an old duvet. On her lower half, above her Doc Martens, her incredibly long and quite shapely legs were encased in black leggings. Her blonde hair, tightly permed, fell to her shoulders in a riot of curls. She carried a backpack, a guitar case, a half-empty bottle of water and a large black plastic bag.

Dirty washing, Naomi thought, taking it from her.

'This is my daughter, Cecily,' she said to the man. 'She's here for the weekend.'

He held out his hand to Cecily.

'Dan Sheridan!'

He turned to Naomi.

'And . . . you?'

'Oh, how silly of me!' Naomi said. 'I'm Naomi Fletcher. I moved in earlier this week.'

'I see. I was away or I'd have offered to give you a hand. Well, I hope you soon settle in. Let me know if there's anything you want.'

'Thank you, I will,' Naomi said. 'Goodnight then!'

'Perhaps you'll come up and have a coffee sometime,' he said. 'Or a drink.'

'That would be nice.'

'Can I give you a hand with your things?' he asked Cecily.

'I'm fine, thank you,' she replied.

Following her mother into the flat, she sniffed the air appreciatively.

'Mmm! Heavenly smell! I'm starving!'

'Lamb stew. I know you like it. I'll just put the dumplings in and we'll eat in twenty minutes. Bring your things into the bedroom.'

She led the way, still carrying the plastic bag.

'I take it this is washing? We'll deal with it tomorrow.'

'You don't mind do you? The machines are quite expensive. And as I was coming home . . .'

'I don't mind at all,' Naomi said. 'I'm used to it. Don't forget, your brother and sister brought dirty washing home whenever they came. I used to think Hugh only came home when he had stacks of washing and needed his hair cutting!'

'Coming home' was the phrase Cecily had used. The words gave Naomi a warm feeling. Perhaps her daughter's home was *still* where she was?

Cecily had piled everything on the bed, then took off her coat, emerging surprisingly slim from its bulk.

'You've lost weight!' Naomi said.

'Oh! Good!'

'Are you eating enough?'

'Of course I am, Mummy!' Cecily said. 'You know I always eat like a horse!'

It was true, and she proved it yet again at supper, demolishing two large helpings, including four dumplings, followed by a banana and an apple.

'Super!' she said. 'Is there some coffee?'

'In a minute. Let's sit by the fire with it shall we?'

'I like the new fire,' Cecily said. 'It's cool! In fact the whole flat's looking good. I never thought it would when I came with you to view it, but I was wrong. You're what I'd call a good homemaker!'

'I'd always *thought* I was,' Naomi heard the chill in her curt voice and quickly admonished herself. There were to be no recriminations against anyone this weekend. No quarrelsome talk. 'What would you like to do while you're here?' she asked in a pleasanter voice.

40

'Nothing very special,' Cecily said. 'Catch up on sleep, so don't expect me to be up early.'

'I won't,' Naomi promised. 'Will it disturb you if I play the piano while you're still asleep?'

'It wouldn't disturb me if the whole of the London Symphony Orchestra played!' Cecily assured her. 'Not if I'm really asleep. I thought later on tomorrow I'd go along to see Isobel and the baby. How *is* Harry!'

'Thriving!' Naomi said. 'I went to see your grandmother yesterday. I dare say she'd like to see you if you have the time. When do you have to be back?'

It was dangerous ground asking your offspring how long they were likely to stay. Either they thought you were shooing them off or detaining them against their will.

'Not for ages,' Cecily said. 'It's reading week, so no lectures. Free as air!'

'Good! Well we'll do whatever you decide on.'

'I quite liked the look of your neighbour.' Cecily poured herself another cup of coffee, nibbled at another chocolate mint. 'He looks . . . dependable. The sort you could turn to if your sink gets blocked or the kettle fuses. Not wildly exciting, but then he's not the age to be exciting!'

He is probably about my age, Naomi thought bleakly. And perhaps her daughter was right.

'I'm not looking for wild excitement,' she said. 'I suppose a sink unblocker is more in my line.'

'Good! So no midnight orgies?'

'I think I can safely promise that, daughter dear.'

A sudden knocking started on the wall, clearly from next door. It was insistent, loud, frantic.

'My neighbour! Her baby's due. I'd better go.' She went to the bedroom and snatched up her coat.

'I'll come with you,' Cecily said. 'What excitement!'

Emily Simpson was at the door the second they rang.

'It's coming!' she said. 'It's the baby! I can't get hold of my husband. He'll be on the train . . .'

She stopped, clutched at herself as a paroxysm of pain hit her.

41

'Please take me to the hospital!' she begged. 'Quickly! I've got a bag packed.'

'I'll get a taxi at once!' Naomi said.

'No, not a taxi! Not on Friday night. We'd have to wait, and I can't wait. I don't want my baby born in a taxi!'

'Of course you don't,' Naomi agreed. 'I wasn't thinking straight. I'll get my car, it's parked quite close. I'll be back quite quickly. Cecily will look after you.' Please God, she prayed, let my car start first time!

Cecily gave her mother a frightened look. 'Wouldn't it be better to call an ambulance?'

'No! My car's already here. I'll be back in five minutes, no more.'

'But, what if . . . ?' Cecily began.

'You'll be all right.' Naomi turned to her neighbour. 'Just hang on, Emily! Everything's going to be all right!'

FOUR

Cecily looked at her watch, again.

'We've been here an hour,' she complained. 'There's not a thing we can do. Can't we go home?'

They were sitting in a corridor in the maternity unit, drinking coffee in cardboard cups from the dispenser.

'Not yet,' Naomi said. 'Not until something happens, either the husband arrives or the baby's born. You can go if you wish but I think I should stay.'

Cecily sighed. 'I'll wait a bit longer.'

A nurse came through the swing doors and walked towards them. Naomi jumped to her feet, splashing her coffee on the floor.

'Is everything all right?'

'Perfectly! A fine baby girl! Eight pounds!' She permitted herself a smile.

'And Mrs Simpson?'

'She's all right. A bit tired, but then not as much as if she'd had a long labour. You can't have it both ways. No sign of a Mr Simpson?'

The remains of her smile gave way to a frown of disapproval. He was one of those, she hadn't a doubt, who chickened out of it at the last minute. She'd met them before and she had a low opinion of them, though they weren't as much of a nuisance as

43

those who insisted on being present then passed out, lying on the floor, cluttering up the delivery room, at the first sign of blood. She had shoved more than one aside with her foot. When she'd first started nursing husbands hadn't been allowed in until it was all over. She preferred it that way.

There was a sudden, slight commotion at the far end of the corridor as a burly red-haired man played a game of dodgems with a porter wheeling a trolley. When they had sorted themselves out he broke into a run. The nurse put up a hand to stop him as he approached.

'In hospital we only run in case of fire or haemorrhage. Would you be Mr Simpson?'

'Yes! Where's my wife?'

He could hardly get the words out. The train had been late. When he'd reached home he'd seen Emily's note on the table. He'd run all the way to the hospital.

'Tucked up in bed!' the nurse said. 'You have a beautiful little daughter!'

He grabbed the nurse, lifted her short tubby body off the floor and swung her around. She submitted gracefully. She was used to it at times like this.

'When you put me down,' she said, 'I'll take you to your wife! She *did* expect you earlier!'

'The train was held up. Trouble on the line. I saw the note when I got home.'

It might or might not be true. She'd heard it all before, but at least he didn't stink of drink, hadn't been wetting the baby's head before its arrival. He seemed, actually, quite nice.

The two of them disappeared through the swing doors. Naomi and Cecily looked at each other.

'He didn't even see us!' Cecily said.

'He wouldn't have known us anyway. I've never met him. I've only spoken to Emily over the garden wall.'

'Well at any rate we can go home,' Cecily said. 'I wonder what they'll call her?'

It was a quiet drive back, it was after all almost two in the morning. How on earth will I find somewhere to park? Naomi

44

asked herself. She needn't have worried, there was her own space, waiting for her.

'I can't think why you worry,' Cecily said. 'People are coming and going all the time!'

'I know,' Naomi agreed. 'But sod's law says not at the right time. Sod's law says I get there three yards after someone has moved into the only available space!'

'You're neurotic!' Cecily said. 'If you can't use your car you might as well sell it – or you could give it to me!'

'You can't drive.' Am I neurotic? she wondered. Really?

'I could learn. You could pay for lessons as a birthday present.'

'If I give you my car I wouldn't have it for emergencies,' Naomi said. 'I wouldn't have had it for tonight.'

They had reached the house. They let themselves in quietly so as not to disturb Dan Sheridan.

'What would he think if he heard us coming in at this time?' Naomi whispered.

'He'd think we'd been clubbing,' Cecily said. 'I wish we had!'

They were in the flat now, it was no longer necessary to whisper.

'I've never been to a nightclub in my life,' Naomi said. Had she ever wanted to? She didn't think so, except that she'd have liked to have done most things once: a parachute jump, sailing silently through the air, landing in a meadow full of summer flowers; flying to New York on Concorde; snorkelling in blue, Pacific waters; eating dinner at the Savoy; playing a Beethoven concerto – the Fourth she thought – at the Albert Hall . . . The list was endless.

Cecily yawned loudly.

'I'm going to bed. I'm whacked! Do *not* call me in the morning.'

When she had gone Naomi moved into the kitchen and made a cup of camomile tea, which she took to bed with her. She was quite tired. It was nice about the baby. She was glad she'd been able to do something. After she'd switched off the bedside lamp she lay awake for a little while, wondering what it was like to float down to earth in a parachute. She closed her eyes, so that instead of the darkness of the bedroom she could see the brightness of

45

the sky around her and the green of the field, dotted with flowers, as it came up to meet her. She fell asleep.

It was eleven-thirty before Cecily appeared, her eyelids swollen with sleep but her hair, because it was so tightly curled, much as it had been when she'd gone to bed.

'I had a lovely sleep,' she said. 'I dreamt I was matron of a large hospital and all the nurses were men, dressed up in aprons and frilly caps, and they were all doing my bidding. Do you think it means anything?'

'I think it's wishful thinking!'

'Did you notice how many of the nurses in the hospital were men? I wouldn't mind having my fevered brow soothed by one or two of them,' Cecily said.

'There are loads of men in hospitals now,' Naomi told her. 'As you'd know if you watched *Casualty*.'

'It's at the wrong time. It interferes with my social life.' Cecily seated herself at the table, where a place had been laid for her, helped herself to Weetabix. 'Were you up early?'

'Much as usual,' Naomi said.

One of the perks she had promised herself in her new life was that of getting up later, at whatever time she wished, at least until she took a job. It hadn't worked out. However late she went to bed she wakened at seven. There was no point in just lying there.

The habit of half a lifetime, she supposed. How long would it take her to throw off those habits? Presumably not until she'd replaced them with new ones.

'I went out to buy milk,' she said. 'There's a shop just around the corner.'

'Buy milk? Don't they deliver milk in Bath, then? Could I have some toast?'

'Of course they do,' Naomi said, popping a slice of bread in the toaster, wondering, as far as she knew for the first time ever, why Cecily couldn't make her own toast. 'Hadn't you noticed, I don't use milk? Not in tea or coffee, and I don't eat cereals. There's no point in having it delivered.'

'So you went out for little me?' Cecily said. 'That was sweet of you, Mummy!'

Was there an edge of sarcasm in her daughter's voice? No,

46

Naomi decided, there wasn't. Cecily said exactly what she wanted to say, straight out: no malice aforethought and no tact either.

In fact, she had quite enjoyed going around to the shop. It was a newsagent's which also sold several other necessities of life; bread, jam, tea – and had a large freezer full of frozen peas, sweetcorn, fish fingers and a few more exotic packeted meals. Chicken Tikka Marsala had caught her eye. One day she would pursue the freezer's depths. The Asian owner of the shop had noticed her at once, smiled and bid her good morning. He probably knew all his customers.

'Are you going to see Isobel?' she asked Cecily.

'Yes. Are you coming with me?'

'I don't think so. You two might enjoy being together.'

'Oh Mummy, you are funny!' Cecily said. 'As if it mattered! I'm only going to say hello to Isso and to inspect the baby.'

On the way back from the shop Naomi had glimpsed Dan Sheridan leaving the house and walking away in the opposite direction. He had a brisk, springing walk, rather at odds with what she had observed of his quiet manner.

Which means I have the house to myself and I can play the piano without disturbing anyone, she thought. She took Cecily at her word that it wouldn't waken her. She had played for an hour, again a mixture of things, as if she couldn't settle down to what she should be playing. But it had been enjoyable, and she promised herself that soon she would get back to her usual way of, while playing a variety of things, always studying something in particular, getting to know it better. Some habits were best not broken.

'Could I have another slice of toast?' Cecily asked politely.

'As much as you like, darling! The toaster's over by the kettle.'

Cecily looked faintly surprised, but rose to her feet.

'I thought perhaps I'd stay until Tuesday,' she said when she came back to the table. 'Then I'd go over to Bristol to see Daddy and Helen.'

'See Daddy?' Naomi couldn't keep the surprise out of her voice.

But why did I think that because Edward had gone out of my

life he'd also gone from my childrens'? she asked herself. Because, the answer came, he deserted me, I didn't desert him. I am the person wronged, I expected my children to take my part, be on my side. Nothing had been put into words, she didn't know whether they had or hadn't. Neither she nor Edward saw Hugh enough for it to make much difference there. As for Isobel, she lived on her own little island with her baby and its father and at the moment that was her world. I can enter it, Naomi thought, but she's not for coming out of it. Unless of course she needs help, and even then she'll simply hoist a distress flag and I'll answer it. Would Edward?

Cecily broke into her thoughts.

'I haven't seen Daddy since Christmas.'

They had still been at Four Winds at Christmas. Edward had by then been spending part of his time with his family, and an increasing share with Helen.

'I thought,' Cecily continued 'now that you've found you *can* use your car, you might run me over.'

'Run you over? And what am I supposed to do while you pay your visit? See a film? Have a meal somewhere? Go shopping in Bristol?'

'Oh Mummy, don't be so silly!' Cecily said impatiently. 'Naturally, I shall stay for a night or two and then go back to Sussex.'

'Aren't you supposed to be in a reading week?' Naomi's tone was sharp. Would it have been if Cecily had been staying with her?

'Not to worry,' Cecily said lightly. 'I'll make it up later. I dare say Helen will be quite pleased to see me. She must be getting to the bored stage, don't you think? Actually, I expect they'd quite like you to drop in.'

'You must be mad!' Naomi tried not to raise her voice, and failed.

'Mummy, don't be so uncivilized! These things happen. It's the way of the world. We have to come to terms with it, learn to deal with it!'

Which of us is the mother and which the child? Naomi wondered furiously. Who is eighteen and who is forty-six?

48

'So will you drive me over? It's only . . . what . . . a dozen miles?'

Naomi took a deep breath.

'At the risk of appearing uncivilized, I will not. I will take you to Bath station and you can get the train to Bristol. You need not bother to give your father and Helen either my love or my best wishes. And if they ask how I'm getting on, as they doubtless will, being civilized people, tell them wonderfully well. Tell them I'm having the time of my life!'

'There's no need to be like that,' Cecily said in a calm voice. 'I'm disappointed you won't run me over, but if that's how you feel . . .'

'It is!'

'Then, Mummy darling,' Cecily said with all the wisdom of her eighteen years, 'you must learn to live in the real world!'

Naomi walked out into the garden. At this moment she would have liked to have chopped down a very large tree or, at the very least, done some hard digging. Neither was possible. The only tree of any size was a winter-flowering prunus, so beautiful now in its delicate pink blossom that there was no way she could wreak her vengeance on it. As for digging, there had been a sharp overnight frost and the ground was too hard.

She had walked out of the house without stopping to put on a jacket and now the biting cold drove her in again.

'I'm just off to Isobel's,' Cecily called out brightly.

'Will you be back for lunch?' Naomi asked.

'Who knows. Perhaps we could lunch somewhere in the town?'

'If you like.'

As she watched Cecily walk away Naomi's whole body was in a turmoil, her insides sick and shaking, her hands trembling. Why did she let it upset her, make her so angry? Anger was not natural to her.

With a sudden movement she crossed the room and sat down at the piano. Her hands crashed down in a horrible discord, and then she paused while her brain sorted out what she should play to rid herself of these complex feelings of anger and regret and confusion. Quickly, her hands descended again in the first

49

crashing chords of the Chopin 'Revolutionary'. He had written this in anger and grief at the fall of his beloved Warsaw and as the notes flowed from her fingers, she felt that, in her own way, in this tempestuous music she shared and reflected his feelings. And then presently, although it was a work she had studied assiduously a year or so ago, memory left her and she no longer knew which notes came next. Tears filled her eyes and ran down her face and the black and white of the keys blurred into one another. She lifted her hands from the keyboard and wept without restraint.

When she had recovered she dried her eyes, and also the piano keys where her tears had fallen on them. Why did I take it out on my lovely piano? she asked. Why did I bash you and crash you as if you had no feelings?

While Cecily watched Isobel feeding Harry she related the drama of Emily Simpson and their late-night dash to the hospital. To say that she *watched* her nephew being fed was not quite correct. She did what she could to avoid seeing anything of the procedure, walking around the room, picking up ornaments and examining them, studying pictures on the wall, looking out of the window. She would have liked to have remained with her back to the room, concentrating on the street scene below, until the whole affair was over, but it would seem rather rude. Not nearly as rude, though, as this primitive earthy ritual which she had by unfortunate timing walked right into.

The sight of her sister's grossly distended, blue-veined breast, nonchalantly displayed as if she was a prize cow, was really quite horrible, and even when she turned away from the sight, which she did as often as possible, there was still the sound. Sucking, gurgling, little grunts of satisfaction. She could swear the baby smacked its lips. It was like a greedy old man with a pint of beer.

She averted her eyes quickly as Isobel moved Harry over to the other side, tucking away one breast, yanking the other out of her bra, pushing the nipple into the child's greedily waiting mouth.

It was disgusting, totally uncivilized! What, after all, were feeding bottles for?

'Who's a good little boy, then?' Isobel cooed with quiet pride.

50

'So how long *was* she in labour then, Mummy's neighbour?'

'Hardly any time at all, thank goodness. Less than two hours.'

'I was twenty-three hours in labour.' Isobel spoke with a touch of complacency. 'From the time the waters broke, that is.'

Don't tell me! Cecily implored silently. I don't want to know! She would never, ever have a child, or at least if by some mischance she did it would be by Caesarian delivery, and bottle fed from the very first moment.

'But he's worth every minute of it, bless him!' Isobel said. She held Harry up against her shoulder and rubbed his back. He belched loudly.

Exactly like an old man, Cecily thought.

'I'm meeting Mummy for lunch,' she said. 'I think she has a real need to talk things through.'

'Harry gained eight ounces this week,' Isobel said. 'They were very pleased with him at the mother and baby clinic! What things?'

'You know! Daddy, Helen, the divorce. Really, Isso, don't you ever think of anything outside of Harry?'

'I think it's best for Mummy if we leave her alone, don't interfere. Everyone should be left to get on with their own life in the way they choose.'

'That's all very well, but it's just not practical,' Cecily said impatiently. Isso was cocooned in her own little world! 'Some people aren't capable of getting on with their own lives. They don't know what to do.'

'You mean you think you can help Mummy to decide what to do?'

Cecily nodded.

'Yes, I do. At least I can help her to face things, see things as they really are.'

'You mean bring her round to your way of thinking. Encourage her to take it all in her stride? Come smiling through?'

Cecily gave her sister a sharp glance.

'I suppose so,' she agreed. 'I do truly believe that it's the healthiest way!'

Isobel put Harry down in his crib, draped a coverlet over him, uttered a few words of love, then she turned to her sister.

51

'And you think, do you,' she asked quietly, 'that out of your own great experience you know the answers?'

'There's no need for sarcasm, Isso! I do read, I do keep up to date. My friends and I often discuss our parents. Mummy's living in a backwater – I mean mentally of course.'

'Really? Well it's not my place to interfere in my parents' lives. Now that I've got Harry my job is to look after him. But if you want to know what I think about Daddy, I think he's a shit!'

'That's not fair!' Cecily cried.

'Oh, I know you think the sun shines on him—'

'Daddy is acknowledging his feelings,' Cecily said hotly. 'He's finding himself. And he's being totally honest!'

'He is a shit of the first water!' Isobel said.

To tell the truth, Cecily thought, she would be quite glad to get away from Isso. Her sister had developed such strange ideas. Perhaps it was a result of childbirth; hormones and so on.

'I have to go,' she said. 'So I take it you don't want me to give your love to Daddy when I see him?'

'Definitely not.' Isobel began to clear away the paraphenalia which accompanied every changing, feeding, washing of her baby. It did tend to take over all the available space. 'What sort of a grandfather model is he for Harry, I ask you? But you can give my love to Mummy.'

'Will do,' Cecily promised. She wondered how high she rated as an aunt to Harry. Probably not very high. She had not begged to nurse him, or examined with wonder the length of his eye-lashes, though he was a nice enough little thing as far as babies went.

Naomi was waiting in Milsom Street, looking at the price of diamond rings in the jeweller's window. I suppose I could sell my engagement ring if I wanted to, she thought. It was quite a nice one, diamonds and sapphires. Edward had never been mean about things like that. She certainly had no interest in wearing it. Come to that, would she continue to wear her wedding ring? She was no longer married.

She looked up and saw Cecily.

'Have you been waiting long?' Cecily asked.

'No, not long.'

'I'm starving!' Cecily said. 'Is this place fairly near?'

'Two minutes!'

Cecily chose lasagne, Naomi rigatone with bacon. 'And a green salad, a tomato salad, and a half-litre of house wine, red.'

While they waited for their pasta they sipped the wine. Cecily looked around the restaurant, half-empty now that most of the lunchers had left.

'It's quite nice,' she said.

'I like it,' Naomi agreed.

Shall I talk to her now, Cecily wondered, or shall I wait until we've eaten? She was full of the desire to help and, in spite of Isso's theories, sure that she could. It was just a case of how to begin and if she spent too much time pussy-footing around she'd never get anywhere.

'I do think,' she said, plunging in regardless, 'if you and Daddy, and Helen of course, were to be more friendly you'd find life much easier, Mummy!'

Naomi took a deep swig of her wine, and refilled her glass.

'You do, do you?' she said, quite quietly.

'I do, Mummy! You'd be less tense. You strike me as being quite tense!'

The food arrived. Cecily eyed it most appreciatively.

'This looks good!' She began to eat, continuing to speak through a mouthful of lasagne.

'You should let go more. You should come to terms with your inner-self, with the core of your being!'

Naomi took a deep breath, and another drink of wine.

If I let go, she thought, if I came to terms with what my inner-self is feeling at this very minute, you would have this plate of rigatone, of which I obviously cannot bear to eat a morsel, right down your front!

Cecily continued to eat steadily and with evident enjoyment.

'Is yours nice?' she enquired. 'Yes of course I know you must be hurt, you've been so used to Daddy, living with him all this time. I quite understand you missing him!'

Got used to him! Naomi swilled down the rest of the wine in her glass, put up a hand to summon the waitress, and ordered another carafe. Was that all her marriage had been about?

53

Through a slight haze of red wine, unadulterated by food, she looked back at the early years, before this . . . chit . . . had been born, and then when she was a baby. Such an adorable baby! How had she grown into this bossy-boots? Life had been wonderful then! The love, the excitement, even the sex. And what was *she* supposed to do about sex? No doubt her know-all daughter, this eighteen-year-old sitting opposite, scraping her plate clean, could advise her.

'You're not eating, Mummy,' Cecily said. 'You must keep up your strength. But if you don't want it all, I'll have a bit. It looks delicious!'

You are lucky, Naomi thought, pushing the plate rather clumsily across the table, knocking over the salt, not to have it on your head!

'Help yourself!' she invited.

But she did love Cecily really! She loved them all. You didn't stop loving your children even when you found them as irritating as she did this one now. She could have smacked her bottom – not that she ever had.

'I thank you for your advice,' she said, enunciating carefully. 'You can be sure I shall consider it!' She drained her wine glass.

'I think perhaps we'd better have some coffee before we leave,' Cecily said.

FIVE

Leaving the restaurant, they passed the theatre. There were posters everywhere for the following week's play.

'I'd like to see that,' Naomi said. 'I enjoy Alan Ayckbourn.'

'Then why not book, while we're here?' Cecily suggested.

'I'll think about it.'

She was not in the mood to do anything definite, not even booking a theatre seat. She was ever so slightly fuzzy in the head and a little bit tired. A leisurely walk home in the fresh air, followed by a nap in front of the fire, seemed about right.

She liked the theatre in Bath. It was cosy, it enfolded one in another, more reassuring age. She and Edward had been there a few times, though mostly they went to Bristol.

But who would I go with now? she asked herself. She could go on her own but it wouldn't be the same. If she were to choose a matinée, would her mother like to come? But would she enjoy Alan Ayckbourn? Almost certainly not!

'And supposing it's a day when she's fighting the Second World War?' she said out loud.

'What?'

'My mother, your grandmother!'

'I don't understand you!' Cecily said.

'I'm sorry! It's too difficult to explain at the moment. In any case, I have to watch the pennies now.'

That really wasn't quite true. Edward paid a reasonable sum into the bank for her on the first of every month, enough for her to live on. She was glad it was paid into the bank. It meant that she could distance herself from it, almost pretend that it didn't come from Edward but arrived in her account by electronic magic from somewhere in outer space.

'No,' she corrected herself. 'It's not as bad as that. Your father is not mean, whatever other faults he may have!' And she could give her daughter quite a list of those, though she would not.

All the same, the sooner she could stand on her own two feet, the better. She felt like a kept woman. No, I don't! she decided. A kept woman sounded exciting, desirable, glamorous. A mistress to be visited late every afternoon on the way home from work; diplomats, men in high office, dropping in on her. The keeper of secrets, a *confidante*. But no, it was not quite like that.

What I feel like, she decided as they waited in the confusing traffic to cross the road to Bridge Street, is someone who has been pensioned off. Redundant. Surplus to requirements. She had once heard on good authority that in France men pensioned off their surplus women by buying them the franchise to lavatories, from which they grew moderately rich on the tips. She could not envisage that happening in Bath.

Did Edward feel that he had pensioned her off, that in doing so fairly and justly he had fulfilled his obligations?

Had he – what a terrible thought! – sat down with Helen and calculated the amount of the pension? What shall we allow poor Naomi? 'We must be as generous as we can,' Helen would say from her unassailable position.

But I have also, Naomi told herself as the two of them walked across Pulteney Bridge, stopping from time to time to look in the shops, to make myself independent in thought and attitude as well as financially.

How did one do that? She had had no practice at it.

'I must buy a *Bath Chronicle*,' she said suddenly.

'Whatever for?'

'They'll advertise jobs, won't they? I mean to start looking for one quite soon. Do you think jobs will be easy to find in Bath? Or difficult?'

'I've no idea,' Cecily said reasonably. 'When my friends want a vacation job in Brighton they go to an agency.'

'I don't want anything temporary. I want a permanent job, but part-time.'

'So what could you do, Mummy?'

Trust Cecily to ask that sort of question! What *could* she do?

'I'm not sure,' Naomi said vaguely. 'Several things, I dare say. I shall make a list.'

When they reached home there was an envelope wedged in the door of the flat.

'Who could have got in at the front door to leave this?' Naomi asked. She liked to know whom communications were from before she opened them, a trait which had infuriated Edward and clearly niggled Cecily.

'The Irishman, of course! Why don't you just open it, Mummy?'

'You're quite right,' Naomi said, doing so.

She read the message out aloud.

While your daughter is visiting I wondered if you might both like to come up for a drink this evening? Sevenish. Give me a ring if it's not convenient.
Dan Sheridan.

'How nice of him,' she said. 'Though really I'm quite tired!'

'Oh really, Mummy, you've got hours to recover!' Cecily said. 'It might be quite fun. You don't have anything else planned, do you?'

'Nothing.'

'Then let's accept!'

It was really too much to hope that it might be fun. The Irishman didn't give that impression. Her mother, however, was in a strange mood. She didn't exactly look forward to spending the evening alone with her.

'Very well,' Naomi said. 'And I think I ought to slip round next door, ask Mr Simpson how his wife and the new baby are. But I shall have a little lie-down first!'

★   ★   ★

Dan checked the cupboard in the kitchen where he kept the drinks. Gin he had, and half a bottle of dry sherry. A few cans of beer and two half-litres of tonic. The beer and the tonics he moved to the fridge. He had no lemon and no crisps. Well, they would have to make do without the niceties. He had asked them on the spur of the moment and now he couldn't be sure why, except that it had somehow seemed better to do so when the two of them were there together.

Perhaps he should nip around to Patel's and buy a lemon and some of those little cheesy biscuit things? And what about orange juice? The girl might not drink alcohol – though he doubted that. He took his anorak from the hook, thrust his arms into it and ran down the stairs. In the shop he wondered if he should have invited them to supper instead of just a drink. Something quite simple. Pasta? But no, perhaps not. He didn't want to make a fuss, didn't want to start something he mightn't wish to continue. He was just being neighbourly.

At ten past seven the bell rang and he went to the door.

'Are we too early?' Naomi asked. She was not sure about Bath hospitality, though there were bound to be rules. Did one arrive on time or was the done thing to be half an hour late?

'Not at all!' Dan said. 'Do come in!'

The room looked comfortable, squashy cushions on the sofa and armchairs, floor-length William Morris curtains at the window. It was not too smart, or too oppressively tidy. A mahogany desk against one wall was piled with what looked like school exercise books. There were more books on the window-sill, on the table, and on the low shelves around the walls. What pleased Naomi particularly was that one corner of the room was given over to hi-fi equipment, with a tall tower of CDs and a shelf of videos. If he was a music lover he wouldn't mind so much that she played the piano. She wondered what kind of music he liked. Nothing, so far, had percolated down to her flat, but then he had only been back a day or two.

'What would you like to drink?' Dan asked. He reeled off the choices. 'You, Mrs Fletcher?'

'Naomi, please! I'd like a gin and tonic if I may.'

'Me too!' Cecily said. She seated herself in an armchair

and looked around with unconcealed curiosity. 'I like your pictures!'

'Probably too many,' Dan replied. 'And a bit of a mixture. I keep adding just one more. I can't resist them.'

'I hate bare walls,' Cecily said.

'I thought all you young people were minimalists,' Dan said, pouring the drinks. 'Everything pared down, no clutter allowed.'

'Not me,' Cecily assured him. 'All I can afford now are posters, but when I earn *big* money I shall collect paintings – and perhaps a few choice, small sculptures!'

Naomi thought it was the room of a man who had decided exactly what he wanted, was not bound by what went with what or what was fashionable, but followed his own inclination. It was eclectic, a pleasing mixture. She doubted that anyone had influenced this room. It was a one-person place. She wondered how long Dan Sheridan had lived alone, or if he had perhaps always lived alone? Although there were pictures aplenty on the walls, there were no photographs in sight.

She smiled at him as he handed her her drink. It was in a no nonsense, heavy tumbler; nothing fancy, a generous long drink.

'I'm happy to see you like music,' she said. 'Perhaps you won't mind so much that I play the piano? You're bound to hear it.'

'I haven't so far,' he said. 'I expect I shall enjoy it.'

'I mostly play in the mornings – occasionally in the evenings. I think in the last day or two I've played after you've left for school.'

He raised his eyebrows.

'Emily Simpson, my next-door neighbour, told me you were a teacher.'

'Ah! Yes, I teach French and history. I heard she'd had her baby. Mr Patel told me. He's our local shopkeeper and the fount of all knowledge – well, all local gossip, though none of it unkind, he's too good a businessman for that.'

'I've met him,' Naomi said. 'I liked him. And I went to see Mr Simpson earlier this evening. Mother and child doing well. He looks better than when we last saw him.'

'Well, here's to them,' Dan said. 'And to you and Cecily. I hope you'll both be happy here!'

'I shan't be here much,' Cecily informed him. 'Just the occasional flying visit. I'm going to see my father on Tuesday and I'll go back to university on Wednesday or Thursday. I'm at Sussex. My father lives in Bristol.'

Tell him the lot, why don't you, Naomi thought. Tell him my husband left me for a newer model. Tell him you're going to have a new little sister or brother! Not that she cared whether he knew or not. She was, after all, curious about him, but she would have preferred to tell him herself, and in her own time.

'My husband and I are divorced,' she said shortly. 'Quite recently.'

'I'm sorry.' He sought for something to say – and found it. 'I'm a widower. My wife was killed in a road accident.'

'How sad,' Naomi said.

Cecily jumped to her feet and began to wander around the room, examining without the least hesitation anything which caught her eye.

'It was a long time ago,' Dan said. 'She was in her twenties, so was I. She was newly pregnant. Our first. She hadn't even had time to tell me. Let me refresh your drink. Tell me what *you* do. Do you have a job? Have you always lived in Bath?'

Naomi took up his questions. He had obviously said all he was going to say about his personal life and no way would she press him.

'No, I haven't, but I've always liked Bath. It seemed the obvious place to come.' Not that she hadn't thought wildly of leaving the country, settling in France, emigrating to Australia, leaving everyone to their own devices, but she had had neither the energy nor the initiative.

'And I don't have a job at present,' she said, 'but I must find one. I bought a *Chronicle* this afternoon, but there doesn't seem to be much in it.'

'That's probably because it's a Saturday,' Dan explained. 'A weekday would be better – not that I'm an expert.'

'I hadn't thought of that,' Naomi said. 'I'll bear it in mind. In the meantime I'll try the agencies. Cecily thinks that's the thing to do.'

Cecily looked up from a book she was dipping into.

60

'Oh, it is!' She spoke with all the confidence of one who had never sought a job.

'What are you looking for?' Dan asked.

He handed around the last of Mr Patel's cheesy bits – they had gone well, especially in Cecily's direction – then relaxed into an armchair, his long legs stretched out before him. He quite liked Naomi Fletcher. He thought it possible that she could turn out to be more lively than she had seemed so far. She was too contained. As for the daughter, 'contained' was the last word he would use about her. She was a pain in the backside.

'I wish I knew!' Naomi said. 'It's more a case of what's available that I can possibly do.'

'I'm sure you'll find something,' Dan said comfortably. 'If you're going after jobs, don't underrate yourself!'

'When I was at Four Winds – that was my former home—' Naomi said, 'I used to teach piano. Not many pupils, mostly the children of friends, but I enjoyed it. I'd quite like to do that again but I'm not sure where to start. As well as a proper job, I mean.'

'I'll keep my eyes and ears open,' Dan said. 'There might be kids at school for music lessons. I'll let you know.'

'Would it drive you mad, hearing children learning the piano?' Naomi asked.

'I don't think so. In any case I'm out a lot.'

Where did he go? Naomi wondered. And was that something *she* would be able to say in a year from now? 'I'm out a lot.'

The conversation dwindled, not least because Cecily had ceased to perambulate and now stood rooted to the spot, staring at nothing, irritating both her mother and Dan Sheridan. In the end Naomi said, 'I think we must be going!'

'Must you?' Dan rose to his feet as she did. They both knew it was a half-hearted question.

'Yes, we really must!' Cecily said quickly. 'We're expecting a telephone call!'

It was patently untrue. All three of them knew it.

'You must come again,' Dan said, looking directly at Naomi.

Back in her own flat, she turned on Cecily.

'How *could* you?' she cried. 'You behaved abominably!'

'I was bored,' Cecily said. 'My God, he was boring.'

'He was nothing of the kind! But even if he had been, that's no excuse. You behaved like a spoilt child!'

'Well if that's what I am,' Cecily said lightly, 'it's got to be your fault! You're my mother. You brought me up!'

'And you have two parents!' Naomi retorted.

She shouldn't have been surprised, though, it was not unusual behaviour for Cecily.

But I was *not* the one who spoilt her, she thought. She has her father to thank for that and I will *not* take the blame. All the same, the accusation niggled her. Had she never been firm enough? Had she been weak where she should have been strong? Could that be why Edward had walked out on her? Should she have fought for him, not just let him go?

Well, it was too late now, it was all in the past. She couldn't even change Cecily at this stage. Whatever influence she had once had – if any – was now no more. But if I can't change the past, she thought, I can change the future, at least my own future. And if being strong was what it took, then she would learn to be strong.

'I think I might go on to Daddy on Monday morning instead of Tuesday,' Cecily said. 'I could go straight to his office and he'd take me out for lunch.'

'Why don't you do just that?' Naomi said crisply. 'In any case I'm going to be quite busy on Monday. I've loads to do and tomorrow you could go to see your grandmother.'

'Must I?' Cecily pleaded.

'I think you should.'

But why won't I say, Yes, you must? Naomi asked herself.

'Make it in the afternoon, then,' Cecily said. 'I refuse to be dragged out of bed on Sunday morning. And you must go with me. Anyway, I suppose it might be more entertaining than visiting Isso again, especially as Patrick will be home. How can *anyone* be an item with a librarian?'

It was one of Doris Campbell's better days. Cecily was also, surprisingly, at her best. Not that Cecily was at any time moody, sunk in gloom for no obvious reason as Isobel had so easily been until Harry had changed her life. No, Cecily reacted to

62

events and made no attempt to hide her reactions. If she was bored, everyone knew it; if she was angry she vented her anger on whoever was there; if she was contented life was smooth and if she was happy she spread happiness around her like the sun on a summer's day. On Sunday afternoon, at River View, she was contented, veering towards happy. Perhaps, Naomi thought, the result of at least twelve hours unbroken sleep. At any rate she listened with every sign of interest to her grandmother's ramblings which, on this occasion, were coherent and rooted in the present.

'We had a very nice morning,' Doris said. 'Bacon and eggs, it being Sunday, and then later on the curate came from St Mary's. He did a nice little service and gave us Communion.'

'I didn't know you liked that sort of thing,' Naomi said. Her mother had never been a churchgoer; Christmas and Harvest Festival perhaps, but not much else.

'Oh, I've developed quite a taste for it,' Doris said. 'We don't have it every week, of course. The third Sunday in the month.' The trouble was in sorting out which was the third Sunday. 'It passes the time!'

'Of course it does,' Cecily agreed. 'One or two familiar hymns. Singing is good for people.'

'The curate's a nice young man,' Doris said. 'Single. And as far as I know, not for the wrong reason, if you know what I mean.'

'You mean he's not gay,' Cecily said.

'I don't think so. Not that that matters except that he wouldn't be in the marriage market.' She gave Cecily a direct look; long, calculating. 'You could do well to marry a parson, Cecily. A nice steady job. Security. Not much of a wage, but a house with it and people in the parish give you presents. A ton of coal, bottles of wine, hampers at Christmas. Yes, you could do much worse!'

'Thanks, Grandma,' Cecily said. 'It sounds an exciting prospect, but I don't think so. In fact I don't intend to marry. It's too long-term.'

'You mean you'll live in sin?' Doris said equably. 'Well, why not? If I had my time to come over I dare say that's what I'd do. Marriage can be very boring.'

I don't know where I fit in, Naomi thought. Suddenly she felt older than the other two put together.

'And what else did you do?' Cecily asked with interest.

'Well, we had our lunch. Roast beef, Yorkshire pudding – not that they know how to make *that*! – peas, carrots, roast potatoes. Quite nice, but I can't think why they never have horseradish sauce. It perks things up, don't you think?'

'Oh, I do!' Cecily agreed.

'And now *you're* both here – though I must say Naomi hasn't much to say for herself. And then there'll be *Songs of Praise* and *Antiques Roadshow*, and *Jack Frost* if we're lucky. Or we'll play bridge.'

'One long round of pleasure,' Cecily said. 'A good place to live!'

'Oh yes!' Doris Campbell looked at her granddaughter. 'How old did you say you were now?'

'Eighteen.'

'Hm! A bit young. But you could put your name down. There's a waiting list as long as my arm.' There was a glint in her eye.

'I might do just that, Grandma,' Cecily said, wide-eyed.

'Well now,' Doris said. 'I don't want to rush you, but I like to have a little nap before *Songs of Praise*, so we'll say goodbye shall we?'

'Why did you tell me she wasn't madly happy?' Cecily asked her mother as they walked back down the hill to the town. 'Why did you give me the idea that she's loopy?'

'I didn't say either of those things,' Naomi protested. 'I said that some days she needed cheering up, and that she gets confused.'

'Well I think she's happy as Larry. As for being loopy, she's as clear as a bright blue sky,' Cecily said. 'You do exaggerate, Mummy!'

On Monday morning, after breakfast, Naomi played the piano for two hours, choosing to ignore the fact that Cecily was still in bed. At half-past ten Cecily appeared, showing no sign of having heard a thing.

'If I'm to get to Daddy in time for lunch I'll have to put my skates on,' she said. 'Are you sure you won't run me there in the car?'

'Quite sure,' Naomi said. 'I'll take you to the station.'

'Lovely weekend, Mummy!' Cecily said as they parted company on the platform.

Naomi waved until the train was out of sight. Was it? she asked herself. Was it really?

She found a car park conveniently close to the station and left her car to do some shopping. Her target today was Boots.

Dressing for the day yesterday morning she had taken a long, cold look at herself in the mirror. She had not liked what she had seen. She'd wanted to turn away and ignore it but she forced herself to look.

Her hair was a mess. She flicked it this way and that, but to no avail. It needed cutting – when had she last even had the split ends trimmed? It was neither one thing nor the other, it had no style.

Her face. Her face was drab. That was exactly the word for it. It was not only that it had that end-of-the-winter look to be seen at the moment on faces everywhere, a look brought on by cold winds and lack of sunshine; no, hers was far worse than that. It was an undefinable colour, a sort of muddy beige or pale sepia. And that was her own fault. Bit by bit, with no definite thought or intention, she had stopped using make-up until now she looked like a blank canvas waiting for colour to bring it to life. Much the colour, almost the texture, of canvas, too. She could do nothing, she supposed, about the fine lines around her eyes, or the ones beginning to appear from nose to mouth. At forty-six they were simply the result of living – and it would be some compensation if it had been riotous living, which it had not.

There were also, she noticed, torturing herself by looking in a magnifying mirror, two distinct frown lines between her brows, and her eyebrows themselves were, to say the least, shaggy.

She had next viewed the contents of her make-up drawer. Depressing, horrible, disgusting! Ends of lipsticks, all in the wrong colour – when in the world had she ever worn pale orange lipstick? Hardened eye shadow in shades long out of fashion;

dried-up mascara. She had used all this stuff once. Presumably she'd liked it then? Why had she stopped, or why hadn't she moved on to something better?

Hence the visit to Boots.

She had half-planned it yesterday morning, though she had said nothing to Cecily, then the afternoon's visit to River View, being with her mother and daughter and yet only half with them, for she had felt herself in a time warp, had strengthened her resolve.

What struck her first as she entered the store was the light and the colour, and then, as she walked around, trying to get her bearings, the various perfumes which assailed her nostrils, though in the pleasantest way. Following quickly on that was her shock-horror at the price of everything. She took a deep breath and deliberately steeled herself against it. This was not a day for counting the cost.

She bought with abandon, eagerly lapping up the advice given by the immaculately groomed beauties behind the counters. She bought foundation, moisturiser, eye shadow, face-packs, blusher, lipstick, eye-liner, tweezers, powder, lip gloss, shampoo, conditioner, rollers, hair lacquer, mascara, cotton wool, tissues, nail polish. She submitted, as she walked around, to being sprayed with a variety of different perfumes. I must smell like a brothel, she thought, but it didn't matter a hoot.

She broke into a conversation between two exquisitely coiffured assistants to seek advice on finding a hairdresser, which they readily gave, while selling her a tube of gel guaranteed to keep any hairdo in place.

At the till she tried not to look at the total as she signed the credit-card slip.

After that, leaving Boots with her two large plastic bags of goodies, there was no way she could bring herself down from her high plateau to shop for household goods. Breakfast cereals, toilet rolls and tea-bags would have to wait. She nipped quickly into Marks & Spencer's, bought salmon fishcakes and frozen chips, then hurried back to her car and drove home.

SIX

There was an edge of desperation in Naomi's desire to reach home with the utmost speed. Queueing to pay to get out of the car park she drummed a tattoo on the steering-wheel, fuming as the driver in front of her fumbled for change. Driving forward along the street she quietly swore at a pedestrian whose erratic movements caused her to slow down. And why, she asked herself, is every traffic light at red? And why do we need all these traffic lights, anyway?

She reached what she had already come to think of as her own parking place just in time to see a red BMW in front of her slide elegantly into it. Glaring at the driver as she passed, she drove around until she found another space, inconveniently distant, manoeuvred into it with none of her usual precision, grabbed her shopping bags and hurried back to the flat.

It was by now well past her usual lunchtime but she had no thought of food. Stopping only to unload the fishcakes and chips in the kitchen, she took the rest of her purchases into the bedroom, cleared the dressing-table and began to unpack. Everything she took out of the bags – and how elegantly they were all packaged – she put into its own group; hair things in one place, skin things – moisturiser, face-pack and the like – in another, and make-up items in a third. The greatest temptation was to start immediately on the make-up. This was what, after all, was destined to transform her, to give her, or so it said on the little boxes, light, colour, radiance, and the rest – but she resisted the temptation. What was the point of a face made up to (and including) the eyebrows, framed by a mane of straggly, dull-looking hair?

No, first things first, so off with her clothes and under the shower and on with the new shampoo, 'to nourish the roots, enrich, fortify and revitalize your hair' and the conditioner 'to leave your hair shining and free, silky, ready to do whatever you want it to do!' This was to be achieved, the small print said, by polyvitamins, tetrasodium, Dimethicone, sodium citrate and a dozen other highly scientific-sounding ingredients, and all dermatologically tested. How could it fail, even on her?

Added to which, she thought as she washed and rinsed, washed and rinsed, massaged the scalp, it certainly smelled quite nice!

Back in the bedroom she wound her hair onto the rollers. How long since she'd last done this? She couldn't remember. Usually she left her hair to dry, straight and thick to her shoulders. When she paid her promised visit to the hairdresser – and that would be soon, she would telephone today – perhaps she would steel herself to have it cut quite short.

What a fright she looked in these rollers, but hopefully all for the good of the cause. Anyway, why were they made in these yucky shades of blue and pink? Why couldn't they be hair-coloured? She looked like a rare blue-headed porcupine.

She reached for the hair dryer and gave her head a quick all-over burst, top power, maximum heat, which would have to do. There was no time to sit here holding the dryer. Far more exciting things awaited her. For a start, the face-pack. With difficulty she penetrated the nail-defying plastic, seemingly laminated to the package, and liberated the fat, squashy tube. 'Cleanses and exfoliates' it promised. 'Removes deep-down dirt and dead skin cells'. It sounded exactly what she needed for her whole life, not just her face. To emerge cleansed, exfoliated, all the dead bits sloughed off.

After the prescribed ten minutes of a by no means unpleasant throbbing sensation she rinsed it away. It was not an easy task, there were bits of it which were reluctant to leave her, but she had to admit she looked better. It was presumably the throbbing which had brought the colour to her skin, though it had also made more conspicuous what had hitherto been quite a small spot on her chin.

She patted her face dry. Now for the skin preparations, which were not to be confused, so the young ladies in Boots had informed her, with make-up. Not at all. These were the foundations which would cherish her skin, leaving it firm, velvety soft, clear and brilliant. Free radicals would race around, reactive molecules would play their part, something called elastin would give supple smoothness and firmness. Exactly what, her mother had always told her, an elastic girdle would do for her figure if only she would wear one. Added to which, she discovered as she read further, hydroxy acids would loosen dead skin cells so that they fell off at greater speed. What with that, and the bits falling off her scalp, she'd have to vacuum the carpet.

Still, there was a discernible improvement. The lines around her eyes were still there, but it was early days yet. And she definitely looked cleaner; oh yes, without a doubt!

Putting on the make-up, the part she'd looked forward to, was quite time-consuming. But then she wasn't just giving a quick lick of foundation, a scattering of powder, was she? No, she was applying anti-ageing, time-defying, light-reflecting liposomes. She looked straight in the mirror and gave herself a broad smile, not because she was pleased with what she saw but because this would show her exactly where to apply the blusher to her cheeks. Next, she brushed on the eye shadow, 'Desert Pink'.

'Pink?' she'd said doubtfully to the sales assistant.

'Pink eyes are the in-thing!' she'd been assured.

Which was strange because she'd thought something called pink-eye was a rather nasty complication of measles.

With the utmost care and a steady hand she outlined the lower edge of her Desert Pink eyelids with eye-liner before deliberately smudging it, and then applied two coats of navy-blue mascara to her lashes. All of which combined, the promise was, would give her a natural, healthy glow. Not that she desired a natural healthy glow. She would prefer to be exotic and alluring.

Well, she thought, looking in the mirror, her eyes held rigidly wide open so as not to smudge the mascara, you may not look alluring but all this, plus the blue rollers, certainly gives you an exotic look! She put up her hand and felt her hair. It was still damp, but if she used the drier now she might disturb her make-up. Also, she was hungry. Perhaps she'd have a cup of tea and a sandwich.

By the time she had snacked – she was saving the fishcakes for supper – her hair was dry. She went back to the bedroom and removed the rollers, not without pain since two of the smaller ones refused to be parted from her hair. Whichever way she unrolled, it was the wrong way and the fine hairs twined ever more tightly around the blue plastic until, at the moment she was contemplating cutting them loose and never mind the hair loss, they obligingly fell out of their own accord.

She brushed out her hair and was moderately pleased with the result. It certainly had, as promised, more volume. With quick movements, chin held high, she flung her head from side to side, checking to see if her hair floated out (as in the television ads) like a silken curtain. It did not. Nevertheless, it did seem overall improved, and would look better still if she were not clad in a grungy brown shirt and a long beige waistcoat purposely designed to be shapeless.

I will change my clothes, she decided. I will wear something decent. She rose, smiled at herself conspiratorially in the mirror, and then as she moved towards the wardrobe the doorbell rang.

She had the same attitude to answering the doorbell as she had to opening the post. She liked to conjecture who might be standing on the mat before opening up to them. Before she could think of a single name – who, after all, knew where she now lived? – the bell rang again, a long, insistent trill.

It was Dan Sheridan.

He wore his usual green anorak, grey trousers, scuffed suede shoes and, wound round his neck, a long scarf which looked as though his mother had knitted it from leftover balls of wool. His hair, blown by the sneaky February wind, fell in wisps over his forehead. He is as dishevelled as I am, Naomi thought. Or at least as I am from the neck down. From the neck up, she reminded herself, she was a new woman, though from the less-than-astonished look on his face that fact had not registered with Dan. He looked into her Desert Pink, mascaraed eyes without the slightest surprise in his own.

Or perhaps – how could she tell, she didn't know him well enough – he was a man who could see her answer the door stark naked and be too polite to say a word?

'Hello,' he said.

'Hello!' she replied.

'I hope you don't mind me calling. I have two bits of news which might interest you.'

'Oh! Well, please do come in!' She stood aside to let him enter. 'I was just . . .' She hesitated. Why would he want to know she'd been about to change her clothes?

'I'm just on my way home from school,' he said. 'I'm a bit early because it's a games period and I'm not in charge.'

He followed her into the living room, stood there until she invited him to sit down.

'Would you like a cup of tea?' Naomi asked.

'Thank you, I won't. I've got a pile of books to mark.'

So come out with the news, she thought.

'Someone in the staff room was talking about her daughter. She wants her to have piano lessons. So I thought of you.'

'How very kind!' Naomi said. 'How old is the little girl?'

'Seven, I think.'

'That's a good age. I expect she can read?'

'Oh, I think so,' Dan said. 'Her mother teaches English.'

'In my opinion,' Naomi said, 'it's good to be able to read first.'

'So shall I ask her to give you a ring?'

'Please do! And I'm really grateful.'

Even to have one pupil would break up her days, give some point to them.

'And the other thing is that I heard on the grapevine that Amersham's might have a vacancy for an assistant.'

'Amersham's?'

'It's a bookshop in the town. Not one of the giants, but not small either. A very good bookshop. The reason I know about it – about the job – is that the wife of one of my colleagues is about to take maternity leave. So it wouldn't be for ever, she reckons she'll return, and I *think* it's part-time.'

'Part-time is exactly what I want,' Naomi said. 'I wonder if I'd have a chance? I've never worked in a shop.'

'I don't see why not,' Dan said. 'Anyway, you could give it a try. But if I were you I wouldn't wait too long. She's already told them she's leaving.'

'Oh, I won't!' Dan watched her face light with enthusiasm. 'Do you think I could meet this lady, find out something about the job before I apply?'

'Jean Fulneck,' Dan said. 'That would be a good idea. I'll tell you what, I'll give her a ring this evening, sort of introduce you, then I'll give her your number. She's very nice, I've met her at a school "do".'

'I could go into the shop tomorrow and suss her out,' Naomi said. It wouldn't be difficult, she'd presumably have a burgeoning figure. Suddenly Naomi felt full of hope and enthusiasm.

'Are you sure you won't have a cup of tea?' she offered again. 'It will save you making one. You could get straight on with your marking.'

'Thanks! I'll change my mind then!'

He was looking at her quite closely now, as if he'd only just seen her, and under his scrutiny her own colour came into her cheeks and mingled with the Persian Rose blusher. What was he to think she was up to, tarted up to the eyeballs in the middle of the afternoon?

'Excuse me,' he said tentatively, 'I hope you don't mind me saying so, but you look – well different!'

'Do I?' she said, widening her eyes. 'I can't think why! Anyway, I'll make the tea.'

She had not felt so foolishly guilty since she was nine years old and had raided her mother's make-up drawer when her mother was out of the house. She had begun by cutting her hair with the kitchen scissors into a longed-for fringe, followed by lavishly using every beauty aid to hand, though there were some things for which she could not imagine a use and which her mother had, even when she'd recovered her temper, flatly refused to discuss. And for the pièce de résistance she had drenched herself in

Coty's L'Aimant. It was that last which had caused her to be sent to bed.

Dan's slightly puzzled expression had, however, nothing of her mother's remembered ferocity.

'I meant *nicely* different!' he called after her as they went into the kitchen.

They were drinking tea when the telephone rang. Naomi sprang to answer it. So far, she had had very few telephone calls here. She supposed it must be Cecily, and if her daughter thought she was going to carry on a long conversation with mother-to-be Helen eavesdropping in the same room, she was mightily mistaken.

It was not Cecily. It was Isobel.

'Oh Mummy!'

She could tell immediately that Isobel was in tears, choked with them.

'Isobel darling, what is it? Tell me at once!' In two seconds flat six frightful disasters chased through Naomi's mind.

'Oh Mummy, you're not going to believe it!'

'Yes I am, darling. Now take a deep breath and tell me calmly. I'm here for you!'

'It's Harry!' Naomi distinctly heard a slight sob.

'*What has happened?*'

'Oh Mummy, he's cut his very first tooth!'

The room spun around Naomi. I will kill her! she thought. She clutched at the telephone table to steady herself. For a moment she couldn't utter a word. But it didn't matter, Isobel was now in full spate.

'Bottom row, right in the middle! Mummy, you *must* come and see it. It's like a little white pearl!'

Naomi found her voice.

'I will. And they usually are – like little white pearls I mean.'

'He was *so* good, Mummy! He didn't cry at all, bless him!'

'Bless him,' Naomi said automatically and put down the receiver.

★　　★　　★

73

A phone call later in the evening from Jean Fulneck had arranged that Naomi should seek her out at Amersham's the next morning.

'I'm small, and red-haired,' Mrs Fulneck had said. 'But you can't miss me. I'm the one with a bump, which is now far too large to disguise! And I work mostly on the ground floor. I go to lunch at twelve-thirty, so why don't you come in a little before that and take a look around, then we'll go for a sandwich or a baked potato and I'll tell you all I know?'

Naomi's first call of the day had been on Isobel, to inspect Harry's tooth, which was truly like a little white pearl, and rather sweet. Indeed, he was a sweet baby. It was his mother who set his grandmother's teeth on edge, which was a terrible thing, Naomi chided herself, to say about one's own daughter. She wondered as she looked at him, lying there dribbling – another tooth on the way, bless him – at what age he would cast off his mother? Or would Isobel have a brood of children and so water down the smother-love process? She rather thought not. Isobel probably had enough of it to deal with a whole football team of progeny.

'You're looking rather smart this morning, Mummy,' Isobel said, taking her eyes off Harry for a moment. 'Where are you going?'

'Nowhere,' Naomi said. 'Well, a bit of shopping in the town, that's all.' She had no intention of telling Isobel about the possible job unless and until she got it. 'I've been thinking it's about time I bought myself a new outfit,' she added.

'You always look nice, Mummy,' Isobel said vaguely.

Clearly, Naomi thought, my new make-up has not hit her right between the eyes. But she had gone a bit easier on it this morning, especially in the eye department, not being quite sure what degree of face paint was acceptable in what Mrs Fulneck had told her was a prestigious bookshop.

'Do you know,' Isobel said, 'I'm sure Harry will be crawling quite soon! When I put him on the floor for his exercise he moves his little arms and legs about like anything!'

'I'm sure he will,' Naomi agreed. Only don't ring up and tell me out of the blue, she thought.

And now here she was at precisely twelve-fifteen, looking in

Amersham's windows at a tasteful display of travel books and biographies, all hardbacks. Could she, if she got as far as an interview, manage to say something percipient about any of them? Not the travel, that was for sure, but there was an Antonia Fraser she had read and enjoyed, also Roy Hattersley – but no doubt better to steer clear of party politics.

There was no mistaking Mrs Fulneck, even if she hadn't been hovering close to the door, arranging books on a shelf. She was, as she'd said, small and red-haired, and looking more than a little unbalanced because of her shape, as if the weight she was carrying might tip her up any minute. Naomi went straight up to her.

'Mrs Fulneck?'

'Sure! Mrs Fletcher?'

'That's right. Am I too early?'

'Not a bit. Why don't you take a look around while I finish this shelf? I'll join you in a minute, then we'll go out at half-past.'

Considering the size of the windows, which was not large, Naomi was surprised at the spaciousness of the shop. Though narrow, it went a long way back with, a yard or two from the front entrance, a staircase rising to another floor of books. It was not difficult to pass the time here. There was something of everything – classics, science, health, travel, politics, crafts, a large spread of fiction, all well displayed and in good order. Notices indicated that the upper floor was largely given over to educational books. She wondered why she hadn't discovered this particular shop before. Perhaps because it was almost opposite to, and overshadowed by, W.H. Smith's?

After a few minutes Mrs Fulneck joined her.

'Finding your way around, are you? It's not difficult, really. Everything's well laid out.'

'Do you always work on the ground floor?' Naomi asked.

'Almost always,' Mrs Fulneck assured her. 'I'm seldom asked to work in educational. It's a bit too specialized for me.'

'It would be for me,' Naomi said.

'I'll go and get my coat, then. There's a sandwich bar just down the road. We have an hour for lunch.'

'What can I say?' Mrs Fulneck asked, fifteen minutes later, biting into a prawn and mayonnaise sandwich. 'I work Tuesdays, Thursdays and Saturdays, nine o'clock until four. I expect they'll want the same. The pay isn't good, but then what shop work is? And at least it's quite pleasant work, better than trying shoes on sweaty feet, wouldn't you say?'

'Oh, I would!' Naomi agreed. 'What would I have to do?'

'Learn the stock, so that you can go straight to something. Keep the place tidy and the books where they're supposed to be. You'd be surprised how many customers pick up a book at one end of the shop and put it back on a shelf at the other end. We spend the first part of every day putting things to rights.'

'What about customers?'

'They're a nice lot on the whole. Civilized. You'll get to know the browsers. They come in most days in the week, read a few pages of whatever book they're on. Never buy it! If the customers want information it's mostly there on the computer.'

Alarm bells rang in Naomi's head.

'I haven't the faintest idea about computers!' she said.

'Oh, that's all right! You'll soon learn.'

'Well, if you say so,' Naomi said doubtfully. 'Though the rest sounds all right.'

'As a matter of fact I did mention your name to Mr Swaine – he's the manager – so he's half expecting you, preferably this afternoon. But if you don't want to go ahead and see him, then no bones broken.'

'Oh, but I will,' Naomi said. 'He might not think I'm suitable but I'll give it a go.'

Walking back up the street, busy with lunchtime shoppers, Naomi said, 'Doesn't the presence of W.H. Smith so close make a difference to Amersham's?'

'I don't think so,' Mrs Fulneck said. 'I've never heard it said, and we don't regard them as the enemy. I expect we have our own customers, though most people who buy books go into all bookshops. They can't keep away. Books are a drug to some people.'

Mr Swaine was available to see Naomi as soon as they were back at the shop. He was tall and thin and didn't look in the least bookish, though Mrs Fulneck had told her he was. He asked surprisingly few questions. Would the hours suit? Would she be able to work extra time in busy periods, Christmas and the like? What books did she read?

'Fiction, mostly,' Naomi admitted. 'But I do read biographies.' She threw in Antonia Fraser and Roy Hattersley.

'Yes,' he said. 'Politics sell well!'

That about wrapped it up.

'Unless there's anything you'd like to ask?' he said.

'No,' she said. 'Not ask, but I have to tell you I don't know how to use a computer.'

'Oh that's all right! Someone will teach you,' he said. 'Quite small children use computers these days!'

So they might, she thought. She had little doubt that Harry would be able to do so even before he acquired his full set of teeth, but it was cold comfort to her. But she would, she thought suddenly, ask Dan Sheridan what he knew about it. His school was probably littered with computers.

'When can you start?' Mr Swaine said, which she took as confirmation that she *had* got the job.

'Next week.'

'Right. Mrs Fulneck can show you the ropes for a day or two before she goes off to have her baby.'

If she doesn't have it in the meantime, Naomi thought. Mrs Fulneck had told her that she was eight-and-a-half months pregnant but was hanging on as long as possible, short of giving birth in the stockroom, because she wanted most of her maternity leave after the baby was born.

On the way back Naomi called in at the hairdressers in New Bond Street. Cut and Come Again it was called, probably the latest, she thought, in a long line of silly names for hairdressers. Soon they would have to go back to the simple idea of using the owner's name. Fletcher, Swaine, Sheridan. She booked herself in for a cut and blow-dry and reserved her options on whether she would have something done about the colour. There were strands of grey in her hair, but not enough to show overmuch, nothing that a rinse wouldn't take care of. On the other hand, she asked herself, how would I look with a broad streak of red sweeping back from my forehead? Bloody silly, she answered herself.

She crossed the road by the Podium and did some shopping in Waitrose before walking down towards the river. She would cross by the Pulteney Bridge, though her flat was so situated that whether she crossed that way or by way of North Parade made little difference. This afternoon she felt like looking at the shops on the Pulteney.

Reaching her own flat, walking up the path, she heard a sharp knocking and there was Emily Simpson standing in her window, beckoning. As Naomi turned back and walked up the next-door path Emily came to the door.

'This is a surprise!' Naomi said.

'It was to me,' Emily said. 'I came home an hour ago. They rang my husband and he fetched me.'

'Is everything all right?' Naomi asked.

'Couldn't be better! And you? How about you?'

'Fine! I've just got myself a job. I shall be a working woman from next week!' It was surprising how good she felt about it.

Now that's rather a pity, Emily thought. She had marked Naomi down as a potential babysitter.

SEVEN

Naomi had not been long in the house before the telephone rang. Surely not Isobel? she thought. Surely not another tooth?

'I'm Clare Morton,' the caller said. 'I believe Dan Sheridan mentioned that I'd like my daughter Lucy to have piano lessons.'

'Oh, hello!' Naomi said. 'Yes, he did.'

'Good! So when could I bring her to see you?'

'Actually,' Naomi said, 'I'd like it if you'd come on your own to begin with. We could discuss it.'

'Oh, I'm quite keen for her to have lessons,' Mrs Morton said.

She sounded slightly surprised, a reaction Naomi was used to. The mother – it was usually the mother – thought it was enough to want the child to have lessons. If they were willing to pay, then they could have them. But it was not so simple.

'Of course,' Naomi agreed, 'so if you and I meet first we can sort out what's best for Lucy.'

'I could come tomorrow, after school.' She still sounded puzzled. 'Are you sure you don't want me to bring Lucy?'

'Not to begin with.' She was politely firm. There were matters other than the mother's desire to have her child taught, some of them best settled in the absence of the child. Was the child teachable was only one of them. 'So why not come at four-thirty tomorrow?' she suggested. 'You know where I live.'

'Yes. Dan Sheridan told me.'

'Right! I'll see you then.'

Things are looking up, she thought as she went to put on the kettle. First a job and then a pupil. Or *possibly* a pupil, she wouldn't decide until she'd seen the parent and then the child. She was long past the stage where she'd take just anyone, and the combination most to be dreaded was the pushing mother and the reluctant child. She would have to see what Lucy thought.

Mrs Morton showed up on the dot of four-thirty, which was good mark number one.

'Do sit down,' Naomi said. 'Would you like a cup of tea?'

Good mark number two was awarded when Mrs Morton refused.

'I arranged for one of the other parents to pick up Lucy from school. I shall have to collect her, so I don't want to be too late.'

'I won't keep you long,' Naomi promised. 'You won't mind if I ask you a few questions?'

'Fire away!' Mrs Morton said.

'You do have a piano? Yes, I can see you think that's silly but I have known mothers who say, "No, we haven't, but she can practise at her grandma's." It isn't the same.'

Mrs Morton nodded agreement.

'I'm sure it isn't. But yes, we do have a piano, and oddly enough only recently. It belonged to my late mother-in-law, though she hardly ever played it. I understand it's quite a good one.'

'Splendid!' Naomi said. 'Have you had it tuned?'

Mrs Morton raised an eyebrow.

'As a matter of fact, no. But she's only going to practise on it, isn't she?'

'But we wouldn't want her to practise on an out-of-tune piano.' Naomi softened the firmness of her words with a smile. 'I can recommend someone if you like. I have mine tuned regularly.'

'Oh! Right!'

'Do you have other children?'

'I do. I have a son of eleven.' Mrs Morton's face said, What's it got to do with you? 'But Lucy's the only one who wants to learn the piano.'

'Of course! I only asked because if I give Lucy lessons she'll

80

need to practise every day and need quiet in which to do it. She can't do it against television, or some other noise.'

'Naturally, I'll see to that,' Mrs Morton said. 'Jack spends a lot of time in his own room, when he's not out playing football. He's at that age.'

'And Lucy can read?'

Mrs Morton drew in her breath. She'd had no idea she'd be given the third degree.

'Of course she can. Fluently! Why do you ask?'

'Because we'll be talking about letters – the names of the notes – and there'll be new words, musical words she won't have come across. It'd not be impossible to teach a child who can't read but it's easier for her if she can. So really, there's only one more question, but an important one. Does Lucy want to learn?'

'Oh yes! Yes indeed she does! She sits at the piano and sings, and accompanies herself. It can sound quite awful because she doesn't know a note she's playing, but she just loves it!'

The tetchiness went out of Mrs Morton's voice as she talked about her daughter. It was a good sign, Naomi thought. It meant she'd got co-operation.

'Then if you bring Lucy to see me,' she said, 'she and I will have a chat, and we'll take it from there. I feel sure it's going to be all right. Tell her it won't be a lesson this first time. It's just so we can see how we get on. And by the way, I don't charge for that.'

'We haven't mentioned money,' Mrs Morton said. 'Do I pay you for a term, or what?'

'Not a term. Put the money in an envelope and Lucy can bring it each week. And if there's ever a time when she can't come – I wouldn't want her to be bothered with a lesson if she weren't well, for instance – then as long as you ring and let me know it's no lesson, no pay.'

'That seems fair,' Mrs Morton said.

'So when would you like to bring Lucy?'

Mrs Morton fished a diary out of her handbag.

'Monday's always a good day,' she said. 'I have a free period the second half of Monday afternoon so I always collect her from school myself. I could bring her straight on to you.'

'Monday is fine. It suits me very well. As a matter of fact . . .' she couldn't keep it back, 'I'm starting a new job on Tuesday.'

'Oh, really? Where? Dan didn't say you went out to work.'

'I didn't. I just got the job today. I'm going to work in Amersham's bookshop.'

'Oh, I know Amersham's,' Mrs Morton said. 'I sometimes buy school books there. They keep a good stock, and what they don't have they'll always get for you.'

'But don't bring Lucy straight from school,' Naomi advised. 'Take her home, give her a drink and some biscuits. If she wants to change into jeans, or something she really likes to wear, then let her. I want her to be comfortable. Get here about four-thirty, if that suits you.'

'Well,' Mrs Morton said, 'it all seems very thorough! We'll be here.'

'And by the way,' Naomi said as she saw the other woman to the door, 'just deliver her here and leave her with me. Then collect her twenty minutes later.'

When Mrs Morton had left Naomi played the piano for an hour. Going off to see Isobel, and then to Amersham's, she had missed her morning session and no day was complete without it. She trusted that this terrace of houses was so well built that Emily and her baby wouldn't be disturbed by her playing. They looked it. Thick walls of Bath stone, with its attractive creamy colour, solid doors, built in an age when quality counted. Of course there was no way Dan Sheridan wouldn't hear her, if he was in that was. She hadn't seen him come home, but then she didn't actually stand in the window watching for him.

On the whole, she thought as she finished playing and went into the kitchen to prepare her supper, it had been one of her better days. The job, the prospect of a pupil, and she supposed she had better include Harry's tooth. And tomorrow morning the hairdresser. Who knew how she would come out of that?

But cooking a meal for one, she thought as she sprinkled a lone lamb chop with rosemary and started to heat the grill, was a bore. It seemed no time at all since she had cooked for five of them. When the children had flown the nest she had found it difficult to cut down to two but at least she and Edward had entertained quite a bit, and that she'd always enjoyed. So, in fact, had he. It was something they'd been good at; finding new dishes, choosing the wines. That was Edward's department, of course. He would not consider a woman opening the bottle, let alone choosing it, but she hadn't minded.

How long would it be before she knew enough people in Bath to give even a small dinner party?

She looked at the potatoes. What *was* the point of cooking two potatoes? You could cook four, common sense told her, and have two cold in a salad tomorrow, but such subterfuges, such frugal planning, went against her nature. She put the potatoes back in the vegetable rack. She would cook a few frozen chips. In no time at all, she realized, she would be hooked on chips. Her skin would go all muddy and she would get fat.

What the hell, she thought, lighting the gas under the chip pan. Chips were comfort, especially if they were crinkle-cut and therefore twice as soaked in oil.

She set out the meal on a tray and carried it into the living room. She was eating her first mouthful of lamb chop, crisp on the outside, gratifyingly pink inside, when the telephone rang. She chewed and swallowed as hastily as possible and picked up the receiver.

'It's me, Mummy!'

'Cecily. Are you all right?' It was unlike Cecily to ring her other than occasionally. 'How's Sussex?'

'I don't know! I'm not there!' Cecily replied.

'Then where are you?'

'I'll tell you if you give me a chance,' Cecily said. 'I'm still in Bristol. I'm phoning to give you the news! Helen's had the baby! A little girl!'

There was a long silence at Naomi's end. What was she supposed to say? Great! Splendid! Bully for her! Give her my love. And your father too, sod him! She felt a slow burn rise inside her which, if it burst into flame, would set the house on fire.

She said nothing. It didn't matter because Cecily was in full spate.

'She's a funny little thing,' Cecily was saying. 'All sort of

83

wrinkled, like a little old man, or in this case old lady. And a bit red, and masses of black hair!'

Naomi continued to hold the receiver to her ear. She wanted to slam it down, but she couldn't. She was hypnotized. She remembered, now, so vividly, Cecily's own birth, which she'd thought she had forgotten. The description was spot on. Perhaps Edward's children were all like him?

'They're calling her Amanda,' Cecily burbled. 'It's a bit of a mouthful, don't you think? Amanda Fletcher. I expect they'll shorten it to Mandy.'

I gave you all names which couldn't be shortened, Naomi thought, inanely. I didn't think that Isobel could ever be Isso.

'But one thing I'm sure about,' Cecily was saying, 'I'll never have children. Too crude for anything! Positively primeval! Of course Daddy's chuffed out of his mind, you'd think no-one had ever had a baby before.'

'Whereas,' Naomi said, breaking her silence, 'he has three other children.'

Quietly, with great restraint, she replaced the receiver.

She had a sleepless night, much of it spent in thinking about her children – she refused to think about Edward and his new family. If she could erase him from her mind for ever she would gladly do so. So many memories of her children, but what had they all come to?

Cecily had more or less gone over to the enemy. Isobel's horizon extended no further than nappies, feeds and teeth. And Hugh? Where was Hugh? He was in Sheffield, of course, being an assistant stage manager and from time to time a small-part actor, waiting for his call to stardom. She knew where he was, but for all she knew of his current life he might as well be in Outer Mongolia.

When he'd first left home they used to write to each other regularly. No, she corrected her memory, I used to write to him regularly, and he wrote back when he had time. Such lovely, funny letters his were, but somehow that had dropped off, on her side as well as on his. Nowadays they telephoned, which in some ways was better, but she hadn't heard from him since she'd moved into the flat. Which was, she reminded herself sharply, less than two weeks ago, and nor had she phoned him.

She was overwhelmed by self-pity, which she recognized for what it was and decided to wallow in it anyway. She squeezed a tear out of her eye, blew her nose, went to the loo, came back and straightened the bed and pummelled her pillow before settling down again. As the dawn broke and an early blackbird sang in the garden, she fell asleep.

When she wakened, it was to remember the hairdresser. To cut or not to cut, she had not made the decision. She went over to the dressing-table and gazed at her reflection, pulling and pushing her hair this way and that, piling it on top of her head, hooking it behind her ears to try the effect. It was impossible to decide, she would wait until she got there. And if she didn't get a move on she'd be late for her appointment.

Somewhere a clock was striking nine as Naomi reached the salon.

'Mrs Fletcher,' she said. 'I have an appointment.'

'Ah yes!' the receptionist said. 'With Ahnree! Will you take a seat? He won't keep you a minute.'

The minute extended to ten, but it didn't matter. She had been handed a surprisingly recent copy of *Harpers & Queen* so that she was able to bring herself up to date with who was newly married to who and where and which balls and/or memorial services the great and the good had attended. She also, while turning the pages, glanced up at the walls of the salon, decorated with large photographs of exquisitely beautiful girls with fantastic hairdos. Presumably they were to give hope and encouragement, but in her case they did not. She knew a lost cause when she met one.

Henri came towards her. He wore skin-tight black leather trousers and a Cossack-like tunic, black with red roses, belted in over an incredibly slim waist. His hair was black-and-silver striped.

'Good morning!' he said. 'And how are we today?' She was surprised to hear what she recognized as a West Riding accent. What mill town had bred this exotic creature?

He sat her in the chair and stood behind her, both of them gazing into the mirror.

'What did you have in mind?' he asked.

'I want a completely new look!'

There! She had said it and she would stand by it!

'Yes, you do!' She thought he agreed rather too readily.

He took hold of a strand of hair, gingerly, as if it might bite him, and held it up away from her head.

'Where did you have your hair done last?' he asked.

'In Bristol. I've only just come to live in Bath.'

He dropped the lock of hair as if it had stung him.

'Ah, well, that accounts for it! Bristol! They think they know it all in Bristol. Not true!'

He turned, and called out to another stylist.

'Mervyn! Come here and look at this! A Bristol "do"!'

Together they examined her hair.

'Wouldn't you just know!' Mervyn said.

'And madam wants to be made over,' Henri said.

'Quite!' said Mervyn.

Henri's eyes, sorrowful rather than angry, met Naomi's in the mirror.

'We'll do what we can,' he said. 'We'll do our best!' With what we've got was clearly implied, though not said. 'Most of it will have to come off!'

'Without a doubt,' Mervyn said, nodding vigorously. 'Well, best of luck, Ahnree!'

Naomi had once had a poodle which, when it sensed she was going to take it to the dog parlour to be plucked, would run away and hide. She knew now just how he had felt. If she had the nerve she would run right out of the door, notwithstanding the fact that she was draped in a pink cotton gown.

Henri handed her over to a young assistant who shampooed her within an inch of her life.

'Don't spare the conditioner,' Henri called out. 'Madam needs it.'

The shampooing over, Naomi sank exhausted into Henri's chair. Eyes narrowed, lips pursed, he studied her image. Mervyn came over and joined him.

'I think really quite short,' Henri said to him. 'Get rid of as much of the old hair as we can, don't you think?'

'Oh, I do,' Mervyn agreed.

'I don't mind having it shorter, but not *too* short,' Naomi piped bravely.

'A sort of cap. Coming forward from the crown into a deep fringe. I *think* that should suit her face,' he said doubtfully.

'It needs colour,' Mervyn suggested. 'I see it with fairly wide strands of red falling over the forehead.'

'I know!' Henri said tetchily. 'But I'm not sure I have the time. I haven't a minute to call my own all day!'

He took a surprisingly small pair of scissors out of his pocket and set to work. Naomi closed her eyes – she could not bear to see all that hair falling to the ground – until, it seemed an age later, he said 'There! That's it!'

Fearfully, Naomi opened her eyes and looked into the mirror.

'Good heavens!' she cried.

'Don't judge it until it's blow-dried. That'll give it plenty of body,' Henri said. 'You have quite thick hair,' he added grudgingly.

I did have, Naomi thought. Most of it was now on the floor.

But Henri was right. When he had finished, and stood back to admire his work, there was a satisfied smile on his face. And also on Naomi's as she looked at her reflection.

Her hair was a buoyant shiny cap on her head. It fell forward from the crown in a fringe over her forehead, which somehow enhanced her eyes, and the absence of thick hair at the sides of her cheeks showed off the perfect oval of her face. The tips of her ears were just visible, crying out for beautiful earrings.

'Thank you,' she said quietly. 'Thank you very much. I feel a different woman.'

Mervyn came over to inspect.

'You've done a good job there, Ahnree,' he said. 'Considering.'

Henri nodded his satisfaction.

'Yeah!' he said. 'Considering.'

When Naomi left the salon the sun was shining. With a spring in her step she walked along the street, pausing frequently to look in the shop windows. Ostensibly, she was looking at the fashions; covertly she was studying her reflection in the glass. When, sometimes, it came upon her suddenly, it was like seeing a stranger, and an attractive stranger at that.

She had planned to do a little food shopping and then go home after the hairdresser. There was plenty to do in the flat. Now, however, she felt like a small celebration, so she decided to have coffee in the Pump Room. There were several places between the hairdresser and the Pump Room where perfectly good coffee would cost less, but none of them had the added attraction of a trio of chamber musicians who she knew would be playing at this time.

The abbey churchyard was, as always she supposed, busy with people crossing and recrossing, small groups gazing up at the elaborately carved west wall of the abbey, now relieved of the scaffolding which had hidden it for so long. In front of the Pump Room another small crowd watched a juggler. She stopped for a moment or two, amazed by his dexterity, then left and went in search of her coffee. With which, she decided she would go the whole hog and have a Bath bun.

There was a short queue waiting for tables.

'There's a place for one person who doesn't mind sharing,' the receptionist said.

Naomi stepped forward.

'I don't,' she said. She was in the mood for anything.

Luck was on her side. She was shown to a table, quite close to the trio, where a man sat alone. She could not believe it. It was an impossible coincidence. But she had to believe it because there he was: Dan Sheridan.

He had been reading a book, and only as she reached the table did he look up and see her.

'Naomi!' he said. 'I don't believe it!'

'Nor do I,' she said. 'Except that it's true! Do you, as they say, come here often?'

'It's my Saturday morning treat,' he told her. 'It's an oasis of civilization after the wildness of the school week. Also, I never see any of the kids in here!'

She sat down and ordered. Dan closed his book.

'Don't stop reading on my account,' Naomi said. 'I'm happy to sit here listening to the music. And eating and drinking of course. I like this Schubert, do you?'

He nodded. 'They play quite a bit of Schubert – at least they do on Saturday mornings.'

'I'm glad to see you,' Naomi said. 'I want to thank you. First of all, I got the job at Amersham's. I start on Tuesday.'

'That's good,' he said. 'I'll come in and buy a book from you.'

'Do,' she said. 'And also I think I've got a piano pupil. Mrs Morton came to see me yesterday and she's bringing her little girl on Monday. I think it will work out all right. So thank you very much.'

She became aware that he was watching her quite intently. Surely what she was saying wasn't *that* interesting.

'Excuse me,' he said, 'please don't think me rude, but every time I see you, you look different!'

'I *am* different!' Naomi said. 'I've been to the hairdresser, had most of my hair chopped off. A young man named Henri has wrought the change.'

'Well I must say he's a clever man. He's an artist!' He stopped short. 'Oh dear, that sounds very rude, as if you were awful before, which you weren't. But I'll be even ruder and say you look ten years younger!'

'Thank you,' Naomi said.

Why don't I thank him properly, she asked herself? He's been so kind to me. Why don't I ask him to supper?

No sooner thought than said.

'Would you come to supper? This evening, if you like. Or any other evening.'

'I'd like to,' he said. 'Not this evening because I promised to visit my aunt. But almost any other evening.'

'Monday then? I can tell you how I get on with my would-be pupil.'

Mrs Morton brought Lucy on Monday as arranged, promptly at four-thirty.

'Thank you, Mrs Morton,' Naomi said firmly, not inviting her in. 'If you'd call back for Lucy in about twenty minutes, that would be fine.'

'Come and sit down, Lucy,' Naomi said. 'Where would you like to sit? Would you like a drink of orange juice?'

'I had one at home,' Lucy said.

'Fine!'

'But I'd like another!'

'Very well!'

She went into the kitchen to pour it, and added a straw. Through the open door she could see Lucy, her body quite still on the chair, but her head swivelling from side to side as she looked around the room. She was small for her age, her short legs not quite touching the floor. A pretty little face, lively, and her dark hair pulled back in a pony-tail. She wore blue jeans, a red sweater, and trainers.

'Here you are then!' Naomi said, coming back into the room. 'I expect your mother told you, we're not going to have a lesson today. I thought we could just get to know each other a bit.'

The straw in her mouth, Lucy nodded.

'You like music, do you, Lucy?'

Lucy nodded again.

'Any special sort? Do you like pop?'

Lucy gave a final deep suck on the straw and when the gurgling had died away she looked up.

'I like the Spice Girls,' she said.

'Good!'

'And sometimes I like sad music.' Now that she was no longer preoccupied with orange juice she seemed quite ready to talk. 'And I like dancey music.'

'And songs?' Naomi asked. 'Do you like singing?'

'Oh yes!' Lucy said.

'Do you learn songs at school?'

'Sometimes.'

'Then I must get you to sing some to me, but not today. So if you like dancey music I expect you like dancing. Do you have dancing lessons?'

'Oh yes!' Lucy's face brightened. 'I do tap dancing. We did a concert once in the church hall. A lot of people came.'

So in that case, Naomi thought, I can presume she has a sense of rhythm.

'Let's go over to the piano,' she suggested. 'Stand right beside me. I'll play one note and then you hum it back to me.'

She played middle C and Lucy hummed it.

'Good! And now I'll play four notes and you can hum them. I'll start on the same one you've just done.'

She played C, E, G and C. Lucy hummed, clear, resonant and accurate.

'Spot on!'

'That last note was the same as the first. Only not quite the same because it was higher,' Lucy said.

'Nothing wrong with your ears!' Naomi said. 'Listen to this. And watch this too.' Starting at middle C she played every C to the top of the keyboard, and then every one down to the bottom.

'All those notes are called C,' she said. 'All the notes have names, but we're not going to learn those today. Now would you like me to play to you?'

'Yes please!' Lucy said.

'Now what shall it be? Do you go to the seaside on holiday? Do you like to play on the beach?'

'Oh yes! And I can swim!'

'Well, I know a nice piece of music. It's got a German name which means "Night on the beach"! So why don't you close your eyes while I play a bit of it?'

Lucy stood there with eyes tightly closed while Naomi played.

'There! Did you like that?'

'Yes,' Lucy said. 'I could hear the sea. But it was a bit sad, a little bit.'

'It was, wasn't it?' Naomi agreed.

She was going to be all right, this one. She was bright, and not afraid. She might well turn out to be a pleasure to teach.

'So do you want to have piano lessons?'

'Yes please,' Lucy said.

'All right then. We'll give it a go. Of course you'll have to work *fairly* hard at it, you'll have to practise every day, but I hope you'll enjoy it. I wouldn't want you to do it if you didn't enjoy it.'

There was a ring at the doorbell.

91

'That will be your mummy,' Naomi said.

When Mrs Morton came in Lucy jumped up and down.

'I'm going to have lessons!' she cried.

Mrs Morton looked at Naomi.

'That's right,' Naomi confirmed. 'Every Monday at half-past four. I'd like you to arrive five minutes before that, if you will. Also, Mrs Morton, will you buy Lucy a new exercise book – choose a nice one – and a pencil, and see that she brings it with her each time she comes.'

'An exercise book?' Mrs Morton looked puzzled.

'Yes. I'll write in it each week what she has to do before the next lesson. I'd like you to read it, and perhaps sign your name when she's done everything.'

Mrs Morton looked slightly mutinous. What a bossy woman this piano teacher was!

Naomi smiled at her.

'Call it one of my little quirks, Mrs Morton. But I do want Lucy to do well, and above all to understand it and enjoy it. You see, it's not just lessons on how to play tunes, it's starting a relationship with music which will hopefully last the rest of her life. I'm sure she and I are going to get on well together.'

EIGHT

With a feeling of satisfaction Naomi watched Lucy and her mother drive away. The lesson had gone well, she looked forward to the next one. Starting to lay the table for the evening meal with Dan Sheridan, she thought the whole weekend had gone reasonably all right except, of course, for those moments, occurring all too often, when thoughts of Edward and Helen and the new baby pushed themselves into her mind. Each time that happened she swiftly and deliberately pushed them out again. Cecily, phoning from Sussex on Saturday evening, had told her that that was quite the wrong thing to do.

'You should go with the flow, Mummy,' she said firmly. 'Be part of it. Don't battle against the tide!'

'That's your advice, is it?' Naomi asked levelly. 'I mean out of the depths of your experience?'

'It certainly is,' Cecily said.

Abashed, Naomi had thought, was not a word in her daughter's vocabulary.

'Of course I don't have the actual *experience*,' Cecily admitted. 'But I've read a lot. In fact there are one or two books I could recommend . . .'

'How kind!' Naomi murmured. 'And now that I'm working in a bookshop I dare say I could get them at a discount.'

'Of course you could. Marvellous! And then, as I've told

you before, I do discuss these things with my friends.'

'You mean you've discussed my case?' She felt sure that that was the way Cecily would refer to her. 'Take the case of my mother,' she would say.

'Oh yes! But it's not unique, you know!'

'It is to me!'

'You have to be positive, Mummy!'

'Oh I am being!' Naomi assured her. 'I had my hair cut today, quite short. I thought that was positive. Next week I might have it dyed blonde. Or red. Or blonde-and-red stripes! Who knows?'

There was the faintest pause at the other end of the phone.

'Well, if it helps,' Cecily said kindly.

'And on Monday evening I'm having Dan Sheridan to supper.'

There was a longer pause.

'Oh!' Cecily said cautiously. 'I wouldn't go *too* far there.'

'I don't know how far I shall go,' Naomi said brightly. 'I haven't thought about the limits. But I shall take your advice and go with the flow! Goodnight, darling! Sleep well!'

She was trembling, mostly from anger, as she put the receiver down. She wished, on the whole, that Cecily would not bother to ring her. A little neglect would suit her better. If my daughter had her wish, she thought, I would be speeding down to Bristol, flowers for the little mother in one hand, bootees for the baby in the other, and an agreement to be godmother tripping from my lips.

She poured herself a generous gin and tonic and hoped that Cecily would not drive her to drink.

On Sunday afternoon, on the way to visit her mother, she had called in on Isobel.

'Harry's second tooth is almost through,' Isobel informed her, busy changing an odorous nappy. 'And he's trying very hard to say "Daddy", or it could be "Mummy". It's not quite clear, bless him!'

Patrick came into the room. He was tall and broad and took up a lot of space.

'Why!' he exclaimed. 'You've had your hair cut, Naomi! It's great!'

Isobel looked up from contemplating her son's navel.

94

'So you have,' she said. 'Is that for your new job?'

'No,' Naomi said. 'It's just for me. And I've asked the man in the upstairs flat to supper tomorrow.'

'Great!' Patrick said.

'How old is he?' Isobel asked.

'Do you know,' Naomi said, 'I never thought to ask him! But he's younger than me,' she added helpfully.

'I hope you know what you're doing,' Isobel said.

'I've always thought I knew what I was doing,' Naomi said. 'Only it turned out I didn't. So how would I know now?'

Walking up the Warminster Road to River View – the hill had seemed steeper, perhaps she should have brought the car – she'd decided she would tell her mother about Dan Sheridan, not because it was the least bit important but because her daughters' reactions had been interesting. Also it would be something to talk about. When it came to her mother topics of conversation were not easy to find.

Mrs Campbell had been wearing a canary yellow jumper and a puce cardigan, both slightly soiled down the front. Two patches of rouge on her cheeks gave her the appearance of a woman with a high fever, or a clown. The clown image won because of the angry gash of scarlet lipstick aross her mouth. Her white hair was lank and wispy.

Naomi swallowed hard and kept back the tears at the sight of her mother, a woman who had been the most fussy of dressers, colours carefully chosen, everything co-ordinated, hair and make-up immaculate. How had she come to this? And the sadness was, did she know that she had? And didn't the payment of well over five hundred pounds a week her mother made ensure that she, who needed no special nursing care and no more than routine attention, would at least be helped to look good? Didn't they care?

Perhaps, Naomi thought, *I* should care more. Maybe an hour or so every Sunday, sometimes, she had to admit, grudgingly given, was not enough. However, if her mother was unhappy it didn't show too much. Possibly she felt worse about it than did her mother, and perhaps that was a measure of her own guilt.

They had talked about the weather. Mild for the time of year. Foggy, especially down by the river, in the mornings. Naomi reported on Harry's progress but her mother seemed not to hold a place for him in her mind. I must really bully Isobel into bringing him here, Naomi thought. It would be a new interest in his great-grandmother's life.

Presently she said: 'I've asked a man to supper tomorrow. His name's Dan Sheridan. He lives in the flat over me.'

Mrs Campbell perked up.

'Is he rich?'

'I don't know. I wouldn't think so.'

'You should find out,' Mrs Campbell said. 'Was he in the war?'

'No, Mother,' Naomi said. 'He's too young for that.'

'I know a song about Dan!' Mrs Campbell began to sing in a high, cracked voice.

> 'Dan, Dan, the dirty man,
> Washed his face in a frying pan;
> Combed his hair with a horse's tail
> And scratched his belly with a six-inch nail.'

'It's not him,' Naomi said. 'This one's quite clean!'

'Cleanliness is next to Godliness,' Mrs Campbell observed. 'Though I'm not sure why.'

'Speaking of Godliness, has the curate been in today?' Naomi enquired.

'Oh, yes!' Mrs Campbell replied. 'He brought Holy Communion for those who wanted it. I always say yes. It makes a change. Anyway, at my age I say yes to most things in case they don't come round again.'

'Perhaps I should do that?' Naomi said. 'What do you think, Mother?'

Mrs Campbell, in full spate now, ignored her.

'I must say, I was a bit disappointed. You see, they don't bring the wine, just those little white wafers and they stick to your top plate for ages. The wine was what I used to like best, though you never got a real drink, and it was sweet whereas I always liked a

96

nice, dry red. Claret. Now one thing your father *did* know about was wine, even though he said it was wasted on women.'

'I'd forgotten you liked it,' Naomi admitted. 'I could bring you a bottle. I expect they'd let you have a glass with your dinner.'

'Some of them drink Ribena,' Mrs Campbell said. 'Filthy stuff! So are you going to marry this Dan?'

'Oh Mother!' Naomi said, laughing. 'Of course not! Nothing's further from my mind. I've only just met him!'

'And also you're married to that solicitor chap,' her mother said. 'What's his name? And you can't have two husbands at once, not in this country, though I think you can in the Middle East. Or is it wives?'

'His name is Edward,' Naomi said. 'And I'm not married to him, not any more. Don't you remember we divorced? He married again and his new wife's just had a baby girl. In any case, I'm not thinking of marriage, not at all.'

Mrs Campbell, looking straight past Naomi, had already lost interest.

'We had pork for lunch,' she said. 'With apple sauce. They don't know how to get the crackling crisp.'

They'd sat in silence for a while, though not an uncomfortable one. Mrs Campbell closed her eyes. Her eyelids were so thin as to be almost transparent. Her eyebrows were grey and wispy, growing in all directions. Old or not, loopy or not, Naomi had thought, she is easier to be with than either of my daughters. Whoever said that the old were narrow and intolerant and the young broad-minded and tolerant had got it the wrong way round.

Mrs Campbell opened her eyes.

'Isn't it time you were off? They don't like you to outstay your welcome.'

'You're right!' Naomi agreed. 'And why don't you change into something else and I'll take your jumper and cardigan home and wash them.'

She had done so this morning, and now they lay flat on a contraption which fitted over the bath for just such a purpose. It might be a nice idea, she thought, giving the wine glasses a polish, wondering whether there would be enough flowers in the

97

garden for a table decoration, if I were to buy my mother a new cardigan when I get my first week's wages. One which would go better with the present yellow than did the puce horror.

She gave a last look at the table and decided it would do. She didn't want anything grand. It was to be a perfectly ordinary occasion with simple food. She planned a lasagne and a salad and had bought a modest bottle of wine in Waitrose. She hoped Dan wouldn't do anything silly, like bringing her a bunch of flowers. Her daughters, if he should do so and if she should tell them, would be highly suspicious. But if he did so, then she *would* tell them. She would quite enjoy that, all the more so because there was nothing in it.

He didn't do so, not quite. He rang her bell promptly at seven-thirty and handed her a small box of chocolate mints. Isobel and Cecily couldn't make much of that.

'How did the piano lesson go?' he enquired.

'Quite well. She's a nice little girl, I think we'll get on. Her mother was the more nervous of the two.'

While she attended to things in the kitchen Dan Sheridan looked around the room. Apart from the gleaming piano, and a pile of sheet music, it said little of her. There were a couple of shelves of books, a small table with pieces of coloured glass, a Chinese lamp, squashy cushions on the sofa and chairs. Perhaps she hadn't had time to unpack?

She caught him looking around as she returned from the kitchen.

'I still haven't finished unpacking,' she said. 'Though as a matter of fact I didn't bring that much.'

She had preferred, at the time of moving, to leave most things behind her. She had not wanted those things which belonged fairly and squarely to Four Winds, many of which she and Edward had bought together, to accompany her into her new life. She had allowed herself only a few personal things – the lamp had been her mother's, the coloured glass she had collected against Edward's taste. Her piano, of course. That was truly hers. Her grandmother, in the hope that her favourite grandchild might turn out to be a concert pianist, thus bringing glory to the whole family, had given it to her when she was still a schoolgirl. If she had her piano, then it didn't matter much about the rest.

'I'm afraid I collect things like a magpie,' Dan said. 'Especially books. I really don't have room for them all.'

'The meal won't be long,' Naomi said. 'Shall we have a glass of wine?'

'That would be nice,' Dan said. 'Shall I open it for you?'

'Already done,' Naomi told him. Why did men think women couldn't open a bottle of wine?

'So you start your new job tomorrow,' Dan said. 'Are you looking forward to it?'

'With some trepidation,' Naomi confessed. 'I'd feel happier if I knew I'd be any good at it, but I've never done anything like it before, so everything's to learn.'

'I shouldn't think you'd have any trouble,' Dan said comfortably. 'I imagine most people find what they want on the shelves and then just pay for it. If they come up with something you can't answer, you just consult a colleague.'

'You're encouraging,' Naomi said. 'And I expect you're right. It's just that it's a new world to me. Oh, it's not that I don't know anything about books. We had a thriving literary group – which sounds pretentious now – where we used to meet fortnightly and discuss specific books. We took ourselves rather seriously. But that's not quite the same as selling them, is it?'

'Selling them might be easier,' Dan suggested.

'Let's hope so. Thank heaven I don't have to add up the bills and give out the change. Arithmetic's not my strong point. It's all done by machine now, isn't it?'

Dan nodded. 'Most things are.'

'Except teaching,' Naomi suggested.

'Bits of that are,' he said. 'But thank goodness not all.'

There was a pause while each of them searched for something more to say.

'And how is the baby next door?' Dan asked, jumping in.

'Absolutely fine. I popped in today.'

'Good!'

'My former husband's new wife has just had a baby,' Naomi said on impulse.

Why on earth had she said it? It was the last thing on earth she wanted to talk about, or even think of.

'Oh!' Dan said.

'Oh dear!' Naomi said. 'You don't know whether to say "Congratulations" or "I'm sorry", do you? It was a potty thing for me to say. Nothing to do with you, and come to that, no longer anything to do with me.'

Dan took another sip of wine.

'How do you feel?' he asked gently. 'But don't tell me if you'd rather not.'

'Furious!' Naomi said. 'Angry and furious! Which is stupid, because anything that happens to them isn't my business.'

She was twisting the stem of her glass round and round so that the wine was threatening to spill over. Dan put out a restraining hand and touched hers. She took a large gulp and put the glass down out of harm's way.

'It's not that I'm one of those women who are always longing for another baby,' she said. 'I don't think I'm over-endowed with the maternal instinct. I even find it difficult to enthuse about my little grandson. Bless him,' she found herself adding.

About to continue, she stopped herself. Why was she going on like this to a man she hardly knew? And, she reminded herself, a man who had lost a young wife and a child not yet born. What had she to complain about in comparison to that? She had a full, and reasonably happy, life so far – and there was more to come.

'I'm babbling!' she apologized. 'Take no notice of me. Let me refill your glass and then I must take a look in the oven.'

'Can I do anything to help?' Dan offered.

'Not really,' she said – and then corrected herself. 'Yes you can. You could toss the salad while I dish up the lasagne. I hope you like lasagne.'

'Love it!' he said, following her into the kitchen.

There was very little room. They skirted around each other, managing not to collide. Naomi took the lasagne out of the oven. It was crisp and golden and cheesy on top, quite good, she thought as she carried it into the living room. Dan followed her with the bowl of salad.

In fact, she thought, taking the first mouthful, the lasagne *was* good, better than usual, and the second glass of wine was just beginning to go to her head, in the nicest possible way so that she felt – how *do* I feel? she asked herself. Carefree! Yes, that was it! Relaxed and carefree.

'How is Cecily?' Dan enquired. Not that he cared.

Naomi pulled a face.

'Her usual self. At least she was when she telephoned on Saturday.'

'Which is . . . ?'

'Ready and willing to put the world to rights, including especially her own family.'

Dan laughed. 'That's youth for you!' he said. 'Didn't we all think like that when we were young? She'll grow out of it!'

'No we didn't,' Naomi argued. 'And I fear she won't grow out of it. I reckon she'll be Chair of everything she gets into, bossing everyone around. Oh dear, I sound dreadful, don't I? It's a sore subject at the moment.'

'Then we'll change it,' Dan said. 'What about your other daughter?'

'Isobel? She's the original earth-mother. For never more than a few seconds does she think of anything other than her baby.' Naomi took another sip of her wine. 'To tell the truth she's rather boring, but perhaps she'll change when Harry grows out of being a baby.'

'She might have another one,' Dan said.

'I dare say you're right,' Naomi agreed. 'And you must think I'm a terrible mother, running down my children like this!'

'It's allowed,' Dan said. 'Once in a while. I expect you're just as fond of them as Isobel is of Harry!'

Am I? Naomi wondered. If she was, she wished she could feel it more. She wished that love, for someone, would wash through her like a warm tide.

'Will you have a little more lasagne?' she asked.

'I will! It's really nice.'

And so are you, Naomi thought. Not totally unlike a lasagne. Warm, comforting, easily digested – not exotic, not *quite* the stuff of a banquet, but exactly right at this moment.

101

'Do you cook?' she asked. 'I'm finding it boring, cooking for one.'

'I have to confess,' Dan replied, 'that I rely heavily on the freezer, and things in packets. Meals for one – toad-in-the-hole, fisherman's pie, that sort of thing. I'm quite an expert on which store does which dish best.'

'I shall come to you for advice,' Naomi said. 'I can see that that's the lifestyle I'll sooner or later adopt.'

'I *can* cook,' Dan admitted. 'And I do if someone's coming. A limited repertoire, of course, but not bad.'

I wonder who he has coming, Naomi asked herself, serving the fruit salad, switching on the coffee. Women friends? Men friends? Colleagues? For some reason she didn't understand she couldn't imagine him being visited by hordes of relatives. There was no feeling that he was part of a family.

'Not that I have many visitors,' Dan said, answering her unspoken question. 'Colleagues from time to time. Friends who happen to be visiting Bath. My aunt used to visit but she's quite elderly and arthritic so she doesn't get out much. I visit her.'

'Does she live in Bath?'

'In Cheltenham, so it's not too far. I have a married sister in Surrey but we don't often meet. That's the extent of my family. My parents died a few years ago.'

'Much like me,' Naomi said. 'Except that my mother's alive in a rest home here. And of course I have the children, even though I do grumble about them. I've always envied people who were part of a large family, all those brothers and sisters, aunts, uncles, cousins. A house bursting at the seams at Christmas, huge birthday parties.'

Dan nodded. 'Me too!'

They drank second cups of coffee, ate a few chocolate mints. What do we do now? Naomi thought, trying to think of another topic of conversation. They didn't know each other well enough to be comfortable with silence. In the end they both spoke at the same time.

'Let me help you with the washing-up!'

'Would you like me to play something!'

Dan decided. 'We'll wash the dishes first and then I'd like it very much if you played.'

They carried the dishes into the kitchen and Dan stationed himself at the sink.

'I'll wash, you dry,' he said. 'You know where to put the things away. On the rare occasions when my sister visits me she insists upon putting things away. It takes me weeks to find them again!'

'What would you like me to play?' Naomi asked when they were back in the living room. 'Do you have favourites?'

'Play whatever you choose.'

She searched through her music. Nothing too romantic. In spite of the drawn curtains, the soft lamplight and the warmth from the living-flame gas fire, which was more like a fire than the real thing, it was not that sort of an occasion. In the end she chose a Scarlatti sonata and an étude by Scriabin.

She played the Scarlatti first. She was pleased to discover that Dan was a person who could sit comfortably and still while listening, no need to tap his feet or his fingers or to look intense. And then when she left the Scarlatti and moved to the Scriabin she forgot all about him. The room was filled with sound; passionate, striving towards a goal, and then suddenly with crashing chords, ending. It still surprised her that the piece was so short.

There was a brief silence after she stopped playing and then Dan said, 'Thank you. That was wonderful! I had no idea you could play like that!'

After only a slight hesitation she said, 'I could play one more piece if you like.'

'Indeed I would like,' Dan said.

Naomi knew now exactly what she would choose, and she didn't need the music for it. She had practised it for years. It was her star piece.

'You said you liked Schubert,' she said, 'so I'll play Schubert.'

She took a deep breath and then, letting her hands fall to the keyboard, began to play the impromptu. At first it was quiet, even, melodic, so totally familiar that it could be whistled on the street, but when the variations began it took off, gathered emotion, plunged into passion. And by now she had once again forgotten Dan's presence. The music was, at one and the same time, an old friend and an old enemy. She had to conquer it while at the same time knowing that *it* was the be-all and end-all. In an arpeggio she slightly lost her place – at exactly the same point as always – and then recovered and went on.

Dan became, after the first few bars, intensely aware not only of the music but of Naomi. As he watched he was amazed by the power which flowed from her slight frame and in her slender hands, by the strength of the chords, by her complete dominance of her instrument; by the light yet precise touch on the arpeggios – he didn't notice her error – and by the thunder of the bass chords. It was as if she was inside the instrument, part of it, making it do exactly what she demanded of it.

Towards the end the music calmed down, and finally came to rest. Naomi lifted her hands from the keys, stretched her head backwards to relax her neck.

'That was superb!' Dan said quietly. 'Thank you very much.'

'I'm glad you liked it,' Naomi said. 'It's a favourite of mine, though I know quite well I'll never do it justice.'

'I think I should go now,' Dan said. 'I've had a wonderful evening but you must be tired by now, and you start your new job in the morning. I wish you luck.'

'Thank you,' Naomi said. 'I've a feeling I'll need it!'

NINE

Naomi was awakened by her radio alarm, the *Today* programme with this morning the dulcet tones of Anna Ford. But why? she asked herself, not yet opening her eyes. Nowadays she never set the alarm. Living alone, no-one to see off to work or to school, what did it matter when she arose? She got up when she wanted to which, following the habit of a lifetime, was in any case sevenish.

By the time Anna Ford had finished her sentence Naomi had remembered everything, had opened her eyes and was out of bed.

Amersham's! Her new job!

She went into the bathroom, stood under the hot shower, felt herself come alive. She hoped, as the lather from the shampoo rinsed off, that her hair had been cut well enough to fall as it should without too much fuss. It had been all right yesterday, but then yesterday had not been an important day.

She stayed under the shower deliberately longer than she ought; isolated, cut off from the world, cocooned in the fast, comforting curtain of hot water. Once she left it, began to dry herself and to dress, she would have to face the world, and about that she was distinctly nervous.

She finished drying herself, draped the towel back on the rail and, on an impulse, surveyed herself in the full-length bathroom mirror, fitted by the previous owner of the flat who, she thought, must have been either a veritable Venus or a masochist. Fortunately her image in the glass was blurred by its steamy surface, no hard outlines, nothing too clearly defined.

Her long neck and her shoulders were reasonably good, she thought, though more suited to a Jane Austen heroine than to today's fashion; sloping shoulders, not broad and square. Her breasts, in spite of feeding three children, were reasonably curvaceous and firm, though the acid test, or so she had read, was to check whether a pencil placed between the breast and the ribcage would fall to the floor or be held firm. In the latter case one had a pair of super droopers.

She decided not to try, not that the bathroom was a place where she would ever find a pencil. In any case, what was there that a well-fitted, underwired bra could not take care of?

She still went in at the waist and curved pleasantly outwards at the hips. Her thighs were long – no sign of cellulite there either – but her legs from knee to ankle were shorter than she would have wished them to be.

Though who cares? she thought. Who is going to see me, who will ever again desire to see me? She turned away from her reflection, and from the question. It was not a thought with which she wished to start the day.

She went into the bedroom. She had decided yesterday what she would wear for her debut into the workers' world. A brown skirt, an inch or two above the knee but not too short, a matching jacket and a cream wool top. She would wear her amber earrings, but decide at the last minute whether or not the amber beads would be over the top. She wished to look smart, but not over-smart. She wanted to be exactly right for selling books. On her previous visit to Amersham's she had noticed with relief that it didn't follow the fashion of dressing its staff in trendy uniforms with first-name badges on chests and bosoms.

Dressed, meagrely breakfasted, and ready for the off, though it was at least forty minutes before there was any need to leave, she pottered around the living room. At one point she heard Dan running down his stairs – it was one of the few sounds which came through from his part of the house – and the closing of the front door as he left. She stood in the window and watched him as he went down the path and walked away along the street. He had a quick, springing walk, as if he was pleased to be going wherever it was. She half hoped that he would turn around, see her and give her a wave. It would boost her confidence, though she was not sure why she so desperately needed it.

She enjoyed the walk to work, liked being part of a surprising number of people presumably on the same pursuit. They were quite different from the throng of leisurely shoppers with whom she usually mingled. They walked briskly, clearly knew where they were heading and were not to be diverted. Also, it was a lovely morning, calm and sunny, the river sparkling; March coming in like a lamb.

She arrived at Amersham's too early, it was not yet open. She hovered in front of the window, pretending to take in the book display until, from the corner of her eye, she saw a man walk up Union Street, turn into Amersham's and unlock the door. Should she follow him in or should she, rather, wait for a sight of Jean Fulneck? The latter, she decided, would make more sense.

She didn't have to wait long. As nearby clocks were striking nine there was Jean Fulneck approaching like a ship in full sail.

'You're an early bird!' she said, catching up with Naomi. 'How long have you been here?'

'Only a few minutes. I wasn't sure how long it would take me. Someone else has arrived but I thought I'd wait for you.'

'That would be Mr Charlton, the assistant manager. Known as "Charlie". He's always here first. You'd better report to him to begin with. He has an office upstairs.'

Seated at his desk in an office which was the size of a roomy dog kennel, 'Charlie' Charlton welcomed Naomi with a flash of quite perfect, brilliant-white teeth in an otherwise homely face, commented favourably on the weather and said, 'I'll leave you in Mrs Fulneck's capable hands for the moment. She'll show you the ropes.'

Jean Fulneck showed her where everything was, told her what was expected of her.

'In any case, I'm here with you today,' she said. 'And on Thursday. Geoff should be back.'

'Geoff?'

'You met him when you came before. He works on this floor.'

'Oh yes, I remember!' Naomi said. It had been no more than a brief nod between them. 'So where is he now?'

'He's got flu. Or maybe just a feverish cold. And there's the other part-timer, Mavis. She works Monday, Wednesday and Friday, so you might never meet her. The only thing is,' Jean said doubtfully, 'I'm not sure I'll manage Saturday. It's all getting a bit near. I might be in the maternity ward by then!'

That, to Naomi, seemed more than likely. In the short time since she had seen her Jean had grown bigger than ever, her bulk lower. She looked, with her bright hair and rosy complexion, like a giant bud which might at any moment burst into flower. Which was how I once reckoned babies came, Naomi remembered. She had thought the navel opened and out popped the child. She could see no other way.

'I dare say I'll manage by then,' she said. 'Or I'll do my best. You shouldn't take any risks!'

She fervently hoped that the child would be born in the comfort of the hospital, not in the ladies' cloakroom here. As a mother of three she would probably be called upon to assist, and it was definitely not her scene.

'Please don't come in even on Thursday if you don't feel up to it,' she urged.

'Well, we'll see!'

The mother-to-be was surprisingly blasé about the whole business. No doubt she would sail through it, Naomi thought.

At Jean's suggestion they had started the morning's work by tidying up the fiction shelves. 'I'll work one stack,' Jean said. 'You do the next, side by side. Everything in alphabetical order by the author. Anything which doesn't belong, put on the table in the middle and we'll sort them out afterwards.'

It was pleasant and companionable. So early in the day there were no more than two or three customers in the shop and when Jean broke off to serve them Naomi went with her to observe how it was done. It seemed easy enough. Not much different from all the Women's Institute stalls she had helped with in her time. Easier, really, because as Dan Sheridan had suggested, they chose the book they wanted and handed over the money. No-one, so far, had asked for advice.

Back at work on the shelves Naomi said, 'I'm just so tempted to open the books and read bits! Do we ever get the time to do that?'

'Occasionally,' Jean replied. 'There's slack times, and others when you'll be rushed off your feet. But I wouldn't let Mr Swaine catch you at it if I were you. He expects you to watch all the customers all the time. You'd be amazed how many respectable-looking people nick books.'

'I hope I never see anyone doing it,' Naomi said. 'I wouldn't know what to do.'

Jean Fulneck finished the stack she was working on and moved to the next. Naomi was only halfway through hers.

'I expect you would,' Jean said. 'It comes to you.'

In the middle of the morning Mr Swaine descended the stairs and began his inspection of the ground floor, which Jean said he did at least twice every day.

'Not that he doesn't trust us,' she said. 'But he's a good manager, he keeps his eye on everything.'

Naomi had been serving a customer, her very first on her own, when Mr Swaine walked through. Though he'd done nothing more than give her a slight nod of greeting she'd felt that his eye was on her. Her knees had knocked, which she'd told herself was stupid. Why should she think that she wasn't totally capable of what she was doing?

The morning flew by. It was as well there were not many customers since there were so many things to learn, in addition to the book stock, which Naomi knew would take her some time to find her way around. Jean was a good teacher, clear with her instructions, and patient. Naomi learnt how to work the till, how to take an order for a specific book, even how to check on the computer whether a book was in stock, or from where it could be obtained.

'You're very quick,' Jean said. 'You'll pick it all up in no time at all.'

Towards lunchtime Mr Swaine came downstairs and made

straight for the counter behind which Jean was showing Naomi how to keep track of orders.

'Good morning, Mrs Fletcher!' he said, formally but pleasantly. 'Welcome to Amersham's! How are you getting on?'

'Quite well, I think.' Naomi looked at Jean for confirmation.

'She's doing *very* well,' Jean said. 'We've covered quite a lot.'

'Good! Good!' Mr Swaine said.

'Though we weren't interrupted much by customers,' Naomi said.

Mr Swaine froze. 'What did you say?' he asked when he found his voice.

'I said we weren't interrupted much by customers.' She spoke clearly; perhaps he was a little deaf?

'I thought that was what you said.' His voice was as cool and as clear as crystal. 'Mrs Fletcher, let me put you right. No customer, even the most trying, is an interruption. The customer is the reason, the only reason, we are here. Without the customer's interruption, as you wrongly choose to call it, neither you nor I would have a job!' His voice rose a little. 'Amersham's would not exist!'

Since the floor did not, as Naomi wished it would, open and swallow her up, she was left facing Mr Swaine.

'I'm sorry,' she said. 'It was an unfortunate phrase, not quite what I intended.'

'Most unfortunate,' Mr Swaine agreed. 'I would not like to think that that was the way your thoughts went.'

'Oh, not at all, Mr Swaine,' Naomi assured him. 'It was a slip of the tongue. I'm sure I'll take pleasure in serving the customers!'

'Good!' he said, turning on his heel, walking back upstairs.

When he was out of sight Naomi turned to Jean.

'Not a good start on my part,' she said ruefully.

'Don't worry, he won't hold it against you,' Jean assured her. 'He says what he thinks, *when* he thinks it. Gets it over. You have to understand that Mr Swaine eats, drinks and thinks Amersham's. It's as well he's not married. His wife would come a bad second. Anyway, it's lunchtime, we'll have to sort out what we're going to do.'

110

'I hadn't thought about that,' Naomi said. Surely she wasn't going to be left on her own? But how could it be otherwise?

'As a matter of fact,' Jean said, 'I brought a sandwich – I do sometimes. There's a little room next to the cloakroom where we can make a cup of coffee, and eat if we want to. It won't take me more than twenty minutes and I'll have a word with Charlie. He'll get someone to cover for me, or maybe he'll do it himself.'

'You shouldn't be cutting short your lunch break,' Naomi protested. 'You need the rest.'

'Oh, I'll be all right!' Jean was all nonchalance. 'Anyway, it can be quite busy at lunchtime. But you can go out when I get back.'

'Charlie' Charlton agreed to take over from Jean himself. 'I think he wants to give you the once-over,' she said. 'Oh, not to criticize! He's easygoing – too easygoing. Not like Mr Swaine, but not as good at his job, either.'

Walking out of Amersham's, Naomi took a deep breath of fresh air. It was good to be free – not that the morning had been difficult, except for the contretemps with Mr Swaine. Since she had decided to take only half an hour instead of the hour she was allowed, she bought a bacon and egg sandwich in Marks & Spencer's, then sat on a seat in the abbey churchyard to eat it.

It was wonderful to be eating outside so early in the year. She must design a small patio for the garden of the flat. Perhaps she might even build it herself – not that she knew the first thing about it. Perhaps Dan Sheridan might give her a hand? Then she would buy a table and a few chairs. She saw a long vista of summer evenings, bottles of wine, a bowl of pasta, salads: friends eating, drinking, gossiping, their features as yet indistinguishable because it was beyond her to imagine who they might be. They would of course be charming, witty, fun to be with, and possibly beautiful.

She jerked herself out of her daydream, glanced at her watch, and started to walk back to Amersham's.

The scene which met her was totally different from the one she had left a little earlier. Jean and Mr Charlton stood behind the counter, each with a short queue of customers in front of them waiting to be served. Several more people, in ones and twos, browsed around the shelves, and even in the few seconds she stood there people brushed past her, going in and out of the door. She hurried upstairs, left her coat, and came down again at once, feeling guilty that she sat in the open air, dreaming dreams, while all this was going on.

'What shall I do?' she asked.

'You can put things into bags for Charlie,' Jean said. 'His queue is longer than mine.' Which was, Naomi decided after the first few minutes, because he was less adept at dealing with things than was Jean. Perhaps life on the upper reaches of the educational floor moved at a more leisurely pace than on the ground with the hoi polloi. Nevertheless, it was nice of him to have helped out and he did it all with good grace and many flashes of his lovely teeth. If the flu-ridden Geoff was still absent when Thursday came and Jean was by some chance in the middle of labour pains – though they didn't call them pains now, they were simply contractions – would Cheerful Charlie help her out? She did hope so.

Back home in her flat Naomi poured herself a weak gin and tonic, and sat on the sofa with her feet up to drink it. I must not, however, she told herself, make a habit of this – the gin, that is. For a start, she couldn't afford it. But today was something special, she had earned it.

What she would have liked would be to have someone there waiting for her, someone who would say, 'How did it go? Was it all right?' Oh well, it *had* gone all right. Perhaps Isobel would phone her?

She had shopped on the way home. Everything was so handy, in that way far superior to Four Winds, and the food shops stayed open later than did Amersham's. She had dropped in on Waitrose and had fallen for several pre-packed exotic meals which promised the tastes and smells of the Orient with no more effort than opening the packet and putting it in the oven. Or the microwave, though in spite of having had one for several years she had not yet come to terms with the microwave. There had been no need to. She had had all the time in the world to do long, slow cooking in the Aga. And Edward liked traditional ways, traditional food. At least he had then. Perhaps now every-

112

thing had changed and they lived entirely out of the microwave.

She drank the last of her gin and tonic, put down the glass, lay back against the sofa cushions and closed her eyes. Now that she had given way to it she realized how truly tired she was. Unused to a hard day's work, she thought. She was verging on the edge of sleep when a knock on her door jerked her awake again. She had heard no-one come in at the front door, so it could only be Dan, and it was.

'I hope I'm not disturbing you,' he said.

'Not at all,' Naomi lied. 'Do come in.'

He followed her into the flat, and sat down.

'Would you like a drink?' she asked.

'That would be nice,' he said. 'But only if you're having one.'

'Oh I will! I'll have a gin and tonic!' Why not have a second one? I've earned it today she told herself. 'What about you?'

'That would be fine,' Dan said. 'Did you have a good day?'

'Quite good.'

She went into the kitchen and busied herself mixing drinks. He was a nice enough man but she hoped he was not going to drop in on her too regularly to ask what sort of a day she'd had.

'What about you?' she asked, handing him his drink. 'Did you have a good day?'

'Passable. There's flu going around so a third of my kids were absent. Cheers!'

'Cheers!' Naomi said.

'Actually,' Dan said, 'I did come with a purpose. I've got two tickets for a concert on Sunday. Classical. I wondered if you'd like to come?'

'Oh! How kind! The only thing is, I usually visit my mother on Sunday afternoons.'

'I see. Well it was just a thought.' He sounded disappointed.

'Though I dare say I could change the day,' Naomi offered. 'Saturday I'll be working, but I could visit on Friday, or Monday if I was back in time for Lucy's lesson!' What a change, she thought happily. Two weeks ago I didn't have an engagement in sight, now I'm having to juggle for time!

'If it's not convenient . . .' Dan began.

'I'm sure it could be. I'd like to go. And actually my mother's never sure which day of the week it is, so I don't think she'll mind. Or even notice!'

'Great!' Dan said. 'It's a good programme. Beethoven; Dvořák's *New World*. Starts at a quarter to three.'

'I look forward to it,' Naomi said. 'Can I top up your drink?'

'Thank you, but no,' Dan said. 'I've got a pile of essays to mark. I'd better get down to it.'

The rest of the week flew by. On Thursday Geoff returned to work, looking white and shaky, but it was good to have him, they were much busier than earlier in the week. On Saturday Jean Fulneck rang in.

'I think this is it,' she said. 'Wish me luck!'

Charlie came down to the ground floor to help. 'On Saturdays,' he said, 'we have more customers on this floor than we do upstairs. I expect they'll keep the three of us going.'

And so they did. When it was over Naomi was tired, but at the same time exhilarated. 'You've done well,' Charlie said – and she felt that she had. She felt she'd earned her very first wage packet, now tucked away in her handbag.

'I'm going straight back to bed,' Geoff said as he was leaving. 'I'll see you next week, if I'm spared!'

He looked terrible, Naomi thought. She hoped he hadn't passed it on to everyone else.

'There's a lot of it about,' Charlie said, reading her thoughts.

He was right about that. On Sunday morning Naomi answered the phone to a barely audible Dan Sheridan.

'I've got the flu,' he croaked. 'I can't go to the concert.'

'Of course you can't!' Naomi agreed. 'So what can I do for you? I'll come up right away!'

'Please don't!' Dan said. 'You'll only catch it from me and I've got everything I need. But there's no reason why you shouldn't go. If you come up I'll just open the door to you and hand you the tickets. Perhaps you could find someone else to go with you?'

Who? Naomi asked herself as she climbed the stairs to Dan's flat. If Isobel were not so closely tied to Harry as if the umbilical cord had never been severed, she might have done. She had once been very much a music lover. Now her criterion was whether it was too loud and would waken the baby.

Dan opened the door immediately. Thin legs emerged from a knee-length dressing-gown. His face was flushed, eyes fever-bright. His hair stood up in spikes, as if he had tossed and turned all night.

'I won't ask you in,' he croaked. 'I feel foul. There's no point in passing it on to you.'

'I could at least make you a hot drink,' Naomi offered. 'A cup of Bovril or something.'

'No,' he said. 'I don't want anything except to be in bed.' He thrust the tickets at her. 'I'm really sorry about this. I hope you can find someone to go with you.'

'If I can't, I'll try to sell your ticket for you at the box office,' Naomi offered.

'I didn't buy them. I won them in a raffle.' He was beginning to shiver.

'All the more reason why you should get something out of it. I'll do the best I can. Go back to bed, and if you want anything, just bang on the floor.'

Why did men, when they were the least bit ill, look so much worse than women? Naomi asked herself as she went downstairs. It was all men. Her father had been the same. Strong, and a bully, when he was well, pathetic at the first sign of a headache. Edward likewise (though he had never been a bully) suffered a head cold as if it was double pneumonia. And the inevitable result was, she thought as she let herself into her flat, that they brought out the maternal instinct in women at its strongest. One actually *wanted* to cosset them; fill hot water bottles, brew hot drinks, soothe the fevered brow. It was strange, really. With part of her she wanted to do all this for Dan, though she hardly knew him.

She set off early for the concert hall, giving herself the best opportunity of selling the spare ticket, though she didn't have high hopes of doing so. There was a queue at the box office, which she joined, and almost immediately a man took his place behind her. The queue moved slowly.

'Do you reckon they might have seats for this afternoon's concert?' he said after a while. 'I only want one. I dare say I should have thought of it sooner.'

He had a deep voice, though soft, and an American accent. Naomi turned around to look at him. He was tall, blunt-featured, cropped hair; not handsome but attractive. Perhaps it was his voice, and his ready smile.

'I don't know,' Naomi said. 'But it so happens I have a spare ticket. The friend I was to have come with has flu.'

'So you could sell me her ticket? That's great!' the man said.

'*His* ticket. I'd be glad to. I think they're quite good seats. It's ten pounds.'

He took out his wallet, gave her a ten-pound note. She handed him the aisle ticket. With his long legs he would need that.

'So we can go straight in?' he asked.

'I think so. We're a bit early, but no matter.'

TEN

He bought two programmes and handed one to her. When they had located their seats, two thirds of the way back in the stalls and luckily at the end of a row, Naomi said, 'You must have the aisle seat. You're taller than I am.'

'Thanks,' he said. 'I'd appreciate that. My knees thank you!'

Though Naomi was not short he topped her by several inches and most of his length was in his legs, so that when they were seated their shoulders were almost level. Does he want to talk, she asked herself, or is he just a man who has simply bought a ticket and is sitting next to me by coincidence? She would leave it to him to decide.

'I'm Tom Lever,' he said.

'Naomi Fletcher,' she replied.

'Nice to meet you, Naomi. Do you live in Bath?' he enquired.

'I do. I haven't actually lived here long, but I've known Bath for some years. Are you a visitor?' It wasn't just his voice. His clothes, though casual, were a subtly different casual from the English; different cut, jacket in a checked pattern which could only be American.

'Yes and no,' he said. 'I live in New York. I'm at NYU, physics, but I'm here at your university as a visiting professor.'

'NYU?'

'New York University.'

117

'Of course! How silly of me! My elder daughter was at Bath University. She's left now, but her husband's there, he's a librarian. They have a small baby . . .'

She stopped suddenly. Why was she telling him all this? She was babbling.

'Well if you say so I guess I have to believe you,' he said. 'But you don't look old enough to be a grandmother. No way!'

She smiled at that which, he thought, made her look even younger and prettier. But in spite of her smile he sensed a slight withdrawal. It was a remark too personal and made too soon and he was annoyed with himself for his misjudgement. In fact, though she told herself she was being silly, Naomi was a mite embarrassed, though only because she felt she had invited the remark. Either way, it served to dry up their brief conversation and they both applied themselves assiduously to perusing their programmes, Naomi reading every word, even the advertisements. She was interested to find one from Cut and Come Again. 'Continental Stylist' it said, which could only mean Henri. She reckoned he hailed from Huddersfield.

The hall was filling up now and the penalty of having seats at the end of the row was that they were constantly bobbing up and down to let people pass. The members of the orchestra filed in, took their seats, tuned up their instruments. The conductor appeared to polite applause, bowed his acknowledgement, turned back to his orchestra and swiftly raised his baton. The first chords of the Beethoven sounded.

In the interval they resumed their conversation.

'That was terrific!' Tom said. 'Did you enjoy it?'

'Very much,' Naomi replied. 'They're a good orchestra, don't you think?'

'Excellent.'

After another pause, in which they both looked around the hall, Tom said, 'How about an ice cream?' There were long queues in front of the two ladies with their trays of ice creams.

'Not really, thank you,' Naomi said. 'It takes for ever.'

'No problem, if you'd like one,' he offered.

'Honestly, no!' She turned to her programme. 'I expect you'll enjoy the second half – Dvořák's *New World*?'

'Oh I will!' he answered. 'It's what attracted me when I saw the posters for the concert. He wrote it when he was head of the national conservatory in New York; it had its first performance there. I think you can hear that he was homesick for Czecho-slovakia. He didn't stay long in the New World. Four or five years.'

'And how long are you to be away from your country?' Naomi asked.

'Not long. Maybe no more than three or four months. They're doing some research here which really interests me. I was invited and I jumped at the chance. Your English universities are first-rate, you know.'

'I believe so,' Naomi said. 'They never have enough money, though.'

The audience was back in its seats, the orchestra filed in again. Listening to the Dvořák, which she had heard before though never actually listened to, Naomi recognized, or thought she did, the homesickness which Tom Lever had mentioned. Was he himself ever homesick for New York? She stole a glance at him. His chin in his cupped hand, he was intent on the music, and she at once looked away again. When it was over he joined enthusiastically in the rapturous applause, and then rose to his feet and called 'Bravo!' in a most unEnglish fashion, though one or two brave souls joined in with him.

When the applause had ended and the orchestra had left, the two of them made their way through the crowded aisles to the exit. It had all been very pleasant, Naomi thought, and not only the music. She would be sorry to see him go. Since the first part of their journey was in the same direction perhaps they would walk that together?

'I was wondering . . .' he said as they reached the door.

'Yes?'

'Well, what I've never had in your country is a real English tea. Crumpets. Cream cakes, strawberry jam . . . the works.'

'I'm not sure that many people here have it these days,' Naomi said.

His face fell.

'Pity! I hoped you'd know where to find it and that you'd go with me. It'd be perfect. An English tea with an Englishwoman. You'd know the ropes.'

'Well . . .' Naomi hesitated.

'Please! If we can't have an English tea perhaps we could have a cup of coffee . . . or a drink maybe, if your bars are open.'

'They're open all day,' Naomi said. 'But as a matter of fact I think I know where we could get what you're looking for and, yes, I'd be pleased to join you!'

Why not? she thought. There was no reason at all why she need go straight home. No-one was waiting for her. It was a thought which yesterday would have left her melancholy. Today it simply gave her a wonderful sense of freedom.

'We'll go to the Francis,' she said. 'I'm sure they still serve tea. And in fair style!'

'This is great!' Tom said half an hour later, leaning back against the chintz-covered sofa, looking at the paintings hanging on the wall, portraits of who-knew-whom from a former age. The waitress, affable, middle-aged, motherly, entirely in keeping with the surroundings, brought sandwiches, scones, strawberry jam, pastries; tea in delicately flowered china. There was a low buzz of polite conversation, and through the long windows the traffic – strangely muted, perhaps there was a nod to the modernity of double glazing – moved around the perimeter of the tree-filled Queen's Square. Two of the trees, she noted, were already bursting into pink blossom.

'Aside from being in someone's private house,' Tom said, 'it's exactly as I pictured it. When I was a kid one of the things we all believed about England was that everyone, from the Queen downwards, stopped whatever they were doing at four o'clock in the afternoon to have tea!'

'No longer, I'm afraid!' Naomi said, laughing. 'Except in places like this. You can travel for miles in the country, looking for a place where they serve cream teas!'

'So long may this continue!' Tom said, passing his cup for a refill.

'My husband and I used to come here for tea when we were in Bath,' Naomi said.

'Used to?'

'We divorced. Actually quite recently.'

'I'm sorry. Is it a difficult subject?'

'I'm getting used to it,' Naomi said.

Some days she was. At other times she felt – 'discarded' she supposed was the word. But who wanted to know?

'And the friend who couldn't come to the concert?' Tom asked.

'I've only known him a week or two. He lives in the flat above mine.'

He heard that with a sense of relief which surprised him.

'And you?' Naomi asked. 'Do you have a wife or someone in New York?' She couldn't believe that it wasn't so. He seemed far too eligible, and at – how old was he, thirty-something she reckoned – how could he not be attached, unless like her he was divorced? That, she supposed, was par for the course in America.

'No wife. Not even a someone,' he said.

So was he gay? And did it matter? Not in the least, Naomi thought. She had met him at the concert, they were having tea together. It was all very pleasant and that was all it was.

'I was engaged once,' he said. 'It didn't work out. Somehow, since then . . .' He left the sentence unfinished.

He was still carrying a torch for her. She was the love of his life, and he would never look at another. Poor man, she thought.

'It would have been a marriage from hell,' Tom said calmly. 'We were totally unsuited. Luckily, we figured that out in time. The thing was that we'd grown up together, boy and girl next door. Everyone expected us to marry. She found someone else pretty quick.'

'And you didn't.'

'Not really,' he said. 'I wasn't averse but it just didn't happen.'

She lifted the lid and looked inside the teapot. 'There's another cup here, would you like it?'

'No thanks,' he said.

'Then I think I ought to be going.'

'If it will make you stay a little longer, then I'll have one more cup of tea!' Tom said. 'Do you have to go?'

Do I? Naomi asked herself. No, she didn't, she was a free agent, a feeling which surprised her, she still wasn't used to it.

121

On the other hand, what would they do next, where would they go? The trees in the square were already etched against a darkening sky, the street lights were switched on. What would they do in Bath on a Sunday evening? She could, she supposed, if she wanted, ask him back to her flat. What was there to prevent that, except that it seemed too positive a statement?

'I think I must,' she said. 'I have things to do.' If he were to ask her what things she would be hard put to it to list them.

'What will you do?' she asked.

'Some work I guess. I have a few things to write up. Perhaps a drink in the bar.'

It sounded a prospect as dull as her own.

'But first I'll see you home,' he said.

He paid the bill, gave the waitress a substantial tip and smiled at her, and they left.

'There's really no need to see me home,' Naomi protested.

'I'd like to. Do you want to grab a cab or would you rather walk?'

'I'd rather walk,' Naomi said. 'It's not all that far, and it's a fine evening.'

They walked towards the river. There was a boat moored on the opposite bank.

'You can take a trip in the daytime,' Naomi said. 'Though I've never done so.'

'Maybe we could, one day?' he suggested. Naomi didn't answer.

He found the Pulteney Bridge interesting.

'Stores built on a bridge!' he enthused. 'It's like the Ponte Vecchio! Have you been to Florence?'

She hadn't. Edward's idea of a holiday had been Cornwall or Scotland, according to the season of the year.

'You should,' Tom said. 'It's magic.'

Ten minutes later she said, 'This is where I live. Thank you for a lovely afternoon.'

'No, I should thank *you*,' he said. 'What a lucky thing that I stood next to you in the line, and what a break that you had a spare ticket. This is the most fun I've had since I came to England!'

122

So why don't you ask him in? Naomi thought. What's to stop you?

'Thank you,' she said. 'I've enjoyed it.'

'When can I see you again?' he asked. 'Tomorrow?'

'Tomorrow,' she said, 'I'm going to visit my mother. I didn't tell you about my mother, did I? And when I get back I have a pupil. I teach piano.'

'How about Tuesday?'

'Tuesday I work. I have a job in Amersham's bookshop.'

'But not all day and all evening? We could have dinner.'

'Thank you,' Naomi said. 'I'd like that.'

'Then I'll pick you up at seven o'clock.'

He waited until she had let herself into the house. As soon as she opened the door she heard the phone ringing. No doubt Isobel, she thought, with some little miracle of Harry's. She was not in the mood for it, nevertheless she hurried through the hall and into her flat, picking up the telephone while it was still ringing.

It was not Isobel. It was Hugh.

'How are you?' he said. 'Have you settled in? Sorry I didn't ring you sooner! It's been hectic here.'

She forgave him at once, as she always did.

'The thing is,' Hugh said, 'I'm coming up to London. There might be something in the offing, I'll tell you later. So I could make a quick trip to Bath!'

'That would be wonderful,' Naomi said. 'When?'

'Wednesday.'

It *was* wonderful. She longed to see him. All the same, she found herself quite pleased that he had not said Tuesday. She would ring Isobel and give her the news. She would certainly want to see Hugh. Or, to put it another way, she would want Hugh to see Harry. He had not yet seen his nephew. She would also telephone Cecily. It was not too long a journey from Brighton, she might come down for the day. Hugh had always got on better with Cecily than with Isobel. They were more alike in character, they had little of Isobel's earnestness which she must surely have inherited from her father, though would she, Naomi wondered, ever go off the rails as Edward had? In a way

123

she had already done so by refusing to marry Patrick, but her very earnestness, and her devotion to her baby, made her lifestyle seem somehow right. Conventional almost. She seemed every bit as married as if she had walked up the aisle in a long white dress and a veil, followed by a bevy of bridesmaids.

Naomi switched on lamps, drew the curtains, lit the gas fire. It was chilly in the room. She had not yet got the central heating under her control. Also, in order to save money, she had developed the habit of turning it off every time she left the house, which was probably quite the wrong thing to do.

I really must go up and see Dan, she told herself. Poor man, he's been alone all afternoon! He's probably dying for a cup of tea or a bowl of soup.

She went into the kitchen, opened a tin of Scotch broth, heated it and poured it into a thermos flask. The very thing for flu! All that pearl barley had an old-fashioned, reassuring look.

She went upstairs – the bottom door was unlocked – knocked on his flat door and called out.

'It's me! Naomi!'

She waited. There was no immediate reply. He must be asleep, and was it sensible to drag him out of his bed simply to drink soup? She was on the point of walking away, leaving him in peace, when he appeared. He was wearing the same beige dressing-gown, his feet were bare, his face was a paler shade of beige than his dressing-gown and adorned, though that was hardly the word, with a day's stubble.

'How are you?' Naomi enquired. 'I've brought you some soup.'

'Come in,' he croaked. 'I've been in bed all day.'

That was evident from the state of his hair. It stood up in spikes, as if he had spent the day tossing and turning.

'Then I don't suppose you've eaten,' Naomi said.

'I've not felt like it.'

'Then the soup will do you good,' she said. 'Where will I find a bowl?'

He stood there helplessly, as if he didn't know the way around his own flat.

'Don't bother,' Naomi said. 'Sit down. I'll find one.'

He did as he was told. Happy to be guided he sank into an easy chair. She found a soup bowl in the kitchen cupboard, toasted a slice of bread, stopped herself just in time from cutting it into soldiers, and took it to him on a tray.

'Drink it up,' she said. 'It will do you good. In the meantime, would you like me to make your bed? I expect it's in need of it if you've been tossing about all day.'

He nodded weakly.

'Was it a good concert?' he asked when she came back. Not that he wanted to know.

'Very good,' Naomi said. 'And I sold your ticket. I have ten pounds for you. I sold it to a very nice American professor who happened to be standing next to me in the queue.'

He put down his soup spoon and closed his eyes. He couldn't have cared less if she'd sold it to a little green man from outer space. He felt awful.

'Well done!' Naomi said brightly. 'You've finished your soup and eaten all your toast. Now I think you should go back to bed and try to sleep again.'

'I'll try,' he said bravely.

'Then I'll go,' Naomi said. She was sure he would have liked her to tuck him in but she wasn't going to. 'Bang on the floor if you want anything.'

What shall I do now? Naomi asked herself, back in her own flat. She had quite a choice. She would like to have played the piano, played something rousing and bright, but because of Dan, poor dear, she wouldn't. She was not in the mood to play a soothing lullaby. She could telephone Isobel, or Cecily, or both, and tell them about Hugh. She would tell her mother when she visited tomorrow. It would be something to talk about. She could make herself some supper, but she wasn't hungry. All those scones and pastries. But she had enjoyed them.

She switched on the television and found herself in the middle of *Antiques Roadshow* watching, as she always did, the anticipation on the faces of those who awaited the valuation of what their treasure might fetch at auction, rejoicing with them when it was fifteen thousand pounds, sharing their disappointment when it was next to nothing. Would I, she wondered, if he were to say to

125

me, 'Your painting should fetch twenty thousand pounds,' go straight out tomorrow morning and sell it, or would I be noble and say 'I shall keep it in the family'? Of course she would sell it, but the situation wouldn't arise. She had left behind almost everything of value except her piano, which was no way likely to be worth twenty thousand pounds.

Thoughts of the piano led her back to the concert. She lost track of the television programme as she recalled the afternoon. She had enjoyed it all. Tom Lever seemed a nice man though of course, she reminded herself, she hardly knew him at all. And there might be very little more *to* know.

Anyway, she would phone Isobel, and then Cecily. They would want to know that Hugh was coming. None of them saw him often.

'Oh, good!' Isobel said. 'I'm sure he'll want to see Harry. After all, he's his first and only nephew!'

'Of course he will,' Naomi agreed.

'I rather expected to see you today,' Isobel said. 'On your way to see Grandma. You usually call in. You'd have seen a difference in Harry. He changes every day, bless him!'

'I would have,' Naomi said, 'except that I didn't go to see Grandma today. I'm going tomorrow. I might not have time to call in on you, but if I can, I will.'

'Oh!' Isobel sounded nonplussed. 'Why didn't you go today?'

'I went to a concert,' Naomi said.

'A concert?'

'Yes. And I had things to do in the flat. This and that. And Dan Sheridan is ill. He has flu. I took him some soup.'

Isobel was suddenly alert.

'Flu? Then I think it would be best if you didn't call in tomorrow, Mummy. Babies are very susceptible to infection when they're teething.'

'I do know,' Naomi said. 'I've had three of them, remember?'

'All the same . . .' Isobel said doubtfully.

'Dan Sheridan isn't living here, darling. He's in the upstairs flat. I simply took him some soup.'

'All the same, Mummy,' Isobel was firm. 'You might have

126

caught it from him. You might already be infected without knowing it!'

'And when do you think I might be ready to circulate?' Naomi asked.

'Well, if Hugh arrives on Wednesday,' Isobel said, 'and comes here on Thursday, and if you haven't developed anything, I suppose that will be all right.'

'Thank you!' Naomi said. 'I'll make a note in my diary.'

Cecily was more forthcoming.

'Good old Hugh! Of course I'll come. I'll get the train on Wednesday. Will you meet me at the station? I wonder what it's all about?'

'I expect he'll tell us when he sees us. It will be nice to see him, won't it?'

'Super! And what have you been doing with yourself?' she added kindly.

'Oh, this and that!' Naomi said. 'This and that!'

'Good!' Cecily said.

The next day Naomi went to River View, arriving at two o'clock.

'I'm afraid I can't stay long, Mother,' she said. 'I have to leave at three because I have a pupil for a lesson at four-thirty.' She felt ashamed of herself because she was really quite pleased to have a time limit to her visit. But not ashamed enough, she reminded herself, to have done something about it by arriving earlier, which she could have done since they lunched at noon.

'I didn't realize you were a teacher,' Doris said brightly.

'I teach piano, nothing else. You remember that, don't you?'

'My daughter gives piano lessons,' Doris said. 'I believe she's quite good.'

'I *am* your daughter, darling!' Naomi said. It was going to be a difficult hour. She was never sure whether to go along with her mother's fantasies or to try to bring her back to reality. Perhaps it was best to let her be where she was happiest on any particular day. She seemed bright in herself at the moment.

'My daughter is younger than you,' Doris insisted. 'I wish she visited me more often but I expect she's busy.'

127

'Hugh is coming. We'll probably come to see you on Thursday. I'm not sure how long he can stay.'

'Hugh?' Doris's face creased into a puzzled frown. Her eyes, which more often than not were serene, had an anxious look.

'Your grandson!'

'Oh!' Doris's face cleared. 'Is he home on leave, then?'

'I suppose you could say that,' Naomi agreed.

'I'm very proud of him,' Doris said. 'The only person in our family ever to be awarded the Military Cross!'

Naomi smiled and nodded. It seemed the best answer. Ten minutes later Doris said, 'You'll have to go now because I have to have a little sleep. But thank you for coming. I'm pleased to make your acquaintance.'

Naomi sought out Matron in her office.

'My mother seems to be having a bad day,' she said. 'She didn't know me at all.'

'Which makes it a bad day for you,' Matron replied. 'Though not necessarily for her. On the whole, Mrs Fletcher, I'd say your mother was amongst the happiest of our residents.'

'I don't know how you cope,' Naomi said.

'We do what we can. We keep them warm, well-fed, clean and, as far as possible, comfortable. But your visits are important, even if your mother doesn't always recognize you at the time.'

'Well of course I would never stop visiting. I might be able to bring my son on Thursday, but would that only confuse my mother further?'

'Oh, do bring him,' Matron urged. 'Who knows, it might be a day when she recognizes you both. And although we see her as confused, that's not necessarily how she thinks of it. She could be quite clear in her own mind.'

I am not a good daughter, Naomi decided as she walked back down the hill, weighed down by a cloud of guilt. Matron is better with my mother than I am. And I'm not all that good as a mother, either. Of course I love my children, of course I do, but Isobel bores me, Cecily annoys me. Hugh? Well, she thought, Hugh is all right, and how lovely it will be to see him.

ELEVEN

Reporting for work on Tuesday morning Naomi felt, for the first time, that she actually belonged. It was something to do with the fact that she had completed a whole week, a week in which nothing, at least not since her tactless remark to Mr Swaine, had gone very wrong. He had not actually spoken to her since that episode but sometimes in his perambulations around the ground floor he would give a slight nod, not unfriendly, in her direction which she liked to think meant that she was forgiven. She more or less knew her way around the bookshelves and took far less time at the beginning of the day in putting them to rights. She could even, now, approach the computer with a degree of confidence though she still dreaded that one day she would hit the wrong key and wipe everything off the screen. The till was less alarming since Geoff had shown her how, if she made an error, it could be corrected and a fresh start be made.

On this morning at ten o'clock Mr Swaine descended the stairs and made straight for the desk with something approaching a smile on his thin face.

'I have just had a telephone call,' he announced, 'to say that Mrs Fulneck has had her baby. A little boy. Eight and a half pounds!'

'Wonderful!' Geoff said. 'We'll send her a card, get everyone to sign it!'

'I think we might rise to some flowers, or a pot plant. Mrs Fulneck was a loyal member of our staff,' Mr Swaine said. 'Mrs Fletcher, perhaps you could see to that? A woman's touch!'

'Certainly, Mr Swaine! I'll do it in my lunch hour,' Naomi said.

That would suit her well because yesterday, in view of the fact of her dinner date with Tom Lever, she had made an appointment with Henri for a blow-dry. If she was late back from lunch it could be put down to the flowers. It was interesting that the news that Jean had had her baby made her feel finally settled at Amersham's, as if the job was now truly hers.

'I'm having a quick hairdo at lunchtime,' she told Geoff when Mr Swaine had left them. 'If I have to get flowers as well I might be a bit late. Is that all right?'

'Sure!' Geoff was nice, easygoing. She liked him.

'But I'll try not to be,' she promised.

Henri was in good form, greeting her with enthusiasm.

'Naomi! Hell-lo!' He kissed her on both cheeks. 'How've you been?'

'Fine!'

In fact, she supposed, she could tell him all her troubles; her mother, her daughters, the difficulty of parking her car. Wasn't it a function of one's hairdresser to listen to the story of one's life? Not that hers would make interesting listening: no scandals, no sexual exploits. Tea at the Francis was hardly in that class.

In any case Henri got in before her.

'You wouldn't believe the time I've had!' he cried. 'A positive nightmare of a morning! I'm totally frazzled!'

I will not ask him why, she decided. I do *not* need to know.

'My car wouldn't start! The washer went wrong. We had water all over the salon floor. The dryer burnt out. The towels were scorched. I promise you I'm totally frazzled.'

'Oh dear!' She could think of nothing else to say.

'Oh dear indeed! But we have to put these things behind us. We have to carry on!'

He studied her intently in the mirror.

'So how do we want to look today, Naomi love? Provocative? Demure? Businesslike? Sexy?'

130

'If I have a choice,' she said, 'the last named.'

'Ooh! Cheeky!' Henri called out to Mervyn. 'Did you hear that, Merv?'

'I did indeed,' Mervyn answered. 'I must say, I'm surprised.'

Why? Naomi wondered. Does he think I'm past it? Or never even reached it? But half an hour later, when thirty minutes of brushing, tugging, drying, teasing, to the accompaniment of Henri's narrative of his horrendous morning, came together, she surveyed the result and was pleased. Not that she saw a vast difference from her previous hairdo except that there were more strands of wispy fringe falling over her forehead. Was that the difference between merely provocative and definitely sexy?

'My oh my!' Geoff said when she walked into Amersham's bearing a yellow begonia in a pot and not more than five minutes late. 'We *are* looking glam! Are we going somewhere special then?'

'Thank you kindly,' Naomi said. 'We are going out to dinner. We don't know where, but we expect it to be somewhere nice!'

When Amersham's closed at five-thirty she hurried home. Usually she took this taste of freedom slowly, lingering in front of shop windows, popping into Waitrose. Not on this occasion. This evening she walked briskly, eschewing temptation. Protecting her hairdo with a shower cap she took a long warm shower. Dressing, she chose a deceptively simple dress, short, with a low neckline, the fine, silky material falling into folds which cleverly concealed a bulge or two and skimmed over a waist which, alas, was no longer twenty-four inches.

She was dressed and ready, blotting the excess lipstick from her lips, adding one more coat of mascara, when she remembered Dan Sheridan.

'Damn!' she said out loud.

She would not have chosen to visit him dressed up to the nines, also it was almost seven. But it would be totally heartless – wouldn't it? – to go swanning off for the evening without even checking to see if he needed anything. He'd probably been alone all day. Not, she argued with herself, that she had any responsibility at all – but he *was* a neighbour.

So what could she take him? There was no time even to heat a can of soup. She looked around the kitchen, opened cupboard drawers; all that came to light was a packet of rather nice shortbread biscuits. It would have to do.

He looked worse than ever. His eyes were red-rimmed, his nose sore, his skin an even closer match to his beige dressing-gown. But surely be could have *attempted* to shave?

'How are you?' she asked brightly. 'Are you feeling better?' A stupid question.

He shook his head, then held the door a little wider open.

'Not really! Come in.'

'I'm sorry!' Naomi said. 'I can't! I have to rush. I'm just going out.'

She needn't have worried that she was dressed to kill. He hadn't even noticed. Perhaps he thought this was her usual sick-visiting garb? But no, she realized. He was a man with a nasty cold and nothing else existed. She could have been stark naked, with a ring through her nose and feathers in her hair, he wouldn't have noticed.

'Oh!'

There was a world of disappointment in one syllable.

'I'm sorry! I've brought you a packet of biscuits. All-butter shortbreads. Scottish.'

She thrust them into his hand.

'If I were you I'd go back to bed,' she said. 'I'll pop up to see you tomorrow!'

She had not reached the bottom of the stairs when the doorbell rang. Tom Lever stood on the doorstep clutching a bunch of flowers – purple irises, pale pink tulips.

'Oh, how lovely!' she cried. 'Do come in. I'm just about ready. I was visiting a sick friend – neighbour.'

'The guy who couldn't come to the concert?' Tom said. 'I hope he's not too bad?'

'Not really,' Naomi said. 'Just a nasty cold.' Poor Dan, she thought, marooned with his shortbread biscuits. How callous I am!

'One man's bad luck is another's good fortune!' Spoken in Tom's deep, attractively husky American voice the words took on an air of profound and original wisdom.

'But for your neighbour's head cold I wouldn't be here right now!' he added.

'That's true!'

Looked at in that way Dan had, willy-nilly, made a worthwhile sacrifice. She would make it up to him. Tomorrow she would cook him a nourishing meal and take it up on a tray.

'My favourite flowers!' she said. 'Irises and tulips!' She had not before realized that they were, but now she knew. 'I must put them in water. Do sit down.'

He seated himself in the armchair, stretching out his long legs so that they took up most of the hearthrug.

'I've booked at a place called The Waterfront,' Tom said. 'A guy in the department recommended it. I hope it's OK. Do you know it?'

'No, but I'm sure it will be,' Naomi said. 'The name suggests it's by the river.'

'That's right. It's on the bridge.'

'Would you like a drink before we leave?' she asked.

'I would, but maybe better not. I don't know just how busy this place gets.'

It was just as well he'd refused, Naomi thought, suddenly remembering that she had the gin, but no tonic water, save for half a bottle opened two days ago and undoubtedly by now as flat as a mill pond.

'Shall we call a cab or do you prefer to walk?' Tom asked. 'It's not far, but whatever suits you. Unfortunately I don't have a car in Bath. I suppose I should get around to hiring one.'

'Well I do have a car,' Naomi admitted, 'but why don't we walk?' Now was not the time to go into her neuroticism about car-parking.

The restaurant was long and narrow, dimly lit. They followed a waiter to a table at the far end, set by a window which overlooked the river, down whose length the lights from the banks were reflected in the dark waters like strings of pearls. The window was large, deep, uncurtained, with no buildings between it and the river, so that there was a feeling, when they were seated with their backs to the other diners, of being on a ship, cut off from the land.

'This is wonderful!' Naomi said.

'Would you like an aperitif while you study the menu?' the waiter asked.

Tom looked at Naomi.

'I'd like a dry martini,' she said.

'Do you mean dry as in American dry? The Martini just waved over the gin?'

'I don't think so!'

'I'll have the same,' Tom said.

They studied the menus – not large shiny ones, with dozens of dishes extravagantly described, fish rushed to you from your local river, served with garden-fresh, organic peas delicately flavoured with home-grown mint – but smallish, enough but limited, handwritten under that day's date. A good sign, Naomi thought.

While Tom scanned the menu, Naomi studied him. He was undoubtedly attractive. How old was he? Early to middle thirties, she decided. Years – at least ten or twelve – younger than she was. And had Edward been a precocious youth, which could never have been on the cards, he would be almost old enough to be this man's father. Sometimes Edward had felt to her like *her* father, until his new-found love had rejuvenated him. Sitting beside Tom at the concert, taking tea with him at the Francis, she had not thought of his age. They were ships that passed in the night. It wouldn't have mattered whether he'd been a school-boy or an octogenarian. Even now age didn't really come into it, she felt no difference between herself and Tom, but it was as well to remember that the gap existed.

Why? she asked herself. So what? She was only sharing a meal with him.

He looked up and caught her eyes on him and she at once resumed her study of the menu.

'What would you like?' he asked. 'I hope there's something to please you!'

There were so many things about her he didn't know – what she liked to eat (apart from cream teas), what she read, did she go to the movies? Where did she go on vacation? Who did she vote for? Was she a health freak? Did she work out at the gym four times a week? He rather thought not. She didn't have that crusading look about her.

They were small things, most of them, and he was surprised at his eagerness to know. She was not so upfront that she would tell all in the first hour, she had that Englishwoman's reserve he'd been told to expect, but that he didn't mind. He looked forward to finding out, to making the discoveries.

'I suppose what I like most in the world is duck,' Naomi said. 'And it's on the menu, so I'm lucky!'

Edward had not cared for duck, she reflected, so she had not had it at home, only when they ate in a restaurant. Stop remembering Edward! she told herself. She was not here to think about Edward and she could, if she so wished, now have duck every day of her life. *Duck à l'Orange,* roast duck, duck with cherry sauce, duck pancakes, duck paté . . .

'So duck for you,' Tom said.

'Please!'

'And I'll have the Dover sole,' he said.

He found the answer to some of his questions as they ate. She read anything she could lay hands on, especially fiction and biographies, and working in Amersham's was like being in Aladdin's cave. She had always voted Conservative, perhaps because Edward had, but she would never do so again, and that had nothing to do with Edward. She thought she might be a Lib-Dem. As for the movies, she did like them, though she seldom went.

'Though I mean to change that,' she said.

'Maybe I could help you to do so?' Tom offered.

She put down her knife and fork. He had noticed her hearty appetite, nothing finicky about her, nothing left on her plate. He liked that.

'Delicious!' she said. 'Was your sole good?'

'Perfect. Would you like dessert?'

She shook her head. 'Just coffee.'

Though the restaurant was filling up, almost every table now taken, they lingered over their coffee and were left alone to do so.

'So you'll go back to New York in . . . when . . . June?' Naomi asked.

135

'That's the plan, so far. It could change.'

'Do you mean you might go sooner?'

'No. I might just stay a little longer.'

Did he want to? he asked himself. From a work point of view, no he didn't. Almost certainly he'd have the results he was looking for by then. He'd want to be back in his own laboratory, his own team working on them. But from a personal point of view he was not so sure. This woman sitting opposite to him, looking up now from her coffee, could change that, perhaps already had.

'Have you ever been to New York?' he asked her.

'I've not been to America at all,' Naomi said. In fact, where have I been? she wondered. Not very far.

'New York isn't like the rest of America,' Tom said. 'I suppose London isn't England. I think you'd like New York.'

'I expect I would,' Naomi agreed. She deliberately tried not to sound too eager. She didn't want to appear as though she was fishing for an invitation, which even if it came she would almost certainly not accept.

In the end the waiter brought the bill, and when Tom and Naomi ceased, for a moment, gazing at each other and looked around, they saw that a short queue of people waiting for tables had formed by the door.

'I suppose we ought to go,' Naomi said.

'I don't want to,' Tom said. 'Though I dare say you're right. Shall I get them to call a cab, or shall we walk?'

'Walk,' Naomi decided. 'Actually, we could go back along the riverside. It's a little longer but rather pleasant.'

Walking along, he took her arm, ostensibly because on this side of the river the path was narrow and not as well lit, but when they reached the main road again he kept his hold on her, drawing her even closer. They walked slowly now, neither of them wishing to reach the journey's end, but when it came, and they stood at the door of her flat, it seemed inevitable that she should ask him in.

'I've offered you a nightcap but I don't know what I'm going to give you,' Naomi admitted as they stepped into the hall. 'I think I might have a little whisky, but that's about all.'

'It doesn't matter,' Tom said. 'A cup of tea would be just fine. I've gotten to like tea while I've been here.'

She dropped her coat onto the nearest chair and went through to the kitchen. She was standing at the sink, filling the kettle, when Tom came up behind her. He took the kettle from her, put it down on the worktop, swivelled her around and folded her in his arms. There was no other thought in her mind than to respond to him. Indeed there *were* no thoughts, only feelings, and over those she felt that she had no control whatever, nor did she wish to have. She was swept along like a paper boat in a fast current. When he bent his head and his mouth fastened on hers she opened her lips to his kiss.

She stretched up her arms to caress the back of his neck, to run her fingers through the thickness of his hair. She pulled his head down to hers and his lips left hers and he was kissing her throat. She had no conscious thought of what his body was doing to hers, only that they were so close that a cigarette paper would not have found room between them, and that she wanted it to go on for ever, never to stop.

She became aware that he had half let her go, took her hand in his, and began to pull her to what he rightly guessed was her bedroom. It was because she stumbled, and he was not quite quick enough to save her from falling, and it all became rather ridiculous and undignified, that she came to herself, suddenly and swiftly. As he helped her up she pushed him away.

'No!' she cried. 'No!'

The strength of her push, the unexpectedness of it, caught him off balance and he sat down, willy-nilly, on the bed, Naomi standing over him. He took hold of her hand and drew her towards him, but she resisted.

'What does this mean?' he asked. 'I don't understand!'

'It's impossible! It's not right!'

'It's not impossible,' he said. 'It happened. It's happening now. You can't say that it isn't.'

'That doesn't make it right,' Naomi said.

'Right? What does that mean?'

'I can't explain,' Naomi said.

'Please try!' He spoke gently now, stretched out his hand again and took hold of hers, lifting her fingers to his lips.

'Please try!' he repeated. 'I need to know. I have to know where I went wrong. I thought . . .'

Naomi interrupted him.

'You didn't go wrong! I did.'

'You? How . . . and where?'

'How old are you?' she asked him.

He looked puzzled.

'I'm thirty-three. Why?'

'I'm forty-six,' Naomi said. 'Thirteen years older than you.'

'You get alpha-plus for your arithmetic,' Tom said. 'Were you doing your sums when you were in my arms?'

'You know I wasn't. I wasn't thinking of anything outside the moment.'

But was there anything outside the moment? Wasn't it just a good dinner, too much wine, a romantic walk along the riverside which she herself had engineered, and a spot of lovemaking to follow? Why should she think there was more to it than that? Because she had felt there was, that was why. And most likely he had felt nothing of the kind. No wonder he was puzzled! She felt hot with shame.

'So?' he said. 'Are you going to tell me what this means?'

'It means,' she said hesitantly, 'that I've been rather stupid. I don't know how to explain it.'

'Then let me try,' Tom said. 'But will you sit down or must I stand? I don't like a conversation on two levels.'

She sat on the bed beside him.

'I think that you're trying to tell me,' Tom said, ' – though tell me if I've got it wrong – that you are thirteen years older than I am and I am thirteen years younger than you, and that makes it all wrong. Is that what you're saying?'

'Everyone knows it is. Oh, it's perfectly all right the other way around,' Naomi said. 'If an old man pulls a woman twenty years younger everyone says how clever he is. "Good old Fred! Life in the old boy yet!" If a woman does it it's disgusting. She's kidnapping! It's the way of the world, I tell you!'

'It's not the way of the whole world,' Tom said. 'Lots of people don't think that way. Ideas change, sometimes for the better.'

'I'm discovering that,' Naomi said. 'But I don't seem to catch up with them. And that's one I'd have difficulty in swallowing. Sometimes I think I'm not living in the present day at all!'

'You don't have to swallow it. Maybe you just have to let things happen. And have you never looked at that from the man's point of view?'

'Do you mean have I said "Good old Fred"? No, not really. If I've thought about it at all, I've thought it was unfair.'

'I didn't mean Fred,' Tom said. 'I meant the younger man. He doesn't have to choose an older woman, so if he does there's something about her that has nothing to do with age. She has something he wants – so is he to be denied that because other people think it's wrong?'

'You make it sound so easy,' Naomi said. 'Anyway, I didn't intend to involve you in all this deep stuff. It's bad-mannered of me.'

He gripped her by the shoulders, so hard that his fingers dug into her flesh. 'For God's sake,' he shouted. 'Stop thinking about manners! I involved myself! I involved myself because I wanted to! Do you think I give a damn, Madam forty-six-year-old, about the rest? Am I to be punished just because I wasn't born soon enough to suit you?'

They both fell silent. He relaxed the fierceness of his grip on her shoulders, though he did not let go of her. They sat thus, without further words. For what seemed to Naomi a long time. She could think of nothing to say, but it didn't matter. Tom was the first to speak.

'I think, now, we should have that cup of tea you promised.'

He pulled her to her feet and they went hand in hand into the kitchen.

They took their mugs of tea into the sitting room. Naomi turned on the fire, it was chilly in the room now, and they sat together on the sofa.

'I'm sorry this tea party isn't as grand as the Francis!' Naomi said. 'I'm sure they'd never serve you with a mug.'

'Naomi, it's the best tea I've ever had.'

'I left all my best china behind at Four Winds,' she said.

'I hope you've left more than that behind,' Tom said, passing his mug for a refill.

'Oh, I have!' Naomi assured him. 'Every day I discover something else I've left behind.'

'Good! Can I see you tomorrow? I've got a lecture in the morning but I'll be free in the afternoon. We could go to a movie.'

'I'd like that,' Naomi said. 'Only I can't. Hugh arrives tomorrow. And Cecily. I don't know what time, I expect they'll ring at the last minute.'

Had she ever before, she wondered, not been 100 per cent delighted that Hugh was about to visit?

'I'll call you tomorrow, sometime,' Tom said. 'Find out when we can meet. I'd be more than happy to meet your family.'

But would I be? Naomi wondered. Even more, would Hugh and Cecily be happy?

Tom put his mug down on the table.

'I must go,' he said. 'Not that I want to, but you look tired.'

'I'm not . . .'

'Don't get me wrong,' he interrupted, laughing, 'you look even lovelier when you're tired. It's those faint blue shadows under your eyes!'

'You're an idiot!' Naomi said.

She saw him to the door. He kissed her gently, ran his finger around the outlines of her face, as if trying to memorize it, and left. She watched him until he turned the corner, out of sight, but he didn't look back.

Two minutes after she was back in the house the telephone rang.

'Sorry to ring so late, Ma,' Hugh said. 'Did I get you out of bed?'

'No.'

Though he might well have done, she thought, and rather wished it had been so, though would she even have answered?

'Good! My train's due at two-fifty. Will you meet me?'

'Sorry,' she said. 'It's not convenient. Get a taxi. I'll pay.'

And when before had she refused a request from her son because she didn't wish to miss a call from another man?

She went quickly to bed, put out the light, and lay awake in the darkness, thinking thoughts which until now had had no place whatsoever in her life.

TWELVE

When Naomi wakened on Wednesday morning it was as if something inside her said that it was to a new world. The air in the room seemed somehow clearer and sharper, there was a tingle to it. The March sun, streaming through the gap where she had failed to draw the curtains together properly, was depositing a strip of shining gold more suitable to high summer across the carpet. There was a buoyancy both about her surroundings and herself. And yet though she observed and felt these things, in those few moments before conscious thoughts came, she did not recognize why it should be so. And then it came to her.

It was Tom Lever who sprang first into her mind, and at once filled it. She felt him almost as if he was there, as if she could reach out and touch him. She recalled with absolute clarity the feel of his arms around her, the slightly stubbly feeling of his skin as her fingers had touched his face, the pleasantly sharp, masculine smell of his cologne. Lying in bed, she closed her eyes, blotted out the room, and saw Tom even more clearly, saw his dark eyes, bright and alive with intelligence, looking into hers, saw his lopsided smile and the perfection of his teeth. Surely Americans had the best teeth in the world?

Her feelings about him were nowhere near as clear as her memory of his physical appearance. What *did* she feel about him? Where was it all going to go? She asked herself whether she would have preferred the whole thing to stay on a friendly level, and the honest answer was no, she would not! When he had held her and kissed her he had awakened something in her which she had thought was dead. Before it had faded away altogether, sex with Edward had been, for several years, a matter of routine, supply and demand. A bit like having a rather dull meal because one needed the sustenance.

Why had she sent Tom away? If she had not, would she have wakened to find him beside her? But it was not in her to do otherwise. After almost twenty-five years of being a faithful wife it was all too sudden, too soon. Nevertheless she turned over and stretched out her arm to the place where he would have been lying, curving it as if she was holding his body.

It was the radio alarm, switching itself on to the *Today* programme, to yet another politician being interviewed and skilfully avoiding the issues, which brought her back to reality, and with it the realization that this was the day she had so looked forward to, and the reason had been, and still was, that this was the day Hugh would arrive. And also Cecily, she reminded herself.

She had a quick shower, dressed in jeans and a sweater, which she would change for something smarter before Hugh arrived, then stood by the kitchen window, looking out onto the garden, marvelling at the daffodils, as she ate her dish of Weetabix. Hugh had liked gardening when he was younger, which she had thought unusual in a boy. He had often helped her in the large garden at Four Winds during the school holidays. She supposed he had grown out of that now. Certainly it was never mentioned. But who knows? she asked herself. Perhaps he might even help her a little with this garden while he was here?

She wished, once more, that she knew how long he intended staying. She could have arranged a little trip in the car – no thought of parking daunted her now. She could have planned the meals, cooked his favourite dishes, which she assumed were the ones they had always been. Wasn't nursery food what young men liked when they came home to Mum?

Well, she thought, she could surely count on him to stay at least two nights, perhaps even until the end of the week, though Cecily would perhaps only manage one night; she would have lectures and things. Naomi felt a small stab of guilt, which she quickly suppressed, that she would be happy if it turned out that way. And if Cecily was here for the shorter time it would be quite reasonable for her to sleep on the sofa, or a camp bed in the sitting room while Hugh had the bedroom.

So now, she decided, I must slip along the road to Mr Patel's. There were various things she needed and probably he stocked everything on her list except for the steak. She would have to go a little further for that.

As she was putting on her jacket she remembered Dan Sheridan. Poor man, she hadn't given him a thought! There must be things he needed from Mr Patel. What am I doing with three men in my life, she asked herself as she climbed the stairs to Dan's flat, when only a short time ago I had none?

A more presentable Dan came to the door. Gone was the dressing-gown, and in its place blue jeans and a bulky rollneck sweater. That he had recently showered was evident from his hair, still wet but combed and plastered to his head.

'I'm pleased to see you looking better!' Naomi said brightly. 'I'm just off to the shops. I wondered if there was anything you needed?'

'I don't think so,' Dan said. 'Or perhaps some oranges and a couple of lemons. Vitamin C's the thing, isn't it? Do come in!'

'So they say,' Naomi agreed. 'And I can't come in. I've rather a lot to do. Hugh is due this afternoon.'

'Hugh?'

'My son!'

'Of course! Sorry.'

She enjoyed, as always, using those two words. 'My son, who is in the theatre', 'My son who lives in Sheffield', 'My son always says . . .'

Suddenly, out of nowhere and with a great rush of pleasure, came the thought of Tom Lever, and it was his name she wanted to mention. My friend, Tom Lever . . . My friend, my would-be lover!

On cue with her thoughts the telephone rang downstairs.

'The phone!' she said. 'Must dash!'

144

She ran down the stairs and let herself in. She was within an arm's length of the telephone when it stopped ringing.

It must surely have been Tom! He'd promised to ring. Unless of course it was Hugh changing his arrangements, something of which he was more than capable. She dialled the recall and listened while the voice at the other end clearly enunciated Isobel's number. 'Damn!' she said again. She supposed she'd better phone Isobel, just in case it *was* important.

'I was phoning to ask when Hugh was arriving,' Isobel told her. 'And what time he might come here. There's no point in coming this evening because Harry will be in bed, bless him!'

'Of course!' Naomi said. 'Bless his little cotton socks!' she added generously. 'Hugh will be here soon after three. I'll get him to call you.'

A bright idea struck her.

'Cecily is coming. Is it possible that you could put her up? My flat's a bit small for two visitors.'

You mean you want Hugh to yourself, Isobel correctly interpreted this to mean. It had always been so and it didn't bother her a bit. Her own life was more than adequate. She supposed other people envied her.

'I might,' she said cautiously.

'Thank you,' Naomi said. 'That would be lovely. I'll give her supper here, of course. I'm just going to the shops to buy in.'

What a bright idea on my part, Naomi congratulated herself as she put down the phone. The question of whether it would seem all that bright to Cecily, she pushed to the back of her mind.

Though the telephone call had accomplished something, she was disappointed that it had not been from Tom; he had said he would call her and she was sure he would, but she hoped he would do so before Hugh and Cecily arrived. Cecily would give her the benefit of her advice on the matter, free, gratis and for nothing, Hugh would . . . well, who knew what Hugh would say, if anything at all? In any case there was really nothing to tell him. She had made a friend, he had taken her out to a meal. That was all.

Hugh, she thought as she walked along the road to Mr Patel's, had made no judgements about Edward, or the divorce, or at

145

least not out loud. It was no doubt easier when one was physically distant. She liked to think that he would be on her side but her experience with Cecily had taught her that that was not necessarily so.

'Are you settling in then, Mrs Fletcher?' Mr Patel enquired kindly.

'Oh yes, thank you!' Naomi said. 'In fact I think you could say settled rather than settling.'

'And you are having a little party?' he asked, wedging a bottle of gin and several tonics amongst the groceries in her shopping bag. 'That's nice!'

'Not a party,' Naomi said. 'My son is coming for a visit. And possibly my daughter.'

'Family. Nicer still! I am a family man myself.'

She knew he was. His wife was often in the shop, her long dark hair in a plait. The bright gold of her dowry in a chain around her neck and rings in her ears. She was like an exotic foreign species of partridge in her colourful saris. And the children, strikingly beautiful with enormous eyes in delicate faces, were frequently seen peering around the door which presumably led to their living quarters.

In the butcher's Naomi bought extra steak, deciding that she would take a nourishing hot meal up to Dan before they started on their own. Though why I should, she thought, I don't know! She just didn't like to think of him living on toast and oranges.

On her way back, heavily laden, she met Emily Simpson, also on her way home, pushing her baby in the pram.

'You look weighed down!' Emily said. 'Here, put some of your things in the pram basket!'

'I'd be glad to,' Naomi said. 'How are you?'

'I'm well enough,' Emily said. 'Except that I'm everlastingly tired because I don't get enough sleep. And madam here is well enough except that she doesn't seem to need sleep. She cries a lot, and she's got powerful lungs. Do you hear her in your flat?'

'I can truthfully say I don't, but it wouldn't matter anyway. Do you hear my piano?'

'Not a lot,' Emily said. 'Do you give lessons? I see a little girl coming.'

146

'Lucy. Yes I do. She's new, and she's doing well.'

She was enjoying Lucy. She was a bright, receptive little girl. She clearly had an ear for music and she seemed particularly to enjoy the short pieces which Naomi always played for her when the lesson was over.

'I haven't seen Dan Sheridan for the last few days,' Emily said. 'Is he away again?'

'No. He's recovering from flu – or a nasty cold.'

Whatever spare time my neighbour has from the baby, Naomi reckoned, she must spend at least half at the front window, watching the world go by. Surely unusual for a woman as young as Emily?

'You must think I'm nosy,' Emily said, as if Naomi had spoken out loud. 'I suppose I am, but it's partly that except when I take the baby out in the pram I'm shut in. Did you feel like that when your children were small?'

Did I? Naomi wondered. She couldn't remember that particular feeling. Looking back, it seemed enjoyable. She had been happy and fulfilled with her three children. Perhaps I used up all my maternal instinct in those first few years, she thought.

Perhaps that's why I can't be bothered much now, not even for Harry. But she still was for Hugh. When she reached her house and collected her shopping from the pram basket she felt a small thrill of pleasure at the thought of the meal she would cook for him. *Boeuf Bourguignonne*. Now *there* was a dish at which she *was* good.

'I would ask you in for a cup of coffee,' she apologized to Emily, 'but I have to get straight on with the cooking. I should really have started it yesterday. It's better done over two days.'

'What is?' Emily sounded bemused.

'*Boeuf Bourguignonne!*'

'Oh! I didn't know that!' She was no less bemused.

Naomi let herself into the flat, put the shopping down on the nearest chair and headed straight for the telephone. She felt sure that Tom would have called while she was out, wasn't it always the way? He had not called, nor had anyone else. Not Hugh, not Cecily, not even Isobel. For a moment she felt bereft, and wondered if she herself should call someone. But whom?

147

Instead she took the shopping into the kitchen, put the tonics into the refrigerator and set to work on the cooking. There was no time to waste. She couldn't think why she'd been so silly as to leave everything until today.

At half-past two in the afternoon she made a cup of tea and sat down to drink it. Everything had been done, she had even changed her clothes, put on her make-up, picked daffodils from the garden and arranged them – if that was the right word for sticking them in the water – in the blue vase. Moreover, the flat was filled with the aroma of the wine-rich casserole, gently simmering away in a low oven.

Three o'clock, Hugh's train was due. Five minutes to get down the station steps and grab a taxi; no more than ten minutes from the station to here. If the train was on time he would be ringing her doorbell at three-fifteen.

And so he did.

She took a quick glance in the mirror in passing, tweaked a lock of hair into place, and flew to the door. He was standing on the step, a wide smile on his face. He stepped into the hall, put down his holdall and took her in his arms in a fierce hug.

'Oh Hugh!' Naomi said when he released her 'It's *so* good to see you! It's seemed ages!'

'It's *been* ages,' Hugh said.

She had not seen him at Christmas. As he'd explained on the telephone, it was pantomime time in the theatre, all hands aloft, no hope of getting away. Christmas Day, the only day the theatre closed, he'd spent with his friends, but he *had* telephoned her. She had still been at Four Winds then and, as it had happened, alone for much of the time. Isobel in Bath with her new baby, Cecily out at a succession of parties, Edward dividing his time as best he could between his wife and his paramour. She had driven over to Bath on Boxing Day to visit Isobel and her mother, although she wasn't able to take another look at the flat which was to be hers because the estate agent was closed for the better part of a week. It had been the worst Christmas of her life, and the one she had missed most was Hugh.

She led him into the flat, a little nervous lest he should not like it, find it poky after Four Winds. He took off his coat and handed it to her; soft black leather, very expensive. She wondered he could afford it on the peanuts salary he earned. But then Hugh had always liked the best in clothes, Naomi thought as she hung it on a peg in the tiny hall.

'Let me look at you!' she said. 'Then I'll make a cup of tea. I expect you're ready for it after your journey!'

'I only came down from London today, Ma,' Hugh reminded her. 'I was there yesterday.'

'Of course you were!' Naomi said. 'You must tell me all about it when I've made your tea. Where did you stay?'

'With a friend. I can't afford hotels.' He smiled ruefully.

'You're looking well,' Naomi said. 'Though you're still too thin.'

But he did look good. He was tall, he held himself well, his reddish-brown hair was well-cut, his clear, hazel eyes shone in his bony handsome face. Surely with his looks he should be acting on the stage, or even in movies, rather than assisting behind the scenes? But he would. One day, hopefully not too far ahead, he would be discovered. 'Oh, yes! Hugh Fletcher *is* my son!' Naomi heard herself saying. 'Yes! *The* Hugh Fletcher!'

He followed her into the kitchen while she made the tea. She opened a tin – it had a picture of a kilted Scotsman on the lid and a pattern of tartan around the outside – and took out shortbreads.

'Your favourites,' she remined Hugh. 'With cherries on top. I remember how you used to like them!'

'And still do,' Hugh said. 'No-one makes shortbreads like you do. And you always kept them in that tin. Happy days!' he said taking a large bite. 'Ah! As good as ever! You haven't lost your touch!'

'I could have,' Naomi said. 'I don't often make them these days. Cecily eschews butter and Isobel thinks they're not good for Harry.'

'Why should Harry eat them?' Hugh asked.

'He doesn't, not directly. She's feeding him.'

'Oh, I see! I must go and see my new nephew,' Hugh said. 'Is Isso as boring as ever?'

149

'That's naughty!' Naomi said. What she wanted to say was, 'Yes she is, only more so.'

'Sorry, Ma!' Hugh said. He looked around. 'This seems quite a nice little place. Are you happy here?'

Am I happy here? Naomi wondered. It was not a question either of her daughters had asked, or her mother. So was she?

'Well?' Hugh prompted. 'Are you?'

'Happy? I'm not quite certain what happy means. And I'm not sure that it's safe to be happy. You see, I thought for years that I was happy and then it all vanished. So now I think I'd rather take happiness in small doses, seize them when they come and not try to hang on to them.

'Good heavens!' she added. 'I'm making a speech!'

'No you're not,' Hugh said. 'And I see what you mean. Or at least I think I do!'

'I'm contented,' Naomi said. 'I like this little flat and I've always liked Bath. I like my new job. Contented is safer than happy; there's not as far to fall.'

'But, darling Ma, I'd like you to be happy,' Hugh said.

'Well right now, this minute, I am,' Naomi assured him.

'Have you made friends?'

'One or two. Well, perhaps not friends because I haven't known them long enough. There's Dan Sheridan, he lives in the flat above. And the people at work. Emily next door, and Mr Patel.'

'Mr Patel?'

'He keeps the corner shop. He's a very friendly man. I told him you were coming to visit me.'

She had not mentioned Tom Lever, nor would she, though she didn't know why. And he hadn't phoned her. Perhaps he didn't intend to do so.

'Is there any more tea in the pot?' Hugh asked.

It was while she was pouring the tea that the doorbell rang.

'That will be Cecily,' Naomi said. 'Now where did I put my purse?'

She found it on top of the television, and extracted a five-pound note before she answered the second impatient ring on the bell.

'Oh Ma, will you be an angel and pay the cab?' Cecily said. 'Has Hugh arrived?'

Without waiting for a reply she dashed past Naomi, in search of her brother. Naomi went out and paid the cab. Emily was leaving her house with the baby in the pram. Naomi stopped to speak to her, peered into the pram, made encouraging remarks, then eventually said, 'I must go. My son's here to stay, and my daughter. They'll wonder where I've got to!'

When she went back into her flat Hugh and Cecily were sitting side by side on the sofa, so deep in conversation that they didn't even look up as she entered. She stood for a moment, then said:

'Would you like a cup of tea, Cecily?'

'What?'

'I said would you like a cup of tea?'

'Oh! Could I have coffee?' Cecily asked.

'Of course! What about you, Hugh?'

'I'd love some coffee. And another bit of your delicious short-bread!' He turned to Cecily. 'Ma's made her special shortbread for her prodigal son.'

'I hope I'll be allowed a piece!' Cecily said.

They went back to their conversation.

How nice that my children get on so well together, Naomi told herself as she made the coffee. It hadn't always been so. When they were growing up Hugh had found Cecily, six years his junior, a nuisance. Absence had obviously made the heart grow fonder.

Naomi carried the coffee into the sitting room.

'I've brought the shortbread tin,' she said. 'But don't eat too many. I'm cooking a nice supper. Oh, by the way, Cecily, Isobel's invited you to stay with them, but I told her you'd eat here first.'

Cecily stared at her mother in astonishment.

'Stay with Isso! I don't want to stay with Isso, Ma! Why didn't you tell her I'd sleep here?'

'Because I thought you'd be more comfortable there, darling. Much better than sleeping here on my sofa!'

'There's no need for that,' Hugh said. 'Cecily can have my room. I'll take the sofa.'

'You can't,' Naomi said sharply.

'Why not, Ma?' Hugh spoke through a mouthful of short-bread.

'Because . . . well for a start you're too tall. You can't stretch out on a sofa. You won't get a wink of sleep!'

And because you're my son, and I haven't seen you for ages, and I had it all planned, and now my selfish daughter is going to mess it up, Naomi wanted to say.

'Of course I will,' Hugh said pleasantly. 'I could sleep on a clothes line! I always could.'

'So that's settled!' Cecily said. 'Thank you, big brother!'

'Then you must be the one to ring Isobel and tell her,' Naomi said to Cecily. 'She'll be most disappointed.'

'That's all right,' Hugh said easily. 'We'll all go tomorrow morning.'

'I can't,' Naomi said. 'I have to go to work.'

'Then Cecily and I will go,' Hugh said. 'And I'll phone Isso and tell her. She won't mind.'

This is not the way I intended it, Naomi thought. It was not working out right. She had so looked forward to this time with Hugh.

Hugh rose, and moved towards the telephone. As he approached it, it rang, and he picked up the receiver.

'Hello!'

He paused, and listened. Then he said: 'No! You haven't got the wrong number. This is Mrs Fletcher's phone. I'm her son. Yes, just a minute. I'll see if she's free. Who shall I say?'

He covered the receiver with his hand and turned to Naomi.

'A Tom Lever. American. Do you want to speak to him or shall I put him off?'

Damn! Naomi thought. Why did he have to ring now? She moved across and took the receiver from Hugh.

'I'm sorry not to have called earlier. I really did want to,' Tom said. 'It's been one hell of a day. Is this a bad time?'

His voice was so warm and friendly. She was suddenly tremendously pleased to hear him. He was just what she needed.

'No,' she said. 'It's not a bad time at all.'

'Good!' Tom said. 'Your son sounded a nice guy. I'd like to have met him.'

She threw caution to the winds. Between them Hugh and Cecily had spoilt her evening and they were obviously going to talk together all the time, so why shouldn't she have her own consolation?

'You can,' she said to Tom. 'Why don't you come to supper? You can meet my younger daughter as well. No, it won't be the least bit inconvenient. I'm doing one of those dishes which will stretch quite easily to another guest.'

She became aware, in the interval in which Tom said 'Are you sure? Are you certain?' that Hugh and Cecily had stopped their conversation and were listening to hers.

'Quite sure! Seven-thirty,' she said. 'Look forward to seeing you!'

She put down the receiver and turned to her children.

'That was Professor Lever,' she said. 'I've invited him to supper!'

'Professor Lever?' Cecily's voice implied, Why have I never heard of him?

'You didn't mention him in your list of friends, Ma!' Hugh's voice was half-teasing, humouring her.

'Didn't I? Then that was remiss of me. I suppose he's one of my best friends.'

A bit of an exaggeration, Naomi chided herself, but then since most of her friends, as she'd called them, were all equally new in her life she supposed there was at least a grain of truth in it.

'I think you might enjoy meeting him,' she said, though she didn't believe what she was saying.

'I look forward to it,' Hugh said in a hearty voice. 'I like to meet my mother's friends!'

'Naturally!' Cecily echoed.

'Good!' Naomi said, gathering up the coffee cups and taking them into the kitchen.

153

THIRTEEN

Hugh and Cecily looked at each other, Hugh with raised eyebrows.

'Did you know about him?' Hugh asked.

'Not a thing!' Cecily said.

'Probably some old fellow she and Dad knew in Bristol,' Hugh said. 'Didn't the two of them go to those town and gown things at the university?'

'I wouldn't know. I was away at school, wasn't I? I never met him in the holidays.' You didn't take all that much notice of your parents' friends. You knew the pair of them went to dinners and asked people back, but school holidays had been kept mostly for family outings. 'Did you say he was American?'

'Definitely. And presumably he lives in Bath.'

'Not necessarily,' Cecily contradicted. 'He could drive over from Bristol. It's not far.'

'True! He didn't sound an old codger, but then one can't tell. Ma sounds like a girl on the telephone. Oh well, we shall see!'

He called out to Naomi.

'Do you want a hand with the washing-up?'

'It's done,' Naomi said. 'I'm going to lay the table. I like to do that in advance.' She came from the kitchen carrying a tray of cutlery and glasses.

'Will you open the table for me?' she asked. 'Both leaves up as there'll be four of us.'

She had brought a small, gate-legged table from Four Winds which, since she took most of her meals on a tray, could be tucked away in a corner of the room but would be adequate when, as now, she had guests. At Four Winds they had had a large dining room with windows opening onto the garden at the back of the house. They had done a lot of entertaining and she had taken pride in her table, enjoyed preparing it – flowers, candles, linen napkins. Well, none of that was necessary, she told herself briskly, as long as the food was good. She had outgrown, or at least *was* outgrowing, that sort of thing.

Even so, the table when finished pleased her. The silver had been a wedding present from her parents, and she had felt quite justified in bringing it with her. The glass had been her grandmother's, of excellent quality but heavily cut which was old-fashioned now. No doubt Helen would already have bought plain, streamlined, modern stuff. But the table's *not* quite finished, she thought. I *will* have flowers. She went into the garden and gathered a few primulas which she arranged in a small green bowl and placed in the centre of the table.

'I'm getting quite hungry,' Cecily said. 'I can hardly bear to wait!'

'We shall have to,' Naomi said calmly, 'we have a guest.'

Tom Lever arrived promptly at seven-thirty. Hugh rose to answer the door, and as he reached it Naomi nipped in front of him and opened it herself. Tom stood on the doorstep, holding a large bunch of flowers wrapped in florist's paper.

'Hi!' Tom said.

'Hello, Tom!' Naomi said, smiling. 'Not *more* flowers! How lovely! And irises and tulips again. You certainly know what I like. Do come in!'

She half turned around, as if she had only just realized that Hugh was only a step or two behind her.

'Let me introduce my son, Hugh! Hugh, this is Professor Lever!'

'Tom!' He held out his hand to Hugh.

Struggling not to show his surprise, Hugh presented a totally blank face as he shook hands. This was not at all what he expected. No beard, no bifocal spectacles, no receding hairline or shoulders rounded from years of poring over books. This man was tall, straight, clean-shaven, maddeningly handsome and, Hugh thought, no more than ten years older than I am. What does he mean by bringing my mother flowers, and clearly not for the first time? And why is she making such a fuss about them?

All he said, in a clipped voice, was 'Good evening!'

How very English my son sounds, Naomi thought, even in only two words. She led the way into the sitting room where Cecily stood by the fireplace, waiting. Hugh immediately crossed and stood beside her.

'My younger daughter, Cecily,' Naomi said. 'Professor Lever.'

Cecily made no attempt to hide her surprise.

'Good evening, Professor!' Cecily said. 'You're not the least bit how I expected you!'

'I'm sorry about that,' Tom said. 'Nice to meet you, Cecily, and please call me Tom. Your mother has talked about you, about you both.'

And what has she said?

Naomi read the question in the faces of both her children.

'Not all bad, I hope?' Cecily said politely.

'None of it bad!' Tom assured her.

'Good!'

The four of them stood for a moment, waiting for the next person to speak. Naomi broke the silence.

'Well,' she said, 'I'll put these beautiful flowers in water. Really, Tom, you do spoil me! And do sit down, all of you!'

Hugh and Cecily sat side by side on the sofa, Tom took an armchair stretching his legs out across the hearthrug, at ease. Naomi put the vase of flowers on a small, round table.

'Beautiful!' she said. 'So nice to be given flowers!'

She was being naughty and she knew it. Hugh had never given her flowers, nor had Edward, but then she had never expected it because that wasn't their way, so really she shouldn't tease like this.

156

'And now for a surprise,' she said, 'I'm going to open a bottle of champagne for the occasion! A little treat!'

'Splendid!' Hugh said with raised eyebrows.

As she walked into the kitchen both men followed her.

'Let me open it!'

'I'll open it for you!'

Their offers were simultaneous. Naomi smiled at both of them.

'How kind!' she said. 'But do you know I have this great desire to open it myself! I—'

'But, Ma, you've never in your life opened a bottle of champagne!' Hugh protested.

'Which is why I want to do it!' Naomi said pleasantly.

'It's not as easy as you might think.'

'I read all about how to do it in one of the Sunday supplements. You keep your right hand curved around the top of the cork, but you don't turn the cork. With your other hand you turn the bottom of the bottle. It sounds easy enough.'

It sounded far simpler than Edward had made it on the rare occasions when he opened champagne, she thought. It had taken him several minutes of intense labour, anything breakable had to be cleared out of the way for fear of which way the cork might choose to catapult, and indeed it had once broken a pane of glass in the kitchen window.

'Cecily, will you bring four glasses from the cupboard!' she called out.

Naomi concealed the fear and trembling in her heart as she took the champagne from the refrigerator and began to follow the instructions she had carefully memorized for this occasion. The three of them stood around the kitchen table; Hugh disapproving, Tom po-faced except for the twinkle in his eye, Cecily incredulous.

It's not going to work, Naomi thought as she turned the bottom of the bottle. Nothing's happening! I'm going to make a fool of myself in front of everyone. Really, one should be able to do this in private before performing in public!

Then, even while in her heart she was panicking, she felt the cork begin to rise, pressing against the palm of her hand.

Moreover, she realized that she was in control. She stopped turning the bottle and waited for the cork, which emerged with a satisfactory pop and without spilling a drop. She gently poured the first half-glass.

'Well done, Ma!' Hugh said. He sounded, she thought, as if she was a small child who, by some luck, had performed a small miracle and must be praised for it.

'Thank you!' she said.

That, at least, was something she would not be afraid to do again. She had mastered it, though how often she would be called upon to open champagne was another matter. She allowed Hugh to take the bottle from her and pour all four glasses – poor lamb, he mustn't be denied all manly tasks – before she fixed the champagne stopper, guaranteed, should it ever be necessary, to keep the bubbles in the bottle for as long as twenty-four hours, which she had cleverly found in a shop in Bath.

'Let's move out of the kitchen,' she suggested. 'I needn't put the vegetables on just yet.'

Once again Hugh and Cecily sat together on the sofa. What is this? Naomi asked herself. They were acting as if they were joined at the hip. But she knew why. They were declaring their solidarity, and was it against her or did they think they were protecting her? It was, of course, against Tom. They were nothing other than totally polite to him, but with a cool, English politeness which he might find difficult to understand.

'Shall we drink to your visit, Hugh?' Naomi said. 'And of course to yours, Cecily dear!' She turned to Tom. 'And to yours,' she added.

'So where did you two meet?' Hugh asked presently.

Before Tom could answer, Naomi rushed in.

'In a queue!' she said.

'In a queue?' Cecily squeaked.

'Yes! For a concert. Wasn't it extraordinary? We just got talking, and then we sat together.'

It was not quite like that, Tom thought, but he wouldn't spoil her fun.

'Do you remember?' Naomi said. 'They played the *New World*?'

'Indeed I do,' Tom said solemnly.

'It was magic,' Naomi said. 'And then afterwards we went to the Francis for tea. Scones and cream.'

'My first cream tea!' Tom said, reminiscently.

'But not I hope your last,' Naomi said. 'And now I really must see to the vegetables.'

Let them sort that out between them, she thought as she went into the kitchen.

She took the champagne bottle from the fridge and filled up her glass, then went into the sitting room.

'Do finish this between you,' she said, handing the bottle to Hugh. 'No, I won't have any more, darling! Work to do and all that!'

Pleasantly light-headed – you couldn't get tight on champagne, everyone knew that – she dealt with the vegetables. Tiny Charlotte potatoes, broccoli, lemon-buttered carrots. There was no pudding to worry about. Fruit and cheese, she had decided, would be quite enough after the rich casserole, nor was she into starters. So no smoked salmon concoction or mushrooms *à la greque*, though Edward would have reckoned that a meal without a starter was a serious dereliction of hospitality.

She tested the vegetables, found them to her liking, which was to say not overcooked, and dished them up.

'*A table!*' she cried, carrying in the hot dishes.

Hugh positioned himself at the chair on her right, and Cecily on her left, which meant that Tom was at the end of the table, which did not matter in the least because he was opposite her, where she could look at him.

When she took the lid off the casserole the smell of it rose into the air, more fragrant than all the perfumes known to man. She passed generous plates around the table.

'Help yourselves to vegetables,' she said. 'I hope you like them not very well done – what my mother would call half-raw, I suppose!'

'How is Grandma?' Hugh enquired.

'Much as usual. Up and down. I'm sure she'd like to see you,' Naomi said. She still didn't know how long he was staying, nor what it was that prevented her asking him outright.

Fear of receiving a disappointing answer, she supposed.

'Will you pour the wine, darling?' she asked him.

'Of course, Ma! I just thought in your newly emancipated state you might wish to do it yourself!' His smile did not quite take the sting out of his words.

'So are you at Bristol University, or here in Bath?' Hugh asked, turning to Tom.

'Bath. On a research visit. I go back to New York in June, or that's the plan at the moment.' He was sure he didn't mistake the slight relief in Hugh's face.

'But your plans could change?' Cecily asked him.

She was more percipient than her brother, he thought.

'Could!' he said easily. 'It depends.'

'On what?' Cecily said.

He shrugged. 'How things go!'

I do not want him to return to New York! The thought rushed into Naomi's mind. She caught his eye and he held her with a look. She felt as if she was being charged from top to toe with a bolt of electricity. She willed him to know what she was thinking. I do not want you to go!

'My invitation here is open-ended,' Tom said. 'But of course I want to take my results back and get my students to work on them.'

'Of course,' Hugh agreed.

'I'm hoping to persuade your mother that she might enjoy a visit to New York,' Tom said.

From the look on the faces of all three of them it was clear that he had said the wrong thing, or perhaps in Naomi's case simply at the wrong time. He was unrepentant. He had nothing to hide, nor had she. It was amazing how much stuffier the young were than their elders.

'I'm not sure that New York is your style, Ma!' Hugh said quickly.

'Why not, darling?' Naomi asked.

She had not been happy that Tom had brought up the subject at this particular moment, but now she was suddenly on his side. Or, even more to the point, she was happy to stand on her own, not let anyone decide what she was to do or not do.

'Because it's big and noisy, violent, crowded. You're a country person at heart, you always were. Quiet places, country pursuits.'

'You mean jam-making for the Women's Institute, the flower tent at agricultural shows, that sort of thing?' She spoke lightly.

'Nothing wrong with that!' Hugh said.

'You always were good at flower-arranging, Ma!' Cecily said kindly.

'Thank you, dear. And I wasn't too bad at jam, was I? But of course I'm not a country person any longer. I live in a city. I rather like it.'

'Bath is not the same as New York, Ma,' Hugh said patiently.

'You've been to New York?' Tom asked Hugh.

'Actually, I haven't,' Hugh said. 'But I know people who have. And of course it's everlastingly on the telly, isn't it? Or in the newspapers. We all know what New York's like!'

Do you? Tom thought. You've seen a few movies, mostly about cops and robbers; you've read a bit of high-life gossip, who's going where with whom, you've read the theatre critics, and about the glitzy stores. What do you know about the real New Yorkers, the people who keep the streets so alive with the business of living? Men and women striding briskly to work, gaggles of kids loafing and joking their way from school. Mothers pushing children in strollers, and the steady stream of shoppers gathering the necessities of urban life from coffee shops, newsstands, corner delis, supermarkets and drug stores. And what do you know about the days when it's so hot and humid you feel as though you're in a warm shower, only not so pleasant, and the other days when the wind blows straight from Canada and all but freezes the skin off you? And those perfect days when the air is so clear and the sun so bright you can stand on a tall building and see for sixty miles? Suddenly he was homesick. All he said, in a quiet voice, was: 'It's not all like the movies!'

'Anyway,' Naomi said briskly, spoon in hand, poised over the meat dish, 'who would like a second helping? It would be nice if we finished it!'

Suddenly, she remembered she had intended to take some supper up to Dan.

'Oh, my goodness!' she cried. 'I'd forgotten about Dan! I meant to take a tray up to him.'

'Really, Ma!' Cecily said, exasperated. 'Do you have to? He's not helpless!'

'I know. But he's not well. He's had a nasty chill – or it might even have been flu.'

'Did you actually promise him?' Cecily asked.

'No. Not him. I promised myself I'd do it.'

'Then it can wait until we've finished,' Cecily said reasonably. 'You can stick it in the microwave. If there's any left, that is. Actually I'd like the teensiest bit more myself.'

Tom refused a second helping.

'Don't hang back, Professor Lever,' Cecily urged. She spoke in a kindlier tone than she had used so far, though as yet she refused to call him Tom. 'Don't let Ma make you feel you're depriving a sick man!'

'Don't be silly, darling!' Naomi said calmly. 'Of course he's not. And I don't *have* to feed Dan Sheridan. It's just . . .'

'Good!' Hugh chipped in. 'Then let's get on with our own meal.'

They were not allowed to. A knock on the door interrupted Naomi's serving of Cecily.

'I'll get it!' Hugh said.

He sprang up to answer the door. Naomi, spoon in hand, paused and looked past him. Dan Sheridan stood on the threshold, pale of face, red of nose, his hair wild, wearing an old grey sweater and shabby sheepskin slippers. She felt a moment of annoyance at the sight of him. Need he look so awful? He was positively wallowing in his indisposition, making the most of what remained of it, and his presence would not in the least enhance her carefully prepared supper party, which was already not going too well. She should have been quicker off the mark with his tray, forestalled him.

'I'm sorry,' Dan said thickly. 'I didn't know you had company.'

'This is my son, Hugh. Professor Lever. Cecily you've already met.'

Dan nodded a greeting.

'I came to borrow some milk. I won't come in.'

Not that he wasn't already in, and advancing a yard or two which brought him close to the table. Out of politeness everyone, except Cecily who continued to hold out her plate until Naomi had served her second helping, stopping both eating and talking. In the sudden silence Dan sneezed prodigiously, then felt about his person for a handkerchief, which he failed to find. Naomi disappeared into the kitchen and returned with a sheet of kitchen roll, handing it to Dan without a word.

'Thanks!' he said, giving his nose a thorough blow.

'You really should be in bed,' Naomi said sternly. 'I intended to bring you a meal, so why don't you go back upstairs and that's what I'll do. I'll be ten minutes at the most.'

'You're very kind,' Dan said morosely. He had hoped for human company but it was not to be.

'Off you go then!'

Oh dear, I sound like a very bossy ward sister, Naomi thought as she went ahead and opened the door for him, leaving him no alternative but to step outside.

Hugh pulled a face at Cecily.

'How very disagreeable. Who is he?'

'One of Ma's boyfriends,' Cecily informed him. 'To be fair, he normally looks better than that.'

'Ma's changed,' Hugh said. 'I can't think what's come over her. At forty-six . . .' he enunciated the words carefully, '. . . it's . . . well!' He left the sentence in mid-air.

'No doubt the start of the menopause,' Cecily said. 'It has strange effects on some women.' She spoke with the assurance of one who had come through it and emerged successfully, or certainly would when the time came. Unless, of course, the menopause by then had been done away with.

Brats! Shitheads! Tom thought. Nevertheless he raised a smile, as though he had not cottoned on to the idea that he was the focus of their remarks.

'Your mother is a terrific woman,' he said firmly.

'Sure!' Hugh said. But did one require one's mother to be terrific?

'Oh, certainly!' Cecily agreed. 'But right now . . . well, new

163

town, new flat, new job. I suppose it's all a bit confusing.' She turned her head and addressed Hugh. 'But I shall try to keep an eye on her.'

'In the meantime,' Tom said, rising to his feet, 'I'm going to clear away these dishes.'

He moved quickly into the kitchen, as if he belonged there, rinsing plates, and had begun to do the washing-up when Naomi returned.

'You shouldn't be doing that,' she said. 'I'm sorry I had to leave. Come back to the table and we'll have some cheese.'

'Poor old Dan!' she said when they were seated again. 'He seems so helpless when he's not well. I do feel sorry for him.'

Why do women feel sorry for helpless men? Tom wondered. It was mildly irritating.

'Oh, I don't think you need, Ma!' Cecily's tone was brisk. 'He must have managed before you lived here. You mustn't pander to him.'

'I will if I want to!' The retort rose to Naomi's lips, but she held it back. It was too childish to utter.

'I suppose if I had a wife I'd quite like her to pander to me,' Hugh said. 'Does yours to you, Professor? Is she here or in the States?'

'I don't have a wife, here or anywhere,' Tom said. Which would come as no comfort to the arrogant schmuck, he reckoned.

When the meal ended they all moved to sit closer to the fire.

'Would you like me to play something?'

The evening was worsening. Perhaps she should not have invited Tom on the spur of the moment, as she had. She should have kept them separate. It was pretty clear that something had been said while she was upstairs. She could feel the tension in the air and it was, without a doubt, the fault of Hugh and Cecily, or more likely the latter. She would like to knock their heads together, but failing that she would try music.

'That would be great,' Tom said.

'Good! What would you like?' She addressed the question to Tom.

'I leave it to you.'

164

She played Debussy, and then a Chopin nocturne. Gentle, soothing stuff. When the last notes died Hugh made no effort to stifle a loud yawn.

'I don't play my son's kind of music,' Naomi said.

'It was really beautiful,' Tom assured her. 'Thank you very much. And I think I must be leaving.'

'Must you?'

The question was perfunctory. It was time to bring it all to a close.

'I must,' Tom said.

She saw him to the front door. Leaving, he kissed her lightly on the cheek, though she would, she thought, have liked him at this moment to take her in his arms and give her a great big reassuring hug, squeezing the breath out of her.

'Should I apologize for my children?' she asked. 'They're not usually like that.'

He shook his head.

'Isn't it interesting how elderly the young can be?' Naomi called after him as he walked down the path.

When she went back into the living room Hugh was standing on the hearthrug, his back to the fire. Cecily sat sideways in an easy chair, her legs draped over the arm.

'Well,' Hugh said.

'Well what?' Naomi asked.

'Just . . . well! A very nice meal, Ma.'

'Thank you, dear!'

'*How* long have you known him?'

'Dan Sheridan?' Naomi said perversely. 'Since a day or two after I moved in. He was away on the actual day.'

'I don't mean Dan Sheridan. I mean Professor Lever.'

Hugh spoke lightly, a slight smile on his face, as if she was a little girl and he was teasing her. But he was not teasing her and she knew it.

'Tom? Oh, about a fortnight – give or take.'

'And you met him in a queue?' His voice rose a little on the last word. 'And you went . . . ?'

'That's right!' Naomi agreed. 'And we went to the Francis for tea and then the following week he took me out to dinner.'

'And now you've invited him into your home? Ma, is that quite safe?'

'Oh, quite safe! After all I had my son and daughter with me!' She smiled sweetly at each of them. 'What harm could I come to? But thank you for being so protective.'

'Ma, you're being naughty!' Cecily chipped in. 'You know perfectly well what Hugh means. He means what about when we're not here.'

'I think I shall be safe with Tom,' Naomi said evenly. 'If the worst came to the worst I could always knock on the ceiling for Dan Sheridan. I'm sure he'd come to my rescue.'

Cecily made a noice which sounded like '*Pah!*'

'Oh, I know Dan didn't look at his best this evening,' Naomi said. 'But I think he's possibly quite fond of me. He's a nice man.'

'I'm sure he is.' Hugh tried to control his impatience. 'We were talking about Professor Lever.'

'Tom,' Naomi said.

'Yes. I think perhaps you should ask yourself – I'm being quite serious – just what is he after?'

'After? You mean he might think I've got money, and he plans to con me out of it?'

'You can't be too careful,' Hugh said. He sounded amazingly like his father.

She had read the phrase 'her blood boiled'. Now she knew what it felt like, or she was beginning to know. Not quite boiling point but on the way up.

'You don't think it's just *me* he's after – horrid phrase – I mean me as a person, a woman? Someone he likes, and wants to be with? It couldn't just be that? Could it?'

'Well of course he likes you,' Hugh said testily. 'You're an attractive woman. He said that himself when you were upstairs with Danny boy. "Charming" was the word he used.'

'How nice!' Naomi said.

'But he's . . . how old? Not all that much older than I am,' Hugh said.

'Oh! Yes! I see what you mean, dear. Actually, he's just eight years older than you are. He's thirty-three. Quite young I

166

suppose for a professor but I do believe they come younger in America.' She started to count on her fingers. 'Which makes him ... let me see ... yes, thirteen years younger than I am. Plus or minus a few months. I don't know when his birthday is.'

'Mother, you are being perverse!' Hugh said. He only called her 'Mother', Naomi thought, when he was cross with her. Well *she* was cross! She was as cross as hell, and with Hugh of all people. She had always thought of Hugh as *hers*. Cecily was Edward's, Hugh was hers. Isobel was ... well right now she was Harry's.

'So you think I shouldn't have him to dinner, or see him alone?' She kept her voice miraculously pleasant.

'You should think about it,' Hugh said.

'I will, I will! What a pity you weren't around to advise your father when he took up with Helen! There's a twenty-two-year difference there. You could have been such a help to him!'

'That's quite different!' Hugh was flushed.

'I'm not sure that it is,' Cecily broke in. 'I think Ma has a point there.'

'Don't be silly, Cecily!' Hugh snapped. 'She *is* our mother!'

Cecily gave it a moment's thought.

'I suppose you're right,' she said. 'One's mother is different. I don't know why.'

'Well thank you,' Naomi said. 'Thank you both. I shall think about what you've said.'

And in the end, she thought, I shall do exactly as I like. Hugh had made up her mind for her on that.

'And now, darling, if you insist on giving Cecily your bed and sleeping on the sofa I'll get you a pillow and some blankets. Don't forget I have to go to work in the morning, but I'll tiptoe around and try not to waken you. I'll see you both when I get home – unless you'd like to come into Amersham's and we could have a quick lunch together?'

'We're going to see Isso in the morning,' Cecily said.

167

FOURTEEN

Isobel was breastfeeding Harry when the doorbell rang. She knew it would be Hugh and Cecily, they had telephoned earlier to say they were coming. Rising from her chair, crossing the room so adroitly that the nipple did not once fall from Harry's mouth, nor was his vigorous sucking interrupted, she pressed the button which would unlock the door on the ground floor, then skilfully, the rhythmic flow of milk in no way impeded, she manoeuvred herself back into her seat. Thus was she revealed when her siblings entered, like a fifteenth-century Italian Madonna, her straight dark hair framing her serene oval face and falling against her over-plump neck to her bounteous bosom.

She held up a warning hand to silence her brother and sister, and waved them to sit down.

My God, Cecily thought, surveying the tableau, does she do this all the time? She opened her mouth to speak but Isobel held a finger to her lips.

'Really, Isso!' Cecily said crossly. 'If we're not to be allowed to speak, we might as well leave at once!'

'One minute!' Isobel whispered.

They sat in silence for a short time, at the end of which Isobel withdrew the nipple from Harry's mouth with a sound like the rubber stopper being withdrawn from a vacuumed wine bottle.

'There!' she said, holding him against her shoulder and gently massaging his back. 'Here's your Uncle Hugh and your Auntie Cecily come to see you!'

She turned to Cecily.

'I'm sorry, but I do like to maintain an atmosphere of peace and calm when I'm feeding Harry, bless him!'

'Well we weren't exactly going to jump up and down or play trumpets,' Cecily said. 'Does he feed all the time?'

'Quite a lot,' Isobel said happily.

'That's why he's getting fat,' Cecily said.

'He is *not* fat,' Isobel informed her. 'He is plump, which all babies should be.' She turned to her brother. 'And how is Uncle Hugh?'

'Uncle Hugh? Oh, you mean me!' Hugh said. 'I'm not quite used to being an uncle! He looks a very nice baby!' Was that the right thing to say? he wondered.

Apparently it was. Isobel smiled happily at him. 'He is!' she agreed. 'Would you like to hold him?'

'Well . . .' he hesitated. 'I'm not . . . I mean, I wouldn't like to upset him . . . but if . . .'

'Perhaps you're right!' Isobel said. 'He doesn't see many strange men. I'll put him down for a sleep.'

She left the room with Harry.

'*She* looks different,' Hugh said to Cecily in a low voice. 'She's put on a lot of weight, hasn't she?'

Cecily nodded. 'I know! And she is different. She's like a *Milch* cow!'

'I can hardly believe it's Isso,' Hugh said. 'Why do people change so? First Ma and now Isso. And we've got to talk to her about Ma. After all, she's the one nearest!'

'And how is Ma?' Isobel asked, coming back into the room. 'How's the new job going?'

'All right as far as I know,' Hugh said. 'Don't you see much of her?'

'Oh, maybe once or twice a week,' Isobel said. 'For short visits. But she's taken up with Harry, bless him. We don't seem to talk about much else.'

Fat chance! Cecily thought.

'Well I think there are things to be discussed,' Hugh said. 'And I suppose I *am* head of the family now.'

'You are no such thing!' Cecily said. 'I'm an independent woman. I stand alone!'

'Patrick and I are joint heads of this household,' Isobel said.

'Or Harry!' Cecily said, *sotto voce*.

Isobel gave her an uncomprehending look.

'All the same,' Cecily said, 'Hugh is right. Ma is not herself. Of course, to be fair, and I do try to be fair, she can't be *quite* herself. There's all the business of Daddy and Helen and the baby—'

'How is the baby?' Isobel interrupted. 'How much does she weigh now?'

'How do I know?' Cecily said impatiently. 'We're talking about Ma!'

'You mentioned the baby!'

'Only in passing! Not as such.'

'Anyway, Isso, it's up to you to keep an eye on her,' Hugh said. 'You're nearest. And even if I do get the job in London I'm going to be frightfully busy. I can't be in Bath every other weekend!'

'I really don't know what you're talking about,' Isobel said. 'I don't see anything different about Ma.'

'Oh Isso!' Cecily snapped. 'The trouble with you is, you don't see anything or anyone except Harry!'

'He *is* my baby.' Isobel spoke in a sweet reasonable voice. 'When you have a baby of your own, Cecily . . .'

'I shall *never* have a baby of my own! Never, never, ever.'

'Oh for God's sake stop squabbling!' Hugh said. 'The thing is that Ma has *changed*. All those years with Father . . . a faithful wife. She wouldn't have looked at another man!'

'For heaven's sake what has she *done*?' Isobel's slightly raised voice was the nearest she ever came to losing her temper.

'She's got very independent, which she never was, and she's got a job, which is all right, of course . . .'

'Every woman should have a job,' Cecily put in. 'No woman should be tied down to domestic drudgery. And I expect she needs the money.'

Hugh gave her a murderous look.

170

'We know all that stuff. The thing is she's got these two men running around her. *And* she's had her hair cut, and *dyed*!'

'Dyed her hair?' Isobel asked. 'What colour?'

'Who cares what colour? Red if you must know! With stripes!' Hugh's voice rose to a near shout.

'Please!' Isobel begged. 'You'll waken Harry.'

'I wouldn't say Danny Boy was running around her exactly,' Cecily said. 'Quite the reverse.'

'Which could be just as bad,' Hugh said. 'She likes looking after people – or she used to. And you can't say the professor isn't running after her. Flowers, dinner dates!'

'A professor?' Isobel said. 'I wonder if Patrick knows him?'

'If it's of the slightest importance,' Hugh said in a tight voice, 'his name is Tom Lever, he's American, he's a research physicist. What *is* more important is that he's thirty-three, he's clearly far too keen on Ma, and I'm not sure she isn't keen on him.

'Oh!' said Isobel.

After which there was complete silence. The three of them looked at each other.

'Well?' Hugh said eventually.

'Well what?' Isobel asked.

'Well what are we going to do?' Hugh demanded. 'We can't just do nothing!'

'Why not?' Isobel asked. 'I would have thought—'

'The trouble with you, Isso,' Hugh interrupted, 'is that you *don't* think.'

'I rather resent that,' Isobel said. 'I think quite a lot. Mostly about Harry, I admit. He's at that age when he needs my thoughts.'

'He always will be,' Hugh said. 'But this isn't about your baby, so could you get your thoughts off him for just five minutes and concentrate on the matter in hand, which is Ma?'

'And could you two stop bickering?' Cecily requested.

'I am *not* bickering,' Isobel protested. 'I do not bicker. Nor do I allow myself to get upset. It's bad for my milk and would give little Harry indigestion.'

'My God, I don't believe this!' Hugh sprang to his feet and stamped across to the window, looking out as if to find calm in

171

the passing traffic, which was not so much calm as snarled up, with a cacophony of tooting horns.

'As a matter of fact,' Cecily said in a clear voice, 'Ma actually has a perfect right to have a friend of the male sex. She is a free woman!'

'We are not talking about rights and all that crap,' Hugh said, rejoining them. 'We are talking about *our mother*!'

'And Harry's grandmother,' Isobel reminded them.

Apart from a dirty look, Hugh ignored her.

'She is not anyone else's mother,' he said. 'She is ours! We owe it to her not to let her do anything irresponsible. We must save her from herself!'

'You have a point there,' Cecily said reasonably. 'I hadn't thought of it like that. You mean we have a duty to her?'

'Precisely!'

'But what is it she's going to *do*?' Isobel asked.

'Hell and damnation!' Hugh shouted. 'And if you weren't a bloody nursing mother I'd put it stronger than that! How in God's name do we know what she's going to do? The mood she's in, she could do anything!'

'You mean . . .' For the first time Isobel sounded perturbed. 'You mean she might *marry* this man?'

'Marriage is an outworn institution,' Cecily said. 'A hundred years from now no-one will marry. I shall never do so. Though to be fair,' she added, 'one has to allow an older generation to live by its own rules. Enlightenment doesn't come swiftly when one is older. Anyway, Isso, you've had the sense not to chain yourself to marriage.'

'It's not so much that,' Isobel said. 'It's more that I haven't had the time, what with Harry and everything. I've nothing against it per se.'

Hugh brought his fist down hard on the small table by the side of his chair, rattling everything on it and sending a small silver-framed very early photograph of Harry skittering to the floor.

'Could we for one sodding minute stop talking about what might happen a hundred years hence, and all your half-baked theories, *and*' – he shot a malevolent look at Isobel, now on her knees rescuing the photograph – 'and your bloody baby!'

172

Isobel raised her head. Her face and neck were flushed as red as a beetroot.

'He's not a bloody baby—!'

Her angry cry was drowned by a louder and angrier one from the bedroom.

'Now look what you've done!' she shouted. 'You've wakened him!'

She rushed out of the room.

'Well, big brother, you have really put your foot in it!' Cecily said. 'Not that I don't agree with you.'

'It had to be said.'

Hugh jumped to his feet again and paced the room, his whole body filled with anger.

'And who says I wakened the baby?' he demanded. 'Don't they waken of their own accord then?'

'I wouldn't know. I wouldn't want to know,' Cecily answered.

Harry's cries, not now at the same pitch of anger, more a long series of noisy complaints which demanded attention, came loud and clear from the bedroom.

'I'm serious about Ma,' Hugh said above the din. 'And I must say last evening was an unpleasant surprise. Ma was never a woman to spring surprises – except pleasant ones of course. Picnics on the Downs, trips to the beach. Not this sort of thing. You knew where you had her. She stuck to the rules.'

He had a great deal more to say but was interrupted by Isobel's reappearance, carrying Harry, still whimpering, against her shoulder.

'He's thoroughly upset,' she said. 'I shall have to feed him.' She sat down in the nursing chair and unbuttoned her blouse. 'Thank goodness I have a good supply!'

'Oh God, no!' The words escaped Cecily before she could stop them. She turned her head away as Harry latched on to the breast with the fierceness of a tiger and the clinging capacity of a limpet on a rock.

'If you don't like what is a perfectly natural function then you are free to leave!' Isobel said in a cold, steady voice. 'I shall feed my baby because, having been awakened from his sleep, he is upset. I myself shall keep quite calm because if I don't then it will upset him.'

'We will all keep calm,' Hugh said. 'We will discuss the matter we started on in a rational manner.' He took a deep breath. How could one discuss anything against this background of rhythmical sucking? How long would it go on?

'You were the one who lost your temper!' Cecily pointed out. 'Not Isso or me.'

'Yes . . . well . . . as I was saying, we've been rather surprised, to say the least. I'm sure we'll all agree on that?'

'And people don't like their parents to spring surprises,' Cecily contributed. 'They don't like them to be unpredictable. They like them to go on doing the same things. All my friends say that.'

'Thank you,' Hugh said. 'As I was saying—'

'But then Daddy sprang a surprise on us,' Cecily continued. 'Given Daddy, that was totally unpredictable.'

'We're not here to talk about Dad,' Hugh said shortly. 'Fathers are different from mothers.'

'Not to daughters,' Cecily argued. 'I mean fathers are to daughters what mothers are to sons.' She allowed herself a small smile of satisfaction at the neatness of her phrasing. 'So I was more affected by Daddy than you were – for a start you're never here – but I don't judge people. I have an open mind. You, brother, if I may say so, are a teensy bit old-fashioned!'

'I am nothing of the kind!' Hugh was indignant. 'I am *concerned* about my mother. Do I take it you are not?'

'Of course I'm concerned,' Cecily said. 'After all, she is my mother.'

'Precisely!' Hugh turned to Isobel.

'And what about you, Isso?'

She did not immediately reply since she was occupied with changing Harry over to the other side. Hugh averted his gaze.

'If you will both excuse me,' she said when Harry was hard at it again, 'I prefer not to join in this discussion while I'm feeding my baby. It upsets both my concentration and his.'

Hugh looked at his watch.

'We don't have too much time. I thought Cecily and I would

174

turn up at this place where Ma works and take her out for a spot of lunch.'

'I didn't know that,' Cecily said.

'I've only just thought of it. But I do think we ought to spend as much time with Ma as we can, while we're here.' He turned to Isobel. 'How long will you be?'

'Ten minutes. I refuse to hurry.'

'No-one's asking you to hurry,' Hugh said. 'Could I use your phone in the meantime? What's the name of this bookshop?'

Isobel finished feeding Harry, winded him satisfactorily, several hearty burps ensuing, changed him and put him in his carry cot in the living room. Ten minutes had stretched to twenty.

'Right!' Hugh said. 'I've come to the conclusion that what we'll do is this. We'll take more care of Ma, see that she's occupied, has plenty to do, is interested in things. Perhaps she should join something?' Or not, he thought. Who knew what unsuitable person she'd meet. She was clearly susceptible, something he'd hitherto not realized.

'What you mean,' Isobel said, 'is that *I* should take more care of her. After all, you won't be here, nor will Cecily that much.'

'Well naturally,' Hugh said, 'you're on the spot. For a start you could get her to take more interest in Harry. Help you out, give you a hand. She'd like that.'

'I doubt it.' About people other than her baby, Isobel could sometimes be quite clear-sighted. 'Besides, I like to look after him myself. You won't realize it, but mothers are so much more knowledgeable now than they were in Ma's generation.'

Hugh sighed.

'Well, we'll have to do what we can. I'll try to talk to her, get to know just how the land lies with this Tom person. For her own good, of course! Entirely for her own good!'

'But don't forget,' Cecily said firmly, 'she's a free person!'

'I know,' Hugh said. It was exactly what he feared.

Geoff it was who answered the phone in ground-floor fiction.

'Yes,' he said. 'I'll get her. Won't be a minute!'

Naomi was serving a customer.

'I'll take over,' Geoff said. 'There's a man on the phone wants to speak to you.'

Naomi's heart did a hop and a skip and a double jump as she went to the phone. Tom! All morning she had been hoping he would call, or even drop in. She wanted, as far as it was possible, to apologize for last night, though if he sought her out for himself she would know in advance that she had been forgiven. Not that she had done anything wrong, except for inviting him in the first place.

'Hello there!'

Her voice was full of warmth, which pleasantly surprised Hugh who, since she had left him sleeping on the sofa when she had set off for work, had not spoken to her since their rather cool exchange last night.

'Hello, Ma!' he said. 'Sorry I missed you this morning. You should have wakened me.'

'You looked too peaceful,' she said.

It was the first time in her life, she thought, that she had been, though ever so slightly, disappointed to hear her son's voice. He would never know, of course, and that at least pleased her, took away some of the guilt.

'I'm at Isso's with Cecily,' he said. 'We thought we might walk down into the town and take you out for a spot of lunch. What say you? Can you take the time?'

'I have an hour,' Naomi said. 'Starting at one o'clock. There are lots of places nearby so there shouldn't be any difficulty. It would be very nice. Do come into the shop.'

She would enjoy introducing Hugh to such of her colleagues as might be around. And Cecily, of course, though she would doubtless be dressed like a refugee from some war-torn land. But no-one could say Hugh was not personable, and with just enough flamboyance in his appearance to mark him out as the actor. Or, rather, the actor manqué, for even if he finally got the job in London it would still be behind the scenes.

They arrived at five minutes to one and Naomi introduced them both to Geoff. Hugh immediately decided that, pleasant though he was, he was not his mother's type, which came as a relief because attraction *plus* proximity would have been the very

176

devil. On the other hand, he asked himself, how did he know any longer what his mother's type was? He had not known until yesterday that such a person existed, except, presumably, his father. The faintest possible doubt now stirred in his mind that his father had not been quite her Prince Charming, not if Tom Lever was anything to go by.

As the three of them were leaving Amersham's – Geoff's parting words had been, 'No need to rush back, Naomi,' – they bumped into Mr Swaine returning from his early lunch, almost literally bumped into since the four of them met in the rather narrow doorway.

'Ah! Mrs Fletcher!' Mr Swaine said agreeably. 'Off to lunch?'

What else, Naomi thought, unless I am leaving your employ for ever?

'That's right!' she said. 'May I introduce my son, Hugh? And my daughter, Cecily?' As compensation for once again having mentioned her last, Naomi added, 'Cecily is reading English at Sussex.'

'Ah!' said Mr Swaine. 'And your son?'

'He is in the theatre,' Naomi said.

'An actor! How exciting!'

Hugh gave a deprecating smile.

'Well, enjoy your lunch!' Mr Swaine said, raising his hand slightly, as if bestowing a blessing.

'Where shall we go?' Hugh asked.

'There are lots of little sandwich bars,' Naomi said.

'Oh, we must do something better than a sandwich bar!' Hugh smiled winningly. 'I don't often get the chance to take you out to lunch.'

'There's a nice little restaurant just up the road,' Naomi said. 'Not too *terribly* expensive, if you're sure that's all right.'

'Of course!'

He took her arm and, with Cecily on his other side, they walked up the road in the spring sunshine.

It was an enjoyable lunch: gazpacho, lamb cutlets, raspberry mousse.

'It was very good,' Naomi said, sipping the last of her coffee. 'And now I must get back. So we'll do as I suggested, Hugh. You

177

meet me outside Amersham's at five-thirty and we'll go straight to Grandma. I know she'll be delighted to see you.'

'I'll be there,' Hugh promised.

'Give her my love,' Cecily said. 'And I'll see her next time. After all, I did visit her only a week or two ago.'

'You did, dear,' Naomi agreed. 'And I do think all three of us might be too much for her.'

Hugh picked up the bill, glanced at the total, and felt in his pocket.

'Hell's teeth!' he said.

'What's the matter, darling?' Naomi asked.

'My credit card. I've come without it!'

'Not to worry,' Naomi said. 'I'll use mine.'

'I'll give you a cheque when we get back to your place,' he apologized. 'I've left my cheque book there too.'

'Right you are,' Naomi said.

She added a tip, paid the bill, and they left, she to hurry back to Amersham's, Hugh and Cecily to wander around the town.

In between selling books, which she had quickly grown to like, Naomi thought of Tom Lever. He did not ring her, perhaps he thought it was not the thing to call her at work, and perhaps he was right. Nor would she ring him from Amersham's. That would be frowned on. And after that, she thought rather sadly, I'm off to see my mother, and then home. In a way she hoped he would not telephone this evening. Hugh had been so charming at lunch, he was a dear boy really and she would not like to upset him when she saw him so rarely.

Doris was in one of her other worlds, though it was not quite clear which one, but most likely Second World War. Or maybe some film, or amalgam of films in which Noel Coward was a brave naval officer, John Mills and Eric Portman were incarcerated in Colditz and Clark Gable, alternating with Gregory Peck, flew planes.

'Dear boy,' she said to Hugh, 'it's so wonderful to see you! I pray for you every night as you set off on your missions. And now you're home on leave. But you should be wearing your uniform,

178

you know!' She gave him a sharp tap on the back of his hand. 'You should be proud to wear the King's uniform!'

'Oh I am, Grandma!' Hugh assured her. 'But they do get dirty in the heat of battle, you know. My batman took it to the cleaners.'

Doris nodded. 'And I suppose the country can't afford to give you all a change of clothing. We need so much money for the war effort. I save all the silver paper from my Kit-Kat bars for that. They make it into Spitfires, you know! Trevor Howard looked wonderful in uniform.'

'I know, Grandma!'

'Mother, it's Hugh!' Naomi said.

'No it's not! It was definitely Trevor Howard in the *Battle of Britain*!'

'I mean *this* is Hugh,' Naomi persisted. Sometimes if you kept at it you could suddenly get through and she'd be back in the present. 'It's Hugh, your grandson. He's come to visit you, all the way from Sheffield!'

Doris nodded sympathetically at Hugh. 'I expect you came to get away from the bombing.'

They stayed a little longer. When they left Doris called after Hugh. 'Wear your uniform next time you come. Are you a wing commander now?'

'That's right, Grandma! And I will!'

'It's a bad day today,' Naomi said as they walked back down the drive.

'A bad day for you and me,' Hugh said. 'Not for Grandma. She seemed happy enough.'

'Oh, she is,' Naomi agreed. 'Sometimes I think she's happier when she's living in fantasy land than she ever is in the real world. But it makes me unhappy. You see I remember her bright and clever, when I was a little girl and she was a young mother.'

'She must be worth a bob or two,' Hugh surmised.

'She is,' Naomi said. 'My father left a lot of money. She couldn't live at River View otherwise.'

'It seems a shame it's being swallowed up in a nursing home,' Hugh said.

'Oh, I don't know. They look after her well. I don't begrudge it.'

'Do you have power of attorney?' Hugh asked.

'No. Her solicitor sees to all that sort of thing. He's very efficient. She's known him for ever. I shouldn't worry about her too much, darling. I'm here for her, and as you say, she's happy enough.'

'Oh, I won't!' Hugh promised.

They had a quiet night in. Both Hugh and Cecily had by now told Naomi that they must leave the next morning. There was talk of going to a movie for their last evening, but nothing appealed. In any case, Hugh told Cecily, in a few moments they had together, he wanted a little talk with his mother.

'I won't be heavy-handed,' he said. 'I've an idea that won't work with Ma. But I just want to set her on the right track. And as I suppose you must be there I don't want you chipping in with your theories of women's freedom and all that crap. So for God's sake keep your trap shut!'

'I make no promises,' Cecily said. 'I shall feel free to say what I think.'

'Don't be such a little fool,' Hugh said. 'I'm doing this for both of us. And, of course, for Ma. By the way, do you know that Grandma is probably stinking rich?'

'I didn't,' Cecily admitted. 'I never gave it a thought.'

'Ma is her only child,' Hugh said thoughtfully.

Naomi cooked a risotto. Italian rice, lightly fried first in olive oil, mushrooms, peppers, bacon, this and that. It was something she did well and a dish Hugh had always enjoyed.

Hugh cleared the plate of his second helping, and sat back in his chair.

'Delicious!' he said. 'I wish I could take it back to Sheffield with me.'

'I wish you didn't have to go back quite so soon,' Naomi said. 'When will you hear whether you've got the job in London? That would bring you so much nearer.'

'In a few days. I'll let you know at once. I'd like to be nearer,

180

see you more often.' In his heart he felt himself unlikely to land the job, but he wouldn't say so.

'But never mind me. Let's talk about you!' he said. 'You seem happy in your new job.'

'I am,' Naomi said. 'They're nice people and I seem to have settled in.'

'Why don't you do it full-time?' he suggested. 'You could carve yourself a nice career there.'

'For a start,' Naomi said, 'I haven't been asked. But even if I were I don't think I'd accept. I don't want to be too tied down. I want to be able to come and go as I please.'

And in which direction? Hugh asked himself. His hope that she might immerse herself in a full-time job seemed unlikely to bear fruit.

'Yes,' he said. 'And I'm sure Isso would like to see a great deal more of you. She as good as said so. You could be such a help with Harry. Grandmas have a very special role, don't they?'

He noted, but ignored, the disbelieving look Cecily shot at him.

'That's probably true,' Naomi conceded. 'Of course I also have roles as a mother, a daughter, an employee, a piano teacher, a friend, and, if there is such a role, an ex-wife. And lastly – no, perhaps firstly, an independent woman.'

'Hear, hear!' It was impossible for Cecily to contain herself.

'I'm glad you agree,' Naomi said. 'It means that in any one of my roles I can actually do what I like!'

Hugh gave his sister a murderous look. Was she purposely making his task difficult?

'Of course!' he said to his mother. 'I only want what's best for you. I'm your son, after all! I just want to feel that you're safe, that you're doing the right things, making the right friendships.'

He means Tom, Naomi thought. She could, if she tried even a little, make him come out with it. She wouldn't, though; it wasn't worth it. She loved Hugh dearly, always would, wouldn't ever want to quarrel with him, but the end of her marriage had taught her one thing and that was never to be too reliant on one person.

Next morning she drove both Cecily and Hugh to the station, hugged and kissed them fondly, watched them borne away on their respective trains.

Back in her flat she picked up the telephone and dialled Tom's number.

FIFTEEN

'Would you like to go to a movie?' Tom said on the phone. 'I'm off to Oxford later today but I'll be back tomorrow, late afternoon.'

'I'd love to,' Naomi said.

Why was he going to Oxford? What was keeping him overnight? She wanted to know everything about him, where he was going, with whom – especially with whom – and for what purpose, but since there was no reason on earth why he should tell her she would hold herself in check and not ask.

'I'm going to the university with a guy from the department here,' Tom said. 'We're taking a look at a very expensive bit of equipment, see if we can get some results from it. I'll call you when I get back.'

For a minute after she'd hung up Naomi basked in the glow Tom's call had given her. Then she brought herself back to earth and looked around the flat, going into each room, wondering where to start. It was amazing how much mess Hugh and Cecily could create between them even over so short a period; half-emptied coffee mugs, newspapers, squashed cushions, damp towels, tissues, unmade beds. And perhaps it was her fault? She hadn't trained them in the ways of tidiness. When they were growing up, and especially in the school holidays when indulgence was to the fore, she (or whoever was helping her domestically) had simply gone around after them, picking up. It was never like that with Isobel, though. She had been the tidy one, the one whose life was ordered – as indeed it was now, Naomi thought, at least according to her daughter's own lights.

She stripped the sofa where Hugh had slept, and which he had left exactly as he'd got out of it. Folding the blankets, putting the sheets to wash, she'd thought she'd perhaps not been as nice to Hugh as she might have been. He'd niggled her, which was unusual. And was that also my fault? she asked herself. Have I already, in such a short time, got so used to living alone, to having my own way, that I don't like anyone else's comments on it?

She dealt with Cecily's bedroom, moved on to the bathroom, putting out clean towels, readjusting the shower which was now all wrong for her, then went into the kitchen to make a cup of coffee. Shall I be nice and neighbourly, she wondered, and ask Dan if he'd like to come down and join me? She was fairly sure he wouldn't have gone back to school.

'That would be great!' Dan said on the telephone. 'I'll be right down!'

He had not felt quite well enough to return to work, he told her as he drank his coffee and ate three shortbread biscuits. You needed to be in first-class condition to face a class of thirty children.

'And since next week is half-term, I'll have a few more days to recover,' he said. 'I reckon it was quite a nasty dose I had!'

Naomi nodded sympathetically.

'So perhaps we could do something together, one day next week?' Dan suggested. 'Go somewhere.'

'Oh! Well, thank you!'

Naomi strove for a combination of pleasure at being asked and disappointment at being unable to accept, while hoping that her reluctance would not show.

'I'm not sure that I can. Aside from working at Amersham's and then giving piano lessons,' – *one* piano lesson, her conscience reminded her – 'I'm a bit worried about my mother at the moment. And then,' she added with inspiration but no truth, 'I

184

think Isobel is beginning to need me more than she has. So I can't make any promises.'

'Oh!' The one syllable contained all Dan's disappointment.

'But I will try!' Naomi said cheerfully. 'Who knows?'

'I expect you enjoyed having your son here?' Dan said. He would say nothing about Cecily. He had his own opinion of her.

'Oh, I did indeed!' Naomi said.

Even so, it had not been quite the same as usual. She returned to the worrying thought of Hugh like a dog to a bone. Hugh had been such an affectionate son, and she'd thought she'd been a satisfactory mother. Surely she'd played her part? Hadn't she also been a dutiful wife, doing everything according to the book, though it never occurred to her that she'd been playing a part. Now her role had changed, it was a different play. She was no longer a wife though, if only Hugh could see it, she was every bit as loving a mother.

All the same, the rest of her life was her own, *had* to be. She had to get through it as seemed best to her, she had to live rather than simply exist. And if her children had any sense at all, she concluded, surely they must recognize that it was better all round that she didn't live only for them. What did surprise her, and pleasantly, was the discovery that she didn't *want* to live only through them. She had glimpsed new horizons, hitherto undreamt of.

'Would you like more coffee?' she asked Dan.

'Thank you, I would!' He was as eager as a puppy. 'This is all very pleasant. I can't tell you how cut off I've felt over the last week.'

'Well, I'm always here!' Naomi told him. And now what am I saying? she wondered. I'm making a rod for my own back. She had no intention of being available on demand.

'So what are you doing the rest of the day?' Dan asked.

'Today? Oh, I have a hair appointment!' Naomi said, improvising rapidly. 'And after that some shopping.'

Come to think of it, she decided when Dan had gone, she would go and have her hair done, though preferably tomorrow, so that she'd look her best in the evening.

'Tomorrow being Saturday, it's totally impossible!' Tracy, the receptionist said on the telephone. 'But if you could come at two o'clock today Ahnree says he'll squeeze you in!'

'I'll be there,' Naomi promised.

Though she could not easily afford them she had begun to enjoy her sessions with Henri, largely, she supposed – and apart from the fact that he made her laugh – because he always sent her away looking better.

So what shall I do now? she thought as she emerged from Cut and Come Again. She had the rest of the afternoon to spare with nothing which absolutely demanded her attention. She could go home and read a book, she could browse around the shops, choosing the new outfit she would buy if only she had the money. She could visit a museum – there were plenty of those to choose from. Really, apart from buying clothes, which was not on, nothing appealed to her. She was restless. What she wanted was for all the hours between now and tomorrow evening to compact themselves into one hour only. You are wishing your life away, she admonished herself.

Walking down the street she stepped aside to avoid a woman pushing a baby in a buggy. The baby was cocooned from head to foot in a furry fabric in brilliant blues and reds, like an exotic caterpillar. The woman was clearly a grandmother. Perhaps that's what I should be doing? Naomi thought. Pushing my grandson out in his pram. What she would do, thus prompted, was to go and see Isobel and Harry. She would be a good mother, not to mention grandmother. Also, and it was an added incentive, she had a small suspicion at the back of her mind that her three children had discussed her. It would be interesting to find out, if she could, what had been said. She quickened her step, walking in the direction of Bathwick Hill.

She rang the bell and Isobel buzzed her in. The hall and stairs smelt even more strongly of dentistry, reminding her that she had done nothing about making an appointment. American women, she thought as she climbed the stairs, always had such impossibly perfect teeth.

Isobel came to the door with Harry in her arms. She raised her eyebrows at the sight of Naomi.

'You've had your hair done!'

'I've just come from the hairdresser!'

'I didn't mean that,' Isobel said. 'I meant . . .'

'Oh! You mean the colour. You didn't know I'd had high-lights, or lowlights or whatever they're called.' Why did she sound as though she was apologizing?

'Highlights,' Isobel said. 'Actually I did. Hugh mentioned it. It's just that you look . . . well . . . different.'

'I don't suppose Hugh liked it?' Naomi asked.

'He didn't say.' Isobel was evasive. 'Actually, it's quite nice!'

'Thank you!' Naomi was pleased and surprised.

'But you don't look like a grandma,' Isobel said in a less approving voice. 'Does she, Harry darling?' she demanded of her baby.

'Good!'

The word slipped from Naomi's lips without thought.

'What do you mean, "Good"?'

'I suppose what I mean is that grandmothers don't nowadays, do they? Sometimes they look young enough to be the mother!'

She waited a second for the compliment, which did not come.

'Oh, I think grandmothers should look like grandmothers, especially to their grandchildren,' Isobel said.

'I don't suppose Harry minds one way or the other,' Naomi said. 'Not as long as I do the grandmotherly things at the right time!' But did she?

Harry waved a hand vaguely in her direction, gave what might have been a smile or a spasm of wind and blew a bubble or two which dribbled down his chin.

'There! He recognized you!' Isobel said.

He's really rather sweet, Naomi thought, suddenly pleased.

'How is he today?' she asked.

'Very well. Just a wee bit constipated, for him that is. It might be because he's beginning to have solids. Lamb and tomato he had at lunchtime. They do all sorts of varieties: liver and bacon, tuna and rice . . .'

'I know,' Naomi said. 'They did when you three were babies. Chicken and rice was your favourite.'

'Really!' Isobel was deeply interested. 'I wonder if Harry will take after me? I'll get that one. I'd no idea you had these things!'

'Oh yes!' Naomi said. 'It wasn't exactly the dark ages. We had electricity at the touch of a switch, running water, and baby foods in sweet little jars! I suppose now it'll be chicken Korma or chicken Masala.'

'I don't think I'd risk chicken Korma,' Isobel said seriously. 'I would think too spicy for his little tummy.' She took a tissue out of the box and wiped Harry's chin again. 'He's teething,' she said. 'He dribbles all the time, bless him! If you'd like to hold him I'll put the kettle on.'

Naomi, tissue to hand, followed Isobel into the kitchen. Harry settled comfortably in her arms.

'I saw a grandmother – now she really *was* a grandmother – pushing a baby in a buggy, this afternoon. Perhaps you'd like me to take Harry out some time?' She could hardly believe what she was saying, especially as she recognized that she really meant it.

Isobel filled the kettle, put two tea-bags in the pot, fetched the milk from the fridge. There was a slight frown on her face.

'To tell you the truth,' she said, 'we don't take him out all that often, especially in the town. I mean there's so much pollution, isn't there? It can't be good for babies, can it?'

'I agree,' Naomi said. 'So what do you do?'

'I open the windows,' Isobel said. 'Since we're reasonably high up from the road I expect the air's a bit better. What we want to do when we've scraped together enough for a car is to take him out into the country quite often. Give him some pure air. But it's so difficult to save enough for a car!'

A wave of guilt swept over Naomi at the thought of her own car doing nothing more useful than occupying its parking space. She didn't want to give it away; she didn't even want to lend it. Nevertheless she heard herself saying, 'You could borrow my car sometimes.'

She had stayed too long. First she had suggested pushing Harry out in his pram and now she had offered to lend her car. Who knew what next?

'That would be wonderful!' Isobel said.

She poured the tea, took digestive biscuits from a tin.

'You take the tea through, Ma,' she said. 'I'll have Harry – though I must say he seems quite comfortable with you.'

'He does, doesn't he!' Naomi agreed, handing him over. 'Though actually he's rather damp, if not worse!'

'I'll see to him while you drink your tea,' Isobel said. 'Did Hugh and Cecily get off all right?'

'Yes. Did you enjoy seeing them?'

'Oh yes! And you could tell they enjoyed Harry. His Uncle Hugh especially.'

'I'm sure,' Naomi said. 'You must have had quite a bit to talk about – I mean aside from Harry. It's a while since the three of you met.' It was the nearest she could get to asking Isobel what they had talked about. And did it really matter if they'd discussed her? Yes, she concluded, it did.

'Did they enjoy their visit in general – I mean to me?' she probed. 'I wasn't quite sure.'

'I think so,' Isobel said.

She laid a large clean towel on the floor and placed Harry on it, lying on his back, kicking his legs in the air, waving his arms.

'I like to give him some time every day to be without his nappy,' she said. 'It's nice for him to get the air to his little botty!'

Since I arrived, Naomi thought with irritation, we have not had any conversation at all which did not include Harry. Perhaps, in fact, Harry was all the three of them talked about. Isobel would have seen to that.

'They did say you'd made new friends in Bath, Ma.'

'Friends? Well, yes I suppose I have. There's Emily Simpson next door. She has a new baby. And Mr Patel. He keeps the corner shop. And then there are the people at Amersham's.'

'And a neighbour in the upstairs flat?'

'Dan Sheridan. Haven't I mentioned Dan?'

'I don't remember. And they said there was an American who came to dinner.'

So they have chewed me over, Naomi thought.

'You mean Professor Lever. Yes, I met him at a concert.' Should she tell her daughter that she was going to the cinema with him tomorrow? No, she would not. She would do that in her own good time, if indeed there was in the end anything to tell.

189

'We're glad you're making friends, Ma. I think Hugh's a bit protective, well we all are.'

'I assure you, dear, there's nothing for any of you to protect me from,' Naomi said, smiling. 'My friends – if I know them well enough to call them that – are really quite harmless, and I'm a grown woman!'

It was not, Naomi was sure, what her children had in mind. But Isobel wasn't listening. Harry had started to cry and she gathered him up from the floor and held him close.

Naomi was weeding in the garden – it was amazing how early in the year the weeds sprang into growth, she could see she was going to have trouble with ground elder – when the telephone rang in the flat. She dropped her hand-fork and rushed inside, willing the phone not to stop before she reached it.

'Naomi Fletcher,' she said.

'You sound breathless,' Tom said. 'What are you doing?'

'Weeding the garden.'

'I called to say I'm back.'

'Welcome!'

'Are you OK?' he asked. 'Apart from being breathless.'

'Perfectly!'

It was wonderful to know that he was here in Bath. Even if she hadn't been going to see him, just the fact that he was within reach meant something. Quite what, she didn't ask herself, nor if she did know would she be tempted to tell him. In her there lurked a small dread of pushing things too far too fast, of frightening him off, which she would not want to do. It was a situation totally new to her and she did not have the confidence simply to follow her feelings. She was unsure where they would take her. But don't be so silly, she told herself. He is simply a friend, and you are a friend to him. Take it easy!

'Why don't I pick you up around six-thirty?' Tom said. 'Choose which movie you'd like. I'm sure I won't have seen any of them.'

'Me neither,' Naomi said. 'Six-thirty will be fine!'

When he had rung off she washed the soil from her hands and went along to Mr Patel's to buy the *Chronicle*.

'I want to check what's on at the cinema,' she explained. 'Do you go to the cinema, Mr Patel?'

'Not often,' he said, smiling. 'We work long hours in my shop, Sundays also. I don't have the time.'

'Of course not,' Naomi said. 'And while I'm here I'll have a bottle of gin and some tonics. And a lemon.'

'We also have limes,' Mr Patel said. 'I understand they are very refreshing with gin and tonic.'

Tom rang the doorbell promptly at half-past six. Naomi felt a rush of pleasure as she opened the door to him.

'I think we have time for a drink,' she said. 'Most of the films don't start until after seven o'clock.'

'Fine!' Tom said. 'So what did you do while I was in Oxford?' He followed her into the kitchen and stood behind her as she started to pour the drinks.

'I visited Isobel,' Naomi said. 'You should meet Isobel – if you can stand babies, that is!'

'I don't know anything about babies,' he said. 'But I'd like to meet your other daughter and I'll risk the baby.'

Do I want him to meet Isobel? Naomi asked herself. He hadn't been a great success with the other two. Wouldn't I rather just keep him to myself?

He moved closer behind her, stretched to take the gin bottle from her, and put it down on the worktop. Then with his hands on her shoulders he swivelled her around to face him, and kissed her.

'I missed you,' he said.

'I missed you too,' Naomi acknowledged.

They carried their drinks into the sitting room and sat in facing chairs.

'So where are we going?' Tom asked.

Naomi handed him the newspaper.

'Choose!'

In fact, she thought, she would sooner stay here with him than go to any film but he was perusing the paper with interest.

'Quite a choice!' he said.

They finished their drinks – Tom refused a second one – and left in time to walk to the cinema. It was a strange little place, hidden away in a maze of narrow side streets. Apparently it had its supporters; there was a queue on the pavement although the doors had not opened. They didn't have to wait long. A small, plump woman came and opened the doors then moved back to take her place in the box office. There was an air of competence about her which said she might well also be in charge of running the film. Once past her Tom and Naomi began to climb the curving stairs which seemed to go onward and upward forever.

'I reckon we're halfway to heaven,' Tom said as they reached the top. 'Do you suffer from vertigo?'

'Fortunately, no!'

'I hope you'll find the film worth it,' he said as they found seats.

It was, though it turned out not to matter to Naomi. Two minutes into the showing Tom took her hand firmly in his and, from time to time, stroked the inside of her wrist with firm gentle movements. From then on her thoughts were too tumultuous to concentrate on what was happening on the screen. For weeks afterwards, when it turned out to be a great success about which everyone wished to give their views, she found she could remember little of it.

When it was over they emerged into a frosty night, so unexpectedly cold that Naomi pulled her coat around her and buttoned it to the neck.

'Let's go and find something to eat,' Tom said, taking her arm. 'I'm hungry!'

They discovered a smallish Italian restaurant not five minutes away from the cinema. It was crowded, and for ten minutes they stood in line inside until a couple left a table in a far corner. The moment they were seated a waitress brought the menu. It was short, handwritten in execrable English, and moderately priced.

'What would you like?' Tom asked. 'There isn't the widest choice in the world.'

She would have eaten dry bread and drunk tap water in order to be with him, she thought.

'I'd like rigatoni,' she said. 'And a green salad.'

'Probably a good choice,' Tom said.

She watched him as he studied the menu further. He looked, suddenly, so young. He was not, after all, that much older than Hugh, and that was, she told herself, something she must bear in mind. But not at this moment. Not for tonight. Tonight she would pretend . . . what would she pretend? That she was younger or he was older or that none of it mattered?

Tom raised his head.

'I'll have the canneloni,' he said.

He ordered a bottle of Barolo. 'Right away,' he told the waitress. 'We'll have a drink while we're waiting.'

While he sipped his wine he studied Naomi over the rim of his glass.

'I've never met anyone quite like you,' he said. 'I thought English women were . . . well I don't quite know what I thought they were, but nothing like you.'

'And I thought Americans were loud and brash and took over wherever they happened to be,' Naomi said. 'Not that I ever met an American man,' she added. 'Did you . . . have you known many English women?' The question was tentative.

'Not many. In the university of course. Mostly scientists. Scientists, male or female, are a race apart. They speak a different language which only another scientist can understand.'

'You're a scientist,' she reminded him.

'I'm different,' he said, smiling at her. His face lit up when he smiled, every part of it infected by joy.

'How different?'

'I'm bilingual. I can speak English and Sciencespeak!'

The meal came, appetizing smells arising from the red-hot plates. The waitress flourished the pepper mill and the Parmesan cheese like a ritual blessing over the food, then left them in peace. For a while they ate in near silence. Tom was the first to utter, through a mouthful of cannelloni.

'I meant what I said the other day.'

'Which bit?' Naomi asked. 'What did you say?'

'The bit where I said I'd like you to come to New York.'

Naomi's stomach did a double somersault.

'I've never been to New York,' she said inanely.

'I know. That's one reason why you should.'

'What are the other reasons?' she asked.

'Because I'm asking you. Because I want you to. You will, won't you?'

Every reason for refusing leapt into her mind, fighting with the terrible longing to say, 'Yes! Yes please!'

'I'm not sure.' She was suitably hesitant, evasive even.

'Why not?' Tom persisted.

'Lots of reasons,' she said. 'I can't go into them now.'

'So what are you going to do?' he asked. 'Give me a new reason each day? If you do I'll demolish them one by one. I'll wear you down!'

She wanted to be worn down, totally persuaded. How could she tell him why she couldn't persuade herself, couldn't allow herself to say 'yes'?

'There's my mother,' she said, clutching at a straw.

'You mean your mother won't be properly looked after if you're away?'

'I suppose she will. But she'll miss me.'

'I'll miss you if you don't come. I shan't be here in Bath all that much longer. I don't want to lose touch.'

For a moment she faced the thought that he would go away and that she would never see him again.

'I wouldn't want to lose touch, either,' she said.

But to be sensible, wasn't it best that she should, best for both of them?

'When do you expect to go back to New York?' she asked.

'Right now it looks like late May,' Tom said. 'You could come along and join me mid-June. A great time of the year in New York. Not too hot, not too humid. And my roof garden is at its best.'

'You have a roof garden. I didn't know!'

'There's quite a bit you might not know. I want to show you everything, and that's one good reason for coming.'

Naomi felt herself weakening.

'How long . . . ?'

'I'd like you to come for a month,' Tom said. 'I'd put up with as little as a week, but I wouldn't recommend it.'

'A month's too long . . . oh, I don't mean I wouldn't enjoy it,'

Naomi said. 'But I have my job to think about. I don't think Amersham's would let me take a month.'

Tom refilled both their glasses.

'Is this another of your barriers I have to break down?' he asked. 'If so I reckon *you* should do it. Just ask them. You might be agreeably surprised, you might not. It would be for you to decide.'

Naomi put down her glass and looked at him. There had been an edge to his voice and now there was a hardness in his eyes. Didn't he know – but how could he – that Amersham's counted for nothing at the side of him? But how could she tell him that she was in danger of falling in love with him, and that it just wouldn't do? It was unsuitable, there was so much in the way, and apart from all that, she reminded herself, she hardly knew him.

'I'm only asking you to visit me in New York,' Tom said reasonably. 'I'm not asking you to go to the ends of the earth with me.'

Which I would do, Naomi thought, though I can't tell you that. But he was right, it was simply an invitation to a holiday in New York. If she let it mean more than that, then it would be her own fault.

'So what's it to be? What are you going to do?' Tom persisted.

'I'm coming!' she said. 'I'm coming to see your roof garden.'

SIXTEEN

They ate slowly, then lingered over their coffee, wanting to draw out the evening though neither of them saying so. It did not need to be said. The queue for tables had long ago vanished and the restaurant was gradually emptying. Naomi was conscious that their waitress was standing with arms folded, waiting for them to finish.

'Would you like more coffee?' Tom asked.

'I think not,' Naomi said. 'I reckon they're waiting to close.'

'You're right!' Tom said.

He signalled to the waitress and she came with alacrity to give him his bill. Tom stood up and helped Naomi with her coat.

'Where do we go from here?' he asked, taking her arm as they left the restaurant.

It was a simple question, and yet it was not, for they both knew it was a question on two levels. Which route do we take to the flat? Do we turn our footsteps to the right or to the left? Which bridge shall we cross? That was easy, because it was immaterial. Either way they would arrive. But 'Where do we go from here?' meant much, much more. How do we go towards the future? Do we go together? Indeed, was there a future for them together or simply a most agreeable present? All these thoughts jostled in Naomi's head in the short time it took Tom to grasp her arm and guide her across the road.

She didn't know the answers. With one half of her, the immediate urgent half, she knew what she wanted. She wanted Tom Lever. But the other half was afraid to reach out, even if he was hers for the taking, and of that she was not sure. It was too soon, too important. She felt ignorant. Twenty-five years of marriage had not prepared her one little bit to deal with this.

They walked arm in arm in companionable silence through streets which, though not deserted, had lost their daytime bustle, past shops whose bright window displays were now no more than dimly lit by reflected light from street lamps. A gang of short-haired, leather-clad youths emerged from a side-turning and made off, singing, in the opposite direction. A solitary cat picked its way purposefully along the opposite pavement, knowing exactly where it was going. An occasional car zoomed by. Otherwise the world, as much of it as was inhabited, seemed to consist entirely of couples, arm in arm, hand in hand, a pair in front of them stopping suddenly to engage in a passionate embrace in the middle of the pavement so that it was necessary to skirt around them, spilling into the road to get by. It was another world from that which Naomi walked through every Tuesday and Thursday morning on her way to Amersham's.

They crossed the road to the river and stopped, as Naomi did whenever she was on her own, to lean on the wall and watch the mesmeric flow of the water, ink-dark now. Nothing was said between them as they contemplated the river. It was not the time for trivialities, that was past, but the time to say more, Naomi thought, was not yet.

Presently, as if there was a signal between them, they made a movement to leave the spot, but before they could make their first step away from the wall Tom's arms were around Naomi and he was holding her close, so close, so hard that when he kissed her she was entirely, gloriously, breathless.

When he eventually let her go he held her at arm's length and raised his hand to touch her face.

'I love you, Naomi Fletcher!' he said in a voice which was not quite steady.

'And I love you, Tom Lever!'

She had said it, and she couldn't believe she'd said it, except that it was exactly what she had wanted to say and nothing had ever been so totally true. The night felt as bright as the day, as if there were a thousand stars, though in fact there were none, and the moon had gone behind a cloud.

He kissed her again, though lightly, then he put his arm around her and they walked quickly, without stopping, over Pulteney Bridge and to her flat. He took her key from her and turned it in the lock. What happens now? Naomi asked herself, though there was no need to ask. Only one thing could happen.

They went in quietly. On the other side of the door he took her hand and pulled her, half dragging her in his urgency, through the sitting room and into her bedroom.

It was the first grey light of morning creeping around the edge of the curtains which roused Naomi. Usually she was slow to waken, resisting the new day, wanting always to fall back again into sleep and dreams. It was not so today. This morning she was asleep one second and wide awake the next and, even before she opened her eyes, conscious of Tom's presence, surprised and delighted by the warmth and weight of his body against hers.

She lay as still as a mouse, not wanting to waken him because when he did waken that would be the next step towards him leaving her. She didn't want him to leave her, ever, but it was inevitable that he would and so she would postpone it for as long as she could.

She was not entirely comfortable. He must, she thought, have been lying on her arm, since it was numb from the elbow down, and she had to move it from under him since now she had the exquisite torture of pins and needles shooting all the way to her fingertips. Stealthily, a minute fraction at a time, she extricated her arm, then raised herself up a little so that she could look down on him as he slept. He lay with his head back, his neck arched.

He was, she decided, quite beautiful. That was the correct word, though it was a totally masculine beauty; a strong, straight nose, thick dark eyebrows. His skin, even though it was only early spring was already lightly tanned, and smooth and taut over his high cheekbones. His cheeks and chin were blue shadowed where he needed a shave. His hair was tousled. Yes, he was beautiful – and in his sleep he looked even younger than his years.

What am I doing? she thought. What *am* I doing? Suddenly she was sure that every one of her forty-six years must show on her face and on her body. It had not mattered last night. They had undressed speedily and she had quickly turned out the light – perhaps without recognizing it as some form of self-defence. Their lovemaking had been urgent and passionate and nothing else had counted, age least of all. If she had been eighteen and he sixty, or the other way round, it would have been immaterial. All they had known was their hunger for each other, and that had been wonderfully and truly satisfied. In the dark, she thought, all cats are black and everyone is the same age.

But it was no longer dark. He would waken any minute and he would see her as she was. She had no need to look in a mirror to know that there would be early morning shadows under her eyes and that her lovely navy mascara would be smudged all over the place, making her first cousin to a panda. It shouldn't matter, but it did.

As for her body, which he would see in the bright light of day, well it was shapely enough and she was slender, but there was no denying the downward pull of gravity. And then there were her disfiguring stretch marks from the births of her children. How could a man so young, so whole, bear to look at a woman with stretch marks?

She was considering whether she would slip quietly out of bed, clean up her face and put on a becoming nightdress when Tom opened his eyes.

'Hello, beautiful!' he said sleepily. 'What are you doing, sitting up there?'

'Looking at you,' Naomi confessed.

'Then you can come here and look closer,' he said, opening his arms to her.

She went into them.

'As long as you don't look more closely at me!'

'But that's exactly what I want to do,' Tom said. 'I want to look at every bit of you. Slowly, I want to savour you.'

He pushed her down gently onto her back and drew down the duvet so that she was naked from head to foot. Then he knelt beside her, regarding her, gently tracing the curves and hollows of her body with his fingers. She closed her eyes and turned her head aside, not wishing to see his face.

'You are beautiful!' he said. 'You are wholly beautiful. Don't you know that?'

'Stretch marks and all?' She couldn't refrain from saying it.

He ran his finger lightly along them.

'Why do you say that?' he asked. 'They're part of you, part of your life. Badges of honour, in fact.'

She opened her eyes and looked into his.

'I say it because I want to be perfect. I want to be new and perfect for you – but I can't ever be.'

He shook his head.

'I couldn't cope with perfection, my love. I want you to have at least a few flaws, to balance mine.'

'I don't believe you have any!'

'And that's not true,' Tom said. 'As you'll find out. The more you get to know me the more you'll discover. Are you willing to risk it?'

'There are worse risks than discovering your flaws,' Naomi said. 'That's not what bothers me.'

'Then what does?' Tom asked. 'Naomi, we've got to be honest with each other. I know there's something, but you've got to say it yourself, come right out with it for once and all.'

And I know what it is, he thought, in the silence which followed. But she has to say it. If she didn't, how could they talk about it?

Naomi took a deep breath.

'Very well,' she said in the end. 'I will. It's the fact . . . well you must know what it is . . . it's the fact that you're thirty-three and I'm forty-six. I'm middle-aged, I'm divorced. I have three grown-up children. You're young, you're free, everything's in front of you. It won't work.'

'You've forgotten something,' he said, smiling at her.

'What?'

'You're also a grandmother!'

200

He drew up the duvet to cover them both – the room was chilly – then he held her close in his arms.

'I told you I loved you,' he said. 'I meant it. I hope you meant it when you said it to me?'

'Oh, I did! I did!' Naomi cried.

'I want you for good,' Tom said. 'And as far as I'm concerned nothing stands between us. Nothing at all unless you let it!'

'Not now I don't,' Naomi said. 'Not at this minute. But it will. While you're still a young man, while you're in your early forties, I'll be pushing sixty.'

'I can't wait for it!' Tom said. 'Except that I want to have all the years up to then with you.'

'I couldn't ever give you children.'

'I don't want children. Oh, I like them, but I don't want my own. I want you to myself.'

Naomi shook her head.

'I don't know that I have the courage. If it didn't work, I couldn't bear to see you change towards me. And I would know, however much you tried to hide it.'

'So you're punishing me because you don't have the courage?' She was surprised by the hardness in his voice.

'You're making – *your* decisions – on some idea that isn't true. What about me? What about trusting how *I* feel? Don't I have any say in the matter? I don't give a shit how old you are. I want you, not your birth certificate.'

She could think of nothing to say.

'I'm going to make love to you,' he said. 'Right now. And in the daylight, not in the dark. Are you going to say no to that?'

She shook her head.

'No! Oh, no!'

When Tom left, an hour or two later, she didn't know the time, it had no meaning for her, she stood in the window, watching him as he walked away down the street. He walked with a swing, with a spring in his step as if the world belonged to him, which was exactly how she felt herself. When he reached the corner he turned and waved before moving out of sight.

Perhaps it was the Sunday morning sound of church bells which brought the words into her mind. She had not read them

201

since she was at school, when she and Mavis Shelley had occupied the twenty minutes of the boring sermon by looking up
the naughty bits in the Bible. Nor had she heard them later in the
church she and Edward had attended with the children. The
Song of Solomon was far too erotic for that. Nevertheless she
recalled them now, as if they were the very words in the world
which were written for her.

' "My Beloved is mine, and I am his." '

She said the words out loud, then turned away and went to the
kitchen. To her surprise – it had been a long time ago – she
remembered the next bit, or a later bit, she wasn't sure of the
sequence:

' "I found him whom my soul loveth:

I held him and would not let him go." '

She and Mavis Shelley had found the whole thing hilarious.
For several weeks of that term they'd been regularly in fits of
laughter. 'Thy two breasts are like two young roes that are twins,'
they would whisper one to the other. Or, if there were others
around, 'Chapter seven, verse three,' would be enough to set
them off.

How little we knew, Naomi thought. How little I knew until
now! But Solomon had known what he was talking about.

She felt refreshed and invigorated. She felt young and new,
and it was not just their lovemaking, though that had been
indescribably wonderful, which had caused her to feel like this, it
was much more that she felt secure in their love for each other.
She was no longer afraid. There would be mountains to climb
she was sure of that, but climb them she would.

She wanted to rush out and thank someone, she wanted to
share her joy. She wanted to take up the invitation of the bells,
still ringing away, and rush into the church and fall on her knees.
But no, she thought. I can hardly thank God for committing
what his Church would call fornication! Or adultery?

Instead, she decided, she would walk around to Mr Patel's and
buy a pint of milk and a Sunday paper.

'It is a beautiful day,' Mr Patel observed.

'Quite wonderful!' Naomi agreed.

'Did you enjoy the movie?'

'Oh yes! It was very good.' She was sure it was, but what had it been about? No matter.

'And shall you be doing something special on this pleasant day?' Mr Patel enquired.

'Not really,' Naomi said. 'I shall go to see my mother this afternoon. She's in a rest home in Bath. She likes to see me.'

'Ah yes! I too have an elderly mother. She lives here with me and my family,' Mr Patel said.

I've never seen her, Naomi thought. Perhaps she never leaves the back room? She might even be bedridden. But at least she was with her family and that was possibly better – at least for her – than being in a home, visited once a week for an hour. All the same, she decided, leaving the shop, this is not a day on which I'm going to feel guilty. It was a special day, in fact everything looked different, smelled different. The sky was higher and bluer, trees were in bud, birds sang louder and even the air tasted cleaner on her tongue. Though from now on, she thought, *every* day would be special. How could it be otherwise?

She made herself coffee and sat down with the newspaper, but it was hopeless. How could she express her own happiness while reading all these dire things? Even her horoscope was gloomy. 'Caution is needed' it said. 'Take great care.' She would ignore it, of course, one only took notice of the good ones, and besides, she was no longer in the mood for caution. Since earlier this morning she had left that behind.

She threw the newspaper aside and went to the piano. What better way to express all the joy that was in her? She played bright, happy pieces; dances, marches, love songs, music written for celebrations. In the middle of a Schubert march the telephone rang and she rushed to answer it.

'Hi!' Tom said. 'How goes it? How are you doing?'

'It goes wonderfully,' Naomi said. 'I was playing the piano.'

'Great!' he said. 'Would you like to go for a walk?'

'I would,' Naomi said. 'Except that I have to visit my mother this afternoon. She expects me.'

'Then you have to go,' he agreed. 'Could I go with you? I've got to meet her some time.'

'I know,' Naomi said. 'But not today. I need to prepare her.'

'You make me sound fearsome,' Tom said.

'No, not a bit! It's just that a new person she hadn't even heard of would confuse her.' But was there anything which wouldn't confuse her? Naomi thought. All the same, she would not take Tom to River View today. Just for today she would keep him to herself.

'Then promise you'll tell her about me,' he said.

'I promise!'

'And could I see you afterwards?' Tom asked. 'Tell me what time you'll be through and I'll meet you at the gate. We could go for a walk. Or whatever you like.'

'Very well,' Naomi agree. 'I'll leave at four o'clock.'

'*A bientôt!*' Tom said. 'I love you!'

She would go early to River View, Naomi decided. It was the least she could do if she was to rush away promptly at four. Also she would take her mother something nice to eat, a sandwich, perhaps. Her mother enjoyed a little snack last thing at night with her Horlicks. It helped her get through the night, she said, though eating so late was not encouraged by the staff and no food was served after seven p.m. Nevertheless, Naomi had discovered, they turned a blind eye to whatever sustenance friends and relatives smuggled in.

She opened a small tin of ox tongue. Her mother would enjoy that, especially with a touch of mustard. She had discovered a new mustard in a small delicatessen on her way to and from Amersham's; coarse-grained, with rosemary and mint. She cut the bread thinly, spread it liberally with butter – her mother abhorred all margarines and spreads – put in two layers of tongue and cut the sandwich into quarters. Physically, last thing at night, it would probably do her mother no good at all, but it would lift her spirits. Naomi, at this moment, desired to lift the spirits of the whole world to the heights of her own.

Doris was having a good day too. Unlike her daughter, she had enjoyed her Sunday paper. She took the *Express* because, she said, having had it for years she knew her way about it. She knew just where to turn to find the latest scandals about vicars and Sunday-school teachers. The Church of England was the worst numerically, she told anyone who would listen, but the Catholic ones made a bigger splash. She also enjoyed the general knowledge crossword. With the aid of her outsize magnifying glass she perused every page except for sports and finance. Even the small ads for strange appliances were of interest, and while she was reading thus she never wandered off into one of her other worlds.

Naomi arrived promptly at half-past two.

'You're early!' Doris complained. 'You know I like to have my little nap after lunch.'

'I'm sorry. You weren't asleep, though, were you?' Naomi pointed out.

'No. But I might have been. And if I had been you'd have wakened me. I can't do with being wakened from my sleep. It leaves me feeling funny for the rest of the day.'

'I came early so as to have more time with you,' Naomi explained. 'I have to leave at four o'clock.'

'You shouldn't have come at all if it was a nuisance to you,' Doris grumbled.

Naomi held back a sigh, managed a smile. Her mother was clear in the head at the moment, and when she was clear in the head she was, unlike her younger self, at her most awkward. Hugh had been right. His grandmother was happier when she was in fantasy land.

'It wasn't one little bit of a nuisance,' Naomi reassured her mother. 'How are you? How've you been?'

'I'm the same as always,' Doris said. 'As to how I've been, that's the same as always. Nothing's ever different. I'm still constipated. They give me all sorts of things – when I remind them – but nothing works.'

'I'll have a word with Sister,' Naomi promised.

'Why are you rushing off at four o'clock?' Doris asked. 'Something more interesting, I suppose?'

Infinitely, Naomi thought.

'I'm meeting a friend,' she said. 'He'll be here at four.'

'He?'

'Yes.'

'So, come on! Who is he? Why don't I know him? I suppose you're ashamed of me?'

'Oh Mother! How silly! Of course I'm not. I haven't known him long, there hasn't been the opportunity for you to meet him. Or the need. He's just a friend.'

'Pull the other one!' Doris said sharply. 'I don't believe you!'

'Mother, how can you say that?' Naomi protested.

'Because you look different, that's why. You can't kid me. I might be old but I'm not daft! But you can't marry him, you know. You're married to that solicitor chap.'

It was the first sign that she was not totally in the present and to Naomi it came as something of a relief. She was learning that she could deal more easily with her mother when she was non compos mentis. There were no arguments then. She could just go along with what was said.

'I'm not married to Edward any longer, Mother,' she said. 'We were divorced. Don't you remember?'

'You can't go marrying every new man you meet,' Doris said. 'Don't think you can!'

'I'm not thinking of marrying,' Naomi said. It was quite true. Nothing whatever had been said between herself and Tom on the subject of marriage. Until her mother had put it into her mind she had not thought of it, and if she had it would have seemed an unimportant detail.

Quite suddenly Doris closed her eyes and seconds later gave a gentle snore. She was fast asleep. Naomi looked at her watch. Ten past three, almost an hour before Tom would be here. But I must stay, she thought. She couldn't just walk out on her, even if she knew where to find Tom now, which she didn't. She just devoutly hoped that her mother would stay asleep for a while.

Quietly, she picked up the *Sunday Express* and began to read.

At five minutes to four Doris opened her eyes.

'You've had a nice sleep, Mother,' Naomi said.

'I was not asleep,' Doris said. 'I was simply resting my eyes.'

'Yes, well – anyway I have to go. I'll be here next Sunday, if not before. Bye-bye, love!'

It was raining steadily when she left the house. Tom was waiting at the gate. He greeted her with a kiss.

'Not the weather for a walk,' he said. 'What would you like to do? Another movie? A museum? Tea at the Francis?'

'Why don't we go back to the flat?' she asked. It was what she wanted, and she was sure he did too.

He took her arm and they set off.

SEVENTEEN

At five minutes to ten on Monday morning the phone rang. Naomi, in the middle of washing her underwear, dried her hands and went to answer it.

'Ma! It's me! Hugh. I've got good news. The best possible.'

'Wonderful! What is it, darling? Do tell me.'

'I'm trying to,' Hugh said. 'The thing is, I've got the job! An offer in the post this morning. Which . . .' he slowed down his voice, 'which I *think* I shall accept.'

'*Think* you'll accept, dear? Why? Is there a catch in it?'

'Of course not, Ma! But one doesn't want to seem too eager. It might give the wrong impression. Start as one means to go on.'

He had, in fact, already written his acceptance, sealed and stamped the envelope, and would walk to the post box with it the minute he was off the phone.

'So when would you start?' Naomi asked.

'Early April. You see what this means, Ma?'

'Why yes! It means you've got the job you wanted, and in the face of quite strong competition. I'm really pleased for you. And proud!'

'Thank you. But I mean do you see what it means for you? It means I'll be living in London. Bath's no distance at all. I'll be able to pop down frequently. Keep an eye on you, old girl!'

'Ah! Yes!'

How could she tell him in the face of his enthusiasm – and was that, or was it not, kindly meant? She couldn't be sure – that she did not wish an eye kept on her. Nor was she sure that she wished him to pop down frequently. Unannounced, bringing his dirty washing. And what a rotten mother she was to think in this way, especially about Hugh.

'Are you still there, Ma?' Hugh asked.

'Yes, dear! And many, many congratulations, darling! I'm so pleased for you!'

'Thank you, Ma. I'll have to ring off now. So much to do, so many people to see!'

'Shall you be phoning Isso and Cecily? They'll be delighted I'm sure.'

'Will you do that for me?' Hugh asked. 'I'm pushed for time.' And it was cheaper for his mother to ring them from Bath, especially considering how long-winded Cecily always was on the telephone.

Naomi returned to the laundering of her smalls. Naturally she was pleased for Hugh. She was delighted. She was also ever so faintly irritated. It was a pity that Bath was quite so handy from London, especially since Hugh would be earning more and would presumably be able to afford the fare.

What she wanted, for the first time ever and for the foreseeable future, was to have her life to herself. She wished to be left free so that she was available, except for Amersham's, whenever Tom wanted her to be. Which would not be today, she reminded herself, since he had told her when he'd left at a very late hour last night, that he had a long busy day ahead in the university.

'But I'll give you a call,' he'd promised.

'Not between about four and five,' she'd said. 'I have Lucy Morton then.'

She enjoyed the weekly lesson with Lucy. She was a bright child, with a natural gift for making music. If they both continued to work at it the little girl might eventually go far.

Naomi went out in the garden and pegged out her washing. As she did so Emily Simpson came out of her house, carrying the baby in her arms.

'Hello!' Emily called out. 'Isn't it a lovely day! I'm going to let Natasha have her sleep outside. She's well wrapped up.'

'It is a lovely day,' Naomi agreed. There was real warmth in the sun and no longer any hint of the wind which had bedevilled them over the last week.

'What are you going to do with yourself today?' Emily asked.

'I haven't decided,' Naomi said.

The day stretched before her, at least until four o'clock, like a blank page on which she could write what she wished. What did she want to do with it? Unbidden, lines from a poet whose name she couldn't recall came into her head.

> 'Christ, that my love were in my arms,
> And I in my bed again.'

Yes, that was what she would like. As it was, no matter what she did or didn't do she would let the memory of the previous evening carry her through the day.

'I wondered if you might be going into the town?' Emily said.

'I might. I don't know. Is there something you want?'

'Actually, yes. I think I might run out of nappies. Boots is the place. Or . . .' her face lit up as a bright idea struck her '. . . I could actually go myself if you'd keep an eye on the baby! I could wheel her round to your garden. She's really no trouble. She'll sleep most of the morning.'

'Well . . .' Naomi began.

'You did say you hadn't any plans, didn't you?' Emily said.

Did I? Naomi wondered. Had she been quite so rash?

'I wouldn't be long,' Emily said.

'Well, all right,' Naomi conceded.

At least it would mean that if Tom were to find a minute to telephone, she'd be there to answer. And how much more like a lovesick schoolgirl could you get than that, she chided herself.

'Thanks a million!' Emily said quickly. 'I'll wheel her around right away.'

She lost no time. Ten minutes later she wheeled the baby in its pram through Naomi's flat and out into the garden.

'I think here, against the wall,' she decided. 'She'll be sheltered if a breeze springs up, though it doesn't seem likely, does it?'

Naomi peered under the pram hood.

'She's fast asleep,' she said, stopping herself in the nick of time from adding 'bless her!'

'She should sleep most of the morning.' Emily spoke with a confidence which Naomi hoped was not a triumph of hope over experience. 'I've left three fresh nappies just in case she wakens and needs changing.'

Three times? Naomi thought. Is there something I don't know about?

'It's ever so good of you,' Emily said. 'I'm truly grateful. What bliss, shopping on my own! Is there anything you'd like me to bring you?'

'I don't think so,' Naomi said. She hated other people doing her shopping.

'Right then! I'll be off.' Emily was out of the house in a flash.

Naomi went back into the garden. She would do a few jobs there, be on hand in case the baby needed attention. But what if the phone rang? Would she hear it, or would she get to it before it stopped ringing?

She retraced her steps, moved the telephone as close to the window as the length of the cord would allow, opened the window, propped open the door to the garden and went back outside. Then she found her trowel and a small fork and began to weed.

She had weeded a square foot of the border when the baby gave a few tentative whimpers, not to announce that she was now fully awake but that she could be quite quickly if she was not given due attention. Naomi put down her tools and gently jiggled the pram. The baby opened her eyes, gave Naomi a steady stare, closed them again and went back to sleep. Naomi felt deeply and truly gratified.

It was not to last. Five minutes later the baby opened her eyes again as if to check who was on duty and found that no-one was. She opened her mouth to its fullest extent, screwed up her eyes to concentrate further, and gave forth a yell worthy of a female sergeant-major drilling the troops. Naomi rose from her knees and hastened to obey.

'Pick me up!' the baby yelled. Though not in so many words, the command was clear.

Naomi jiggled the pram again, gently at first, then more frantically, but the baby was not in the least pacified. It was not the treatment she had requested.

'Very well,' Naomi conceded. 'I'll pick you up, honey, but I must wash the soil off my hands first.'

The baby screamed on a high, steady note during Naomi's absence. By the time she returned its puckered face was a deep shade of puce and its clenched fists beat the air.

'All right! All right!' Naomi said, lifting her out of the pram. The crying ceased as abruptly as if a tap in full flow had been turned off. 'There! That's better, isn't it?' The baby began to whimper again.

'Ah! I see the problem! Or rather I smell it. You are damp, if not worse!' There was none of the sweet, fragrant baby aroma of good soap and talcum powder. 'Very well' Naomi said. 'I shall change you. Hopefully for the first and last time before your mother returns!'

She took the baby inside, laid her on a clean bath towel on the sofa, and set to work. It was a doddle. To her surprise she found she had lost none of her skill, last employed eighteen years ago on Cecily. And thank heaven, now as then, for disposables. She had heard her mother's horror stories of terry-towelling nappies and was glad she had not been born too soon to suffer with her own children.

'And now that you're sweet and clean,' she said 'I shall put you back in your pram and you'll have a nice little sleep until Mummy returns, which we both hope won't be long!'

Nor, she realized, hearing herself, had she lost the habit of talking to infants as if they understood every world.

If this one did, she did not agree. As Naomi laid her with great gentleness in the pram she started to scream again. Naomi sighed deeply and shook her head. 'I can't have you doing this when your mother walks in!' Though that might not be a bad idea, she thought, looking to the future. Nevertheless, she picked up the baby again, lay her over her shoulder which had almost always worked with her own children, and returned to the house. It did work – except when she stopped to sit down. Here was a child who liked, and demanded, continual movement. Naomi therefore obligingly paced the floor and was so doing when Emily returned half an hour later.

'Come to Mummy then!' Emily cooed. The baby gave several residual sobs, then little gulps of satisfaction as her own true mother took over.

'Has she been good?' Emily enquired of Naomi.

'Perfectly!' Naomi lied.

Lucy Morton, on arrival, was highly excited. Her mother dropped her at the gate and watched while she ran up the path. Naomi, who had seen their arrival, opened the door before Lucy had her finger on the bell push.

'You look pleased with yourself!' Naomi said. 'It's not your birthday or anything, is it?'

'My birthday's in July,' Lucy said. 'I'm to have a very special birthday present only it can't be a surprise because Mummy has had to make arrangements.'

'And is that why you're looking so pleased?' Naomi enquired.

'Yes. And the special thing is that we're going to Disney World! I mean for our holidays in the summer! In Florida.'

'Why, that's wonderful!' Naomi said. 'No wonder you look so happy!' Though in fact, she thought, Lucy was for the most part a happy little girl, although today she had an extra special shine about her, as if she was lit up from inside.

'Well, that's all quite wonderful,' Naomi said. 'I'm so pleased! And now to the piano. Did you do all your practising?'

'Yes,' Lucy said. 'And I've brought my notebook and Mummy's signed it.'

The lesson went well, as it always did. Perhaps I should try to get more pupils, Naomi told herself. She did so enjoy it. But no, not now. While Tom was here she wanted to spend every possible minute with him. What she would do when he finally returned to New York she could hardly bear to contemplate. But at least having decided to visit him there she would have the memory of him in his own setting to bring back with her.

'Because it's such a happy day for you,' she said to Lucy when

213

the lesson was over, 'I'm going to play you a happy tune. A dance, I think. In fact you *can* dance to it if you like.'

She played a polka. Lucy immediately picked up the rhythm and danced to it, adroitly avoiding the furniture as she moved around. Rhythm ran through her whole body, as natural to her as breathing. How would she choose in the end, Naomi wondered, from so many different ways of expressing it?

At five minutes to five Mrs Morton's car drew up at the gate.

'Off you go!' Naomi said to Lucy. 'See you next Monday.'

No sooner had the car pulled away, Lucy waving to the last second from the passenger seat, than the telephone rang. Since she had forgotten to move it back from the window-sill Naomi had, for a second or two, to look for it.

'Hi there!' Tom said. 'What have you been doing all day?'

'Minding next-door's baby,' Naomi said. 'Giving Lucy her piano lesson. She was in great form today. She's been promised a trip to Disney World.' And I've been thinking about you, she wanted to say.

'We're invited to a dinner party,' Tom announced. 'Next Friday.'

'Both of us?'

'Sure! Melanie Clarke. She said to bring you.'

'How did she know about me?'

'It could be that I told her!' She could tell by his voice that he was smiling.

Dr Clarke was a colleague, a member of the group with whom Tom was working. He had spoken of her more than once without ever actually saying what she was like, though clearly he found her compatible. She was married to a research chemist working in Bristol.

'She sounds frightfully clever,' Naomi said.

'You mean because she's asked you to dinner?'

'Idiot! But she does sound clever.'

'She is,' Tom said. 'So you'll come?'

'If you want me to.'

Tom's sigh came down the telephone like a gentle wind.

'Of course I do! I'd rather just be with you, you know that, but we have to step into the world sometimes. Especially you do.'

Step into his world he meant – which so far she had not done at all, not even one tentative toe. University life was like a foreign country to her, inhabited by a different race, even though she had been through it all those years ago. She had her degree but what had she done with it? University equips you for life, they'd said, though she'd not found that it had particularly equipped her for life with Edward and three children.

'How about I meet you from Amersham's when you finish work tomorrow?' Tom asked.

'That would be lovely. Come into the shop. I won't make you buy anything.'

'I have to go now. I love you,' he said.

'I love you too,' Naomi replied.

She went into the kitchen and put on the kettle. What should she wear on Friday? Would it be jeans and sweaters, or something formal? And if the latter, how formal? And what did she have which would fill *that* bill? She had, in what she now realized was a ridiculous pet, given most of her collection of little black dresses to Oxfam. And could she afford to spend on something new, and did she even want to? Oh well, she would ask Tom. But one thing was sure, she must have her hair done, though she was spending far too much money with Henri these days.

She poured boiling water into a mug, waved a tea-bag through it, then sat down at the table. Almost immediately the telephone rang.

'Hello, Ma!' Cecily said brightly. 'I thought I'd come down Friday evening, stay overnight, then move on to see Daddy on Saturday.'

'Oh!' Naomi said. 'Friday evening? I'm sorry, sweetheart, I won't be here. I'm out to dinner. But I'll leave a key somewhere – perhaps next door – and you can let yourself in. There'll be food in the fridge.'

'There's no point in that if you're not going to be there,' Cecily said testily. 'Where are you going?'

'I'm not entirely sure,' Naomi admitted. 'University people.'

So it must be the American. The real reason Cecily had proposed herself was that Hugh had said, 'For goodness' sake keep an eye on Ma!' For herself she was torn between her belief

215

that all women must be free to make their choices and the fact that Naomi was not really all women. She was her mother. And now her mother was messing up her generous gesture by going out to dinner.

'Perhaps you could stay with Isso or go to Daddy first,' Naomi suggested. Not all that long ago she had been furious at the thought of any of her children spending time with Edward. Now it seemed less important. 'Then you could come to me on Saturday evening, or even Sunday. We could visit Grandma on Sunday.'

'Thank you very much! I'll let you know!' Cecily's tone was heavily sarcastic. So much for trying to help one's parent.

On Tuesday Tom came into Amersham's fifteen minutes before closing time. He smiled at Naomi, who was serving a short queue of customers, wandered around the shelves and bought a paperback.

'A new Sarah Paretsky,' he said presenting it to Naomi for payment. 'I don't like her usual main character very much but she's a good writer.'

'She's very popular,' Naomi said. 'Like most of the American crime writers, though I prefer Patricia Cornwell.'

'How soon will you be free?' Tom asked.

'Five minutes.'

'Then I'll wait outside.'

'Where would you like to go?' He asked when she joined him. 'It's early for a meal but we could have a drink somewhere and eat afterwards.'

'I'd like that,' Naomi said.

They found a small pub, dark and dingy inside, the ceiling yellowed with years of tobacco smoke, though now only two people were smoking. Tom went to the bar and collected drinks.

'There you go!' he said. 'A G and T. And the same for me.' He had not learned to appreciate British beer, it was seldom cold enough for his taste.

'Tell me about Friday,' Naomi said. 'For a start, are you sure I'm invited?'

Tom shook his head in exasperation.

'What a damned silly question. What do you expect me to say?

216

"No, you're not, but in spite of that I'm going to smuggle you in!" Of course you're invited! In fact I think Melanie's looking forward to meeting you.'

'Does she know anything about me?'

'Nothing, except that you're my friend.'

And your lover, Naomi thought. Melanie would probably be disappointed. If Tom had told her nothing, then she would expect someone quite different: young, beautiful, clever.

'What shall I wear?' she asked.

'What does it matter?' Tom said. 'Anything from a grass skirt to a diamond tiara. Both if you like!'

'I only want to do the right thing by you, in front of your friends,' Naomi explained.

'Just be there,' he said. 'Just be there!'

'Who else will be?'

'I don't know,' Tom said. 'Could be anyone. Mostly university, I guess.'

In the end Naomi went shopping and bought a new dress, dark blue, simple and understated, but the fabric was silk. It would do for other occasions should they arise, indeed it would have to since it had set her back a pretty penny; more than she could afford, more than she should have allowed herself to spend.

Melanie Clarke and her husband lived in a spacious flat over an antique shop within a stone's throw of the Assembly Rooms. When a young man opened the door to them, Tom and Naomi stepped into a lofty hall and from there he led them into a large room with a high ceiling, elegantly moulded cornices and a delicately painted ceiling rose. It was plainly furnished, which made it seem even more spacious. Two large sash windows looked out, since the curtains were not drawn, over the lights of the city. The room seemed, to Naomi, full of people when they first entered though in fact, when she came to sort them out, there were no more than eight, plus herself and Tom. It was just that they all clustered together, near the door. Melanie separated herself and came to greet them.

'Hi, Tom!' she said. 'And this must be Naomi! Nice to meet you!'

She was young, thirty at the most, with thick blonde hair

cascading over her shoulders, and wide-set, green eyes. A stunning combination, Naomi thought, not to mention being a brain box, but her smile was warm and friendly.

A man stepped forward. He was small, plain to the point of ugliness, with receding hair and an unhappy expression on his face.

'I'm Jacob Clarke,' he announced. 'Glad you could come. What can I get you to drink? White wine or red?'

'White please,' Naomi said. She could have done with a stiff gin and tonic but there was none in sight. Everyone was sipping wine from elegantly plain glasses.

'Tom, you must introduce Naomi to people,' Melanie said. 'I have to disappear into the kitchen.'

She left them, as did Jacob. Tom took Naomi's elbow and guided her further into the room, introducing her as they moved around. 'Though I don't know half of these people myself,' he whispered to her.

They were a mixed group. A couple in late middle-age turned out to be Jacob's parents. There were two postgraduate students, one of whom had opened the door to them, who, they told her, worked with Melanie. A young couple in their mid-twenties seemed at odds with the rest of the company. The wife was anxious because they had left their baby in the care of a sitter for the very first time.

'Of course we only live in Gay Street so if the baby doesn't settle and the sitter phones I can nip down quickly,' the young mother said.

'Relax, Angela!' Her husband chided her. 'Of course he'll settle. Why shouldn't he?'

Because they don't, Naomi could have told him, but she would keep totally quiet about her experiences with Natasha.

'You young parents fuss too much,' Jacob's father said. 'When Jacob was a baby we were quite strict with him, weren't we, Dahlia?' he asked his wife. He pronounced her name with a long 'A', as in darling.

'Indeed we were,' Dahlia said. She had the firm, crisp voice of a games mistress in a girls' high school. 'Crying exercises the lungs! If he was warm and dry and well-fed, we left him to it.'

Perhaps that accounts for his miserable expression, Naomi thought. And how was it that everywhere she went they talked about babies? Even Amersham's was not immune. On Thursday Jean Fulneck had brought in her baby for them to see and the whole staff had been gooey with admiration, including Mr Swaine who had touched him with a hesitant finger and said what a fine little chap he was.

Melanie now returned from the kitchen and directed them to a table laid for ten at the far side of the room.

'You must sit here, Naomi,' Melanie said. 'Next to Jacob.'

In fact Naomi found her host was not nearly as morose as he looked. He was pleasant and entertaining, keeping up a smooth flow of conversation. Tom sat opposite to her with Angela, the little mother at his side. She spoke mostly about her baby but a little about her husband who was something, though Naomi never found out what, to do with museums. On Naomi's right sat one of the two postgraduate students, not the one who had let them in. Michael by name, he ate hungrily through smoked salmon and shrimps, rack of lamb and Marks & Spencer's individual syrup sponge puddings with custard sauce without uttering more than a dozen words, six of which were 'Would you pass the pepper, please?'

'We've quite taken to these old-fashioned puddings,' Jacob confessed. 'And Marks do them so well.'

'A good old-fashioned pudding never did anyone any harm,' Dahlia said with the voice of authority. 'My favourite is spotted dick!'

'Spotted dick?' Tom sounded incredulous.

'It's sort of whitish, with currants and raisins in it,' Angela explained. 'Perhaps you don't have them in New York?'

'I guess not,' Tom said gravely.

Michael came suddenly to life.

'My favourite is sticky toffee!' he said.

Melanie spoke up from the far end of the table where the other student, equally silent, sat next to her.

'It so happens that I have a couple of sticky toffee puddings in the fridge. Would you two boys like them? They take less than a minute in the microwave.'

How kind she is, Naomi thought. She probably invited them just to give them a good meal. She couldn't think why she'd been so nervous about meeting Melanie.

When coffee was served – for which they remained at the table – the telephone rang in the hall and Jacob went to answer it.

'I'm afraid it's your babysitter,' he said to Angela. 'Would you have a word?'

Angela went white, jumped to her feet and rushed out of the room, returning a minute or two later, apologetic but no longer frightened.

'Nothing terrible has happened,' she said. 'But I'm sorry, we'll have to leave. The baby just won't settle.' She looked to her husband.

'Really, darling, what's the point of having a sitter if she can't deal with him?' he said testily.

'I'll leave on my own,' she offered. 'I don't mind!'

'No you won't!' he said, getting up. 'I'll come with you.'

'She is making a rod for her own back, of course!' Dahlia said when they had left. 'Begin as you mean to go on!'

Melanie brought in a fresh pot of coffee, the students finished their sticky toffee puddings and drained the custard jug, the talk resumed.

They spoke of Manchester United, Diana Princess of Wales, science versus the arts, the Booker Prize, Europe, the traffic problem in Bath, New Labour, and crime in New York. It was amazing how most of them knew something about everything. Naomi spoke up on traffic in Bath, and car parking, and was listened to with respect.

What nice people they are, she thought. None of them had shown the faintest surprise that she should be partnering Tom. No-one had asked a personal question she didn't want to answer. She had simply been accepted. How very civilized!

She smiled across the table at Tom and unobtrusively raised her glass – she had accepted a little Grand Marnier – to him. He returned her look with one which sent her into shivers of expectation.

EIGHTEEN

A phone call from Hugh interrupted the late, leisurely Sunday breakfast Naomi and Tom were taking.

'What are you doing?' Hugh asked.

Naomi prevaricated.

'I'm reading the Style section of *The Sunday Times*.'

'You should read the *Observer*,' Hugh advised. 'Anyway, I'm ringing to tell you I'll be down next weekend. I have to find somewhere in London to live. It'll be the last chance before I move there. So I'll be with you late Saturday and leave Monday after lunch. I'll let you know the time and perhaps you could meet the train? Anyway, no time to talk now. All news when I see you.'

Naomi put down the receiver and related what he had said to Tom.

'But it's not convenient,' Tom said quickly. 'We're going away for the weekend. You can't possibly have forgotten.'

'Of course I haven't,' Naomi said. 'But what could I say?'

'It's quite easy. You could have said that you had other plans. It wouldn't be convenient.'

They had decided to take the car, go to Bristol and across the bridge into Wales, where Tom had never been. They would stay somewhere for Saturday and Sunday nights and return on Monday in time for Lucy's piano lesson and Tom's seminar.

'I thought you were looking forward to it,' Tom added.

'You know I was.'

'Then why, just because Hugh chose *his* date do you have to abandon yours and mine?'

She recognized his irritation – they were intimate enough by now to know each other's signs – by the deliberate, measured tone of his voice, which he did not raise in the slightest but spoke as if to a backward child. She also admitted the logic of his words, but logic had nothing to do with it, at least not for her. She was simply following the habit of more than twenty years in which the needs of her children, but of Hugh in particular, had been paramount, closely followed by those of Edward. There had been no difficulty about it then. She had taken such a course for granted, even taken pleasure in it. She was as conditioned as a Pavlovian dog to respond to Hugh's requests.

'I don't know,' she said. 'I suppose it's because it's what I've always done.'

'Then you'll have to change,' Tom said flatly.

'I know that too. It's just that it's not as easy as you make it sound.'

Of course she wanted to change, and on this occasion especially. She had so looked forward to this weekend with Tom, the two of them together, no other duties, no visit to her mother, no telephone. And now she had cancelled it entirely for want of saying 'I can't'.

'OK,' Tom said. 'I'll go along with it – reluctantly – this time, but you've got to spell it out to Hugh, and to the rest of your family, just where things stand. I mean between you and me.'

'I will!' Naomi promised. 'I will!'

'Why are you like this?' he asked. 'Why all this dithering?'

'Because it's a situation I never envisaged.'

She didn't suppose it was a situation Edward had envisaged, yet he was the one who had broken away.

'You are *free*!' Tom reminded her. 'You are no longer married. You are a free woman, no longer answerable to anyone. You are not answerable to your children. You've brought them up and now they're independent.'

'A mother always feels answerable to her children,' Naomi

222

said. 'She never quite believes they're independent, that they don't need her any more.'

'They might need her from time to time,' Tom conceded. 'And no-one's saying you shouldn't help where help is needed, but you should not – *must not* – live through your children. In the end it's not fair to them.' He brought the palm of his hand flat down on the table, so hard that the cups rattled.

Is that what I did with Edward? Naomi asked herself. Did I concentrate on the children and exclude him? She didn't think so, but if she had then she hadn't meant to. It was probably just another of the things you didn't notice at the time it was happening.

'You seem to know a lot about children for a man who's never had any, never been married!' she said to Tom.

He's not married, she thought suddenly, but there was no way at the age of thirty-three he wouldn't have had affairs. Of course he would. He was too attractive for it not to be so. Also, she thought, a wave of desire coursing through her body, his love-making was that of a man who knew what he was doing, who had been there before and knew exactly how to please a woman. She wanted to ask him about the women he had loved before her, she would like to know about them, but that she daren't do.

She could, though, imagine them. They would be bright. They would be intellectual; he had moved too long in university circles for that not to be the case. They would be pretty. While walking with him in the street she had seen his head turn at the sight of a good-looking woman. Above all, she told herself, they would have been young. She hated the way it always came back to this question of age. She was sure, too, that that would be what alienated her from her children. She might not feel too badly about being alienated – though surely that was too strong a word? – from her daughters, but she could not easily take it from Hugh. He had always been so close to her.

'I do have to get to know your family,' Tom said. 'You can't keep me under wraps for ever.'

'I know,' she agreed. 'And you will, I do promise. You've already met my mother.'

The previous weekend at Tom's request, almost at his

insistence, she had taken him to River View on her Sunday afternoon visit. She had done it without warning her mother beforehand.

'This is my friend, Professor Tom Lever,' she'd said.

'Please call me Tom, Mrs Campbell,' he'd said, holding out his hand.

'My word, Tom, you have a nice strong grip!' she said. 'And you can call me Doris. There aren't many left who call me Doris. Come to think of it, practically no-one!'

'It'll be a privilege, Doris,' Tom said.

'You've got a funny accent,' she said. 'Are you a foreigner?'

'American.'

'Oh! Oh yes, I remember the Yanks in the war. They were a cheeky lot and no mistake! Overpaid, oversexed and over here, that's what they said about them. I remember that bit. So what regiment are you in, or do you fly bombers? Clark Gable flies a bomber.'

'Neither,' Tom said. 'I'm a scientist. I'm here at the university for a little while.'

'Oh!'

'I've brought you a few flowers.'

'That's nice!' Doris said. 'I don't get many flowers these days!'

You get them every time I come, Naomi thought, but no matter.

There was a silence while Naomi found a vase and dealt with the flowers. Doris closed her eyes and began to nod off while Tom sat quietly beside her. Suddenly she opened her eyes again.

'Are you Naomi's young man, then?' she asked sharply. 'Are you two courting?' Without waiting for a reply she continued. 'You know she's married to that solicitor fellow? She keeps forgetting, but I don't.'

'Mother,' Naomi said patiently, 'I am *not* married to Edward, not any longer. We divorced. Don't you remember?'

Doris ignored her entirely. Her attention was on Tom.

'I reckon you'd be good in bed,' she said. 'I can usually tell.' If a look could be interpreted, she was undressing him with hers.

'Mother!' Naomi protested.

'Thanks for the compliment!' Tom said, smiling.

Doris turned to her daughter.

'Your dad was good in bed,' she said. 'He was a bugger in most ways. Bossy, short-tempered, wanted everything his own way, pompous – you should have heard him give his little speech at the Masons' Ladies' Night. But he was certainly good in bed and I forgave him a lot for that. I remember once . . .'

A gleam came into her eyes but in fact she didn't remember. She closed her eyes again and that was the end of her rationality for the afternoon. Soon afterwards they'd crept away, leaving her fast asleep.

Walking home, Naomi found herself surprised by her mother's revelations. She had never spoken like that before, indeed she'd always been prim and proper, using euphemisms for those things which were not to be said out loud. No-one in their house ever went to the lavatory, they went to wash their hands. She had never thought of her parents as having a sexual relationship, even though her own presence was proof that it had happened at least once. They had never exchanged endearments, they had addressed each other as 'Mother' and 'Dad'. How could lovers do that?

Was it possible that her own children had seen she and Edward in a similar light and thought that, now they had brought up their family it was all over and done with, that they were too old to start again (except for Edward, of course, but he was a man)? Cecily, with her liberated outlook, might not take that view, except that her theories would most likely not include anyone over the age of twenty-five, and certainly not one's mother.

'One's mother,' Naomi said out loud as they were crossing the bridge, 'can suddenly become as sacred as Mary, the Mother of God.'

'An interesting observation,' Tom said. 'Especially coming out of the blue. I must say, your mother didn't strike me in that light.'

'I wasn't talking about my mother,' Naomi told him.

They covered the rest of the way to the flat in companionable near silence, walking arm in arm. Putting the key in the lock,

Tom said: 'I guess I should now prove to you that I'm good in bed.'

'You already have,' Naomi said. 'But further proof wouldn't come amiss.'

Later she said: 'I reckon my mother would be proud of you!'

'I enjoyed meeting your mother today,' Tom said. 'She's an interesting old lady.'

'Sometimes I think she's more interesting now than when she was younger,' Naomi said. 'She's less buttoned up. I just worry that she's losing her faculties. She was such an efficient lady when she was younger. Now half the time she doesn't know where she is.'

'When are you going to tell her, and when are you going to tell the rest of your family, that you're going to visit me in New York? Isn't it time you did?'

'I will. I'll do it soon,' Naomi promised.

'So you should, it's not much more than two months away,' Tom pointed out.

What he did not point out was that in two months' time he would be gone. She could hardly bear to think of it, yet it was scarcely ever out of her mind.

'If it's any help, I'll do it,' Tom said. 'I'll drop it into the conversation. Though why there should be any hole-and-corner business about it I don't understand. It seems straightforward to me.'

'I've told you, I'll do it,' Naomi said. 'Just let me choose my own time.'

That had been a week ago. They had not brought up the subject since. He had stayed with her three nights since then. One morning she found herself seeing him off at the same time as Dan Sheridan came downstairs on his way to school. What the hell, she thought a minute later as she stood by the window, waving to them both as they walked along the road together.

The day before Hugh was due for the weekend he phoned Naomi and gave her the time of the train. She had determined that when he did so she would tell him to take a taxi – or even a bus – but when he spoke she changed her mind. It seemed so mean when she had a car.

226

On the way back to the flat Hugh talked about what he would be looking for in London.

'I'd like a flat somewhere near the theatre, but it would have to be quite a small one, I expect rents are sky-high. I might even have to live further out, but I don't want to. I want to be at the centre of things.'

'Will you be better paid?' Naomi asked.

'Yes, I'll be better paid but it won't go as far in London, will it? And I expect I'll have to make a hefty deposit. I might ask for your help with that, Ma.'

She found a parking space almost opposite to the flat. She hadn't replied to his remark.

'Would you like a drink?' she asked when they were in.

'I could use a gin and tonic,' Hugh said.

Naomi walked into the kitchen and began to mix the drinks. She supposed she might help him with money in the end but it was the way he took it for granted which niggled her. She came back into the living room and handed him his drink.

'Cheers!' Hugh said.

The word slipped out, he knew it was no longer the phrase to use. Too provincial – which was something he must watch.

Naomi raised her glass and took a longish drink.

'At any rate,' Hugh said, 'I'll be down to see you more often – if I can afford the fare.'

'It's always nice to see you,' Naomi said levelly. 'But I'd prefer it if you'd given me due notice, or check that it was convenient.'

'Convenient?' He sounded puzzled.

'Yes. I might have other plans.'

'Other plans?'

'I might already have something arranged.' She took a deep breath and dived in. 'As a matter of fact I had for this weekend. I had to put them aside.'

'Well, that was nice of you, Ma,' he said kindly. There wasn't the least hint of sarcasm in his words. Her behaviour was no more than he expected. 'I'd have been happy to join in, still would if it's congenial. So what were you going to do?'

'I was going to drive up to Wales with a friend,' Naomi said. 'Spend the weekend.'

'I didn't realize you'd kept up with any of your old friends,' Hugh said. 'I hope she wasn't too disappointed.'

'He, not she,' Naomi corrected him. 'I was going with Tom Lever. Actually, he *was* quite disappointed.'

She watched Hugh's face as she spoke. As a child, when he had been angry, he had never flushed, as the girls had. He had turned pale, caught his breath, said nothing at all until he was in control of himself, which was exactly what was happening now. She knew by the whiteness of his face that he was furious.

She said nothing, waiting for him to speak.

'Is that wise, Mother?' he said in a stiff voice. He called her 'Mother' only when he was angry with her.

'Wise? I don't think that occurred to me. It was just something we thought we'd like to do. Tom hasn't been to Wales. However, he was very understanding and gave it up for this weekend in favour of you. I expect we shall go another time.'

What have my sisters been doing to let this happen? Hugh thought furiously. She was their mother as well as his. Why didn't they take some responsibility? That stupid cow Isso was living on the spot. Why couldn't she turn her gaze away from that bloody baby for ten minutes and think about their mother? And why wasn't Cecily here more often, why didn't she telephone more, know what their mother was doing? He would insist on seeing them *tout de suite* and telling them what he thought. As for his mother, what was she thinking of, taking off for the weekend with a man almost young enough to be her son? But he read the expression on his mother's face as she slowly sipped the rest of her gin and tonic and knew that he must tread warily. It was no use blowing a fuse.

'I don't think it was quite the best of ideas, Ma,' he said, as calmly as he could. 'You don't know him all that well. He's, well, he's foreign for a start. He doesn't know our conventions.'

'I never think of American as being foreign,' Naomi said conversationally. 'After all, we speak the same language, give or take a few words like "shades" for sunglasses and "drapes" for curtains . . .'

'Mother!'

228

He was finding it difficult to keep his temper but he knew he must if he was to get anywhere.

'You don't mean . . . surely not . . . that I might actually come to some harm?' Naomi said.

'I'm saying you don't know what might happen.'

Oh, but I do! Naomi thought. I do! And I was looking forward to it.

'He shouldn't have asked you,' Hugh said. 'He shouldn't have put you in this position.'

'He didn't. It was my suggestion.'

If he heard her interruption he took no notice of it.

'He was simply using flattery, which is dishonest. After all, Mother, he's almost young enough to be your son!'

She had known that had to come.

'Not unless I was *very* precocious!' she said.

'Mother!' He had lost his cool at last. 'You are deliberately misunderstanding me! You know perfectly well what I'm trying to say.'

'Yes, I think I do.' Naomi was as suddenly quiet as Hugh was noisily angry. 'You're trying to say that I'm forty-six years old, old enough to know better than to think that an attractive young man of thirty-three could possibly have a genuine reason for paying attention to me other than to indulge in some game of flattery. You're saying it loud and clear!

'But let me tell you, dear, that you are wrong! Also let me remind you that, though I appreciate your concern for me, I am old enough to make up my own mind.

'And now I'm going to make some supper and we're going to eat it in a civilized manner. Will you be an angel and go along to Mr Patel's to buy a bottle of wine? I meant to get some and forgot. Choose what you like, he has quite a reasonable selection.'

It was not true that she had no wine in the house. She had two bottles in the rack in the kitchen which, as soon as Hugh had gone to Mr Patel's, she must put out of sight. How childish she was being to go through this petty deception, but the truth was that for a while, just a little while, she wanted Hugh out of the flat, she wanted to be on her own. The scene she had had with him had left her shaking inside. She needed time alone to recover.

Most of all, more than anything in the world, she wanted Tom, and if that was right now physically impossible she wanted to hear his voice on the phone. While Hugh was out, she would try to reach him. He might be in his lab, but since he had arranged not to work this weekend perhaps that was unlikely. He might be in his digs, which were close to the university. He had not said how he meant to spend the weekend they had planned to be together. *And which I ruined for both of us*, she thought as, the moment she heard Hugh close the outer door behind him, she picked up the telephone.

For his part, leaving his mother's flat, Hugh made straight for the nearest public telephone, which was at the end of the street, only yards from Mr Patel's. He dialled Isobel's number, tapping impatiently with his fingers on the glass door while he listened to the ringing in her flat. Damn her! She was out! How dare she be out! But she was not out, and seconds before he decided to put down the receiver she answered.

'Isso?'

'Hugh? Where are you?' He scarcely ever phoned her.

'I'm in a phone box. Where were you? Why didn't you answer the bloody phone?'

'I was changing Harry,' she said. 'And don't shout. He can hear you. Why are you phoning from a call box? Is something wrong?'

'It damn well is! Our mother has gone off her rocker. If I hadn't been here she'd have been off for the whole weekend in wildest Wales with that Yank who's after her. We've got to do something, Isso!'

'What can *I* do?' she asked, not sounding in the least worried.

'I don't know, but we've got to do something. After all, you're nearest, though I can tell you I'll be glad when I'm living in London. I'll not allow this sort of thing to happen!'

'In the meantime,' Isobel said, 'Harry's crawling around the floor. I can't stand here talking to you!'

'We've got to get together, all of us with Ma. We've got to be kind, but firm. The only thing I can think of right now is that you

230

ring her this evening, tell her you'll be bringing Harry around to see her tomorrow. Better make it later in the day because she goes to see Grandma.'

'But I never take Harry to see Ma!'

'Precisely! So now you will, we all will. Get that sister of yours on the phone and tell her she has to be down here tomorrow!'

'She's your sister as well as mine. You call her!'

'How can I? I'm in a public call box, I've run out of change and obviously I can't call her from Ma's place. So for God's sake get on with it! I think—' What he thought was never expressed. The money ran out.

Had Mr Patel's signboard not been the first thing which caught Hugh's eye as he left the call box he would have forgotten all about the bottle of wine. As it was, he made a swift and the most expensive choice from what was on offer and hoped that his mother would pay for it.

A laboratory assistant answered Naomi's call.

'You're lucky! Professor Lever's here, but he's just leaving! I'll call him back!'

'Hi!' Tom said. 'Is everything all right?'

'Not quite,' Naomi said. 'But I'm dealing with it.'

'Is Hugh there?'

'Not at the moment. He's gone to Mr Patel's to buy a bottle of wine, which is why I'm calling you. I'm missing you!'

'And I'm missing you. So don't do it again!'

'I won't,' she promised. 'I won't ever. But I did tell Hugh that it hadn't been convenient, that I was going away with you for the weekend. I asked him in future to consult me first.'

'Good for you! And how did he take that?'

'Not all that well. I sent him out to buy a bottle of wine so that I could telephone you.'

'I'm glad you did.'

'I wondered . . .' Really, the thought had only just occurred to her.

'Yes?'

'What if you come to supper tomorrow evening and I invited as many of the children who could come – and I broke it to them

231

that I intended visiting you in New York? Is that a good idea or isn't it?'

'A very good idea,' Tom said.

'That's all I'll tell them, at least for now. Not that we're lovers, though there's no way I'm not proud of it.'

'They can work that out for themselves,' Tom said. 'They'd have to be blind not to see it.'

'That's the doorbell. It'll be Hugh,' Naomi said. 'I must let him in. I love you.'

'I love you,' Tom said.

Who did this guy think he was, throwing his weight around? Tom asked himself as he left the university. Hang on, he answered himself. This guy was Naomi's son. She cared about him, unlovable though he might seem to everyone else. Probably in his own peculiar way he cared about her, or at least wanted to protect her. So there was no point in going in with all guns blazing, though go in he would.

Naomi and Hugh tried to converse normally as they ate supper, but it was not easy. Naomi's mind was on Tom, on how he would behave when they all met the next day. He could come on strong and she wasn't sure that that was the way to do it. In any case she had yet to invite them. She would telephone Isobel and Cecily immediately after supper, first telling Hugh what she proposed to do, though no way would she inform any of them that she had already invited Tom. Hugh's mind was on Isobel. Surely she'd had time by now to contact Cecily? Why didn't she phone?

They had finished supper. Naomi was in the kitchen washing the dishes when the phone rang. It must be Tom. She rushed to answer it.

'Hello, Grandma!' Isobel said. 'How are you?'

Naomi frowned. Was she to be addressed as Grandma from now on? Was she no longer Isso's mother?

'I'm well,' she said. 'And you?'

'OK,' Isobel said. 'Harry's cutting another tooth, poor little mite! Actually, I'm phoning to say I thought I'd bring him to see you tomorrow. Early evening is the best time for him.'

'How extraordinary! No, darling, not that you'd thought of

232

coming.' (Though it was.) 'Just that I'd decided, since Hugh is here, that I'd ask you all to supper, that is if I can get hold of Cecily. If not, then the rest of you.'

'Another coincidence!' Isobel said. 'I spoke with Cecily this evening. She's coming!'

'Good! Will Patrick come?'

'Oh, yes!' Isobel said. If it was to be a family conference then she'd insist.

'I'm not sure I'll get you all around my table, but we'll manage.'

'I'll bring Harry's solids with me,' Isobel said. 'You don't need to worry about that. He's on ham and spinach now, bless him!'

'Would you believe it?' Naomi said, putting down the telephone, turning to Hugh. 'Isobel was coming here with the baby, tomorrow! And Cecily. And at the same time I'd decided to ask everyone here for supper.'

'What a good idea, Ma!' Hugh said. It hardly mattered where they got together except that his mother was likely to provide a far better meal than Isobel.

'I shall have to visit your grandmother in the afternoon,' Naomi said. 'Shall you go with me?'

'If you like,' Hugh said, 'I'll go on my own.'

It had occurred to him in the train on the way down that he had neglected his grandmother, and that was not the thing to do. He was determined to put it right. A visit whenever he was down this way, an occasional letter or postcard, or even a theatre programme with his name on it.

'Why, that would be very nice! She'd enjoy that,' Naomi said.

If she had the faintest idea who I was, Hugh thought. But it was up to him to make certain that she did know.

NINETEEN

The moment Naomi wakened on Sunday morning, even before she opened her eyes or raised her head from the pillow, she remembered that this was the day she was to have six people for supper and she had no idea what to give them, not the faintest. Also, would the food shops be open? Some of them would, including Mr Patel's but she would have to look around.

Wide awake now, she got out of bed and put on her dressing-gown. She would like to lie back, close her eyes and drift off to sleep again, not only in order to put off all thoughts of providing food but to push away the second, and in a way more difficult, thought that had come into her mind which was that this evening was to be the showdown with her family. However polite they all were, including Tom, there was bound to be confrontation. Had she been right to arrange it so, everyone present, everyone putting in their two pennyworth?

Oh well. It was done now. Short of fire or flood, or her catching the next plane out of the country, it would happen.

She went into the living room, drew back the curtains onto a bright day, heard a single church bell ringing close by for early service, then went into the kitchen. She moved quietly, not wishing to waken Hugh, though unless he had changed his ways it would take a near earthquake to arouse him before he had slept his fill. Also, she didn't particularly want him around before

234

she'd straightened herself out. Who knew what his mood would be?

While the coffee was filtering she took cookery books from the shelf and began to leaf through them. Everything seemed to call for ingredients she didn't have or couldn't be sure of finding anywhere on Sunday morning, or to be too complicated to make, though complications in the making shouldn't worry her since she had all day in which to do it.

In the end she decided on a curry. The evenings were chilly, so it would be suitable. She knew her own family enjoyed curries and though she didn't know about Tom, he seemed amenable to most foods. And to be on the safe side she would make it a vegetable curry since there was never any knowing with Cecily whether she might or might not have turned vegetarian overnight. She felt happy with her choice since almost everything she needed she could get from Mr Patel, and she would go along there as soon as she'd finished her breakfast, leaving Hugh to sleep.

She was right in thinking Mr Patel would have it all. There was nothing the recipe called for – split red lentils, tumeric, cumin, pineapple chunks, pastes and powders, vegetables of various kinds – which he didn't stock. He also had coriander growing in a pot.

She bought ice cream and fruit for dessert and tomatoes for a salad starter.

'And I think I'd better have some beer,' Naomi said to him. 'It's better than wine with curry, don't you agree?'

'Certainly,' Mr Patel said. 'Or water.'

'I'll have some bottled water also,' she said.

'You cannot carry all this,' Mr Patel said.

'You're right,' Naomi said. 'I should have brought my son with me.'

'There is no need to worry,' Mr Patel told her. 'If you can wait an hour I will bring it along myself. My wife will look after the shop. She is busy with the children at this moment, but later she will not be.'

'That's very kind!' Naomi said.

'It is a pleasure, Mrs Fletcher.'

She was without doubt one of his favourite customers and recently she had seemed a much happier lady than she'd been when she'd first come into his shop.

By the time Naomi was home Hugh was stirring. He emerged from his bedroom on the way to the bathroom wearing striped pyjama bottoms, his eyes bleary with sleep, his hair tousled. He looked, for a moment, like the little boy he had once been and, as she looked at him, Naomi's heart melted. The last thing on earth she wanted was for them to quarrel.

That's not true she reminded herself, the *very* last thing on earth she wanted was to lose Tom, even though she knew that she perhaps must. But she was not going to lose him one hour before she need, and certainly not because of anything her children might think or say.

Hugh came out of the bathroom.

'Do I smell coffee?' he asked. 'Do I smell bacon?'

'You soon could, if that's what you'd like.'

'I certainly would. I never get a *real* breakfast,' Hugh said.

'Then why don't you cook yourself one occasionally?' Naomi asked.

'No time, darling,' he said. 'Always too busy!'

'If I know you, what you mean is that you stay in bed until the last minute and then you've no time left to eat breakfast, let alone cook it!'

'Oh Ma,' he said. 'You know me too well!'

A little later he sat down to bacon, two eggs, tomatoes, fried bread and a fresh pot of coffee, all of which Naomi had enjoyed preparing, as she now enjoyed watching him demolish every last morsel, cutting a piece of bread from the loaf to wipe his plate clean.

'What are you going to do today?' he enquired.

'I was going to ask you the same thing. I'll be quite busy preparing for this evening. I'm going to make a curry.'

'Oh, good!' Hugh said. 'I'll get out from under your feet, then. You won't want me around if you've things to do. As you know, the kitchen's not my place. What time do we have lunch?'

'I hadn't intended a Sunday lunch today,' Naomi told him. 'Just a snack, bread and cheese.'

'Then I'll have another slice of toast now,' Hugh said. 'And this afternoon I'll pop along to see Grandma. In the meantime I'll go and get the Sunday papers.'

'And I'll ring Isobel,' Naomi said. 'Make sure everything's all right.'

And why should she be doing that? It wasn't something she would normally do and there wasn't the slightest reason why everything shouldn't be all right with her daughter. It was just this feeling that she wanted to be on the best possible terms with all her family before the evening came. She would have telephoned Cecily except that she could hardly ever raise her on the phone.

'I'm OK,' Isobel said, slightly surprised. 'Harry is very well. He had wind at four o'clock this morning but he's better now.'

'Good! I'm making a curry,' Naomi said.

There was a short silence before Isobel replied.

'I'm not sure curry will suit Harry!'

'I hadn't thought of Harry eating it,' Naomi said. 'You said you'd bring his food. Ham and spinach, you said.'

'Spinach and rice today,' Isobel said. 'What I mean is that I breastfeed him at night. I'm not sure curry won't give him indigestion.'

'Not my curry!' Naomi said. 'Anyway, I reckon little Indian babies must be fed on curry all the time – after it's been filtered, so to speak. It doesn't seem to do them any harm.'

'Harry is *not* a little Indian baby,' Isobel said. 'Indian babies are different. Their stomachs are different.'

'I never knew that!' Naomi said brightly. 'Anyway, darling, I must rush.'

She put down the telephone.

'I will *not*', she said out loud 'change my menu for little Harry! He must learn to deal with cosmopolitan food!'

Hugh, as he walked up the Warminster Road to River View, was in a thoughtful mood. This visit to his grandmother was something he had to get right. Of course there'd be other visits, he had no intention of neglecting the old lady, but today's must set the scene, establish who he was and his place in the family. Her only

237

grandson. His mother, he feared, though she would always be on his side, and he knew he had the edge over Isso and Cecily, was too easygoing. She would simply let things take their course and who knew what that might be?

Lawyers, he reckoned, were sharks. They preyed on their clients, especially if their clients were rich old ladies, slightly dotty in the head. Who knew what his grandmother's solicitor, probably half-senile himself, had persuaded her into?

He smiled sweetly at the young woman who opened the door to him.

'I'm here to visit my grandmother!' he informed her. 'Mrs Campbell.'

'Is she expecting you?' she asked.

'Not exactly. But I'm sure she'll be pleased to see me!'

I'm sure she will, the young woman thought as she directed him to his grandmother's room. Who wouldn't?

Doris, for once, was wide awake, sitting in her chair. Moreover, she recognized him after only the slightest hesitation.

'How nice of you to come!' she said.

'A pleasure! A true pleasure! I expect Ma's told you I'm going to be working in London. I'll be able to see you much more often.'

'She might have told me,' Doris said. 'Sometimes I forget.'

But you're not going to forget me, not if I can help it, Hugh thought.

'Where is your mother?' Doris asked.

'She couldn't come today. She's rather busy. All the family are coming to supper this evening. What a pity you won't be there, Grandma! You would complete the party!'

'We have a very nice supper here,' she said. 'Not as much on Sunday as other days because we have the roast lunch. Lamb, baked potatoes, peas and carrots we had today. Apple sponge and custard to follow, though I think the sponge would have been better if they'd used Bramley apples. You can't beat them for cooking. Bramley Seedlings. Can you still get them?'

'I don't know, Grandma. I shall look out for them in London. If I can find them I'll bring you some.' He wanted to reintroduce the subject of London because it had occurred to him that she just might help him with his deposit. Why not? He was her grandson, and she wasn't by any means short of the ready. But he wouldn't push it too hard today, just mention it if the opportunity occurred.

'You sound as though you're pretty well fed,' he said.

'Not bad at all! Yesterday we had pork chops, cabbage, beans—'

He interrupted the menu. The whole afternoon could go in a description of meals.

'Do you get many visitors?'

'Not a lot. Your mother reckons to come every Sunday, but sometimes I don't see hair nor hide of her.'

I expect she comes and you don't remember, Hugh thought. It was exactly what he was afraid of.

'She was here last week,' Doris said. 'She brought her young man.'

'Young man? You don't mean Mother, it must have been another visitor.' But even as he said it, he had a nasty feeling.

'Are you telling me I don't know my own daughter?' Doris demanded.

'Of course not, Grandma. I just thought you'd made a mistake about the man. I mean who—'

'I didn't make a mistake. I'm not daft!'

'Of course not! So what was he like, this man?'

'Oh, he was very nice. An American he said. He brought me some flowers. He's a professor.'

The worst was true. His mother had brought that Yank to meet his grandmother! Moreover, he'd wormed his way in, bringing her flowers.

'Only an American professor, Grandma. Not quite the same thing.' With difficulty he managed a tight smile. 'And he's not her young man. He's just . . . well . . . an acquaintance.'

'Is that so? It didn't look like that to me. Your mother reminded me she was no longer married to that solicitor fellow – I forget his name. Let's see, he'd be your father wouldn't he?'

She was going off. He could tell by the faraway look in her eyes.

'They'd make a lovely couple. I told them so. I mean your ma and the professor. Not the solicitor. I never liked him!'

Hugh laughed as heartily as he could, and suddenly realized what the phrase 'hollow laughter' meant.

'Oh, there's no chance of that!' he said. 'He's far too young! He's not much older than I am!'

'You're as young as you feel!' Doris said. 'I think your mother could be made to feel quite young again.'

It was precisely what Hugh feared. For two seconds he closed his eyes against the horror of it all. When he opened them his grandmother was asleep.

As he sat there watching her he faced the awful prospect of his mother marrying Tom Lever, then inheriting her mother's fortune, and spending it all on Tom. It was a nightmare. It was unbearable!

He was about to pull himself together and leave when his grandmother opened her eyes and was instantly awake again, though in another country.

'I'm sorry,' she said. 'I fell asleep. Have you brought me my Communion?'

'Your Communion?'

'You usually come straight after morning service, don't you? I expect you got held up?'

'Grandma! It's me!' Hugh said desperately. 'Hugh!'

'I never knew your name was Hugh,' she said in a kindly voice. 'I have a grandson called Hugh! And you mustn't call me Grandma, you know. I'm not your grandma. It was one of the first things I said to the staff when I came here. Just because I'm old you mustn't call me Grandma! And they never have. They respected my wishes.'

'But really, I am—'

She took no notice.

'And you're not wearing your dog collar,' she scolded mildly. 'I know it's trendy for the clergy not to wear their dog collars but I never think it's right. You should be proud of it!'

'*But I'm not—!*' Hugh shouted.

'I expect you ride a motorbike,' Doris said. 'They nearly all do. I don't really like that either! A bicycle when you're a curate, a modest car when you get to be a vicar.'

She was asleep again, her chin sunk on her chest. This was
terrible. She had no idea who he was! He rummaged in the
drawer of her bedside table and found a sheet of paper. She had
to know who he was and that he had visited.

Darling Grandma (he wrote)
   I hope you had a good sleep. It seemed a pity to wake you.
I very much enjoyed being with you and I hope to see you
again before too long.
      Your loving grandson
      Hugh

Was it a bit over the top, 'Your loving grandson'? But if he
signed it 'Hugh' she might confuse him with the clergyman,
whoever he was. And he would say nothing to remind her of their
earlier conversation about Tom Lever, though he would certainly
have something to say to his mother.

He tiptoed out of the room, tapped on the door of a room
marked 'Matron', and entered when she called out the invitation.

'I'm sorry to disturb you, Matron,' he said pleasantly. 'I'm
Hugh Fletcher, Mrs Campbell's grandson. She's fallen asleep,
poor darling, so I wonder if you'd be kind enough to see that she
gets this note. It's important. She's a little confused and I do
want her to remember I've been.'

'Of course! I'll give it to her myself,' Matron said. What a
charming young man! she thought. 'I'm sure your visit will have
done her good.'

'Well, I hope to visit more often in the future,' Hugh said.

'Good!'

As promised, she later took the note to Doris.

'What a charming young man your grandson is!' she said.

'Oh yes!' Doris said. 'And he's quite clever too. He's a professor at the university!'

Hugh's rage propelled him at great speed down the hill and
back towards his mother's flat. How could she? How could she
be so silly? It must be something to do with her age and if that
was so he didn't know how to tackle it, though tackle it he must,

241

or at least they all must, it wasn't just up to him. Anyway, he thought, he would phone Isso from the call box, put her in the picture.

'You have no idea how bad it is!' he said when Isobel answered the phone. 'Ma is behaving in the strangest way and this so-called professor is wading right in, taking advantage of her. Something has—'

'He isn't a so-called professor,' Isobel interrupted. 'He's real – quite well thought of. Patrick told me—'

'Don't interrupt!' Hugh yelled. 'He might be Einstein for all I care! It's simply a question—'

'But you'll get nowhere if you call him a so-called professor when he's a real one—'

'For God's sake stop nit-picking!' he shouted. 'We have to take this seriously.'

'Which I am doing,' Isobel said. 'And *you* have to keep calm. You won't get anywhere with Ma by shouting at her.'

Hugh drew a deep breath.

'I do not intend to shout at her. I am shouting at you because you will keep interrupting! We have to decide how to tackle this. You must see it affects all three of us: you, me, Cecily.'

'And Harry!' Isobel said.

'Fff—'

'Do not say that word!' Isobel broke in sharply. 'He might well hear you. He's quite close to the phone.'

'He won't bloody well understand it, will he? Not unless it's his second time around!'

'Even so, Patrick and I have a rule that we don't swear in front of Harry. Not even a "damn".'

'My money's running out again,' Hugh said. 'Just think about what I've told you and arrive with some ideas. And ring that sister of ours and warn her!'

'She won't be in,' Isobel said. 'She never is. I'll do—'

What she would do Hugh was never to know. All was silence. Leaving the call box he tried to slam the door but it was heavily weighted and refused to be slammed.

Mr Patel, outside his shop arranging a display of fruit, observed Hugh. There is Mrs Fletcher's son, he thought. A very

242

angry young man. I wonder what can have upset him? Perhaps Mrs Fletcher might one day tell me?

As he walked the rest of the way Hugh slowed his pace. Isobel was right, he must keep calm. It would avail him nothing to take the wrong line with his mother. When anyone came down too heavily she would quite quietly do her own thing. He had observed it when his father got mad at her. It had driven his father crazy and it would drive him crazy too. You could not have a fierce argument with her. She was not stupid, far from it. She was emotionally capricious, like most of her sex, but in her case she knew how to contain it. So he knew that if he was to win – and win he must – he must go carefully.

He was at the door. He took a deep breath and rang the bell.

'*A bientôt*, darling!' Naomi said, and put down the receiver.

She was so pleased that Tom had phoned her and glad that he'd done so when Hugh was out. Though after today, she thought as she went to answer the door, it would all be different, everything would be out in the open. Or just as much of it as she and Tom wanted to be.

'Sorry, darling!' she said. 'I was on the phone!'

He waited for her to tell him with whom, but she didn't. That was another thing, Hugh thought, she was getting secretive. He wanted to ask her who it was but didn't quite dare to do so.

'Have you heard from Cecily?' he asked, fishing.

'Not a word. But you know Cecily,' she said with a laugh. 'She'll phone from the station just when it's most inconvenient to me. And by the way, I meant to ring Isobel and tell her you'd fetch them in my car. We can't have them struggling with Harry and all his paraphernalia. Will you phone her, tell her you'll pick them up?'

So it hadn't been Isso, which only left the Yank. Hugh dismissed the thought that anyone else might have called his mother.

'So how was Grandma?' Naomi asked. 'Excuse me a minute while I go and add a drop more liquid to the curry. It soaks it up like a sponge! But it smells OK, don't you think?'

'Delicious!'

'So how was she?' Naomi repeated from the kitchen.

'Difficult to say. Some of the time she seemed quite with it, some of the time way off.'

'I'm afraid that's par for the course,' Naomi said. 'Did she know you?'

'Part of the time, not all of it. She asked after you.' He was getting nowhere. The problem was he didn't know how to begin.

'I went last Sunday, as usual,' Naomi said.

'Yes, she said so. She said – I didn't know whether this bit was right or not – she said you'd had a man with you, a young man.'

For a second Naomi ceased to stir the curry, then started again, quite carefully. She was pleased to be in another room.

'That's right!' she said. 'I took Tom!'

'Tom?'

'Tom Lever. You met him. You had supper with him.'

She put the lid back on the pan, adjusted the gas, and walked into the living room. If Hugh was going to play silly fools, she was ready to face him.

'Oh, the American?'

'That's the one.' She sat down in a chair opposite to him. 'You're rather young to forget names so quickly,' she said lightly. 'I hope you're not going to take after Grandma!'

Hugh flushed. He'd not played that one well.

'I was rather surprised,' he said stiffly.

'What? That I took Tom or that Grandma remembered him?'

'Actually, that you took him. I wouldn't have thought that Grandma was in any fit state to meet strangers.'

'Oh, but she enjoyed it!' Naomi said. 'It does her good, makes a nice change for her to see a fresh face.'

In future, Hugh thought, mine will be the face she sees most of. I'll see to that.

'In any case,' Naomi said, 'Tom isn't a stranger. He's my friend.'

'He's not family. That's the point. I don't think she's well enough!'

'How considerate you are, darling. But she seemed all right. One mustn't make too much of a friendly visit to an old lady,' Naomi said.

'She made it sound rather more than that!'

Oh dear, Naomi thought. My dear mother's gone through all that business of 'good in bed'!

'You mustn't take too much notice of what Grandma says. You know she's not entirely lucid, poor dear. She makes things up as she goes along!'

'It didn't sound like that to me,' Hugh said stubbornly. 'She was quite clear.'

'So what did she say?' And do I want to know? she asked herself.

'If you must know, she referred to him as your young man. As if there was something serious going on.'

'My young man! What a funny, old-fashioned phrase! No-one uses it these days, do they?'

'Boyfriend' they said now. She hated that. In any case, she thought with a warm feeling of satisfaction, he *is* my young man. My mother is right, that's exactly what he is. Suddenly the phrase seemed perfect.

'You're being facetious!' Hugh said crossly. 'It's not a laughing matter. You shouldn't have done it. Not only that, but—'

Naomi held up her hand and silenced him.

'Before you go any further, Hugh, I just want you to know that you are not to tell me what I should or should not do, in any department of my life. I am grown-up and free. It would be nice if you happened to approve of what I did, and if you liked my friends but, in the end, it doesn't matter if you don't, though I expect you to be polite to them. Do you understand me?'

Hugh didn't answer.

'Then I take silence for consent. And now I must go and make the tomato salad. Will you phone Isobel, dear?'

Her hands trembled as she sliced the tomatoes, chopped the onions, made the dressing. More than anything in the world she longed for Tom to be there at this moment. This was not simply about a visit to her mother, it went deeper than that. With her children she now felt, rightly or wrongly, that they stood solidly against her and she was deeply hurt by it. With Tom beside her she felt she could face the world.

Hugh came into the kitchen.

'If you'll give me the car keys I'll go and collect them now,' he said. 'We shan't be back quickly. You know how long it takes Isso to get ready for anything.'

'There's no hurry,' Naomi said. She knew he and Isso, and Cecily if she was there, would discuss her ad nauseam.

As soon as Hugh had closed the door behind him Naomi dialled Tom.

'Can you possibly come fairly soon, love?' she asked. 'I'd quite like you to be here when they all arrive.'

'I'm on my way,' Tom said.

TWENTY

Within twenty minutes a taxi dropped Tom at the door. They embraced in the hall even before they had walked through into the flat.

'Oh Tom, you don't know how glad I am to see you!' Naomi said. 'It's been a shitty day and I've a feeling it's going to get worse!'

He followed her into the flat.

'So tell me about it!'

'Well for one thing, Hugh went to see my mother this afternoon.'

'And?'

'She told him you'd visited with me.'

'Does that matter?' Tom asked.

'Apparently it does to Hugh. She went into details he didn't like.'

Tom's mouth stretched in a wide grin.

'I'll bet she told him I'd be good in bed! Great!'

'I'm not sure she told him that precise bit,' Naomi said. 'If she did he didn't bring himself to repeat it to me. What seemed to upset him most was that she referred to you as my young man and told him she thought it was serious.'

'No harm done,' Tom said. 'Quite the reverse.'

He took her hand and pulled her over to the sofa. They sat down side by side.

'Don't you see, the more your family see us together, the more they'll learn to accept the situation. And if they don't accept, too bad. It exists and they'll have to put up with it.'

'That's all very well,' Naomi protested. 'But it's not a situation you have to face. They're my family, and no matter how awkward they are I do love them. I don't want to be at cross purposes with them.' She paused, then began again. 'On the other hand perhaps I *am* making too much of it. All we're really talking about is me about to break the news that I'm going to visit you in New York. It's no big deal, so why am I nervous?'

'Because you know perfectly well that's not all we're talking about,' Tom said. 'That's what you've decided to say this evening, it's all you need to say for now, but don't tell me you think that's all it's about!'

She didn't answer. Of course she'd thought beyond the visit to New York, time and time again. She'd dreamt impossible dreams and then made herself put a stop to them because they *were* impossible. In any case Tom had said nothing which gave her cause to believe that his own thoughts went any further than her visit. It had been a boundary across which neither of them had strayed, at least out loud.

'Well?' Tom said.

'Well what?'

'Do you seriously think that's all it is, that that's the end of it? I go home to New York, after a week or two you come and visit with me. You return to England. We send each other a few letters, birthday presents, cards at Christmas. We remember each other kindly. End of story. If you believe that you don't have nearly as much perception as your mother. She knew different.'

'So what should I believe?' Naomi asked quietly.

'Do you think I'd let you go? Don't you know that I want to keep you for ever?'

'Do you mean . . . ?' Her heart was thumping. 'Are you saying you want to marry me? Because if you are it would be quite unsuitable. Everyone would rush to tell you that, not only my family.'

'No they wouldn't,' Tom contradicted her. 'I reckon you've got that wrong. But that's not what I'm saying. I'm not asking you to marry me because I don't know exactly what I think about marriage. I think it's right if you want kids, but I don't want kids . . .'

'And I'm too old to have them.'

He ignored her.

'I only know I want to be with you, and I don't see any end to that.'

'With you in New York?'

'That's where my work is.'

'Leave my family? Is that what you're asking?'

'Yes. But there are planes and telephones and faxes. As far as I know America isn't cut off from England!'

'What about my mother?'

'That would be the toughest part. I know that, my love!' He spoke gently. 'But your mother was the one who saw it was serious. Remember what she said? She said we'd make a lovely couple.'

'Yes,' Naomi said. 'She called you my young man.'

'So I am,' Tom said. 'Isn't it a sweet old-fashioned phrase? But I'm totally serious. I'd be mighty troubled if you weren't. So come here! Let me show you just how serious I am.'

When she was in his arms nothing else mattered. She was afraid of nothing and no-one because no-one else existed. If she gave the slightest thought now to her family it was to wish that they wouldn't come, that Cecily would remain in Sussex, Isobel would stay at home with her baby and Hugh would be miraculously beamed back to Sheffield.

It was not to be. Even the present moment was not to last. It was shattered by the telephone bell.

'Don't answer it!' Tom urged.

'I must,' Naomi said. 'It might be Isobel or Hugh and they know I'm here. It might be urgent.'

'It might be nothing of the kind,' Tom said, but she had already lifted the receiver.

'Oh! Dan! Yes I'm fine. It was just that . . . of course I can lend you a cup of sugar. I'll bring it up!'

'No, no!' Dan said. 'I'll come down right now!' He was off the phone at once.

'It's Dan Sheridan,' she said. 'On his way for a cup of sugar.' Even as she spoke she heard him running down the stairs.

'Don't ask him in,' Tom said.

'I must. I can't keep him standing outside the door. He won't stay.'

It was wishful thinking. He stepped inside, empty teacup in hand, the second she opened the door.

'You've met Professor Lever!' She waved a hand in Tom's direction as she went in search of the sugar. When she returned Dan was comfortably seated in the armchair.

'I haven't seen you for a day or two,' he told her. 'Are you all right?'

'Very well, thank you! And you?'

'Oh, I'm fine. Busy, of course.'

'How's school?' Why was she asking him these unnecessary questions. She didn't wish to hear the answers, she just wanted him to go.

'That's fine – except we've had an epidemic of head lice amongst the kids.' Involuntarily, he lifted a hand to his head and scratched. 'It's over now,' he added.

'I'm pleased,' Naomi said. If she were to tell Isobel that he had so much as set foot in her flat she would not cross the threshold.

'There's a delicious smell coming from somewhere!' Dan said.

'I'm making a curry. My family are coming to supper, all of them. I'm sorry I can't ask you to join us. We just don't have the room. In fact I'm not sure we have enough chairs to sit at the table!'

'Oh, that's no problem,' Dan said eagerly. 'I'll lend you a couple of chairs. Oh, I don't mean so you can invite me, I wouldn't dream of it! I'll bring them down.'

'Please don't bother!' Naomi said. 'I'm sure we'll manage.'

'I insist!' Dan said. 'One good turn deserves another.'

Naomi thrust the cup of sugar several inches closer to him so that he was obliged to rise to his feet and take it, and finding it in his hand, he left.

'Why did you have to apologize for not asking him to eat with us?' Tom asked. 'You're under no obligation to feed the world!'

'I know. It was silly. I thought for one awful moment he was offering chairs so he could come!'

What a pity, Dan thought, climbing back upstairs. She's such a nice woman. He had thought they might have been friends, real friends; have little outings, go on trips. But it was not on the cards. He had seen the light when he'd met up with the American leaving her flat the other morning but he'd told himself it could have an innocent explanation, though just what he couldn't conjure up. Now that he had seen them together he knew that that wasn't so. Everything was there in the way they looked at each other, stood together, spoke.

'I must check the curry,' Naomi said to Tom. 'Every time I add more liquid it sort of rears up and sucks it in, like some predatory, deep-sea monster.'

'Can I do anything to help?'

'You can help me lay the table,' Naomi said. 'Better still, you could collect the chairs from Dan, otherwise he'll be down here again.'

In Isobel's flat, while she methodically, with calm deliberate movements, gathered together the equipment needed for Harry's visit to his grandmother's home, Hugh alternatively sprawled full-length on the sofa or sprang to his feet and paced the floor (as far as he could for impedimenta) giving vent to his feelings. Patrick was reading the *Sunday Express*.

'Have you thought about it at all, Isso?' Hugh demanded. 'Have you considered what it will mean if Ma takes up with this . . . this . . . *American*?' He invested the word with all the horror of a murderous swindler.

'Not really,' Isobel said. 'I don't have the time. I don't see why Ma has to take up with anyone when she has us, but I suppose she ought to be allowed a friend if she thinks she needs one.'

'A *friend*? Who said anything about a friend?' Hugh stormed.

'In any case,' Isobel said, viewing the contents of the holdall she was packing, 'I hadn't thought it particularly alarming.'

'Alarming is exactly what it is!' Hugh said. 'You should be hearing warning bells loud and clear!'

251

'I suppose three nappies will be enough?' Isobel spoke to herself as much as to anyone else in the room. 'And I'd better take Fluffy Bunny. Harry's taken a real shine to Fluffy Bunny these last few days, which is really interesting because he didn't take to it at all at first!'

'Riveting!' Hugh said. 'Could you just concentrate on the fact that the thing about Ma *is* serious? I told you what Grandma said, "They'd make a lovely couple . . . I think your mother could be made to feel quite young again." Grandma clearly sees the light. It's just terrible that she approves!'

'Why?' Patrick asked, not raising his head.

'Because . . .' Well, who would want their mother young again? It was against nature. And what has it to do with him? Hugh thought irritably. But he must talk sense into Isso, if anyone actually could.

'Because for one thing, and to put it bluntly, there's a lot at stake. Ma stands to be a rich woman when Grandma – unfortunately of course – dies.'

Isobel broke off her packing and looked at her brother. There was something in what he said, not that she wanted anything for herself, but there was Harry to think of. He had a right to his inheritance, and surely as a great-grandson he was something special? Perhaps Hugh was more sensible than she'd given him credit for?

'She's well into her eighties for heaven's sake,' Hugh said. 'She can't last for ever! And would we want the Yank to lay his hands on what's rightfully ours?'

'You mean your mother's?' Patrick said.

'Well of course but eventually ours. And Ma wouldn't want us to go short.'

'I wouldn't count on your grandmother not lasting for ever,' Patrick said laconically. 'She's being fed and watered, regular meals, regular attention, not a care in the world. She could live practically for ever. They do in rest homes. There was a woman in the paper last week. A hundred and seven, still going strong!'

Hugh did a rapid mental calculation. Twenty years. Well, halve it and say ten years – at five hundred pounds a week. A quarter of million, more or less.

'I don't think that's likely,' he said firmly. 'Grandma didn't seem all that robust to me.'

'Not that you wish her to die,' Patrick said, turning the page.

'Of course not! Not before her time. And of course I want Ma to be happy. It's just that I don't see her happiness lies with this . . . stranger . . . we don't know anything about.'

'You only want what's best for her,' Patrick said evenly.

'Precisely! You see my point?'

'Of course I do,' Patrick replied.

'There! I think that's everything,' Isobel said. 'Shall we start packing the car? Everything over and under the table and over by the door. You and Patrick take it all downstairs and I'll bring Harry when you're ready.'

Hugh looked in disbelief.

'We'll be three or four hours at the most. What does he want with this lot?'

'There's nothing here that Harry won't need, or want,' Isobel said. 'You haven't the slightest idea about babies, have you?'

'What about Cecily?' Patrick asked. 'I thought she was coming here?'

'Who knows where Cecily is?' Hugh said. 'I'm definitely not waiting. Besides, how would we fit her in the car? As for you, Isso,' he added, 'I expect you to back me up in this business. I can't do everything on my own.'

When the doorbell rang Naomi went to answer it, leaving Tom standing by the fire in the living room. She was really quite nervous. Had it been a good idea not to tell her family that he would be there, to spring a surprise on them? Oh well, it was too late now!

Isobel stood on the top step, holding what at first appeared to Naomi to be a bedding roll. Surely she hadn't suggested them staying the night? On further inspection it proved to be Harry, wrapped up against the night air, his little face just visible several layers down into the roll. Behind Isobel Hugh and Patrick stood with their arms full of bulky objects.

'Do come in out of the cold,' Naomi said. 'Hugh, love, you'll have to park the car properly. It can't stay there.'

'We haven't emptied it,' Hugh said dourly. 'It's not so much a car as a removal van! Where can we put this lot?'

'Well . . .' Naomi said uncertainly, 'perhaps leave them in the hall to begin with?'

'Oh no!' Isobel said. 'We'll need them. They're Harry's bits and pieces. Put them down in the living room, boys, then you can bring the rest in!'

They advanced into the living room, Naomi leading the way, Isobel close behind her with the animated bedroll – Harry having decided to kick his way out of it – Hugh and Patrick bringing up the rear with their assorted bundles.

Tom stepped forward, holding out his hand in greeting. No-one could accept his offer of a handshake, no-one had a hand free.

'There you are, Tom!' Naomi said inanely as if he had just come down the chimney. 'Let me introduce you. This is . . . well, of course you know Hugh! And this is my daughter Isobel and her partner, Patrick. And inside the packing is my grandson, Harry. And this is Professor Tom Lever!'

'Hi there!' Tom said. 'Pleased to meet you all.'

Patrick nodded affably.

Isobel returned Tom's smile. He looked quite nice at first sight, not at all like a man who would rob Harry of his inheritance. All the same, she hadn't expected to see him here. Hugh looked murderous, and gave a grunt. How could his mother spring this on them? She wouldn't dare! He had to believe, therefore, that she had not done it, that the fellow had arrived unexpectedly. And I will see to it that he leaves quickly, Hugh resolved.

'Why don't you two men get rid of your bundles . . .' Naomi began.

'. . . and bring the rest in?' Isobel said.

'Er . . . yes. You sit here, Isobel, and unwrap Harry,' Naomi said. 'He must be baking. It's quite warm in here.'

'Can I do anything to help?' Tom offered. 'I'll get some of the stuff in from the car?'

'Thank you. We can manage,' Hugh said sharply. 'We mustn't keep you. I expect you're on your way.'

'No really,' Tom said. He turned to Naomi. 'Let me help you with the drinks?'

'Thank you,' Hugh said. 'I'll be back in two minutes. I will do the drinks.'

Hugh was going to be at his most difficult, Naomi thought, though it was no more than she expected. He could quite quickly ruin the whole evening. Then she thought, suddenly changing her mind, no he can't, I won't let him. This is *my* evening and I am going to be in control!

Tom turned to Isobel. She had unwrapped Harry, dropping the layers in a heap on the floor beside her, and he lay across her lap, kicking vigorously, waving his arms in the air, saliva dripping down his chin.

'He's cute,' Tom said. 'My sister has a son who's just three months but she lives in Colorado so I haven't seen him.'

'Oh, how sad for you!' Isobel sympathized. 'I didn't know you were an uncle.' It was a point in his favour with Isobel, who saw most people in terms of whatever relationship they had – or regrettably did not have – to a baby.

'I've seen photographs,' Tom said. 'I hope to see him in the flesh before too long.'

'How nice!' Isobel said. 'Have you any photographs with you?'

'Not at the moment,' Tom said. 'Can I do anything to help you? Maybe open up some of these things?' He waved a hand towards the bundles.

'What *would* help would be if you'd just hold Harry for a minute while I get out his play mat. Then he can go down on the floor. He enjoys that.'

She felt she did trust him. He seemed a nice person, clearly fond of babies.

'Why don't you sit here and I'll put him on your lap? He's quite dry,' she said kindly. 'Which makes a change. Little boys do wee-wee such a lot!'

She positioned Harry, wiped his damp chin with a tissue. 'You keep the tissue,' she said to Tom. 'He's teething. He dribbles all the time, bless him!' She moved away in search of the mat.

It was at this moment that Hugh entered, Patrick behind him. He saw his nephew, *his nephew*, gurgling happily on Tom's lap while Tom, a satisfied smirk on his face, gently dabbed at him with a tissue. Hugh walked across to his sister, who was on her knees opening things.

'Traitor!' he hissed.

Then he walked into the kitchen where his mother was getting out glasses.

'How could you, Mother?' he demanded.

'How could I what, dear?'

'How could you invite that man? I thought this was to be a family occasion? I can only hope he was rude enough to drop in uninvited, in which case he doesn't have to eat with us, he can leave.'

Naomi put down the glasses she was holding, otherwise, she thought, she might drop them. Or even throw one or two!

'Oh no,' she said in a quiet voice. 'I invited Tom. He wanted to meet my family and it's what I wanted too. So will you shut up and try to act like a grown man instead of a spoilt child! And just let me add that if anyone is asked to leave it won't be Tom!'

She couldn't believe she was saying these things. She had never ever in her life spoken to her son like this. Perhaps she should have? And in spite of the fact that she was still shaking inwardly it was as though her outburst had somehow strengthened her.

'He is nursing *my nephew*!' Hugh said. 'He has no business to!'

'How nice of him,' Naomi said. 'Did you want to nurse Harry, then? I expect Isobel will let you. And now, since you are my son, will you please find out what people would like for aperitifs while I sort out the rice. But if you think you can't do it with any grace, then Tom or I will do it.'

'I will do it,' Hugh muttered. 'What do you have?'

'Most things, I think. Gin, vodka, sherry, Martini, wine.'

She put on the pan for the rice then followed Hugh into the living room. Patrick chose gin, Isobel orange juice. 'It suits Harry best!' she explained.

'And I'd like a Martini,' Tom said.

'I'll make that. I know how you like it,' Naomi said. She was being naughty and she knew it. 'Does anyone know why Cecily isn't here? Wasn't she supposed to come with you?'

'You know Cecily,' Hugh said. 'She's always late. I expect she'll turn up here just when we're halfway through the meal.' Cecily, he hoped, might at least be on his side. He was disgusted that Isso had let him down. And how were they going to say any of the things he'd planned with the American sitting at the table?

'Harry is just loving this,' Isobel said happily.

Harry was by now lying on his special rug. It had all kinds of attachments built into it; a mirror in which he could view himself, devices which twirled, bells which rang, a frame from which things hung down. Nearby was a musical box which, at a touch, played Brahm's 'Cradle Song', and in other places were soft toys of every kind, including Fluffy Bunny. He had only to move, to stretch out his hand, and there was some new delight.

When the time came for the adults to have their supper there was a special seat which clamped onto a dining chair so that he could sit with them. There was his special place mat, dish, plate, spoon – and a plastic bib which neatly caught in a pocket all the detritus which fell or he spat out of his mouth.

'He just loves eating at the table, bless him!' Isobel said.

Hugh was handing out the drinks – he debated whether he would accidentally trip and spill Tom's down his rather smart waistcoat, but seeing his mother's eye on him thought better of it – when Cecily arrived. She was accompanied by a young man.

'This is Sean!' she announced with pride.

Sean was tall, thin, with aristocratic features and extremely pale skin. His hair was razored close to his scalp in an interesting zigzag pattern, with alternate zigs and zags in blond and dark hair. Henri would like that, Naomi thought. He wore a gold drop earring in the shape of a cross in one ear and a gold stud in his nose. Naomi was slightly shaken to see that Cecily had had her nose pierced and wore a gold stud which matched Sean's in her left nostril. All the same, she told herself bravely, it looked quite pretty – and was there any real difference between an earlobe and a nostril?

She wondered if the matching studs of the two of them had any special significance. Were they, for instance, love tokens, like matching rings? Or had they just purchased a pair and divided them between them? She hoped to find out.

257

She shook hands with Sean, who had a surprisingly strong grip.

'You just have time for a quick drink before we eat,' she told him. 'What would you like?'

'Would beer be convenient?'

They were the first words he uttered, in an exquisite, melliflu-ous voice and a high-class accent. Winchester, she thought.

Hugh dragged Cecily off into the kitchen.

'It's all ruined!' he said. '*He's* here! The American!'

'But why?' Cecily asked. 'I thought he was specifically *not* to be.'

'Ma invited him. Not a word to any of us. Of course it's ruined the whole thing! And why have you brought a complete stranger? You knew it was family only!'

'He's not a stranger. We're an item, Sean and I. We do everything, but everything, together. He's wonderful, don't you think?'

'Not particularly,' Hugh said.

'You should have a relationship, brother dear,' Cecily said. 'Everyone should! Or perhaps you're gay? I've only just thought of that. Even so . . .'

'I am not gay!' Hugh said fiercely. 'It so happens that so far I haven't met the right person. I happen to be more choosy than every other member of my family!'

Naomi came into the kitchen.

'The rice will be done,' she said. 'Shoo, the pair of you! I like my kitchen to myself when I'm dishing up. You two can get people to the table.'

'Where do you want them to sit?' Cecily asked.

'I've thought of that,' Naomi said. 'I've actually put little place cards on the table.

'Sean must sit by me,' Cecily said. 'We always sit together.'

Looking around the table, Naomi felt moderately pleased. The curry had been delicious, the rice – and she had never considered herself good at rice – had been suitably fluffy. Everyone had eaten well and Cecily and Sean had each demolished two large portions. How did they stay so thin?

I arranged the seating quite cleverly, she thought with satisfaction. Isobel and Patrick sat on either side of Harry, who perched on his special chair. Isobel had insisted that he should be at the table with the rest of them. 'His very first family meal, bless him!'

'Not exactly family,' Hugh muttered from the other end of the table. Naomi had placed him there partly because it was correct, he was her son, but more because it made him immediately in line with her. She could look him in the eye. Hopefully, though she was not sanguine about this, she could if it became necessary quell him with a look. Also he was physically separated from his sisters, his natural allies, having Patrick on his right and Sean on his left.

There was no way she would not have sat as close to Tom as possible. He was on her right. She need only to stretch her hand a few inches to touch his, which she now did under cover of the tablecloth.

On Tom's right was Cecily, but since she was next to Sean she was happy, that is she was except when she looked at Harry, sitting immediately opposite her, his face and his special table mat liberally spread with a gooey mixture of spinach and rice. Cecily looked at her nephew as little as possible. Most of the time she was entwined with Sean. But she was happy, Naomi thought, watching her youngest child. And happy people wanted everyone else to be happy, so perhaps she would be kind to her mother.

Naomi disengaged her hand from Tom's and cleared the empty plates, returning with a fruit salad.

Patrick, a resigned look on his face, wiped the table in front of his son while Isobel went to work with a wet-wipe on Harry's hands and face. Cecily averted her eyes and gave Sean a little kiss.

Naomi served the fruit salad. She could not put off any longer what she had to say. It was, after all, the reason why she had invited them. But how to introduce it naturally, casually, into the conversation? 'Tom and I are thinking of . . .', 'Tom and I have this idea . . .' She grabbed Tom's hand under the table and held on to it. He smiled, raised his eyebrows in what she knew was saying, 'Shall *I* do it?' She shook her head.

It was Sean who unwittingly came to the rescue. Finishing his

259

second dish of fruit salad and ice cream he put down his spoon, then leaned across Cecily to speak to Tom.

'You live in New York, I believe, Professor?'

'That's right,' Tom said.

'I've always wanted to visit New York but never got around to it. What would you say was the best time of the year?'

'Why, I reckon any time's good,' Tom said. 'But June is the best. It's warm, but not too hot, not too humid.'

Naomi cleared her throat.

'As a matter of fact . . .' She stopped.

'You were saying, Mrs Fletcher?' Sean prompted. He was exquisitely polite.

Naomi felt Tom prod her in the thigh, under the table. She then realized that, perhaps because she'd stopped speaking, everyone had gone quiet, waiting for her to answer Sean's question. It was as if they were all keeping totally still, waiting for the camera to click.

'As a matter of fact,' she said, 'I've been invited to visit New York – *and* in June!'

She couldn't believe it was her own voice saying it, but it was because six pairs of eyes were turned in her direction.

'Who . . . ?' Isobel began.

'Why, I've been invited by Tom of course! Who else? And I've accepted. I'm hoping to stay for a whole month!'

'Now isn't that wonderful!' Sean said. 'I do envy you!'

'Are you sure that's wise, Ma?' Hugh said.

It was a totally inadequate thing to say, expressing nothing of the outrage inside him, but in this company – and half of them not family so they should keep out of it – he could for the moment think of nothing else. He had to get his mother to himself, stop her doing this. There was no telling where it would all end.

Tom stepped in to save Naomi's reply.

'I'll be leaving England in May. My research has gone as far as I can take it here. I want Naomi to see New York.'

'Well, lucky you, Ma!' Cecily said. 'Perhaps Sean will take me one day?'

You little rat, Hugh thought.

'You don't know what you're talking about, little sister,' he said furiously. 'Ma's never done anything like that. She shouldn't be going all that way without a member of her family. If you'd wait until the autumn,' he said, turning to his mother, speaking more gently, 'I'll get a few days off work and you and I will go together.'

'How sweet of you, darling!' Naomi said. 'Thank you. But I'd really prefer June. And you know you can trust Tom to look after me!'

'It'll be my privilege,' Tom said.

Hugh looked as though his recent meal had turned to lead in his stomach.

'Well, Ma,' Isobel said, 'you seem to have it all worked out! But Harry will miss you.'

'And I'll miss him,' Naomi said.

'Yes, you're bound to,' Isobel agreed. 'So much will be happening to him. He'll be cutting more teeth, eating new foods, starting to crawl more and to stand. Why, he'll even be completely weaned by the time you get back!'

'Thank heaven for that,' Cecily muttered.

'I think it's a great idea,' Patrick said from his end of the table. 'Do you the world of good!'

'Thank you, Patrick!' Naomi said. What a nice boy he was! She wished Isobel would marry him.

Hugh was, for the moment, vanquished. Both of his sisters had let him down. Where was their loyalty? He would have words with them when he got them alone, and in the meantime he would salvage what he could.

'Well if you must go, Ma, the least I can do is pop down here as often as possible, keep an eye on things for you. Especially on Grandma. Someone must look out for Grandma!' And he would make sure that it was he.

TWENTY-ONE

Naomi parked her car and walked back to the flat. She had just deposited Hugh, Cecily and Sean at the station, Hugh to go to London, and from there to Sheffield, Cecily and Sean back to Brighton. She was glad they had chosen to leave reasonably early in the day. Relations with Hugh, though not at all with the other two, were still strained and enough was enough. For the same reason she had been quite pleased when Cecily had announced last evening, out of the blue, that she and Sean proposed to stay the night.

'We'll sleep in here,' she'd said. 'The sofa, the armchairs. Just as long as you can find a blanket or two.'

It would save her a session with Hugh, on his own, Naomi thought, he reinforcing his objections, she adamant, refusing to move. As it was he had followed her into the kitchen when he saw the chance.

'I truly don't think it's a good idea, Ma,' he said. 'I don't think you can have thought it through. Why not wait a few months and let me take you?'

'That's very generous of you, dear,' Naomi said. 'Can you afford it?'

'You are wilfully misunderstanding me,' Hugh protested. 'You know I can't. I didn't mean take in that sense. Simply why don't you and I go together? We'd have a wonderful time.'

'I'm sure we would,' she agreed. 'But on this occasion I want to be with Tom. He asked me and I accepted.'

'Where will you stay?' Hugh asked sharply.

'Why, with Tom of course! Where else?'

Cecily had walked into the kitchen.

'I think it's a wonderful idea!' she said. 'Don't be so stuffy, Hugh! Women are free spirits. They can do what they want, live their own lives. Sean would never try to tie me down.'

'Spare us your freedom for women crap!' Hugh said. 'We are talking about my mother!'

'She's also my mother – and I approve!'

'You've changed your tune,' Hugh said.

'Well, I'm glad you approve, Cecily darling, and I'm sorry Hugh doesn't,' Naomi said pleasantly. 'But in fact I'm doing what I want to do and neither approval nor disapproval matters at the moment. So why don't we stop talking about it? Why don't we leave this mountain of washing-up until the morning, when I can do it quietly on my own after you've gone, and why don't we all go to bed? It's quite late.'

'Isso approved. Or at least she didn't disapprove,' Cecily said.

'Isso is nothing more than a baby-rearing machine,' Hugh said angrily. 'I should have known better than to expect any support from her! But she'll live to rue the day and so will you! Neither of you can see any further than your stupid noses!'

'At least we don't think of nothing but money!' Cecily said.

'Money?' Naomi queried. 'What has money to do with it.'

'Nothing,' Hugh said. 'She's talking rubbish!'

'Oh no I'm not, brother!' Cecily countered. 'Who wrote the scenario that Grandma would leave all her money to Ma, and Ma would go off and spend it all on the divine Tom? You did!'

Naomi stared at them as they confronted one another. Two spots of colour burned in her cheeks.

'That is more than enough from both of you!' she said in a voice icy with rage. 'I hope with every bit of me, Hugh, that your grandmother lives long enough to spend every penny she has, and failing that, she gives it all away to a home for stray cats! I shall encourage her to do so! As for you, Cecily, it would have been better left unsaid. It's not something I've enjoyed hearing!'

'I'm sorry, Mummy!' Cecily said.

'I'm sorry,' Hugh said. 'It wasn't really like that.'

'I'm going to bed,' Naomi said. She had walked out of the kitchen and left them to it, pausing only to wish Sean goodnight as she passed him.

Until then, she thought, now going into the kitchen to face last night's horrendous pile of washing-up, the evening had not gone badly at all, far better than she'd expected. Hugh had been the only fly in the ointment and he had been held back by the presence of others, most of whom did not see eye to eye with him.

After the meal Isobel had extricated a papier mâché bath, just big enough for Harry to sit in, and had given him a much-needed, top-to-toe wash down on the hearthrug. Soap, flannel, creams and lotions had appeared from various places, even a fluffy white towel which Isobel commanded Patrick to warm in front of the gas fire.

'I could have supplied a towel, darling,' Naomi said. 'And you could bath him in the bathroom if you wished. There's room enough.'

'Thank you, Ma,' Isobel said. 'He's just fine here. He likes to be where the action is!'

When Harry, before a mostly admiring audience, was bathed, nappied, nightclothed, Patrick was detailed to prepare his carry-cot and he was put to bed, for which he demonstrated his disapproval, indeed strong dislike, by crying lustily.

'It won't last long,' Isobel said. 'He's exercizing his little lungs!'

'And his little arms and legs,' Naomi observed. He was kicking and fist-fighting furiously.

'I'll put his musical box on,' Isobel said. 'That'll soothe him. He likes his musical box.'

It might have soothed him had he been able to hear its delicate tones over his own stentorian yells, but he could not.

Without saying anything, Naomi went and sat at the piano, and almost immediately picked up on the Brahms, playing it loudly at first, so that Harry could not fail to hear it over his own cries, then more and more quietly as his crying quietened and finally ceased. He was fast asleep. Patrick switched off the musical box, Naomi played to the end and then quietly left the piano.

Isobel looked down at her sleeping child, touched his rosy cheek with one gentle finger.

'Why that was truly wonderful?' she said. 'I never knew my darling Harry was so musical! What a clever little boy he is!'

Naomi washed and dried the glasses and put them away, then turned to the cutlery. How could seven people possibly have used so many knives, forks and spoons? And there were plates, dishes, cups, pans still to come. Not a single surface in her small kitchen had enough space to put down so much as an egg cup. Perhaps it had not been the most brilliant idea in the world to leave it all until today.

Arms up to the elbows in Fairy Liquid suds, Naomi thought about her children, especially and predominantly about Hugh. She had not been particularly nice to him, there had been a lot of straight talking as well as nasty little digs, but she had felt that she had been fighting – it was not too strong a word – for something she very much, almost desperately, wanted. She didn't remember having felt quite like that before. But she couldn't just throw Hugh aside, she *did* love him, and she realized that in hurting him she had inevitably hurt herself. She had got her way over the New York business, but as a result there was now a distance between herself and Hugh which had never been there before.

She dried the silver and put the best of it away in its baize-lined cabinet. How nice it had been – other things apart – to use it once again.

My children are quite different from each other, she thought, and no matter how tiresome they can be, they all have their redeeming features.

Isobel's redeeming feature was clearly her love for Harry. She was besotted by him. She could be, and frequently was, boring, deadly boring, but she was devoted to her child and it seemed unlikely, given her nature, that she would ever be actively unkind to anyone.

Cecily's redeeming feature was her openness. She was incapable of hiding behind anything. She thought she was truly sophisticated yet, in fact, Naomi thought, her younger daughter was naive. She thought she was mature but she was not yet grown-up. It was part of her charm. Sean would probably be good for her. He seemed so self-possessed, reliable. She was pleased Cecily was going to spend most of the Easter vacation with him, at his home in north Yorkshire. Cecily was selfish, of course, but not as selfish as Hugh. Naomi's thoughts had gone full circle and were back with Hugh again.

Yes, he was selfish. No doubt he had been spoilt and no doubt she had done the spoiling. Hugh saw everything from his own point of view.

Isobel saw everything from Harry's point of view, Naomi thought, and Cecily had not yet formed her own points of view so she saw everything from whichever view was fashionable at the time among her contemporaries.

And what about me? Naomi asked herself. She supposed that up until recently she had seen most things from a mother's stance – although secondarily as a dutiful wife.

Not for long these days did her thoughts stay away from Tom, and today was no exception. Tom was sure of himself, moreover he could judge other people well, though he didn't condemn them even if he didn't like them. He was, of all the people she had ever known, the most whole, the most real, the most mature.

She thought of Tom's sister, who had a baby and lived in Colorado, she thought of Amersham's – she would have to consult Mr Swaine about her trip – she thought about her mother.

Sometime later, it might have been a long time or a short one, she had no idea, she found herself drying the very last plate.

She spent the rest of the day working in the flat, working in the garden, giving Lucy her piano lesson and, through most of it, dreaming. Dreaming of what it would be like, a whole month with Tom, only each other to think about. She did not allow her dreams to take her beyond that period. No thought of coming home, alone, of leaving him behind, was allowed to intrude. Not for today.

At six o'clock in the evening he telephoned.

'Can I come over this evening?' he asked.

'I was hoping you would.'

But when he arrived an hour later she knew at once something was wrong. It was there in his face.

'What is it?' Naomi said quickly. 'Don't say nothing! I can tell!'

'I'm not saying that. Nothing we didn't expect, only not quite so soon.'

'You're leaving!'

She felt sick inside. Her whole body sagged and she thought she would fall. Tom took her in his arms and held her tightly against him. She could feel his heart thumping against hers.

'When?' she whispered.

'April sixteenth. There's a conference in NYU on the seventeenth. I have to be there. I tried to opt out but I couldn't.'

'Did you know this yesterday?'

'Of course not! I had a call this afternoon.'

'I can't bear it!' Naomi said.

'I know,' Tom said quietly. 'Nor can I. But you will, we both will. Perhaps you can join me earlier, earlier than you planned, I mean.'

'I don't know,' she said miserably. 'I can't think straight!' All she could think was that whether she went out earlier or not, the final parting would be sooner. There must be a limit to the time she could stay in New York.

Tom released her, held her at arm's length and looked into her tear-bright eyes.

'I know what you're thinking,' he said. 'It doesn't have to be like that, but we won't talk about that now. From now on we'll just live every day we have together to the full. Agreed?'

'Agreed,' Naomi said.

'And every night?'

'Oh yes!'

'Can I move in with you? I want to experience living with you, being with you all the hours I'm not working. I don't want just to be a visitor.'

'You can move in the minute you want to,' Naomi said. 'You can stay until the hour you leave for the plane.'

'And your family?'

She shook her head.

'It doesn't matter at all. They must take me as I come. And if they take me they must take you. For the rest of the time you're here they won't separate us. Nothing and no-one will.'

Only a short time ago it would have been different, not because of her family but because she would not have had the confidence to allow him to be with her all the time, to see her when she was not at her best, tired, untidy, no make-up, possibly cross – all the pitfalls of everyday living in fact. She would have been afraid that some small thing might put him off. Now she was no longer afraid of that and perhaps that was because she could, in any case, only allow her expectations to be short-term. He would not see her when she was older, and he was still a young man.

'I'll move all my things down tomorrow,' Tom said. 'Are you sure you won't mind that – I mean me cluttering up your place?'

'Of course I won't mind. I'll collect you in the car. Will everything go in the car?'

'Oh yes,' he said. 'I travel light, not too much excess baggage. But this place won't be as neat and tidy as you keep it.'

'It doesn't matter a bit,' Naomi said.

The worst time of all would be when he finally moved out, taking his belongings with him, removing every sign that he had ever been there. Her flat would be neat and tidy then. It would also be empty as it had never been before.

'Would you like to go out to eat?' Tom asked. 'Or go for a walk?'

'Not a meal,' Naomi said. 'I'm not in the mood this evening. I'll cook. Something simple.'

'No,' Tom said. 'I'll cook. If I'm sharing your bed I'll also share your kitchen. Let's go for a walk by the river, stop by your Mr Patel and pick up some mushrooms. I'll do a mushroom omelette and a salad. Does he carry mushrooms?'

'He sells everything,' Naomi said.

They had a brisk walk, it was too cool by the river to linger, and called in on Mr Patel on the way back.

'This is my friend, Professor Lever,' Naomi said. 'He's going to be staying with me for a week or two.'

I am glad Mrs Fletcher has a friend, Mr Patel thought, but why then does she look so sad?

It was a good omelette – 'Better than I could have cooked,' Naomi admitted – but the atmosphere was heavy.

'Part of my fairly limited repertoire,' Tom said. 'But I'm willing to learn more. I eat out a lot at home, or pick something up and bring it in.'

Like most men he left behind him a messy kitchen, even though he had made no more than an omelette and a salad. She didn't mind, in fact, Naomi thought, clearing away after him, she was almost glad. She clung to the intimacy of his imperfections almost more closely than to his virtues.

Conversation between them, after supper, was difficult to sustain. There was so much to be said and most of it impossible to say.

'Let's go to bed,' Tom said.

They made love. They made love with the passion of desperation, and were comforted. Afterwards they lay in each other's arms, wide awake, not wanting the day and the night to end.

'Tell me about New York,' Naomi said.

'What do you want me to tell you?' Tom asked.

'Anything and everything. Where you live, where you work, where you shop. What sort of apartment you have, who your neighbours are. Everything!'

'I've told you a lot of this before,' Tom said. 'I don't think there's much new to tell.'

'It doesn't matter. If you had children you'd know that what they like best are the familiar stories, the ones they've heard a hundred times, the ones they could probably recite to you, word for word.'

She had, at the moment, that childlike desire to seek comfort in the familiar, even though it was familiar only through Tom's telling and not her own experience.

'Tell me again!' she said.

He told her. He told her that he lived in SoHo, which was nothing at all like London's Soho and simply meant that it was an area south of a wide thoroughfare named Houston Street, a wide crosstown street. That its imposing buildings, seemingly made of pale stone, pillared, finely and elaborately carved in classical designs, were in fact made of moulded cast iron and were nineteenth-century relics of what had once been a thriving industrial area. It was now, Tom said, largely an area for artists and craftsmen, for fashionable restaurants and, surprisingly, for small shops.

If you knew which was the hottest restaurant, he told her, and you chose to stand outside where the TV stretch limos and photographers congregated, you could be fairly sure of seeing the glitterati of stage, screen and the fashion world arriving to eat (and to be seen).

'But only while it's hot,' Tom said. 'It can be all the rage in September and it'll be somewhere different, just three blocks away, before Christmas!'

The huge buildings which had once been noisy with manufacturing industry were now divided into expensive and sought after lofts, usually one vast floor being a single loft.

'But I only have half a floor because a professor's salary doesn't run to a whole one,' Tom said.

'And you live on the top floor,' Naomi said, for all the world like a child prompting the bedtime storyteller.

'That's right! And the other half of the floor is rented by Mary-Beth Constantine,' he said. 'But I have the whole of the roof garden because Mary-Beth doesn't like gardening, though she's looking after it while I'm away.'

'Shall I meet her?' Naomi asked.

'Of course.'

There was a pause.

'And your parents live upstate?'

'They do. And you'll meet them.'

'They won't approve of me,' Naomi said.

'Of course they will! They'll just love you.'

He waited for her reply but it didn't come. She was fast asleep. The following morning when Tom left for the university

270

Naomi set off for Amersham's. She was not looking forward to the day because she had promised Tom, over their cornflakes, that she would definitely speak to Mr Swaine. Nice and polite though he was, she did not think he would take kindly to her request for a month off when she had been working only a few weeks.

He did not.

'It will be quite awkward, Mrs Fletcher,' he said. 'By the middle of May Bath will be full of visitors, we could be quite busy. You have only just found your way around things and begun to be useful. What will I do with someone completely new?'

'I'm sorry,' Naomi said. 'It's very important to me.' If she lost her job, then she lost it.

Suddenly, the idea hit her.

'Perhaps Mrs Fulneck would come and help out?'

'She has her baby. It's the reason she left us,' Mr Swaine pointed out.

'She left to have it. Perhaps now her mother would look after it for a while. It is only eight working days – ten at the most. Would you like me to ask her?'

'No,' Mr Swaine said. 'I'll ask her myself. It would be the best solution, but I don't hold out any hope, none at all!'

He had been quite wrong, he admitted later in the day. He had telephoned Mrs Fulneck and she had jumped at the chance.

'In my day no mother would have left a young baby, even with its grandmother,' he said. 'But I suppose it's as well for us that things have changed.'

'So there you are!' Tom said when Naomi told him that evening. 'I told you it would work out!'

He was pleased for her simply because it stopped her worrying about it. In his scenario she would not go back to Amersham's because her place was to be with him in New York.

'Clever clogs!' Naomi said. 'And are you going to tell me how it will work out with my mother? I thought of going to see her tomorrow.'

'Wait until the weekend,' Tom said. 'And I'll go with you.'

Naomi shook her head.

'I must break it to her myself. I owe her that much. We can both go together at the weekend but not until I've been first.'

She was thankful, visiting her mother next day, to find her in a reasonable state of mind, quite able to take in what Naomi was saying to her, though she was not happy about it.

'Four weeks is a long time,' she said. 'Who's going to come and see me?'

'Well Hugh will for one,' Naomi said. 'You know he'll be living in London well before I leave. He intends to visit you much more often. Hugh's very fond of you!' She hoped that last bit was true.

'And who else?' Doris asked.

'I expect Isobel will.'

She would bully Isobel into it. She would just have to come. If she didn't want to bring Harry, then Patrick would have to look after him.

'And I'll write to you, and telephone you, Mother!' Naomi promised.

Doris looked suddenly afraid. She reached out and grabbed Naomi's hand.

'You will come back, won't you?' she said. 'You won't stay out there for ever?'

'Of course I'll come back!' Naomi promised. 'You'll see, the time will pass quite quickly!'

All too quickly, she thought. All too quickly.

How could I leave her for ever? Naomi asked herself as she walked home. It would be like abandoning a child. But she would say nothing of this to Tom. There was nothing he could do to solve it, and in their time together her firm intention was to introduce no note of sadness about those things for which there was no solution. Those she would keep in her own heart, bring them out only when she was alone.

On an evening later in the week Hugh telephoned. Tom was at a meeting in the university or he might well have answered the phone. He and Naomi had decided that there was to be no fudging about the fact that they were living together, which included that whoever was the nearer to the telephone would answer it, whether it rang in the middle of the day or the middle of the night. They would make no announcements about their new life together, nor would they make denials. 'In fact,' Naomi asked, 'who cares?' 'Hugh does,' she answered herself. So because she wanted no more arguments with him she was pleased she had picked up the receiver.

He was, strangely, all sweetness and light.

'How are you, Ma? Are you well?'

'Very well, dear. And you?'

'I'm fine!' Hugh said. 'You'll be pleased to hear I've found a place to live. A small flat, minuscule really, but near to the theatre.'

'Why, that's wonderful!' Naomi said. She was truly pleased.

'The snag is,' he said, sounding rather less cheerful, 'I have to find fifteen hundred pounds, rent in advance. It's quite usual, all above board, but naturally I can't lay hands on that amount . . .'

There was a pause. He is waiting for me to offer it, Naomi thought. And why couldn't he lay hands on it? He'd been in work, not highly paid it was true, but regular, ever since he left university. No doubt he had not saved a penny. A year ago it wouldn't have been a problem, she and Edward would have found it – money hadn't been one of their problems, but that was no longer the case now.

'So I wondered, Ma, if you could let me have it? I'd be eternally grateful!'

'Of course you would,' Naomi agreed. 'And I'd like to help, but I'm not sure I can. How would you propose to pay it back? I'd need something regular because I have my own expenses.'

'Pay it back? Well, I hadn't thought about the details. We'd have to discuss it.'

'Yes.'

It was as clear as crystal. He had not thought at all in terms of a loan. It was to be a gift.

'As a matter of fact,' Hugh said, 'I could ask Grandma! I'm sure she'd help!' And there'd be no nonsense from his grandmother about paying back. She wouldn't need it, would she? The only problem with Grandma was catching her in the right mind for as long as it took her to do it.

'I wouldn't want you to ask Grandma,' Naomi said firmly.

'She's not fit to be bothered. And of course you'd have to go through her solicitor. She can't just hand out amounts like that.'

'I can't wait for the due process of the law,' Hugh said, trying not to show his impatience. 'I'd lose it!'

'I understand that,' Naomi said. 'Leave it with me and I'll see if I can work out something. I'll ring you.'

'Thanks, Ma. I knew I could rely on you!'

'I haven't said you can. I've said I'll try,' Naomi reminded him. 'Oh, by the way,' – (it was not 'by the way' she thought, it was central to her life) – 'I have news for you. I'm going to New York mid-May instead of in June. Tom has to leave here on April sixteenth.'

'He's leaving for good?'

'Yes.' That will please you, she thought.

'Well, you know what I think about this whole thing,' Hugh began.

Naomi cut in.

'Yes I do. So we won't go into that any further.'

She was right, Hugh thought. At any rate for the moment. He was desperate for the fifteen hundred pounds. And in spite of what his mother said, and even if she came up with the goods, he would sound out his grandmother. That was the one good thing about his mother haring off to America for a month; he would have a clear field with Grandma.

When Tom came home Naomi told him about Hugh's call. 'I can't quite decide what to do,' she confessed.

'Could you let him have the money?'

'Actually, yes. It's not highly convenient, but I could.'

'Then why don't you? It's a good enough reason for him to ask, and even though he should be able to do it himself, the truth is, he can't. Tell him you'll sort out a way for him to repay you, but let him have the money now.'

'You're right,' Naomi said. 'It would make me feel better, too!' And how nice Tom was, she thought. Hugh had never been anything other than rude to him.

A little later they had finished supper, which had been a plate of tagliatelle eaten while sitting in front of the fire, balancing trays, when the telephone rang. Naomi stretched out a hand to answer it, hoping that it was not Hugh.

'Edward!'

She shouted in surprise. Tom rose to his feet to leave the room but she motioned him to sit down again.

'I'm quite well, Edward,' she said. 'But I'm quite sure you can't be phoning to enquire about my health.'

'I'm not,' he said. 'Except that what I hear makes me ask if there is actually something wrong with you!'

'So what do you hear? And from whom?'

She could guess what he'd heard – and from whom. Cecily was the only one who kept in touch with him.

'I hear that you're off to America with a man you hardly know, you've only just met him and you're going to *live* with him. Have you taken leave of your senses?'

'I would say, rather, that I've come to my senses. Not that it has anything to do with you. Anyway, since you're interested, let me give the correct version.'

Tom looked up in surprise at the steeliness of her voice. He had never heard this in her before.

'I'm going to stay for a month in New York with a friend who lives there, though at the moment he is here. I am going of my own free will, indeed I'm looking forward to it. And yes, I shall be living with him while I'm there – if by living you mean sharing his bed, and I'm doing so now, until he leaves. But you know all about that sort of thing, don't you? How is the baby, by the way?'

'I was concerned about you, that's all,' Edward said. 'I just hope this man is trustworthy.'

'Oh absolutely!' Naomi said. 'He's right here now. Would you like me to introduce you? And there's another thing, since you're concerned about your family. Hugh – remember Hugh? – is in need of fifteen hundred pounds for his new flat. I'll give you his telephone number in case you're able to help him.'

'I've always told Hugh that when he got himself a proper job I'd be right behind him,' Edward said. 'I'm not pouring money into the theatre!'

'Thank you for ringing,' Naomi said. 'Goodnight!'

'Wow!' Tom cried. 'You scared me to death!'

'I hope I did the same to Edward,' Naomi said. 'But I doubt it! Anyway, *I* feel better for it! So why don't we just forget him? Why don't we forget everyone? From now on do what we said we'd do. Concentrate on ourselves, on being together.'

Afterwards, thinking back – she had just seen Tom off on the afternoon flight, waving to him through the glass-panelled doors, which cut off those who were travelling from those who remained behind, until he was no more than a speck in the distance – that was exactly what they had done in those too few precious weeks. Tom, his work in the university winding up, had taken days off when Naomi was not working at Amersham's. They had visited Bristol, Cheltenham and other places; they had taken a boat on the river, gone to the theatre, the cinemas, museums and exhibitions. They had shopped. They had visited restaurants and they had cooked for each other lovingly at home. They had visited Naomi's mother, together or just Naomi on her own. Sometimes she had known them, sometimes they had been strangers to her. They had made wondrous, exciting, passionate love.

Everything they had done together Naomi had stored in her mind against the time when all she had would be memories.

She never knew how she had made the journey back from the airport to her empty flat, but from that moment she began to mark off on the calendar, in her diary, in her head, the days which must elapse before she would see Tom again.

TWENTY-TWO

'Chicken or lamb, madam?'

Naomi was awakened from what, she felt, had been the brief-est of naps by the voice of the stewardess who was standing patiently by her stainless-steel trolley.

'I'm sorry. I didn't realize . . . lamb, please!'

Quickly, she unclipped and pulled down the folding table, and in perfect synchronization with her the stewardess – or should it be flight attendant, Naomi asked herself, they changed their job titles didn't they? – deposited a plastic tray full of goodies. Naomi made a close inspection. Everything, except a little foil box, warm to the touch, which presumably housed the lamb, was in sealed, see-through plastic containers. A tomato salad, bread roll, pat of butter, a square of cheese, two crackers and a mousse-like dessert with a blob of cream on top. There was a small carton of fresh spring water, a container of milk, a plastic cup, a small tumbler, salt, pepper, knife, fork, two spoons, serviette and toothpick. And now the stewardess was at her side again.

'Red wine or white, madam?'

The wine, in a dinky little bottle, was the only commodity for which there was no designated space on the tray. Naomi pondered on how she might move things around but the designer had been there before her. A place for everything and everything

277

in its place. In the end she stood the wine bottle inside the teacup.

Did other people eat this amount of lunch every day? she asked herself. All these courses? It was a far cry from her usual cheese sandwich and she was sure she couldn't manage the half of it, yet when she looked around the other passengers, those who were not opening recalcitrant plastic wrappings with their teeth were steadily munching as if they might never see food again.

Perhaps that was it? Suppose for some reason the plane didn't reach New York when it should? Suppose for some reason they were diverted? Or there wasn't room for them to land? Or some other reason far too awful to contemplate?

She had had a beagle once, Flora, which ate everything in sight, and when there was nothing in sight would break loose and ransack dustbins, returning home with a swollen belly and, if the food had been suspect, throw up liberally in the garden.

'The beagle is a hunting dog,' the vet had told her. 'He eats whenever he gets the chance in case there should be no food tomorrow. The beagle,' he added sternly, 'is not suitable for domestication.'

She had better join the pack. Several of those around her – and from her aisle seat she had a view of her fellow passengers – were well on with lamb or chicken, some starting to open the dessert. She had the feeling that if she didn't get on with it her tray might be snatched away before she had eaten.

She opened the foil container. New season's lamb, the menu had promised, with mint sauce, fresh garden peas, baby new potatoes and julienne carrots. The sight of it reminded her of something, and then it came to her: Meals on Wheels – which she had delivered every Friday morning for several years and about which her elderly clients had constantly grumbled. She now knew why, but she said to herself what she had so often said to them – 'Come on now, eat it up! It will do you good!'

She ate most of the dessert, it was surprisingly good, but the hermetically sealed cheese defeated her. She contemplated whether she would risk her teeth on trying to bite it open, but remembering that she had still not visited the dentist, and the likely cost of dental treatment in New York deterred her. All that remained was the coffee which, apart from the fact that in opening the little carton of milk she splashed it liberally over the tray and her person, was good.

Looking around she wondered where all those people were she met from time to time who said, 'Of course, I never eat a *thing* on the plane!' Not on this flight, for sure!

She had hardly settled down to her book when the hot towels came. Always something to divert one, spread out through the long hours of the flight to relieve the boredom. Next there would be the film and later, no doubt, the duty free, which would bring them nicely to the tea trolley.

She buried her face in the hot, steamy towel. Delicious! And never mind what it wrought with this morning's careful make-up. She would repair that when she ventured to the loo, which would not be yet as there was a long line waiting.

She smiled at the young woman who collected the towels, handling them with a pair of tongs. She was so slender, they all were. Two of them could easily pass in the aisle without touching each other, which would be more than any two passengers, taken at random, could manage.

Air hostesses, she remembered they had been called when she was at school. That was it! Everyone in her form, except for Hilda Grange and Carol Branch, the form swots who had gone to Oxford and Cambridge respectively and were now high up in the civil service, had wanted to be one and, hopefully, end up marrying the pilot.

The woman in the seat next to her rose.

'Will you excuse me?' she said politely. 'I'm sorry to disturb you. There's not a lot of room, is there?'

'That's true,' Naomi agreed. 'And you're not disturbing me.'

The woman, though pleasant enough, and having made a few desultory remarks at the beginning of the journey, had not seemed to want to talk, and this suited Naomi. Looking backward over the weeks since Tom had left Bath, and even more to what was now only a few hours away, she had more than enough to occupy her mind. It was good just to sit and think, or even just to drift into sleep if that should happen. And she supposed it was because of everything else going on in her head that she found herself unable to watch the movie, unable to keep on watching, that was. She did try, but it was complicated, all about a more-than-human dolphin. The sound quality through her headset was not good and before long she lost track, and gave it up. It was clearly enjoyable to people around. There were ripples of laughter and from the woman next to her, who had made it back to her seat minutes before the movie started, a few quiet chuckles.

Naomi closed her eyes and thought about Tom. She longed so much to be with him, not only to be in his arms – which she did – but to talk with him, eat with him, discover New York with him. He had telephoned, of course, and they had chatted – or rather he had chatted and she had listened. She was never totally at home with the telephone unless for business matters. She did not have the gift for chatting to someone she could not see. It was a gift all her children had in abundance. The size of the telephone bills when they were at home had been a bone of contention with Edward. It appeared that Tom had the same facility as her children. Born of practice, he'd said, 'Americans spend half their lives on the phone!'

Hugh, as she'd told Tom, had been down to Bath twice. Each time he'd gone to see his grandmother and each time on his own. When she'd suggested going with him he'd pointed out that if he and she went separately, then it made extra visits for his grandmother.

'You can go on a weekday, and when I'm here I can go on a Sunday. It makes sense!' he'd said.

It did of course. Naomi didn't quite know why she was uneasy about it. 'I can't see that he can be after her for money,' she said. 'I let him have the fifteen hundred pounds.'

'Loaned or given?' Tom asked.

'Lent – though I've not yet worked out the details of repayment.'

'You should have. Anyway, I don't think you need worry about him with your mother. When she's all there I reckon she's a match for Hugh any day. And when she's not all there she's even more than a match because he can't get through to her.'

'I hope you're right,' Naomi had said. 'I dare say you are. Anyway, he's going to come down and visit once or twice while

I'm with you. And Isobel says she'll visit her grandmother, though she could hardly refuse to do otherwise, since I've offered her the use of my car while I'm in New York! She was pleased about that.'

Cecily, too, had said she would try to fit in a visit to River View, if Sean was free, but at the moment he was working quite hard. 'And we don't like to be separated,' she'd added.

Whatever happened to Cecily? Naomi asked herself as the film ended and all through the plane the window blinds clicked up, letting in some welcome daylight. The answer was that Cecily had fallen in love, and out had gone reason. She hoped that wasn't true of herself. But surely not? Surely she was older and wiser, though there were times, thinking of Tom, when she felt like a young girl again, younger by far than his thirty-three years. It was at these times she had no qualms whatsoever, she knew everything would be all right.

The flight information was being shown on the screen again. They were now more than halfway through the journey and the thought gave her a surge of happiness, as if she already had one foot in America. It seemed an appropriate time to alter her watch. Five hours back, almost as though she had been given five extra hours of life to spend with Tom. Her neighbours had been surprised by her decision to go to New York, though Dan Sheridan less so than Emily. 'If you'll trust me with a key,' he'd said, 'I'll keep an eye on things for you. Take in the post and so on.' Mr Patel had wished her well and presented her with a small phial of a delicately scented liquid which, he said, was made from many different essences and spices. 'It is good for travelling,' he said. 'Or if you are tired or have a headache. Rub a few drops on your wrists and you will be refreshed!'

What nice friends and neighbours she had! How fortunate she was to have them after so short a time living in Bath. Except that every minute was taking her nearer to Tom, she might almost be sorry to be leaving them.

She wished she could be as happy about her mother as she was about others, but she was not. She had visited her assiduously over the last few weeks, trying to prepare her for the fact that she would be going away. 'I'll write to you,' she promised. 'I'll

281

telephone you. It'll be quite exciting to have a phone call from New York, don't you think?'

Doris had refused to be mollified, refused even to talk about the prospect, as if ignoring it meant that it would not happen.

'The time will fly!' Naomi assured her. *That* was all too true.

She was aware her mother understood her, or did so most of the time, though there had been two occasions when she had not known Naomi at all, had treated her as if she were a complete stranger. On the first of the two occasions she had been quite polite.

'It's nice of you to come and visit me,' she'd said. 'Are you from the Women's Institute? I'm a lifelong member of course! People keep coming to see me,' she'd confided. 'It's very nice of them but I don't know who they are or why they've come!'

On the second occasion she'd been openly rude. 'I don't know who you are and I don't want you here,' she'd said. 'I shall have to ask Matron not to let you in!'

Naomi had talked to Matron, who did not offer a great deal of comfort, simply stating the obvious.

'Sometimes,' she'd said, 'your mother is as clear and bright as either you or I, sometimes the reverse. There's nothing to be done about it. Don't worry about her while you're away. You've earned a break and we'll take good care of her.'

'I know you will,' Naomi said. 'I'm grateful for that.'

'She enjoys your son's visits,' Matron said. 'She doesn't always know who he is but she is markedly happier after he's been.'

Is she so with me? Naomi wondered. Do I make the slightest difference? But whether she did so or not was beside the point. She's my mother, she thought. I wouldn't be in the world without her, I wouldn't be speeding towards Tom. I can't abandon her because she shows no gratitude, because half the time she doesn't even know who I am. Gratitude had nothing to do with it. How much gratitude did I show her for bringing me up? You did things from duty, because it was the way the world worked, and from love.

She wished, not for the first time but certainly more fervently than ever before, that she had siblings with whom she could share all this. What must it be like to have a sister or a brother?

She took her book out of the seat pocket, found the place and began to read again, and in no time at all fell asleep.

Once again she was awakened by the stewardess, this time pushing a trolley laden with all the enticements of duty-free goods, which Naomi politely waved away. Much more fun, if she wanted to shop, to do so with Tom in New York. In any case, or so she'd heard, things were at the moment cheaper there than in England.

There was a curious atmosphere in the plane now. It felt quite different from the way it had before she'd fallen asleep, her thoughts full of her mother. There was a feeling in the air of excitement, a buzz, almost tangible as if one could raise a hand and touch it. And it was not only a feeling. People, so many of them, in small ways, were behaving differently. They were walking up and down the aisles, they were talking to each other. She looked at her watch and was amazed to see that she must have slept for more than an hour. That was it! They were getting near, they were getting so near.

All her thoughts of England, of her mother, her children, of Lucy for whom she'd had to find a substitute teacher for a month, a situation about which neither she nor Lucy had been madly happy, were now left behind. Far more than three thousand miles of land and sea separated her from them. Every feeling, every thought in her head, was going forward now. When she'd been a small child she would lean forward in the car, believing that by so doing she'd make it go faster, they would reach the seaside sooner. That was the feeling she had now.

Duty free over, tea was now being served in a rush, and then equally quickly cleared away, but not before she had eaten a dainty ham sandwich and a doughnut. Almost before the last tray had vanished people were beginning to check their belongings, collect them together. Although the information board showed quite clearly that forty-five minutes must pass before they would land, hair was being combed, shoes fastened, lipstick reapplied.

My passport! Naomi thought. Where did I put my passport?

It was exactly where it should be, in the inner compartment of her handbag. And where else would it be? she chided herself.

How could it have escaped and gone walkies while she had been sitting here, practically immobilized, for the last six hours? She checked the details, leafed through it. Minorca 1988. That had been a good holiday, the children young. France 1992. She and Edward, most unusually, had gone to Paris for three days. Hugh had been away from home by then, Isobel in her first year at university. Cecily had stayed with her grandmother. Cecily and my mother adored each other then, Naomi thought. For that matter, so did I with Edward, though she recalled that the holiday in Paris had been spent largely in museums. She closed her passport and put it away again.

Surely, she thought, the plane is losing height? They were asked to fasten their seat belts. Was that normal, so far away from landing? She supposed it was. A man rose from the seat in front and began to retrieve belongings from the overhead compartment, an anorak and a carry-on bag, determined that when the starting pistol went for the race off the plane he would be first off the mark. A flight attendant with a tight smile moved swiftly towards him.

'I'm sorry, sir! That's not allowed just yet!' She spoke as one who was saying it for the thousandth time and was only just restraining an impulse to smack his hands. Nevertheless he had won. Wearing his anorak, clutching his bag, he was ready for the off.

It was strange how the last twenty minutes seemed the longest of the entire flight, and not because nothing was happening. In a way it was action-packed, the plane descending, almost dropping, Naomi thought, then levelling, rising a little, dropping again, so that landing seemed inevitable – but no, it wasn't to be, not just yet. When it came, a quiet gentle thud, it was an anticlimax.

If the landing time had seemed drawn out it was as nothing compared to the time from leaving the plane, stepping out into the air which, though fuel-laden, seemed fresh after the confines of the plane, until all the formalities were through. She went through it like an automaton, steeling herself to endure each trying stage which stood between her and her goal. She stood in a long, long line which snaked its way around to the immigration booths where she was questioned so closely, so fiercely, by an unhappy-looking man that she wondered whether she would be allowed into the country or immediately deported. Do I look like a woman who will burst into the White House and kidnap the president? she asked herself. Eventually, however, he stamped her passport, reluctantly she was sure, with a thud which shook his counter. 'Have a nice day!' he said.

Compared to that, getting herself through baggage claim, finding her suitcase, clearing customs, though time-consuming and tedious, were a doddle. And then all her tedium, fatigue, misgivings, worries and cares vanished like the snow in summer as she wheeled her trolley through the automatically opened doors and saw Tom, not a dozen yards away, waving to her.

He pushed the trolley to one side and took her in his arms, holding her tightly as if he would never let her go. It was, Naomi thought – though she was hardly capable of thought – the crowning point of her life so far. Nothing, *nothing*, had ever been like this before. No words were said on either side. There were none which could express such feelings. They had no idea, either then or afterwards, how long they had remained there, locked in each other's arms. The trolley could have been stolen, wheeled away never to be seen again. People bumped into them. It didn't matter. In the end Tom said, 'Let's go! Let's get home!'

He grabbed the trolley, Naomi clung to his arm.

'The car's in the parking lot,' he said.

Sitting beside him as he manoeuvred his way through the rush hour New York traffic, Naomi saw nothing of her surroundings clearly, though later she had impressions of wide, many-laned highways, bridges, tunnels, a river, toll booths. There was little conversation between them, now was not the time for what they had to say to each other, if indeed it could be expressed in words. Eventually he drove into a shabby-looking, busy street with broken pavements, rough roads, black plastic bags on the sidewalk piled against trees in large planters. He turned the car into a parking lot and the man in charge came forward to greet him.

'Hi, Tom!' he said.

'Hi!' Tom said. He helped Naomi out of the car. 'This is a

friend from England, Naomi. She's staying for a few weeks. This is Mark.'

'Have a good visit,' Mark said.

'Thanks!' Tom said.

They crossed the road. Immediately opposite the parking lot Tom unlocked a street door, unprepossessing, shabby, not at all what Naomi expected.

'At least we have an elevator,' Tom said, following her in. 'Ancient, but it works. Otherwise you'd have to walk up five floors.'

It didn't matter. She would have climbed Mount Everest with him.

The elevator came to a shuddering halt and they were in a narrow passage with two doors.

'This is mine,' Tom said, unlocking it with a series of twists and turns with two keys. 'The other door is Mary-Beth's. I told you she has the other half of the floor. You'll meet her later.'

Not this evening, Naomi hoped.

'Not this evening,' Tom said, catching her thought. 'This evening is ours. There's no-one in the world except you and me. I won't even answer the phone.'

Tom's door opened into a large room of which Naomi's immediate impression was space and light. There was no time to register more. She was in Tom's arms and this time there was no waiting trolley, no milling crowds. As Tom had said, they were alone in the world.

TWENTY-THREE

When Naomi opened her eyes next morning her very first thought was to wonder what had happened to her bedroom curtains, pale turquoise with a silk stripe. They were not there. Instead the early light was filtering into the room through a cream, narrow-slatted venetian blind, throwing a pattern onto the opposite wall. The confusion lasted no more than seconds, and then she knew she was in New York, in Tom's bed, and he was asleep beside her.

She lay still, not wishing to disturb him, reminding herself that his body clock was five hours behind hers and that though to her it felt like the middle of the morning, for Tom it was no way near time to come to life. Last night it had been the other way. She, in spite of her longing to savour every moment of her first evening in New York, and never mind that she had had two naps on the plane, had nodded over the meal Tom had prepared for them. He had taken pity on her, they had gone to bed early and she had fallen asleep quickly in his arms. Now she was awake and refreshed and looking forward with a mixture of excitement and contentment to the day ahead.

Already the traffic had started with the rumble of heavy trucks. Tom had explained that the loft was no more than thirty yards away from Broome Street which was a main route to the Holland

Tunnel to New Jersey, and that the noise of trucks was a fact of life.

'You'll get used to it,' he'd said. 'We do. And we're constantly trying to get the city to do something about it.'

She raised herself on her elbow and turned to look at him. He slept so peacefully, his breathing hardly moving the bed sheet, half on his back, half on his side, his right arm stretched out towards the wall, his shoulders bare. He looked so strong, so young; his skin shone with life and health. There was a faint blue stubble around his cheeks and chin. She wanted to touch it. She loved him so much. She had missed him desperately in the short time they had been apart. How would she bear it when the time came to leave New York?

She must try not to think so far ahead. She must, and she was determined she would, grasp each day and enjoy it to the full. And to begin with she would leave the bedroom now, quietly so as not to disturb Tom, and make a cup of tea.

She tiptoed along the short corridor, from which she knew doors led to a small study, an even smaller bedroom and a bathroom, towards the living room, one corner of which was fitted as a kitchen. The blinds had not been closed yesterday evening; they had spent time looking out into the busy street, noisy with traffic, full of people, vibrant with life, and now the daylight, lit by the early morning sun, streamed in along two sides of the room through tall sash windows, picking out the high ceiling, elaborately embossed in designs from the classical age. But it was not, Tom had told her, a plaster ceiling however much it looked like it. It was made entirely of tin, moulded tin. It was its own work of art, manufactured in the nineteenth century, at the same time the ironmasters were creating the classically inspired, magnificent buildings with their columns, friezes, architraves, mouldings which, looking out from Tom's loft, met the eye in every direction.

The floor of the loft, in contrast to the ornate ceiling and the pillars which went up to meet it, was plain and functional; wooden boards with the patina of years, solidly constructed to bear the weight of the machinery which, all those years ago, had been placed on them.

Not without a search, she found Earl Grey tea-bags in a tin. Last night Tom had shown her where everything was including, she was fairly sure, the tea caddy, but she'd been too tired to take it in.

'But in any case,' he'd said, 'if you want anything, anything at all, waken me. I don't want to be asleep when you're awake. I want to spend every possible minute with you!'

Even so, she thought, carrying her tea to the table which stood in front of a window, I shan't waken him yet.

Looking down towards Broome Street the traffic was beginning to build up, still mainly large trucks but now also vans and cars, and far more bicycles, roller-blades and skateboards than she had ever expected so early in the day. There was also a great cacophony of car horns, blaring, impatient, and in the near distance, possibly from Broadway she thought, the piercing noise of a siren – police or fire engine, she didn't yet know the difference, but louder by far than anything she had heard in England. Broadway, in the short time she'd been here, had been her greatest surprise. They had driven a short stretch of it on the way from the airport. Tom had laughed at her.

'What did you expect?' he'd asked.

'I hadn't really thought about it,' she confessed. 'But not all shops and offices and not a sign of a theatre!'

'Broadway's very long,' he said. 'It takes in most things. I promise you'll see the theatres later!'

Facing the window, she neither saw nor heard Tom as he came, barefoot, into the room. When his hands came down on her shoulders she jumped to her feet with a small scream and he twisted her around to face him, and kissed her, long and hard.

'You left me!' he accused her. 'Didn't I tell you never to leave me!'

'You were sound asleep,' Naomi said. 'I didn't like to disturb you. Would you like some tea?'

'Not right now,' Tom said.

When he finally released her she went across to the kitchen, poured a mug of tea and brought it back to him at the table.

'It still surprises me that you drink tea,' she said. 'I had thought all Americans drank coffee.'

'And Americans think the English drink tea all the time,' he said. 'Not true in either case.'

He'd told her when they were in Bath that an English visitor to New York had brought him a packet of Earl Grey tea as a present and he'd been quickly hooked on it. 'And then I discovered you can buy it just about anywhere in New York – for a price,' he'd said.

They sat for a little while then Tom asked, 'What would you like to do today? Where would you like to go?'

'There are all sorts of places I'd like to see eventually,' Naomi answered. 'Museums, galleries, stores, parks – everything in fact, but more than any of that I want to do the things you normally do, the everyday things. I'd like to see the place where you work, the local shops you go to. I'd like to walk in the neighbourhood. I'm sure there are terrific places to visit, but I don't want to go back home having been only a tourist.'

'You won't,' Tom promised. 'That's the last thing I want. You know I want you to feel this is your home. Here, in New York, with me.'

'I'd like you to promise not to talk about that,' Naomi said. 'You know I can't make any promises. I don't want to spoil what time we do have.'

'There is no way I can promise not to talk about it,' Tom said firmly. 'No way at all. If you think I'm going to let you go without putting up a fight, you're crazy!'

'It's just that—'

'So be prepared,' Tom interrupted. 'I'll talk about it whenever I have to. I don't want to make you unhappy, but the worst unhappiness for both of us would be if we lost each other. Admit it, Naomi!'

She couldn't answer him. There was no answer. They sat in silence.

'OK,' Tom said. 'I won't mention it for the rest of today.'

'Thank you,' she said.

'But after that,' Tom said 'I can't promise.'

'What I would like to do, fairly soon, is phone home,' Naomi said. 'Just to say I'm here and everything's all right.'

'Sure! Who will you call?'

'Oh, Isobel.'

'Then I'll take a shower while you do that.'

Naomi dialled Isobel's number and was surprised by the speed with which her daughter answered.

'Just to tell you I'm here,' Naomi said. 'Everything's fine. How about you?'

'I'm fine,' Isobel said. 'So is Harry. He's just finished his lunch. Spinach and tuna. You might look around in New York, Ma, see if they have anything new in the way of baby foods. He likes variety, bless him!'

'I will!' Naomi promised. It would be a riveting experience. 'And what did you do in New York?' 'I searched for baby foods!'

'Have you been to see your grandmother?' she asked.

'Good heavens, Ma, you only left yesterday! Of course I haven't. I'll go in a day or two. It's a case of when I can leave Harry. I really don't think I'll risk taking him there.'

'I hope she's all right,' Naomi said.

'Of course she will be, Ma! Why wouldn't she be? And if she weren't they'd call me. They have my number.'

Isobel's tone was brisk, and what she said was true, even so Naomi was not completely reassured. Perhaps she should ring River View herself?

When Tom came out of the bathroom she said: 'Do you mind if I ring my mother? I'd feel easier if I did.'

'Sweetheart,' Tom said, 'there's no need to ask me every time you want to pick up the phone! You're living here. You're not a three-day guest!'

She was quickly through to River View.

'I'd like to speak to Matron,' she said. 'It's Mrs Fletcher, Mrs Campbell's mother. I'm ringing from New York.'

'Good afternoon, Mrs Fletcher!' Matron said.

'Good afternoon,' Naomi said, 'though it's not far into the morning here. I wondered how my mother was?'

'I saw her earlier,' Matron said. 'She's quite well.'

'Oh, good! Is she missing me, do you think?'

'I wouldn't think so, Mrs Fletcher. She saw you only the day before yesterday.' Matron's voice was unusually gentle.

'Of course! Do you think I could speak to her?'

'Certainly!' Matron agreed. 'Though it might not be totally satisfactory. Most of our ladies here aren't used to receiving telephone calls, let alone from New York. But I'll have you put through.'

Naomi waited a minute or so and then her mother's voice came, surprisingly clear and strong.

'They tell me someone's telephoning me from New York. I think there's some mistake. I don't know—'

'It's me, Mother!' Naomi interrupted.

Doris took no notice.

'. . . anyone in New York, and I *never* take calls from strangers!'

'I'm not a stranger . . . !'

'I think you must have the wrong number! In any case, I've had my lunch and it's time for my sleep!'

There was a click, and silence.

'What happened?' Tom asked.

'She hung up on me! She didn't know me. She thought I was a stranger. Oh Tom!'

She turned away from the telephone, her eyes filled with tears. Tom took her in his arms, stroked her hair.

'I'm sorry, Naomi! But it's no different from when you're there. Some days she knows you, some days she doesn't. As far as we know it doesn't trouble her. You're the one who feels it, and it's the same whether you're in New York or Bath.'

It wasn't, Naomi thought. It was different. But she wouldn't try to explain it. It was her problem.

'Take your shower,' Tom said. 'I'll make breakfast and then we'll decide what to do.'

In the end they decided to stroll around the neighbourhood, do a little light shopping, perhaps lunch out, perhaps not.

'We'll take it as it comes,' Tom said. 'Then this afternoon, as it's a beautiful day, I'll show you my roof garden.'

They walked two or three blocks to the east.

'Mulberry Street,' Tom said. 'This is where SoHo gives way to Little Italy.'

Turning south, Little Italy became Chinatown, the signs in Chinese, though Naomi could not have said precisely where one merged into the other. And somewhere between them was Canal Street. It ran, Tom told her, from east to west right across downtown Manhattan. It was wide, heavy with traffic moving in both directions and at crossing places at the corner of every block, when the lights changed in their favour, scores of pedestrians, every colour and nationality, though Asians predominated, swept across the road like an immense tidal wave, finally to be cast on the opposite shore.

She had never seen so many different shops, all of them packed with goods from floor to ceiling and frequently spilling out onto the pavement.

'I guess you can buy just about anything on Canal Street,' Tom said. 'Anything from a live lobster to a sofa bed or a fine diamond to a small screw. Which reminds me I need some picture hooks and a few coat hangers. I don't have enough hangers for you.'

They found both, the screws in an Aladdin's cave of hardware, the hangers on a table on the pavement, five for a dollar. Then Tom took her arm and they waited to cross the road.

'It's real easy,' he said. 'It says "Walk" or "Don't Walk". You do just as you're told. But New Yorkers ignore them. They cross when and where they want to.'

'Where are we going now?' Naomi asked.

'To buy fruit and vegetables,' Tom said. 'The best and cheapest are in Chinatown.'

So they were, on pavement tables and in abundance, every variety she had ever seen and almost as many she had not, all exquisitely displayed. Tom made a careful selection, examining each item, discarding some, choosing others.

'And now,' he said, 'I'll show you something you might or might not be familiar with!'

It was a collection of live lobsters, on a bed of crushed ice, moving lethargically, though every so often the vendor pulled a too adventurous one back into place.

Naomi shuddered.

'You don't like lobster?' Tom asked. 'You don't want to choose one?'

'You mean we take it home live?'

'Of course! In a shopping bag.'

'Actually, I do like lobster,' Naomi confessed. 'Though I've only ever seen it on the plate, ready to eat. Or out of a tin. Would you have to . . .' She hesitated.

'Plunge it into boiling water? I'm afraid so.'

'Then no. I couldn't be around when you did that.'

'Then we'll pass on lobster,' Tom said. 'For today. But I'm glad you're tender-hearted! Are you ready for some lunch? A beer and a sandwich?'

Tom led her off Canal Street, into a dark crowded bar. She chose a pastrami sandwich on rye, with pickle. Tom laughed at her expression when it was served.

'This is quite the biggest sandwich I've ever seen!' Naomi said. 'What do your countrymen think when they're served a sandwich in England?'

'I won't tell you,' Tom said. 'Except that it comes as a shock.'

They finished lunch. Tom drained his glass.

'What would you like to do next?' he asked.

'Go home,' Naomi said.

They walked two short blocks and turned onto Broadway. Cheap shops, expensive shops. Crowded displays of gold, amber, flashing crystal jewellery, real or not. Discounted designer perfumes, leather goods at what seemed to Naomi give-away prices. Fashion stores, all with sales. It was difficult to pass by. Naomi stopped in front of a display of amber jewellery, glowing in the sun.

'It's so lovely,' she said to Tom. 'And not at all expensive. A brooch each would be perfect for Isobel and Cecily.' She was hovering, halfway to purchasing.

'Wait!' Tom said. 'You've a lot to see yet. Anyway, they're here every day. We can come back.'

She tore herself away. 'I suppose you're right,' she said.

'It's a nice day,' Tom said as they turned the corner to Broome Street. 'Warmer than I reckoned it would be. We'll go up on the roof. In fact I must, I've got plants to water.'

'I can't think of anything I'd like better,' Naomi said.

In the apartment Tom put away the shopping, then they

gathered together cushions, newspapers, a bottle of water and binoculars.

'There's a pair of sparrowhawks nesting on a nearby roof,' Tom explained. 'They've got four fledglings. I watch them whenever I can.'

He led the way out of a door at the rear of the loft and up a steep flight of steps, at the top of which a door opened onto the flat roof. Naomi gasped with surprise as she stepped through the doorway.

'Why, it's beautiful! Who would have thought . . .'

'I suppose I'm quite proud of it,' Tom said. 'Half of it is Mary-Beth's, it goes with whoever rents the top floor, but she's not interested in gardening, she leaves it to me.'

'Doesn't she come up here to sit?' Naomi asked.

'Occasionally in the evening. Not often. I'll ask her while you're here.'

The roof was perhaps a hundred feet long and about thirty feet wide, with two wooden decks a foot or so high, one at either end of the roof and a walkway between them. On the deck where Naomi and Tom now stood was a wrought iron table and four chairs. On the far deck was a lounger and more chairs. But it was not the architectural features which took Naomi's breath away, it was the profusion and colour of things growing, lush and abundant, on this high plateau over the city streets. There was a breeze here, even though on the ground the air had been still.

'There's always a breeze,' Tom said. 'It's great in the hot weather, not so good when it grows into a roaring wind. That's one reason why everything's in heavy pots and planters, or tied down.'

'Did you do all this?' Naomi asked.

'Yes. Over a period.'

Along the tops of the walls he had fixed a strongly secured trellis, now further strengthened by its cover of Boston ivy. In wooden planters and whisky barrels small trees grew; a purple-leaved prunus, an acer or two, a crab apple, a Mountain Ash. Naomi recognized all except one.

'That's a European birch,' Tom said. 'A clump birch.'

In the bases of the barrels, the soil was covered with white and purple alyssum and blue lobelia. Over the sides of planters junipers grew down to the ground. From the middle of a planting of conifers and other shrubs a small fountain sprayed the air. Everywhere, or over at least two thirds of the roof, colour sang. Blue geraniums, white and red dianthus, orange and yellow nasturtiums, white potentilla. There was no end to it.

'The peonies are the most spectacular at this time of the year,' Tom said. 'But they didn't last, not up here. But come with me, there's a plant I can't identify and I don't know how it got here.'

She followed him to the far deck.

'Do you know the names of plants?' he asked.

'Quite a few,' Naomi admitted. 'I used to have a big garden.'

'Then tell me what this is!'

She felt a stab of pleasure because she recognized it at once.

'It's an aquilegia,' she said. 'I can tell by the leaves, and by the spur on the back of the flower. But I've never seen a yellow one before. It's quite beautiful. Mine are sort of purple.'

'So where did it come from?' Tom asked.

'Who knows? They sprang up all over the place in my garden. I reckon the birds carried the seeds.'

They continued to walk around the garden, identifying the plants, admiring them, dead-heading as they went. That was second nature to Naomi, who had seldom walked around the garden at Four Winds without a pair of secateurs in her hand. When the tour was completed they went and sat at the table.

'I'll go and fix some tea,' Tom said.

'No, let me!' Naomi said. 'Let me do something for you!'

The days flew by. The nights also. Days of joy and fun and pleasure. Days of museums and visits and walks by the harbour, of meals and shopping and gardening. Nights also of joy, and of love and passion and tenderness and fulfilment. Days and nights also, on Naomi's part, of anxiety, of fear for the future, of indecision, of argument.

She had found the Metropolitan Museum totally splendid, awesome, and the Frick, in spite of its grandeur, somehow intimate. It was her favourite so far. She had walked in Central Park. She had been dazzled by Fifth Avenue stores and then

Tom had taken her clothes shopping on the Lower East side where she had brought just a few beautifully tailored garments – a pants suit, a jacket, a skirt, at unbelievably cheaper prices.

She had particularly wanted to see where Tom worked and one day during her first week he had taken her up to the university. It was no more than a fifteen-minute walk up Broadway to West Fourth Street.

'I need to check something in the library,' he said. 'We can't take visitors in there. But I won't be long. You could wait for me in Washington Square Park – or perhaps you'd prefer to have a coffee in the Violet café? It's quite close.'

The day had been cool, spotting with rain, so she had chosen the latter. It lived up to its name. The colour violet was everywhere, not least on the low window-sills which were crammed with artificial violets.

'But why this particular colour?' she asked Tom when he joined her later.

'It's the NYU colour,' he said. 'All the teams are called the Violets – the women's teams are the Lady Violets – which perhaps explains why we don't have a football squad! How could you call an American football team "The Violets"? They've been trying to change it for a hundred and seventy years, but they never do.'

Since then they had been once to the theatre, once to a concert, twice to the movies. She had done everything, in fact, that could be expected of a visitor and much that would not have been, and it was the latter things which she knew she would cherish most. Quiet hours spent together in the apartment, meals cooked for each other, errands to the supermarket or the local deli. Perhaps the best of times had been those spent on the roof. Part of every fine day had seen them up there, working on the plants, playing Scrabble, reading, talking, or even just sitting quietly, saying nothing. They had quickly reached a stage where words didn't matter and silences were comfortable.

They talked in bed. When they had made love, when she was lying secure and happy in Tom's arms, in the dark, Naomi could say what she couldn't at other times. She could spill out her hopes and her fears without the restraint she felt at other times.

297

'I love you more than I've ever loved anyone in my life,' she confessed. 'I didn't know it was possible to love like this, or to be so loved.'

'I know,' Tom said. 'I know because it's the same for me. Truly it is. I'll love you as long as I live. I'd die for you.'

'And I for you,' Naomi said.

'But you won't live with me, now and for ever?' Tom said. 'You won't take the risk. You won't trust your own feelings, or is it me you won't trust? You're still afraid of what people will say because I'm younger than you are. You're afraid of the future with me!'

'No, I'm not!' Naomi protested. 'I've left that behind. Truly, I don't care about that any more. You're you and I'm me . . .'

'Made for each other,' Tom said softly.

'It isn't that. You know what it is, Tom.'

'It's your mother,' he said. 'So what about a man must leave his father and his mother and cleave only to his wife? Don't you believe that? Doesn't that apply to women, then?'

'Of course I believe it and of course it does,' Naomi said. 'But long before it applied to me I thought it was something easier said than done.'

'Nobody said it was easy,' Tom said. 'What about whether it's right? And your mother would be affected far less than many other parents. Half the time she doesn't know who you are!'

'But don't you see, Tom, that's the point,' Naomi said. 'If she was sensible, if I could talk to her, if we could discuss things rationally, if she could understand, but it's not like that. It's as if she's not my mother, it's as if the roles were reversed. She's my child. I'd be abandoning my child. We'd be at opposite sides of the world.'

The next day they were at breakfast, planning, later in the morning, to take the subway down to Battery Park and walk by the harbour.

'We could go over to Ellis Island,' Tom suggested. 'I went a few years ago when it was first opened. Now *there* are stories of people who weren't afraid to start a new life in a new country. Who knows what or who they had to leave behind?'

'I'm not afraid, not the least bit,' Naomi said sharply. 'And I don't need a trip to Ellis Island to prod me. Nothing there's going to solve my problem!'

Tom took her hand, kissed her fingers.

'I'm sorry! It wasn't my intention . . . I hadn't planned to go. It just entered my head, but we won't go. Perhaps we could—' He was interrupted by the telephone.

He listened for a moment, then handed it to Naomi. 'It's for you! Isobel!'

'I've got news for you, Ma!' Isobel said. She sounded unusually full of life.

'I'm listening, dear!'

'I'm pregnant, Ma! I thought I might be before you left, but I wanted to be sure. Well now it's confirmed! I'm so thrilled, and so is Patrick.'

'Well then I'm pleased for you,' Naomi said. 'It *is* a surprise . . . I mean Harry so young . . .'

'It will be wonderful for Harry!' Isobel enthused. 'A little sister for him! He'll be able to look after her.'

'You know it's a girl?' Naomi queried.

'Not exactly *know*, but I'm quite sure it will be. Selina, we thought we'd call her. Or Harriet, after Patrick's grandmother.'

'Well it's all quite unexpected news,' Naomi said.

'I was going to wait to tell you when you were home next week, but I just couldn't,' Isobel said.

'Well thank you for that,' Naomi said. 'Have you seen your grandmother?'

'Yesterday! She was quite well. We had a nice chat. She enjoyed hearing about Harry. I didn't tell her about the new baby. I wanted to tell you first – but you can pass it on if you like.'

'Thank you. I will,' Naomi said. 'I intend to ring her later in the day. Are you . . .' she hesitated, '. . . do you and Patrick think at all of getting married? I mean, now that . . .'

'Oh, I dare say we shall!' Isobel said happily. 'When we have time!'

'I don't know whether I'm pleased or not,' Naomi said to Tom when she gave him the news. 'Not that it's anything to do with me. But it won't be easy for Isobel. They never have two

299

ha'pennies to rub together. And the flat is quite unsuitable. No garden. And ferrying two babies up and down those stairs!'

'I guess they'll manage,' Tom said.

Later in the day Naomi telephoned her mother. She calculated the time so that it would be mid-evening in England, probably the most convenient time of the day for her mother. To her surprise and delight she was in good form, her mind as clear as crystal.

'You'll be home next week,' she said. 'I've marked the days on the calendar. I'll be glad to see you back, love!'

'I'm looking forward to seeing you,' Naomi said – and that part at least was the truth, no matter how she felt about the future. 'And I've got a bit of news for you!'

She told her about Isobel's baby.

'She could call it after me if it's a girl!' Doris said.

'Why don't you suggest that to her?' Naomi said.

'You can tell if it's going to be a girl or a boy,' Doris said.

Really, my mother is up-to-date medically, Naomi thought. She must know all about scans.

'Yes!' Doris continued. 'You thread a needle with a length of cotton and then the woman lies on her back and somebody holds it in the air over her belly, and according to which way it spins around you can tell the sex. I forget which way is which but I can find out. They'll know here.'

'Well, that's something else you can suggest to Isobel,' Naomi said.

'I will. And I'm going to drink my cocoa now, and go to sleep,' Doris said. 'I'm quite tired. Thank you for phoning, love!'

'Goodnight. God bless!' Naomi said.

It was four o'clock in the morning when the telephone rang in the apartment. Naomi heard it fractionally before Tom wakened but it was he who stretched out a hand and picked it up, and almost immediately handed it to Naomi.

'Tell your family how to calculate a five-hour time difference,' he said sleepily.

It was Matron.

'I'm afraid I have sad news for you, Mrs Fletcher. Your mother died in her sleep, some time during the night. I saw her

300

myself just before she went to bed. She told me she'd spoken to you. She was very happy, looking forward to seeing you soon.

'I've informed your elder daughter, but I wanted to speak to you myself. I wanted you to know that your mother died peacefully.'

TWENTY-FOUR

Naomi put down the telephone. She sat at the table, saying nothing, not moving. Staring ahead.

'What is it?' Tom said. 'What's happened?'

'My mother. She's dead. She died, in the night, in her sleep. That was Matron.'

He stood up, moved towards her and enfolded her in his arms, but she was rigid. Why am I not crying? she thought. Surely that was the thing to do? But there were no tears in her. She felt as if she was turned to stone. It was as if her whole body was dry, impervious.

'What happened?' Tom said gently. 'Tell me about it.'

'There's nothing to tell. They found her this morning. She'd been very happy, Matron said. She'd talked about me going home.'

'I see.' He stroked her hair, kissed her lightly on the top of her head. 'I guess it doesn't help to say it was the best way to die, my darling, but it was.'

'No, it doesn't help,' Naomi said. 'I know it's true, but I don't feel it. I don't feel anything – anything at all.'

There was silence then which Tom did not try to break. He pulled a chair close and sat beside her, holding her hand in his. After a while she spoke, the words pouring out of her.

'You see I've never had to deal with death before. I wasn't

around too much when my father died. I didn't want to be. I didn't like him. I thought the world would be a better place without him. In any case my mother was there. There wasn't anything she couldn't cope with. I wasn't responsible for anything. Now I am. All of a sudden I'm responsible and I don't know what to do.'

She was babbling and she knew it, not making any particular sense even to herself.

'I must go home,' she said. 'I must go home right away!'

'Of course!' Tom agreed. 'We'll both go. I'll ring the airline right away, see how quickly we can get a flight.'

'No,' she said. Suddenly she knew what she must do and, even more, what she must not do. It was clear. 'No. I must go on my own. You mustn't come with me. I have to be on my own. You must understand. I have to be with my family. I'm head of the family now. Me, head of the family! Doesn't that sound silly!'

'Sure I understand and I won't intrude,' Tom promised. 'I just want to be with you, I want to look after you. *You* need someone.'

'Thank you,' she said. 'But you can't. I know that for certain.'

Her brain was beginning to function. Matron, she remembered, had told Isobel and Isobel would have phoned Cecily and Hugh. Hugh would come straight down to Bath, she was sure of that. He would want to look after her and it was his place to do so, not Tom's.

'Will you get me on a plane?' she said. 'Do you think I might get a flight this evening?'

'I'll try. It's Friday – always busy – but I'll try. Oh, sweetheart, I'm so sorry! Are you sure I can't come with you? I want to help. I wouldn't get in the way. I'd stay in a hotel. I just want to be there for you.'

'No. Really not. I'm quite sure about it. Just get me a seat on a plane.'

With every bit of her she wanted to be back in England. She felt as though she could not bear the time which must past until she set foot in Bath. She felt – she knew it was stupid – that if she hadn't left Bath in the first place this would not have happened.

'I'll do it right away,' he said.

She listened anxiously while he telephoned. It was clear that he was having difficulty. Presently he turned to her.

'There's nothing to Bristol. If you want to go this evening the best they can do is a flight to Gatwick. You'd have to get yourself from there to Bath.'

'I'll take it,' Naomi said. 'I don't want to wait until tomorrow. Hugh or Isobel can pick me up at Gatwick. She has my car.'

'Let me call her,' Tom offered when he had made the booking. 'Or Hugh.'

'No. I'll do it,' Naomi said.

She was saved the trouble. Within minutes the phone rang, Tom answered it, and passed the phone to Naomi.

'Hugh,' he said.

Naomi's conversation with Hugh was brief. When she hung up there were tears running down her face.

'What did he say?' Tom asked.

'He said he'd meet me at Gatwick.'

He looked at her intently.

'What else?'

She was in full flood now, hardly able to get the words out.

'He said . . . he said, "What a pity you weren't there, Ma!" He was right.'

Tom took a sharp breath, controlled his anger. It was not the time for it.

'He's wrong,' he said as calmly as he could. 'What could you have done? Your mother passed from life to death in the best possible way. In her sleep. She needed no-one.'

'How can we possibly know that?' Naomi sobbed.

That was true. But since no-one could, or ever would, Tom thought savagely, why couldn't the selfish bastard have kept his mouth shut?

'We can trust,' he said.

The rest of the day, or much of it, seemed to be spent in packing.

'There's no need to do all this,' Tom said. 'Surely you can leave most of it here?'

'No!' Naomi said. 'I must take everything!'

She was quite determined on that, as if it was some kind of

304

penance. Which it was, Tom thought as he watched her cram every sign of her presence in the apartment into her bags.

There came a point, though, in the afternoon, when there was nothing left to pack.

'The sun's shining,' Tom said. 'Let's go up on the roof for a while.'

Between them they did the odd jobs which needed to be done there, working in near silence. Then they sat at the table and picked up their books, trying to behave as if today was just a normal day, a day like yesterday had been and as tomorrow would be also. But it isn't and it won't be, Naomi thought. Everything is different now.

Late in the afternoon Tom drove Naomi to the airport. As she was leaving the apartment she stopped at the door, and looked around. It was a long look, as if she was committing everything there to memory. Nothing was said by either of them. Tom put the baggage into the elevator and they were carried down to the street.

At the airport Tom, short of something to do, bought her a magazine.

'In case you don't sleep on the plane,' he said.

'I don't suppose I shall sleep,' Naomi said. Nor would she read the magazine.

'I wish I was coming with you,' Tom said. 'If you change your mind I'll be on the next plane.'

'I'll call you tomorrow,' Naomi said.

'Promise you'll come back soon!'

'I can't promise that. I don't know. We've gone through this before. Please don't ask me.'

When she went through into the departure lounge he watched until she was totally out of sight, swallowed up in the crowd. Why did he feel, he thought as he turned away, that he might not see her again? It was illogical. Her mother's death, much though he regretted it for Naomi's sake, had freed her from what she had so recently admitted was her chief obligation, the reason why she had to live in England. Now, suddenly released, she seemed intent on putting herself in chains again.

Did she actually love him as much as he loved her? he asked

305

himself, searching for his car in the car park. But when he thought of their days and nights over the last three weeks, how could he believe otherwise? He tried to comfort himself with what he hoped was the truth, that she was in shock from the suddenness of her mother's death, and the fact that she had been so far away when it had happened – though the shock had been more severe than he had expected – and that she would recover, perhaps quite soon. And that when she recovered she would come back to him.

He could not, for the moment, bear to go back to the silence of his empty apartment. On Broadway he turned into West Fourth Street, found a parking spot and went into the university. Even in the vacation there were people around and he could always find work to do.

The hour and a half in which Naomi waited for take-off felt to her like the longest in her life. What could be going on, she asked herself fretfully, that they could be kept hanging around like this? It had happened on the way out, of course – indeed there'd been a double dose then because, flying from Bristol, she'd had to change planes at Dublin. But it hadn't mattered, she'd been on her way to Tom, alive with happy anticipation, every minute which passed taking her nearer to what she most desired.

It was totally different now. Though she dreaded what she must face when she stepped off the plane she wanted to be there at once. Common sense told her that time was not desperately important, that whatever was most urgent would have been dealt with, but common sense didn't come into it. Nothing could bring back her mother. And nothing, it seemed, could rid her of the feeling, which she knew to be irrational, that she should have been there. Now all she could do was get there as quickly as possible in order to support her family. If she could have afforded to have flown by Concord she would have done so, just to save a few hours.

In the end her flight was called, in the end it took off, into a sky crimson red from the setting sun. From her window seat she looked down at the city spread out beneath her, buildings etched against the sky, strings of street lights like diamond necklaces, the dark water of the harbour. She looked at it as she had eyed the apartment in those seconds before leaving, as if she wanted to imprint the whole scene on her memory. She looked until darkness and distance together had blotted it out and there was nothing below her but blackness.

When it came she turned down the offer of food. Long before the plane quietened down for the night she put on her eye mask and tried to sleep, and indeed did so, fitfully, at intervals through the night, waking frequently, surprised always to observe that something was happening. People reading under subdued lights, people walking about as if sleep was the last thing on their minds.

Hugh was at Gatwick to meet her. The moment she walked through the exit doors after being waved nonchalantly through customs she saw him standing there behind the barrier. He rushed to meet her and when he put his arms around her, pushing the luggage trolley aside, she knew her first moment of comfort.

'It's so good to see you, Ma!' he said.

'And you,' Naomi said. 'It's good of you to meet me.'

'What else would I do?' Hugh demanded. 'Do you really think I'd leave you to get a train to Brighton and another one to Bath? Let's go to the car – or would you like a coffee or something first?'

'No,' Naomi said. 'I had coffee on the plane, and something of whatever they give you for breakfast.' She had hardly noticed what it was, had eaten it because, to her surprise, she had been slightly hungry.

Not without difficulty, Hugh located the car in the semi-darkness of the huge car park, and they set off. It was comforting to be in her own little car even though, unusually, she was not driving.

'How long to Bath?' she enquired.

'About three hours,' Hugh said. 'We'll be there by lunchtime but we can stop whenever you want to.'

'Thank you,' Naomi said. 'I don't suppose I shall.' All she wanted now was to be in her flat, her haven. She had lived there less than six months yet she felt it had been her home for years and years. She would never quite forget Four Winds – how could she, she had had her children there, she had been, for the most part, happily married there – but the memories were no longer as sharp as they had been. Each week, each month, dimmed them a little, made them less painful. Besides, since she had been with Tom she had discovered a new outpouring of happiness against which her marriage to Edward had been like that of a candle flame to the full light and warmth of the sun.

'Did you let your father know?' she asked Hugh. 'In his own way he was quite fond of my mother.'

'I did,' Hugh said. 'He said he'd telephone you once you were back. He might not get to the funeral. They're going away.'

'They' presumably included his wife and baby. Would they be going somewhere exciting, Naomi wondered, like the Riviera or the Caribbean, or would their new domestic bliss with the child mean that they would settle for somewhere more staid? Somerset or Devon.

'Does that mean you've fixed the day of the funeral?' she asked.

'Oh no, Ma! I wouldn't do that without your say-so,' Hugh assured her. 'But Matron gave me the name of the best under-taker and I agreed to let Grandma be moved to his chapel of rest. Apparently they don't like them to stay in the home after they've died. It upsets the residents. You can quite see that, can't you? It's too close for comfort!'

'Yes. So you've not made any arrangements.'

'No others. I said you'd be there the first minute you could.'

'I'll go this afternoon. Will you go with me?' Naomi asked.

'If you want me to.' He did not look forward to it. The trappings of death were not for him. He would be glad when all that was over, everything settled.

'I did visit Grandma,' he said. 'I visited her twice while you were away. I think she appreciated that.'

It was not quite true. On the first occasion she had been pleasant enough but he had not got any closer to her nor made the impression he had hoped to. On the second occasion she hadn't known him at all and had been barely polite, making it quite clear when she wanted him to leave after only twenty minutes. It had been a wasted journey as well as costing him his fare from London, which he had hoped she might reimburse.

'I asked Matron for the name of Grandma's solicitor,' he said. 'She didn't know it, which rather surprised me.'

'Why should she?' Naomi said. 'She would get in touch with me if she needed to.'

'You were not available,' Hugh said rather sharply. 'You were out of the country, which was why I thought that I therefore, being in charge, so to speak, ought to make his acquaintance. *Not* that I expected anything like this to happen, of course. But it just goes to show that you never know. Perhaps you ought to fill me in on him.'

'His name is Henry Jackson, of Jackson, Straw and Jackson, of Cheltenham,' Naomi said. 'Though now that I'm back you won't need to know, will you?'

'Perhaps not,' Hugh conceded. 'Will he come down for the funeral, do you think? I mean there'll be the will and so on, won't there?'

'I think he might, out of respect,' Naomi said. 'My mother's been his client for many years, and before him of his father.'

'And I suppose she's quite well off?'

'Oh yes!' Naomi agreed. 'My father made a lot of money. He was in the right place at the right time. And my mother was never a great spender. The interest paid her fees at River View and whatever other bits and pieces she wanted. Actually, I never gave much thought to what she was worth.'

You didn't need to, Hugh thought. My father kept you in comfort, even though he was as mean as hell with me because I wouldn't follow in his footsteps. But clearly he wasn't going to get any closer at the moment to finding out what his grand-mother was worth, and to whom she might have left it. But surely as her only grandson . . . ?

'We'd better stop for petrol,' he said. 'I hope you've got your credit card with you, Ma dear. I'm skint, and I'm up to the hilt on mine. It wasn't cheap coming down to see Grandma.'

When they were on their way again Naomi said: 'I suppose you've heard Isobel's news? I mean about the new baby?'

'I have,' Hugh said. 'I think she's off her rocker. They both are. How can they afford it? And that flat's awful!'

'She seems happy enough,' Naomi said. 'Though I do worry about the flat myself. No place for two babies.'

'Oh, I don't *worry* about it,' Hugh said. 'It's their choice. They don't have to have swarms of kids.'

'Two is hardly a swarm, darling,' Naomi remonstrated.

'It could be the start of one,' Hugh said.

The rest of the journey passed with little conversation between them. Naomi was tired after the night flight and worried about what lay ahead. More than anything she was missing Tom. She looked at her watch, calculating what he might be doing. He would still be in bed, of course. Would he be lying on his back with his arms flung wide? Or would he perhaps be awake, thinking of her as she was of him? When would he telephone her? She longed for him to do so, but part of her thought it would be better if he did not. All reason, all straight thinking, all sense of duty would go out of her head when she heard his voice on the phone.

'Here we are then!' Hugh said, coming to a halt at her door. 'What a bore that last fifteen miles is. Nothing but bends, and never enough room to pass anything!'

'You drove very well, dear,' she said. The truth was that she had noticed none of it. She had been in another country.

'I'll take your cases out and then I'll find a parking space,' Hugh said. 'Or try to.'

At least it was good to be in her own home again. Welcoming. While waiting for Hugh she put the kettle on.

When he came in she asked him for the undertaker's number, and telephoned at once.

'He'll see us at three-thirty,' she told Hugh. 'In the meantime I'll make some lunch. Will an omelette suit?' She didn't want any, but there was no reason, because she was jet-lagged and not in the mood for eating, why Hugh should go hungry.

'Fine,' he said. 'Three eggs. I warn you I'm hungry.'

The undertaker – funeral director, she learned to call him – was a nice man, much younger than she had expected. She wondered what moved a young man to do a job like this. Whatever it was, he did it well. He was businesslike, practical, and at the same time compassionate. He directed his questions to her, without shutting Hugh out. In a short time, not that he hurried her, everything was arranged and she knew that it would go well.

'Next Thursday, then,' he repeated as they left. 'And if you have even the smallest question, please come back to me. And don't forget that you can come in to see your mother whenever you want to. Feel free.'

She had dreaded seeing her mother, no longer alive, but the ordeal was not really as bad as she had expected. There was no doubt that her mother looked at peace, more than she sometimes had in life. Where is she? Naomi asked herself. Where did she go to?

All she desired when she returned home was to go to bed, but everyone said that the best way to deal with jet lag was not to give in to it, to wait until it was your normal time before going to bed. She wasn't sure she could last out, but she'd try.

In the evening Isobel rang.

'Come round in the morning, Ma! Come and see Harry,' she urged. 'It will do you good!'

'It probably will,' Naomi said to Hugh. Young, new life, she thought, including the new life in Isobel, was probably the best antidote to old age and death.

'Shall you come with me?' she asked Hugh.

'No,' he said firmly. 'I'm going back to London in the morning. Will you give me a lift to the station?' He would be glad to leave. Death and mourning were not his scene and pressure of work was a good reason to opt out.

'But I will be back for the funeral,' he added. 'I wouldn't dream of missing that.'

For a moment it occurred to Naomi that he was almost looking forward to it, but of course she must be wrong.

'I'm sorry about Grandma,' Isobel said next morning. 'But I'm not going to dwell on it because of the new baby. I have to think positive, happy thoughts. And she was an old lady, she'd had her life. I'm sure she wouldn't want us to mourn.' She spoke in the kindest possible voice. 'But I will be at the funeral,' she

311

added. 'Taken in the right way, funerals can be reasonably happy occasions.'

How nice to be so certain about things, especially about life and death, Naomi thought.

'It was wonderful having your car while you were away,' Isobel said. 'It made such a difference. Harry enjoyed it.'

He looked up – he was playing on the rug with a large frog covered in green and yellow velvet – and smiled on hearing his name. He really is a very nice baby and I have missed him, Naomi decided.

Leaving Isobel she made a detour and went to River View to see Matron.

'I do want to thank you so much for all you did for my mother. She was happy here.'

'I do believe she was,' Matron agreed. 'We were pleased to have her. She was a nice lady.'

'I'm sorry I was away when she died.'

'Mrs Fletcher,' Matron said firmly, 'you have nothing to apologize for, or feel guilty about. We are all entitled to take a break from time to time and I suspect you needed one. And I had very few arrangements to make. The rest will fall to you, but how fortunate that you have your son. Such a nice young man!'

'He's gone back to London,' Naomi said.

'Ah well!' Matron observed. 'Men must work and women must weep! But I'm sure you have work to do!' She rose from her chair, gracefully bringing the meeting to an end.

Back at home, Naomi telephoned Mr Jackson, apologized that she hadn't been able to do so earlier and gave him the arrangements for the funeral.

'I shall attend, of course,' he said. 'And afterwards I would like to see you and your family, if that's convenient.'

Tom telephoned.

'I called yesterday,' he said. 'Hugh answered. He said you'd gone to bed, you were asleep, he said he'd rather not disturb you.'

'Oh Tom!' Naomi cried. 'I didn't know! He must have forgotten to tell me! I suppose I was fast asleep or I'd have heard the phone, but I'd have been happy for him to have wakened me.

You know that.' Hugh had deliberately not let her know. There was no way he could have forgotten.

'Is he there now?'

'No, he's gone back to London. He'll be here for the funeral.'

'I love you like hell,' Tom said. 'Let me come over!'

'Oh Tom, it won't do!' Naomi said miserably. 'I'm best left to sort things out for myself. And you know what Hugh's like!'

'I don't care about Hugh,' Tom said.

'But I must. And about Isobel and Cecily. I'm their mother.'

'When are you going to stop being their mother and come back to being my lover?' Tom demanded.

'I can't just stop being a mother,' Naomi said. 'I'm needed here. Please try to understand.'

'I am trying. It's just that it seems simple to me. So remember I love you. I'll call you every day, no matter who's there.'

Do they need me, my family? Naomi asked herself when she had put the phone down. Isobel's life is firmly set. So is mine to her. I am the grandmother. Cecily took pride in being free from all restraints, though this seemed not to apply to Sean since she had telephoned Isobel to say that when someone let her know when the funeral was, she and Sean would come down together. I must phone her this evening, Naomi thought.

As for Hugh, did he need her, and if so for what? For material gain only, she decided. She shared his life at no other point and now, when she needed him, he had left. Reluctantly, she didn't want to believe it but she had to, she saw through his intention to be there for the funeral and his eagerness to know if Mr Jackson would be there. He wanted to know what was in his grandmother's will, in particular what was in it for him.

He would be disappointed. She knew what was in the will. Two or three years ago her mother had told her, and she doubted she had changed anything since.

In the days leading up to the funeral it was astonishing how many things there were to be done, and all it seemed by her. It was with difficulty that she slotted in a quick visit to Henri – she must look as good as possible for her mother's sake.

As funerals go it went well. There were few mourners, Doris Campbell had outlived most of her friends. Matron, and one or

313

two of the residents of River View came. A very elderly lady in Cheltenham sent flowers, as did Edward. The service was taken by the young clergyman who had visited Doris at River View. 'My mother would have liked that,' Naomi told him.

Afterwards, when everyone who had gone back to Naomi's flat to drink sherry and eat bits and pieces had gone home again, leaving behind only the family and Mr Jackson, he looked at his watch and said, 'And now I'm afraid we must get down to business!'

He sat in the armchair by the fireplace, his papers on a small table in front of him. The others sat in a semicircle around him. Naomi glanced from one to the other as they waited for him to begin. Isobel balanced Harry on her lap, more intent on her baby than on the lawyer. Patrick sat on a chair beside her. Cecily sat close by, but not with Sean who, not being a member of the family, had tactfully gone out for a walk. Cecily was looking apprehensively at Isobel. She was thinking – though Naomi had no way of knowing this – if my sister pulls out a tit and starts feeding that baby in front of everyone, I shall scream!

Naomi's glance moved to Hugh. He was sitting on the edge of his chair, directly opposite to Mr Jackson. Naomi was quite sure she knew what his thoughts were. She had learnt a lot about her son in the last few months, sometimes more than she wanted to.

'I am here to speak to you about the will of your late mother and grandmother,' Mr Jackson began.

He was swift and businesslike. There was really little to be said. Mrs Campbell, he said, had left her entire estate to her only child, Mrs Naomi Fletcher.

Hugh went chalk-white. He looks as though he will faint, Naomi thought.

'Except,' Mr Jackson continued, 'that she leaves the sum of five hundred pounds to each of her three grandchildren and a like sum to the River View rest home.'

Hugh's pallor changed to a bright red.

'Five hundred pounds!' he spluttered. 'And the same to a bloody rest home?'

'I think we should moderate our language,' Mr Jackson said.

314

'These are the wishes of the deceased. It is my job to carry them out.'

'And are we, her grandchildren, allowed to know the value of her estate?' Hugh asked fiercely.

Mr Jackson glanced at Naomi for her permission. She nodded her head.

'In all,' he said, 'though one cannot be precise . . . it could be more, it could be less, depending on the market . . . but I estimate that the estate will be in the region of four hundred thousand pounds. Give or take either way, as I said.'

Hugh exploded.

'And we, her grandchildren – me, her only grandson – get five hundred measly pounds out of a near half-million?'

'That is the wish of the deceased,' Mr Jackson repeated. Where there's a will there's a quarrel, he thought – but did not say. It was commonplace to him. There was someone like Hugh Fletcher in most families.

Hugh turned his venom on his mother. She felt nothing but sadness as she met his gaze.

'And I suppose your fortune will be spent on that bloody Yankee? He probably knew about it all along!'

She had no need to answer. Mr Jackson intervened.

'If you will allow me to continue, I have something else to say.'

Reluctantly, Hugh quietened down. Cecily and Isobel looked at the lawyer with renewed interest.

'Mrs Fletcher, who knew the contents of Mrs Campbell's will, spoke to me on the telephone yesterday. She made what I consider to be one of the most generous proposals I have ever heard. It is her wish that, when her mother's estate is finally settled, the net sum should be divided into four equal parts – one part to go to herself and one to each of her children, namely Hugh, Isobel and Cecily.'

He closed his file and sat back in his chair. He didn't approve of what Mrs Fletcher had done. He would gladly have seen the son cut off without the proverbial shilling, but it was her wish, and his place to carry it out.

'How long—' Hugh began.

'It will take time,' Mr Jackson said frostily. 'The due processes of the law cannot be hurried!' And if they could, he thought, I wouldn't hurry them for you, though I might well for the young lady with the baby.

When they had all gone home, her children, it must be said, in varying transports of delight and disbelief, Naomi picked up the phone and dialled New York.

'Tom?'

'Hi!' he said. 'I was about to call you. How did it go?'

'Everything went well,' Naomi said. 'I'll tell you the details later. The main thing now is that tomorrow I'm going into the town to book my flight to New York!'

There was a long silence.

'Did you hear what I said?' Naomi asked.

'Yes,' he said. 'I did. One question. Will you book a round trip, or one way?'

'One way!' Naomi told him. 'Eventually.'